Postcards FROM Summer

Postcards
FROM
Summer

CYNTHIA
PLATT

SIMON & SCHUSTER BFYR

NEW YORK LONDON TORONTO SYDNEY NEW DELHI

SIMON & SCHUSTER BFYR

An imprint of Simon & Schuster Children's Publishing Division
1230 Avenue of the Americas, New York, New York 10020

SIMON & SCHUSTER BOOKS FOR YOUNG READERS
and related marks are trademarks of Simon & Schuster, Inc.
For information about special discounts for bulk purchases, please contact
Simon & Schuster Special Sales at 1-866-506-1949 or business@simonandschuster.com.
The Simon & Schuster Speakers Bureau can bring authors to your live event.
For more information or to book an event, contact the Simon & Schuster Speakers Bureau at
1-866-248-3049 or visit our website at www.simonspeakers.com.
Interior design by Hilary Zarycky
The text for this book was set in Perpetua Std.
Manufactured in the United States of America
First Edition
2 4 6 8 10 9 7 5 3 1
Library of Congress Cataloging-in-Publication Data
Names: Platt, Cynthia, author.
Title: Postcards from summer / Cynthia Platt.
Description: First edition. | New York : Simon & Schuster Books for Young Readers, [2022] |
Audience: Ages 12 up. | Audience: Grades 7–9. |
Summary: Seventeen-year-old Lexi travels to her late mother's majestic summertime home
to learn of the romance—and the tragedy—that changed her life forever.
Identifiers: LCCN 2022002382 |
ISBN 9781534474406 (hardcover) | ISBN 9781534474420 (ebook)
Subjects: CYAC: Mothers—Fiction. | Secrets—Fiction. | Love—Fiction. |
LCGFT: Romance fiction.
Classification: LCC PZ7.P7124 Po 2022 | DDC [Fic]—dc23
LC record available at https://lccn.loc.gov/2022002382

To Mike, who asked for this dedication
(and whom I love more than I can say)

Postcards
FROM
Summer

Emma (Then)

The night air is so humid I can practically touch it. Air isn't something that you're supposed to think about. It's just . . . there. That's the way it should be anyway—just something that you take for granted as you breathe it in and out. Not something you have to actively ponder. But tonight, the air's so hot and dense that it feels as if it's pressing up against me, holding me back from where I really want to be.

I love the summer, but I hate this night.

My hair plasters itself to the back of my neck, and when I bend my elbow to tie it back up again, the skin on my upper arm sticks to my forearm. Blisters chafe themselves into painful bubbles under the straps of both my shoes. Nothing *works* the way it's supposed to right now.

Even the hotel feels off tonight. The lawn is usually crawling with guests playing games under the lights or laughing as more and more alcohol seeps into their systems. But as I trip across the grass, no one's doing what they should be. Instead, they wilt on the verandah as elegantly as they possibly can. Not that elegance is easy to maintain in this heat. But they've paid through the nose for a vacation *from a bygone era*, as the brochures promise, and they're all determined to have one no matter what.

Through the open ballroom doors, a waltz by Strauss streams out into the night air. I should be in there right at this very moment, swirling around the dance floor in that dizzy haze that only a waltz can provide.

I'm going to be in such enormous trouble when I get back.

I still have to get out of here.

This whole night seems to be conspiring against me. It even isn't just the heat and the humidity and the sweat. It's the way the air hangs with the aroma of orange day lilies that burst to life this morning and then shriveled up and died by nightfall. Hovering on top of that is the smell of freshly cut grass and smoke from the bonfire by the lake.

Sounds from guests who are scattered around the lawn and by the pool mix with the buzz of cicadas. The chirping of crickets. The off-key songs of the frogs at the edge of the little fishpond.

It's all too much. Too close. My brain can't process this kind of sensory overload right now.

And I know it's not the island's fault, or even the hotel's, that I'm feeling this way. I know it's just circumstances beyond my control.

I slip into the rose garden, then run down the darker, more secluded part of the lawn. I can't handle any more polite small talk tonight.

Honestly, I'm not sure what I can handle anymore. So many people expect so many things from me that the line between where their expectations end and I begin is starting to blur.

I make my way to the greenhouse, but its long shadows and the whistling sound of the hot wind through one of the boarded-up windows push me back out the door again. So I run. Around the grounds, through the playground, the pool area, even the rose garden again. A small pit of despair starts to form in my stomach.

The lake. All I need is a little quiet time by the water and everything will be okay. Just as I get to the end of the path there I hear it: a low voice singing my favorite old Gershwin song, "Embraceable You."

Relief, fear, worry, and something that feels like a pure burst of joy take hold of me all at once. I had no idea up till now that I could feel all those emotions at the same time, and I'm not sure the discovery is doing anything to make me feel better.

As soon as I turn the corner, I see him. Even with all the other emotions jumbled inside me, something else entirely takes hold in my chest.

He sits where the sand meets the trees. The half-moon shines in his hair and casts him in a silver light. For a second, it's like looking at a ghost, as if he could evaporate into thin air and slip through my fingers forever.

"What're you doing here?" he asks.

I take a deep breath. "How did you know it's me?"

"I always know when it's you."

He always knows when it's me. What am I supposed to do with that?

"What are *you* doing here?" I ask, throwing his question back to him.

He doesn't say a word, so I walk over and sit down in the sand next to him. It's pretty clear that I'm the one who's going to have to keep the conversation alive.

"I had to escape," I tell him.

"Me too."

"Your dad?"

He picks up a stone and tosses it into the water. "Yours?"

A pathetic little laugh escapes from me. "How did you guess?" I ask. "Too many expectations."

"Too many demands," he adds.

"Too many ways I'm supposed to live my life."

"Too many ways I'm not supposed to live mine."

We turn at the same time and look at each other, and he gives me a sad smile.

"So what're we going to do about it?" he says.

There's no easy answer to that one, though. As much as I hate all of my parents' expectations for me, I also hate the thought of letting them down. I'm all they have, after all. I know what that means. It's just that they've gone from telling me what they *wish* I'd do and moved right into *demanding* that I do what they want me to do.

If I think about it too much, I start to feel sick. I need to *move*—to run or to swim or to make something.

After raking my hands over the pine needles on the ground, I finally pick up a handful. They're still the soft, pliable texture of newly fallen needles. I wrap one around my pinkie and then tie it into a knot, warping tiny pine needles into the spaces I make between the needles.

"What's that?" he asks.

"A gift," I tell him. "For you."

He leans in closer to see what I'm doing. His leg, his arm press against mine. His damp skin sticks to mine, but I don't mind this time. Even in this heat I still feel something like a chill as I lean into him more. He takes the basket from my hand, his fingers brushing against my palm.

"Only you can make something out of nothing like this," he says in a quiet voice.

I shrug just a little. Not enough so that I have to move away from him.

His fingers close gently around the little basket I gave him and he looks over at me again, this time with serious eyes. "Thanks for this," he says. "I'll keep it with me. Always."

Always.

He'll keep it always. He always knows it's me.

I have no idea how to respond, so I don't say anything at all.

Something is swirling inside me—something has been for a while now—though I've never quite been able to figure out what. I can feel it in my stomach, moving upward to fill my chest. Ready to explode if I can't find a way to just . . . release it.

A fear lurks inside my brain that the explosion would be less like fireworks and more like a nuclear bomb exploding if I ever let myself go.

I want this and don't want it, all at the same time.

The moonlight glimmers in his eyes as he watches me.

He understands. I know he does. I can tell just from the look in his eyes.

Nothing about that is comforting.

My chest begins to ache as the feeling that I'm about to explode grows even stronger. It's so huge now—so overwhelming—that I have to do something to make it stop.

So with one last, desperate look at him, I lean in and press my lips to his.

And the world explodes.

Not with fireworks or nuclear bombs, but with something I don't even have a name for.

Because with this one kiss, everything has changed.

CHAPTER 1

Lexi (Now)

Sometimes when I was little I'd spin in circles till I got dizzy. Partly I liked the thrill of the spinning, like I'd created my own little hurricane with me at the eye of it. But I also liked what happened after my body stopped but my brain hadn't caught up to that fact yet. Everything would still be twisting and turning. I'd look at the world around me, and it would be the same as it had been before I'd started spinning, but everything would look different, too.

I sort of feel that way right now, but without needing to spin to make it happen. Even on a quiet night, our kitchen looks a little like it's swirling from the off-kilter blur of color that is my half brother Connor's art taped onto every possible surface. Tonight is not a quiet night.

Dad chops veggies and hums as Connor literally runs in circles around the kitchen table fetching ingredients for him. My stepmom, Abby, smiles at them from her work-cluttered seat at the head of the table like nothing makes her happier than her two guys (as she calls them) making dinner. It's a heartwarming scene, really.

As I stand in the doorway, though, it's hard not to wish that some of this familial warmth was aimed at me. It's not fun to feel jealous of a five-year-old, especially one I love as much as I love this kid. But a tiny pang of envy hits me anyway. I barely remember my mom, and would've killed to have this kind of relationship with my dad when I was little. Or even now.

Connor starts reciting the poem he "read" at his kindergarten graduation as he runs.

"Kindergarten
Is now done.
On to first grade,
Oh what fun!"

He stumbles on every other word but since he's five and adorable (even I can't resist those dark brown curls and dimples), Dad and Abby don't care.

"Can you do it again?" Dad asks.

"Really?" Connor's eyes are wide with happiness.

"Of course really," Dad tells him. "It's my new favorite poem."

Abby stops going through her work to listen to Connor recite the millionth rendition of this poem she's heard over the last couple of weeks. "Wonderful, sweetie," she says. "Just like you were at graduation today."

To be fair, Connor did do a pretty great job at his graduation ceremony, even if his paper graduation cap slipped over his eyes during his recitation. As the true child of two lawyers, he just kept talking like nothing had gone wrong.

Even if he hadn't, Dad and Abby would still tell him he's the best.

The pang of envy returns. When I turn back to look at the stairs, it becomes a wave of nausea. Because while everything's swirling around down here, I know what's waiting up there.

The package arrived while Dad, Abby, and Connor were at the store, so none of them saw it. It's addressed to me, or at least to some alternative-universe me: Alexandria Roth. My first name and my mom's last name before she married Dad. The return address lists a nursing home in Michigan.

I turn and glance back toward the living room. To the stairs that lead up to the bedrooms. All I have to do is get through dinner and I can go see what's inside the package to alternative-universe me.

"Lexi, did you hear me?" Dad's voice cuts through my thoughts.

"No . . . what?"

"The table?" he says. "Can you set it? The pizza's already in the oven."

"Oh . . . of course," I mumble. "I just zoned out for a second."

"Well, try to zone back in, okay?" he says. "It's Connor's graduation celebration." Nothing about his tone sounds angry or even annoyed, but resentment that he's now dad of the year gets under my skin, making the nausea even worse.

Without another word, I set the table while Connor recites the poem again. Then I sit down across from him. The seat next to him has been empty since my stepsister, Chloe, left for school in California. Just looking at it makes my stomach feel worse. If she were here, we'd open the package together. If she were here, I wouldn't feel this lonely in my own family.

But she's not even coming home this summer except for a long weekend in August. As I look at her empty chair again, the smell of Connor's chosen meal for tonight, veggie pizza and French fries, makes me gag. I push the food around on my plate, hoping that no one notices.

"Aren't you hungry, Lexi?" Abby asks.

"My stomach's not feeling great," I admit. "I'm not sure pizza and fries are going to help."

She reaches over and presses her hand to my forehead. "You don't have a fever," she tells me. "Maybe you should go upstairs and lie down for a little while."

This couldn't be better if I'd planned it. And I really didn't plan it. My mind is about as diabolical as . . . well . . . a ladybug.

"Maybe I should," I agree. I get up from the table, only to find my dad looking at me with a crease between his eyebrows. Before he starts in on me, I hurry upstairs. The sooner I get to my package the better.

When I close the door to the room I used to share with Chloe, I grab the package from the floor of my closet. Placing it carefully on my bed, I run my fingers over the address label. *Alexandria Roth*. It could be some weird scam. It could be anthrax for all I know.

I'm going to open it anyway. Besides, who sends anthrax from a nursing home? I grab a pair of scissors from my desk and slit the package open. I don't know why I'm so nervous about this. It's probably just a promotional thing, or even something that got ordered under the wrong name. But then, my eyes snag on the return address again: *Refuge by the Lake Nursing Facility*.

I take a deep breath and sift through the layers of bubble wrap inside the box.

Just under it all lies a note.

Dear Alexandria,

Let me begin by offering my condolences. Your grandmother was a fascinating woman, and I enjoyed getting to know her over the past few years. She had been talking for ages about writing you a letter and sending this to you, but she put it off too long. I'm sure you're going to hear from her lawyer about her will, but I wanted to send this to you myself since I know it had been on her mind.

I'm very sorry for your loss.

Sincerely,
Amanda Siedler
Head RN
Refuge by the Lake Nursing Facility

My hand shakes so much that the note falls from it. Her will. I'll be hearing from her lawyer about her will. My grandmother wanted to send me whatever's in this box, but she died before she could.

Probably this is the part where a normal person would get all teary-eyed, but I'm like that song from *A Chorus Line*: I feel nothing.

I remember going to see the play when I was ten and Chloe was twelve. Abby took us for a girls' night out a few months after she started dating Dad. That song stuck in my head and wouldn't leave me. Because unlike the woman who sang it, who didn't feel anything she was supposed to, I felt everything. Every emotion, every minute of the day. And I wanted it to stop.

Now, here I am, thinking about that song again because it's impossible to feel any sense of loss about my own grandmother.

I guess maybe I should say my estranged grandmother? There are only three things I know about the woman, after all.

I never met her, even when I was a baby.

My parents never talked about her and my grandfather, though I know he died a couple of years after Mom did from the same heart defect. (I had to get tested for it afterward.)

She and my grandfather tried to take me away from Dad after Mom died. This was the one time I ever laid eyes on her. Even then she never said a single word to me.

From stuff Abby's told me, the custody case got nasty fast. A couple of months after Mom died, I had to appear in court. The judge asked me flat out who I wanted to live with.

There aren't many things I remember from this time of my childhood, but I remember my dad holding my hand a little too tightly as we walked into a big, empty courtroom. My grandparents sitting at one table surrounded by men in fancy suits and Dad sitting by himself at another. He looked terrified. I hadn't felt scared at all that day till I realized he was.

A bitter sigh escapes from me. After my grandmother fought to get custody of me, she didn't want anything to do with me for twelve whole years afterward. There's nothing she could send me now that could make up for that.

The only emotion I can conjure is disappointment that the one person who might have been willing to talk to me about my mom is gone.

God knows Dad's never going to.

I pick the letter off the floor and read through it again before looking at what's in the box. Underneath more bubble wrap is a small chest, about the size of a jewelry box.

The top is painted a deep blue-green, and the four sides of it are covered with intricate mosaics made of tiny rocks and glass and bits of shells. One side of the mosaic pictures a beach; on the other, a garden full of flowers. The front has four people on canoes under a dark night sky. The back is a greenhouse.

"What the hell?" I whisper.

Then I lift the cover.

The hinges creak as if no one's opened it in a really long time. I gently rest the top of it against the cardboard box so that it doesn't break off.

Inside, it's filled to the brim with hoards of stuff: letters, a datebook, fliers. And on top is a postcard with an enormous blue Victorian building with lacy white woodwork and a bright green lawn on the front. It looks fancy and old-fashioned. At the bottom of the postcard are the words:

Palais du Lac Hotel

Mackinac Island

I've never heard of this place before, but it's pretty. I flip the card over and freeze. Because this isn't just a postcard. It's a postcard from my mom.

The days I spent with you here will always be the best of my entire life, no matter what else happened. I thought nothing could ever come between us. I never intended to hurt you, but I know I did. Then everything fell apart and you were gone.

If you've somehow forgiven me, I'll be waiting here for you in our palace by the lake. But if not, I understand.

Either way, I already miss you and hope to see you again soon, even if it's just in my own memories.

Love,

Emma

Underneath it lies a napkin, yellowed with time. On it is a whole conversation, like a series of texts but in ballpoint pen.

I'm the worst.

Lots of things are worse than you.

I just stole stuff.

Like Robin Hood, remember? Steal from the rich and give to the poor.

Except I stole fudge. And the poor is me.

I stole fudge with you, JR. Am I the worst too?

Do you really want me to answer that?

Maybe you ARE the worst.

I knew you really thought so.

Both sets of handwriting are in smudged ink, and it looks like the writers were young. But as I hold the postcard in one hand and the napkin in the other, one thing is clear: Mom's handwriting is on both.

"What. The. Hell?"

My door bursts open and Connor runs in with his purple blanket. "I brought you Oscar to make you feel better!"

"Jesus, you're supposed to knock, Connor!" I yell as I shove everything back into the blue chest and slam it shut.

The words come out more harshly than I mean them to. Connor's bottom lip starts trembling. His little fingers knead into Oscar the blanket's purple yarn, which he only does when he's had a nightmare or is *really* sad.

"Sorry," he says in a cracking voice.

I shake my head and sigh. "It's okay. Just knock next time."

He nods, but still won't look at me.

"Thanks for bringing Oscar," I say, trying to make this right. "He always makes me feel better."

Connor finally looks up. "Me too."

"Want to be an Oscar sandwich with me?" I already know the answer to this question, which is why I ask it.

Connor wipes his tears and climbs onto my bed next to me. "With pickles and mustard?"

I grab my old yellow sunflower pillow and my even older Grinch stuffy. "Got them. Now get ready, because it's sandwich time!"

Connor giggles as I grab him, the sunflower, and the Grinch up in my arms and wrap the blanket around us. "OSCAR SANDWICH!" he yells.

"Best kind ever."

As soon as his giggling subsides, though, he peeks out of the blanket. "What's in your blue treasure chest?"

I glance down at the Grinch. Like him, I have to think up a lie and think it up quick. "Sneakers," I say.

There's only one problem: Connor may be five, but he's no slouch. "Sneakers came in *that*?" he asks. "I thought sneakers came in cardboard boxes."

My eyes shift uncomfortably through the hole Connor's made in the blanket sandwich and realize he's right. Sneakers don't come in wooden chests with mosaics on them.

"They're special edition sneakers," I tell him. There's no choice but to keep it going now. "That's why they came in that box."

Connor's eyes widen. "Wow," he breathes. "Can I have the treasure chest after you're done with it?"

I am the worst sister ever. Seriously, the worst.

"Um . . . well . . . they don't fit," I reply. "So I have to return them. The box, too."

His whole face droops in disappointment.

"But maybe we could make a box just like it this summer?" I offer, and he's instantly smiling again. It seriously takes so little to make him happy.

"With little rock pictures?"

"Definitely with little rock pictures," I say.

Connor gives me one of those full-body hugs only little kids can get away with. "You're the best."

A knock sounds at the door and I unwrap us and throw Oscar on the mosaic box just as the door opens to reveal Dad.

"Bath time, kiddo," he tells Connor. I should've known he wasn't coming to check in on me. Connor hurtles himself at Dad. "Bath time's the best!" he yells.

Dad laughs and swoops him up in his arms. I watch them, wondering if Dad acted like this when I was little, too, or if a different side of him came out when he started a new family. Did he sweep me up and swing me around like I was the best thing in his world?

Even if he did, I don't remember it. It's hard to remember lots of things that happened before Mom died. It's like the edges of everything got rubbed off and a little blurry after I lost her.

"Lexi and me are going to build a treasure chest," Connor tells Dad. "With little rock pictures on it!"

Suddenly a wave of panic hits me that Connor will tell Dad about the blue chest. If all the stuff in there really belonged to Mom, I want to keep it for myself.

I have to keep it for myself.

Dad's already gotten rid of almost everything that reminded him of her. I won't let him take another piece of her away from me.

Time for a diversion.

"After we make it, we can play pirates," I tell Connor. "Won't that be fun?"

The dimples come out in full force. "Argh, matey, it will!"

Just as I think I've thrown Connor off the scent, Abby appears in the doorway, laying her hand on Dad's shoulder. "What's this I hear about a pirate chest?"

"With rock pictures!" Connor says again.

"Rock pictures?" Abby smiles. "I've never heard of that before. How will you make them?"

"Lexi knows," Connor says with utmost confidence. "She'll show me."

Both Dad and Abby look my way.

"Oh . . . um . . . maybe we can make sand art," I tell them. "Or mosaics."

Suddenly Dad's eyebrows knit together. "What did you just say?"

"Um . . . sand art?"

"Or mosaics!" Connor yells in Dad's ear. Then he looks at Abby. "What's mosaics?"

"It's a kind of art where you make pictures from tiles. Or in this case, rocks," she tells him.

"Oh!" Connor practically sings. "Just like—"

"Or we'll do sand art," I interrupt him. "As long as it looks like a pirate chest, it doesn't matter how we make it, right?"

Connor agrees as he squirms out of Dad's arms and pulls on Abby to pick him up instead.

Dad, on the other hand, still stares at me like I'm some giant, annoying puzzle he can't solve. "Since when do you know how to make mosaics?"

I shrug. "I don't. I just thought it would be a fun thing to do with Connor."

Abby beams at me over Connor's head. "You're such a good big sister, Lexi."

I don't know how Abby does it, but somehow she manages not to see any of Dad's moodiness. Ever. It's like she put on a pair of rose-colored glasses the first time she asked him out and never took them off.

Dad glances at me again. "You really are a good big sister." Then he starts to usher them out of my room.

"You can keep Oscar for now, too," Connor calls back to me. "To help you feel better."

"Thanks, matey."

Through the closed door I can hear them talking and laughing as they get ready for bath time. I wait a few minutes to be sure they're not coming back. Then I lift Oscar off the mosaic box, careful that none of the tiny pieces of the chest get stuck in the yarn.

I need to know what else is in this box.

Just underneath the dirty old napkin is a small notepad that hotels leave in rooms, with *Palais Du Lac Hotel* printed at the top of each page. A tiny sketch of a short pink dress with a high lace collar covers the top page. The lines and angles Mom used to draw the lace are harsh. Etched around it is a gravestone with *RIP* in formal lettering written on it. On the next page is my mom's young handwriting.

> Today I had to wear a scratchy lace dress for 3½ hours. JR told me I should build a Viking funeral pyre for it. He was kidding but I talked him into doing it for real so I never have to wear it again. Once we have it built I'll steal marshmallows from the kitchen to roast over the dress's pyre. It's a more honorable way to go than this dress really deserves.

I laugh out loud for a second as I read it, trying to picture my mother as a girl doing something as reckless as burning a dress. I hope she didn't get in trouble. I hope she and whoever JR was got to roast marshmallows as they watched the dress go up in flames.

Mom sounds like she was a handful.

Then I look into the chest again and see it: a single piece of watercolor paper. In the middle of the page, there's a painting of a pitch-black sky dotted with stars—so many of them that it's hard to imagine how she even painted something so intricate. The creamy slide of the Milky Way runs through the image, a soft mix of purple and white and even pale yellow. And swirled all around all of this is my mother's tiny, much more grown-up writing.

> The four of us went canoeing tonight. There was no moon so the stars were impossibly bright. It felt like if we just looked hard enough we could see into the universe and understand something important about it—something that no one else had ever discovered. Ryan sang with his annoyingly perfect voice as Linda rowed their canoe. The night was so beautiful that it made my chest ache. Right at that very moment, everything seemed exactly as it should be. I wish I could have put it in my pocket like a piece of lake glass so I could feel it warm and smooth in my hand whenever I needed a reminder that life could be this way.

I put the paper down and run my fingers over her writing and the rough texture of the painting. I wonder who Ryan and Linda were. Who JR was. Then my mind wanders back to Mom herself. Her writing spirals around the page as if she'd tried to create her own little galaxy with her painting at the center of it.

Being able to read this is like getting a part of her back I didn't know existed before. I'm missing someone I barely remember, yet here she is, through her art and her writing, giving a piece of herself to me.

Mom was beautiful. I can tell even from the tiny note about her dress and this peek into her impossibly beautiful night. She seemed cool and funny and creative, all things I'll never be. Sadness hits me so hard that it's paralyzing for a little while. It's not fair that I don't know how beautiful she was for myself. It's not fair that she died so young.

Or that Dad won't ever talk about her.

Or that I'll never have a chance now to ask my grandmother about her.

My stomach turns. I'm going to throw up. I grab my recycling bin and hold it against my chest. I focus on the air entering and leaving my lungs. Without my phone, I have no idea how much time has passed, but after a while my stomach starts to feel less queasy.

I return Mom's stuff to the chest, before stowing it in my closet. Then I slump onto my bed, closing my eyes to try to block everything out.

My grandmother is dead.

My mom's mosaic chest is here in my room.

My stepsister is halfway across the country.

My dad and Abby are probably going to have a great night without me.

The world starts spinning again, but this time I'm not sure how to make it stop.

CHAPTER 2

Lexi (Now)

I try to sleep but it doesn't stick. My mind is too restless. Turning on the light, I get Mom's mosaic chest and place it on my bed again. The postcard, the napkin, the painting. I need to see what's beyond that.

But what's beyond it is . . . weird?

There's an award ribbon that says *I Survived Mackinac Island* for some reason. Just underneath that lies a flier for a gallery looking for local artists to submit for a new exhibit. It's been folded over and over again into a tiny square. Some of the ink has worn off in the creases.

Underneath that is a tiny watercolor painting. In it is a girl who looks strikingly like me. Same dark eyes, same sharp chin. Same unruly black hair. She's dressed in what looks like a long, flowy Snow White dress. A bird perches on her finger singing out music notes while another nests in her messy hair. Over the top of the picture, in neat calligraphy, are the words I am a perky princess!

I laugh out loud but it quickly turns into something else. Something a little too much like crying. I flip this little painting over to see if she wrote anything else, but it's not her handwriting I find there. Instead, it's the same writing as on the napkin.

It was supposed to be an insult. Not an invitation to turn yourself into an actual perky princess.

This makes me laugh wetly again. I guess I just love the fact that Mom was the kind of person who'd turn an insult into . . . this. This joyful, funny picture owning the insult. Smoothing it out on my bed, I take a closer look. The watercolors are delicate and soft, but the ink lines that she drew around them are thick and bold. The calligraphy looks like something out of a Disney movie.

She was an artist. I already knew that. But I didn't *know* what that meant before. Now . . . now I can see how brilliant she was.

I shake my head and dig in even further. There's a flier for a karaoke night at someplace called First Church of the Lake. At the top of it is some clip art of microphones and the lines *Your wife won't do karaoke with you? You can* duet *yourself!*

Does this mean my mother could sing? I don't remember her ever singing to me, but what do I know? I can't even remember what her speaking voice sounded like at all anymore. It's just . . . a void. Where her voice should be in my memory there's nothing. Why can't I have even this tiny piece of her? Why did my brain have to erase that for me? There's an ache in my chest at the thought that I'll never hear her voice.

I turn the flier over to see what's under it in the mosaic chest, only to find these words written on the back of it:

So much better than karaoke.

I wish she'd left more information, written some other detail to help me piece together what she ended up doing that night. But this is all I have.

A sob escapes from me. I heap everything back in the chest and slam it shut. Then I open it again. And close it. Over and over and over again . . . dozens of times, probably. I can't do this anymore. The chest goes back into my closet and I shut off the light.

Even curled up in the fetal position with the light off, I can't sleep. It's like I'm being haunted without there being any ghost to make it creepy. I want my mom back, just not this way.

But there is no other way.

I should have gone through more of her stuff before I got in bed. I owe it to her to get to know her better. I'm letting her down. Oscar the blanket, who Connor never sleeps without, is still in my bed, which means I'm letting him down, too. The thought of him alone in his room being brave without his Oscar makes my stomach churn again.

I go to the window. I get back in bed. I curl around Oscar, willing myself to get the same comfort from him that Connor does.

It doesn't work. So I pick up my phone. SOS, I type in. Call me. Then I wait.

It takes all of a minute for my phone to buzz.

"What's wrong?" Chloe huffs out. "What happened?"

"Nothing's *wrong*," I tell her. "Not really."

For a long second or two Chloe doesn't say anything, but there's music blaring in the background wherever she is right now to fill the silence.

"So . . . what?" she demands. "You sent me an SOS at two in the morning your time just to say hello?"

"No . . . sorry . . . I . . ." But somehow I can't get out any other words. "I just . . ."

"Lex, hold on, okay?"

I nod like somehow she can see me and wait for her to come back. The music in the background gets progressively less loud as the seconds drag on.

"Now spill," she says.

Somehow I still can't figure what to say or how. Like talking about it will make everything too real.

"All right, you were pissing me off before," Chloe says. "But now you're making me worry. Talk to me, Lex."

I can do this. I tell Chloe everything.

"Okay," I begin. "Well . . . the thing is . . . my grandmother died."

"Oh my God," she says. "Are you okay?"

The force of her concern hits me, even from a couple of thousand miles away. "I mean . . . you know I didn't know her at all, so . . ."

"That doesn't mean you're not upset," Chloe counters.

"So . . . she died," I say again. "And the nursing home where she'd been living sent me a chest full of my mom's stuff and now I want to read all of it because I've wanted to have something of hers for so long but I'm feeling overwhelmed and I can't seem to sleep and I just . . ."

"Lexi, breathe," Chloe says, her voice softer now. "Just breathe, okay?"

I nod into my phone. "Okay."

It takes me a minute to get myself together. I try to focus on the music in the background, less blaring than it had been but still a constant presence on this call.

"Chloe, where are you?"

"At a bar."

"But you're not twenty-one."

"Did you call to lecture me about where I go at night or to talk about your mom and grandmother?" she replies.

"No . . . no . . . I'm not . . ."

This is going all wrong. Everything is. I'm back to where I was a few minutes ago, not knowing where to begin.

"So why don't you tell me what's in the chest?" Chloe asks, giving me the starting point I need.

"I . . . I haven't looked through all of it yet," I admit. "But there's an old postcard she never mailed. And a dirty napkin that has—"

"Your grandmother sent you a *dirty napkin*?" Chloe sounds totally indignant over this. "Not much of an inheritance."

I huff out a laugh despite myself. "There's writing on it," I tell her. "My mom's and someone else's."

"That makes it slightly better, I guess," Chloe says.

I flip over the hotel postcard again. "And the postcard was to an old boyfriend or something," I continue. "Asking if he could forgive her and if he wanted to meet again."

"Wait . . . was it addressed to Matthew?" Chloe demands. "Did they break up before they got married?"

"I have no idea," I tell her. "It has an address written on it but no name."

"What's on the front of the postcard?" she demands. "You're leaving out all the important details!"

"Because I'm in emotional turmoil!" I remind her. "And it's the middle of the night and I didn't eat dinner and I can't sleep and . . . !"

"Lex?"

I sigh. "Yeah?"

"Sorry I got impatient."

I nod again like an idiot. Then I turn the postcard over. "The front of the postcard is a big, old hotel called Palais du Lac on Mackinac Island in Michigan."

"Okay . . . ," she says, drawing out the last syllable. "Never heard of it."

"Me either," I admit. "But there's a notepad from the hotel that she wrote all over, too." I take the notepad out. "The writing on it looks like she was much younger than when she wrote the postcard."

"So your mom clearly went there on vacation, right?" Chloe says. "Probably more than once. You know what this means?"

For a second I try . . . I really do try . . . to figure out what she's talking about and what it could all mean, but I come up empty. "I have no idea."

"It means you have to go there!" Chloe tells me. "You need to go dig up more about your mom."

I wince in surprise at her words. "No, I couldn't—"

"Yes, you could," Chloe cuts me off. "Matthew never talks about your mom and you want to know more about her, right?"

"Right."

"Then here's the perfect opportunity," she says. "You have to go."

Go to Mackinac Island and learn more about Mom. Be somewhere she's been . . . where she's walked and made friends and *lived*. Somewhere her memory might linger.

We don't live in the same apartment that she and Dad and I shared together. Dad and I moved into Abby's place after they got engaged. So I can't even walk around the house and *be* somewhere she used to be. The idea of going there almost tears me in two, I want it so badly right now. I open my mouth to agree with Chloe, but then reality sets back in. Reality is pretty crushing sometimes.

"Dad would never me let go."

"Matthew's such a pain in the ass," Chloe sighs. "You'll just have to lie to him about where you're going."

"Chloe!"

"What?" she says. "Do you really think my mom or Matthew always knew where I was in high school? Because they didn't. You know they didn't."

"I know but . . ."

But Chloe is *Chloe*. And I'm me. Abby probably wouldn't have even minded if she knew what Chloe had gotten up to in high school. She's always full support, full steam ahead. Chloe wants to move across the country to go to college with her girlfriend, Kiera? Abby doesn't freak out that her daughter's making major life decisions based on a high school romance. *It makes me happy to see you so in love.*

Connor wants to spend the summer at a local eco camp so he can muck around and be with frogs every day? Abby doesn't fret over him dragging mud into the house all summer long. *You'll be just like a real scientist, sweetie!*

I have no idea what I'm going to do with my life or where I want to go to college? *You don't need to have all the answers right now, Lexi. You just need to be yourself.*

But Dad . . . Chloe didn't have to grow up with him. All the rules to follow and expectations to meet. It was exhausting. I remember yelling at him once that he spent every day defending actual criminals in court and trying to get them off the hook, but he never let me off the hook about anything.

He was *not* pleased.

Just the memory of how upset and disappointed he was that I'd use his work against him like that makes my eyes tear up again.

"I can't do it, Chlo," I say sadly. "He'll see right through it and he'll be so mad at me."

"Then you have to come up with a *really* convincing lie," she counters. "An ironclad one. Something he'll never suspect."

Silence falls on the phone. I have no idea what would constitute something Dad wouldn't see through. Something he'd wouldn't suspect even though he's a public defense lawyer and his actual job is to pick apart arguments and evidence.

"You could tell him you're going to look at colleges!" Chloe shouts into my ear. "That's it!"

"Chloe, that's a terrible idea," I protest. "Even if he goes for it, he'll ask all kinds of questions about the schools afterward that I won't be able to answer."

Chloe makes a dismissive *pfft* into the phone. "I can research them for you and send you intel," she replies. "Like Ed in *Cowboy Bebop*!" She sounds a little too excited about this. "And I'll feed you the intel during your trip so that you can feed it back to him." She laughs out loud. "This is the best plan ever!"

I shake my head in the darkness of my room. "You are so scheming."

"My mom and stepdad are both lawyers," she replies. "Nature and nurture both doomed me."

This makes me laugh, just a little. But it's hard to give her joking my full attention because . . . maybe it would work? Maybe between the two of us we could pull it off?

"Lex, are you still with me?" Chloe asks. "'Cause Kiera just offered to help do the sleuthing with me. We're going to be . . . like . . . a crime-solving duo."

"Except we'd be *doing* the crime!" I hear Keira call out gleefully in the background. "Like *Ocean's 8*, but without Rihanna!"

"I mean, sadly without Rihanna," Chloe adds. "Even if she just sat there and did nothing but *look* like Rihanna, she'd make this whole thing a thousand times better."

This time I laugh out loud, then clamp my hand over my mouth to muffle the sound.

"Okay, if . . . and that's a BIG if . . . I want to go along with this plan," I say, "how would I actually get there? It's not like I have lots of money lying around to buy a plane ticket."

Another *pfft* meets this statement. "What're you, the queen of England?" Chloe scoffs. "You don't need a plane ticket. Get in my shitty old car and drive there."

"Your car is really shitty and old," I protest. "What if it doesn't make it there and back?"

Chloe lets out an exasperated sigh. "Then you call for a tow truck," she says. "Or you call me. What's the worst thing that can happen?"

That is a sadly easy question to answer. "Dad finds out where I've really been and freaks out?"

A long, long pause follows that statement. If I couldn't still hear the music pulsing in the background, I'd think she'd hung up.

"Lexi, how old are you?"

I sigh. "Chlo, you know how old I am."

"You're seventeen. Seventeen is old enough to make your own decisions," she tells me. "You want to learn more about your mom and you have a lead on where to find more. So get a damn oil change and go."

Once again, I'm at a loss for words. This time, though, it's because what she's saying might actually be possible. I might be able to fake my way to Mackinac Island. I might be able to actually walk in Mom's footsteps and . . .

My eyes stray to the blue chest and the mosaic of the greenhouse. That picture might be of a place Mom knew. Someplace she'd been, not just something she imagined up for her mosaic. I want to be there, too. I need to be.

My heart thumps in my chest a little too quickly. Tears stream down my face. I'm terrified and excited and so many other things at once that my stomach hurts again.

I could go to Mackinac. I could . . .

"Lexi, did you zone out?"

"Yeah," I tell her. "But I've zoned back in."

"So what're you going to do?"

I squeeze in a shallow breath. It comes back out as a nervous sound. Half sob, half laugh.

"We'll be your wingwomen," Chloe continues. "Kiera and me . . . we'll make sure you have what you need to keep Matthew in the dark. We'll have your back the whole time."

Somehow this makes me wish she was here so desperately that it's painful. My chest hurts. My whole body does.

"I miss you so much, Chlo," I tell her, trying to hold my tears back.

"I miss you too," she says. "I wish we could come with you."

And then it hits me. Chloe's not coming with me. No one is. If I do this—if I go to Mackinac Island—I'll be entirely on my own for the first time in my life. It's both terrifying and thrilling to think about.

Mostly terrifying, if I'm being honest.

Dad'll kill me if he ever finds out, that's a given. And he's going to find out eventually. The only credit card I have is an emergency one that's linked to his account and I'm guessing the hotel's not going to take a reservation without a credit card. When the bill comes in a few weeks, I'll be toast. It'll be a miracle if he lets me leave the house again before I go to college. I'm not even exaggerating.

Maybe this isn't worth it after all.

"You're not chickening out already, are you, Lexi?" Chloe asks. She knows me way too well. "Because I'm not going to let you. You have to go. It might be your only chance to find out more about her."

My eyes stray to the mosaic box. I run my fingers over the greenhouse again. I take out the postcard and the notepad and the painting.

Mom was so funny and beautiful and *alive* when she put all of this on paper. I want to know her like that. I ache to.

Chloe's right. I know she's right. This is too important to just let go of.

"No, I'm going," I reply. "No matter what the consequences are, I'm going."

CHAPTER 3

Lexi (Now)

There's no possible way that I'm going to pull this off.

I hit Google and look up Mackinac Island as soon as I wake up since I've never even heard of the place and it's . . . something. Horse-drawn carriages. Quaint little shops. It looks like a movie set, but it's real. People actually live there. I can't believe Mom used to go on vacation in a place like this.

Then I look up the hotel itself. It looks like a kind of castle, with its turrets looming over everything else in sight. The kind of place that would have false bookshelves with doors that lead to secret places. It also costs hundreds of dollars a night, which only includes breakfast. While I could eat simply, I'd still need to actually *eat*. And eating takes money that I don't have. Plus I'd need to pay for gas and the ferry to get there. The money I make at my part-time job at the supermarket isn't going to cut it.

I put my phone down, a surge of disappointment coursing through me. Why couldn't I be from some rich family whose parents would never even notice all the huge fees racked up on the credit card? Why does it have to be so hard to do something as simple as find out more about my mother?

Lying back on my bed, I press both hands over my eyes and try to envision how I can still make this trip happen. My phone dings with a text message, but it's probably Chloe and I don't have the energy to face her right now. I can't bring myself to put into actual words just how impossible this idea would be in reality.

Instead I get up and lift my mom's mosaic chest out of the closet.

Maybe it'll be enough to just read everything in here. Maybe I won't have to waste tons of money I don't have and get grounded for my entire senior year of high school.

With great care, I open the lid of the chest and rifle through what I've already read until I find something new.

There's a sketch of a blond girl lying on a bench that has the name VIOLA BENSON carved over her. Under that, I find a piece of paper wrapped around two friendship bracelets. One's clearly homemade, an elaborate pattern woven together from pieces of twine or something. The other's definitely *not* homemade. It's got pale blue cording, the kind you find on bracelets in places like The Paper Store, with a silver charm in the shape of the island hanging from it.

The paper they're wrapped up in has a completely different handwriting from Mom's or her friend from the napkin and the painting.

I know it seemed at first like I didn't care that much about the friendship bracelet you made me. But I did. I just always act like I don't care about anything. Bad habit, I know.

Anyway, you and I both know I'd never be able to make one friendship bracelet, let alone two. And if I did, neither of us would want to wear them. So I did what you're supposed to do as a good, red-blooded American and bought these for us instead. What can I say? Capitalism runs through my veins.

L

I slip both bracelets onto my wrist and hold my hand over them. Mom must have worn them at one point. They're hers. Actually hers. I squeeze my eyes shut and try to feel something . . . anything . . . of her. Like these two pieces of cord and string could still hold a trace of her I could grasp on to.

But they don't and I can't.

I sit with them on my wrist for a while anyway as I keep looking through the chest.

The next piece of paper contains a list of places she wanted to run away from home to. Spreading her stuff out over my bed, I compare the handwriting. It looks younger than her writing on the postcard, but older than the chocolate-stained napkin. Just like with the napkin and the perky princess, this list has someone else's writing on it, too. The same someone else's writing. JR's.

Where I'd like to run away to:

1. Paris
2. Peru
3. Prague

Why're you starting with all these P places? Does alphabetical order mean nothing to you?

They're just what popped into my head. I'm not done plotting my escape yet.

4. Johannesburg
5. New York City
6. Rome
7. Mt. Everest

Mt. Everest? People die climbing that thing.

Not if they're very, very careful.

Um . . . yeah. Even if they're very, very careful. Climbing Everest is like asking to die.

Did I invite you to come with me?

Yeah. You did.

But you didn't want to. So mind your own business. These are my places I want to disappear to!

8. Both islands of New Zealand
9. Tokyo (or Kyoto) (or really anywhere in Japan)
10. Mumbai

It's not like your parents are poor. Can't you actually just go to these places?

When I asked my dad about going on vacation in Paris

he got annoyed and said, "We're already in the most beautiful place in the world."

So you can go to Paris when you're older.

And if you're **really** nice to me, I might let you come with me.

I'm never nice to you.

Then you can stay home.

I read through the places Mom wanted to go and their little notes back and forth.

Mom did actually go to Paris when she got a little bit older, but she didn't go with her friend JR. There've never been many pictures of her lying around, but when I was in fourth grade I found one of Mom, Dad, and me when I was about three at the top of the Eiffel Tower. Dad's wearing me in one of those kid carrier backpacks. In the picture, Mom and Dad looked thrilled. I, on the other hand, appeared to be howling like someone was torturing me.

When I found it, I was so happy to see a picture of her that I ran to show my dad so he could tell me about the trip.

"I didn't know we went to Paris!" I told him, handing the picture to him. "Did we have fun? Did Mom like it there? It doesn't look like I liked it."

His whole face froze when he realized what I'd given him. His jaw tensed in that way it always does when he's upset about something.

"Where did you find this?" he asked in a low voice.

"In one of the boxes in the closet," I replied. "How old was I when we went?"

He gazed out the window, away from me. "You were three and a half," he said. "We took a belated honeymoon."

This seemed like a funny idea to me even at the time. I picked up the photo again, eager to see every detail I could. "You took me on your honeymoon?"

Dad snatched the picture back. "Why don't you go do some coloring?"

I reached for the picture again, but he put his hand over it like a cage. "But Dad, I—"

"Lexi, I told you to go do some coloring."

I shrank back from him and did exactly what I was told. I found a coloring book, then sobbed into it for about half an hour.

That night, after I went to bed, I heard Dad crying in the room next door. Even then I knew he wouldn't want me to go in there to help him feel better.

I felt so lost, so alone when I was little. I still do now.

I wonder sometimes if I was a birth control accident he didn't want to have to deal with. They were really young when Mom got pregnant. Just a couple of years older than I am now. They didn't get married till I was a year old. Maybe he didn't want to get married. Maybe he didn't want me. The very thought makes me clench my fists to keep my hands from shaking. But honestly, it would explain a lot if that were the case.

Part of me wishes I knew where Dad had hidden that picture so I could look at it again now that I'm older. But probably he threw it out. He threw out a lot of her stuff after she died. He packed the rest away.

There's been so little left of her for such a long time.

Now there's more.

I lay the list out on my bed along with the other bits and pieces I've already looked at. Then I dig back in.

There's a watercolor painting, done on the inside of a little, flattened paper plate, of a girl with wild black hair just like mine. She's got her back to me as she looks at the Eiffel Tower, so you can't see her face, but it's clear who it is.

The word "Someday" is inked underneath it.

Well, at least Mom's *someday* came true. She went to Paris with Dad and me. Mom who I barely remember, and Dad who never smiles the way he did in that picture.

Someday.

The word slides around in my head for a while. I try to force my mind to focus on what my own *someday* might be, but I come up empty. Anger . . . frustration at myself for not even being able to formulate a single wish for the future . . . sweeps over me. Heat moves from my face down my neck and into my abdomen because I have no answers.

Someday I'll figure out who I am and what I want to do with my life. *Someday* all of this will make sense.

Unfortunately, that day isn't today.

A nagging thought pulses in the back of my mind right now as it has so many times before: If I'd known Mom better, longer, would I know myself better, too?

I put the paper plate aside and tear into the mosaic box, needing to find at least some of the answers. There are more hotel notepads with her scribbling all over them. A practically empty datebook, some fliers.

There are no answers, though.

I pile everything back into the mosaic chest and close it gently. I can't deal with this now.

After a full afternoon watching a *Thomas the Tank Engine* marathon with Connor, my mind feels like it's turned to jelly. That show is seriously weird. Like, slow torture weird. But he can't resist the talking trains, so I watch it anyway. It gives me time to think if nothing else.

I have to at least try to talk to my dad before I even consider doing something as stupid as sneaking off to a strange island. I haven't asked him about Mom for a long time. Maybe now he'd tell me more. Maybe now he'd be ready to talk.

So I go in the kitchen while he's getting dinner ready.

"You going to set the table?" he asks.

"Yeah, sure."

Plates. Cups. Napkins. Utensils. I get them in place on the table. The whole time I try to figure out how to bring Mom up. How to make him talk to me.

In the end, with no other brilliant ideas for subterfuge, I go with bluntness.

"Dad, can I ask you a question?"

"Shoot."

He doesn't look up from the stir-fry chicken and veggies he's making. I wipe my sweaty palms on my shorts.

"What was Mom like?"

Dad looks up abruptly. His eyebrows bunch together. For a long second or two, I'm not sure he's even going to answer.

"What do you want to know?"

It's a good question. One I should have worked out ahead of time. Still, I know what I want to hear. I just have to ask the right way.

"I mean, what was she like as a person? Was she funny? Was she shy?"

Dad stirs the chicken and veggies in the wok. He adds in sambal to make it good and spicy. He doesn't say a word.

"Dad?"

With a quick nod of his head, he says, "She was wonderful."

It seems at first like more might be coming. Like he's just taking his time with his answer. But then the seconds drag on and on and . . . nothing.

"But . . . I mean . . . *how* was she wonderful?" Hope wells up in my chest that this might be it. That he might actually talk about her.

Instead he turns and opens the fridge to get out some ginger. His shoulders are as bunched up as his eyebrows are. He looks like he's going to shrivel in on himself.

"Dad?"

With another nod, he says, "There was no one like her. She was . . . well . . ."

And that's it. That's all he gives me. Now it's me who feels like I'm shriveling into myself.

I stand by the kitchen table. Dad stands by the stove. Neither of us says a word. This goes on for God knows how long before he finally turns around. The pain in his eyes makes me wince.

"Lexi, I . . ."

Dad wipes his forehead with the back of his hand. He drops his eyes down to the floor. "Can you go let Abby and Connor know that dinner will be ready soon?"

Our eyes meet, but he quickly looks away. He's not going to tell me anything. He's *never* going to tell me anything.

"Sure, Dad. I'll go let them know."

But instead I head straight to my room. Then I check my phone. Two messages from Chloe.

You are NOT going to wuss out of this, the first message says.

Then I scroll to the second text.

Are you?

With a grim smile on my face, I write back: **No, I'm not.**

I'm not sure I can wait anymore for some distant day and time when I'll know more about Mom. The time is now.

Scrolling through my browsing history, I find it: the Palais du Lac Hotel.

One room with a double bed, back of the hotel, no water view, no frills. I hit reserve.

Since my dad is a stickler for rules and organization, I hit him where it counts: with my planning. He wants shiny binders and typed-up agendas? I give him that. If there's one way to convince him (and by that I mean trick him) into letting me do this, it's going to be beating him at his own game.

"What do you think?" I ask as he looks through the file I prepared for him. The road is mapped out; the colleges I'll go see are, too. I even used sticky notes to separate out the different schools.

He sifts through all of it. "I think you've done your research."

I wait for him to say more, but he doesn't.

"Some of the schools are pretty close to each other," I continue. "So I can probably hit the six of them over the seven days." I pick up the ballpoint pen I brought to the table with me in case I needed to take notes, but instead of writing anything, I just keep clicking the tip of it in and out of the pen itself as I wait for him to respond.

"And you'd be with Tabitha the whole time?" he asks.

"Of course."

My classmate Tabitha Friedman is in Ann Arbor visiting her grandparents all summer long, so she's not here to tell any tales.

Then I hit him where I know is his sensitive spot.

"And then you wouldn't have to take time off to drive me around," I tell him. "I know you have a lot of cases up in the air right now."

Abby puts her hand on my arm. "You're so sweet to think about your dad's workload. He does have so much going on."

My guilt levels skyrocket. My palms sweat so much the pen slips out of my hand.

"Yeah," Dad agrees, making it even worse. "It would be bad timing." Then he gives me a searching look. "Are you sure you'll be okay on your own? I could probably take a little time off later in the summer so we could go together."

"I won't be on my own," I lie. "And it will be good practice for my first year of college."

Abby wipes a tear away from her eye. "I can't believe you're all growing up so quickly," she says. "Chloe's gone and you will be too in another year. But we don't want to hold you back." She smiles first at me and then at Dad. "What do you think, Matthew?"

He nods at me. "I think it's a solid plan," he says. Then he dives into logistics: getting my car serviced before I go, calling the credit card company to let them know my plans, having emergency plans in place in case anything goes wrong.

"I'll be fine, Dad," I tell him. "I promise."

He gives me a long, serious look. "I know you'll be responsible,

Lexi," he says. "But I'm your dad. I'm supposed to worry about you."

This makes Abby swoon a little and me glance his way, puzzled. *Does* he worry about me? Somewhere deep down I know he loves me. But deep down doesn't count for much. At least not to me.

Honestly, the thought makes it easier to keep lying.

"I'll take care of everything," I assure them. "It'll be great. And I'll get a jump start on college tours."

My mind strays to the chest. To the memory of the night that Mom loved so much she wanted to carry it around with her like a piece of lake glass. The notes she wrote and the friends I've never heard of before. My resolve hardens.

I am going to Mackinac Island and nothing is going to stand in my way.

CHAPTER 4

Emma (Then)

There's something about the beginning of summer that makes me want to jump and dance and even skip. It's not just the weather—though that certainly helps. It's that the whole island feels as if it's thrown open its doors and burst back to life.

As I walk into town, everyone and everything is practically vibrating with the beginning of summer. By the end of the season, every single person who lives here year-round will be complaining about the tourists, but right at this moment shopkeepers are smiling widely through ice cream parlor windows and greeting people from off-island who are eager to experience the island down to the very *taste* of it at the doors to the fudge shops.

And why shouldn't everyone be smiling, islander and tourist alike? They're here, in the most beautiful place on the planet.

The steady clip-clop of horse hooves sounds behind me and I turn to wave to Martin, one of the older folks who drive the carriages around town.

"Heading to the dock?" I call to him.

"The very place, Emma," he tells me.

"Then I'll see you there!" I wave as he passes me on the road.

If Martin's heading to the dock, that means the ferry must almost be here. And since the ferry never, ever runs late—and I always do—that doesn't bode well for me.

I kick off my flip-flops and take off at a run, holding my sundress up over my knees to keep myself from tripping over it. This time I pass Martin—along with two other horse-drawn carriages—on my way to the dock.

As I catch my breath, I notice that the ferry is still a white dot out on the lake, which means I probably didn't have to sprint here. And after a few minutes of standing around with nothing to do, it starts to eat at me that, well, I'm standing around with nothing to do.

The summer's officially beginning and I have far too much energy right now not to have anything to do.

I march toward a patch of tall dandelions growing out from where the pier meets the town landing. One by one, I pick them all, weaving them into a crown. The stems tightly wind around each other and the flowers point out *just so* around the greenery. I place it carefully on my head, hoping it might make my hair a little less unruly, even though I know it would take a lot more than a dandelion crown to manage this mop.

The ferry's so close now I can see the faces of the tourists as they gawk at the carriages and stores and everything that makes Mackinac *Mackinac*.

At two o'clock on the dot, it pulls up to the dock and passengers begin streaming off the boat, pointing at all the charming, old-fashioned sights that the websites and brochures promised them they'd find here. It's sort of cute—even a little heartwarming—to see them disembark with so much enthusiasm.

But they can't hold my interest for long because I'm here for a very specific reason—or at least a very specific person—and he's not new to summers here at all.

Finally I spot JR.

He has the same too-pale whiteness to his skin he arrives with every summer, as if he hasn't stepped foot outdoors for the entire school year. He also has an eager expression on his face as he scans the crowd for his dad, though I know for a fact that Terry isn't here to meet him. It's funny and almost sweet to see JR excited about something because . . . well . . . he's not the most excitable human being I've ever encountered.

I wait till he sees me to wave at him.

The hopeful expression on his face fades and for a split second his shoulders seem to deflate. He looks away, forcing his face into his usual mask of indifference. Not that this is anything new. If I lived and died by JR's indifferent looks, I'd have shriveled up into nothingness long before now.

"What're you doing here?" he asks as he approaches.

"Happy to see you, too, JR."

He gives me a stern once-over. "I didn't say I wasn't happy to see you," he clarifies. "I just asked what you're doing here."

An eye roll is the only possible response to this, so I give him one. "I came to meet you," I inform him. "To welcome you to this glorious summer."

He drops a book and I bend to pick it up for him.

"Are you reading that same book *again*?" I ask when the I see the author's name.

"It's the Earthsea series," he informs me. "If you'd ever bothered to ask me about them, you'd know there are tons of them."

"Hm . . . maybe you can tell me later."

He shoots me an aggrieved look before he stuffs a book into his duffel bag and shoulders it. "Are you welcoming me to summer by making me walk to the hotel with my stuff?"

"Looks that way."

JR sighs but doesn't argue. "Are you at least gonna help me carry this thing?"

Instead of replying, I pull the bag off his shoulder and take one of the short straps while he picks up the other. With it hanging between us, we start making our way up the hill toward the hotel.

"Well, it's definitely lighter this way," he mumbles.

I elbow him gently over the bag. "Why are you so grumpy?"

JR looks up at the sky as if he's asking some higher power for strength to deal with me today. "Why are you so cheerful?"

I grin at him. "Because the sun is shining, the weather is perfect, the lake is beautiful, and everything is exactly the way it should be!" I tell him a little breathlessly.

A grim look meets this declaration. "You're not going to start skipping, are you?" he gripes. "'Cause I regret to inform you that you're way too old for that anymore."

"I'm seventeen as of two months ago," I remind him. "Not that you called to wish me a happy birthday or sent a card or anything."

He grunts—then he blushes, of all things—but doesn't respond otherwise. I take this as an invitation to keep talking.

"Besides, you're never too old to skip when your joy is too much to contain," I tell him. I drop my strap of the bag, letting it sag to the ground at his feet. Then I toss my dandelion crown onto JR's head and twirl away from him, skipping up the road to the hotel.

"Why do you always have to be like this?" he calls after me, but when I turn around, JR looks like he's trying really hard not to smile.

"Because I have a delightful joie de vivre!" I yell back to him. "Ask anyone who knows me. It's one of my best qualities!"

Finally the smile comes out in full force. His smiles are so rare that it makes me laugh just a little bit.

"What's so funny?" He instantly drops the smile.

"You are, JR," I tell him. "Don't be such a grump!"

"Don't be such a perky princess," he replies.

I laugh out loud this time. "You think I'm a perky princess?"

"Like you've stepped out of a Disney movie," he tells me. "I'm just waiting for a little bird to perch on your finger to sing you a happy song."

I close my eyes for a second and spread my arms wide. "God, I'd *love* it if that happened. Can you imagine being friends with the birds?"

JR stops in his tracks. Stares at me as if I have ten heads. This would be more imposing if it weren't for the fact that he's still wearing a dandelion crown.

"Know what I think?" I ask him.

"Nope," he says. "And I don't want to."

"Alas for you, I'm going to tell you anyway," I reply. Then I put my hands on my hips and look him squarely in the eye. "I think you're happy to see me, but too much of a dork to admit it."

Shouldering his bag again, JR begins to walk past me on the road to the hotel. I watch him go, wondering if he's really going to leave me here. We haven't seen each other in months, and he's just going to take off without me? Who does something like that?

But then he calls over his shoulder, "I am happy to see you." For some reason, this makes a warm feeling bloom in my chest . . . which he promptly ruins by saying, "But if you tell anyone I said that, I'll definitely deny it."

I sigh and start skipping again, elbowing him a little too hard this time as I pass him. Now it's me outstripping him as I pass under the *Palais Du Lac Hotel Centennial Celebration* sign that hangs over the gates.

"There's someone I want you to meet," I call back to him.

"I don't want to meet anyone."

"And there's a whole slate of activities we can join after you've caught up with your dad," I yell. "More than usual because of the hotel's anniversary."

"I don't want to do them."

JR can be so, so sulky sometimes. So annoyingly stubborn. But I know him too well to think this is his final answer.

"And yet you know you will," I say as I turn to face him again. There's a good bit of distance between us now, so I stop to let him catch up to me.

"And yet I know I will," he sighs.

I grin at him. "Want to skip with me?"

"Yeah, I *totally* want to skip with you," he says. "It's all I've been dreaming about for weeks."

"Really?" I don't want to sound as eager as I do but . . . well . . .

"No, Emma. Not really."

I know he's never actually going to skip with me, but I can't help trying to convince him anyway.

"Maybe you could consider it just this once," I say in a wheedling voice. "Just to make me happy?"

I look at him expectantly. For a second, I wonder if he's actually considering skipping, but he shakes his head. "How 'bout I just walk fast while you skip?"

I take a good look at him. The old jeans and beaten-up sneakers he won't let go of even though they're falling apart. The dark hair hanging over his eyes that's in dire need of a cut—and that I'm very sure he won't get cut any time soon. The barest hint of a frown teasing at the corners of his mouth. This concession is clearly the best compromise I'm going to get.

"Deal."

We walk on till we get to the staff housing where his dad lives. "Greenhouse at seven?" I ask.

His eyes widen for a second before they drop to the ground. A crease forms between his eyebrows. "Let's just meet at the bonfire."

"But . . . we haven't been there for so long and . . ."

"Emma?" he says. "Let's meet at the bonfire, okay? I've got stuff to do this afternoon."

Something very tiny deflates in me. The first thing we always do when he gets here is go to the greenhouse. Always. And now . . .

"Oh . . . okay."

He lets his dark hair fall over his face as we walk. Finally JR pushes it behind his ear again and looks at me for a long second or two. "I thought you were going to skip?"

I take in a deep breath and let it out again. It almost feels as if he *wants* me to skip, but that doesn't make any sense at all. But I'm not sure what else to do right now. I want to feel the happiness I did just half an hour ago. As if this is going to be the best summer ever.

So I do it—I start skipping. But I've lost some of my zeal for it. JR keeps his word and walks as fast as he can to stay by my side till he turns off to the staff housing. JR is a grump and a cynic, and a million other things that drive me bonkers. But he's here and so is the summer.

As I keep skipping, some of the earlier happiness seeps back into me, as if each bouncing step pushes more and more of it back into my chest. This summer will be extraordinary.

CHAPTER 5

Emma (Then)

E ven though my dad seemed determined to make dinner unpleasant, as soon as I step out onto the verandah and into the deepening twilight, I try to put my conversation with him out of my mind. It's not hard to do because twilight is, of course, the best part of the entire day. The light is that perfect in-between of not-too-bright and not-too-dark. The sky contains a whole palette full of colors, as if it got bored with the deep blue it wore during the day and dressed up for a spectacular night. Maybe I should have dressed up, too, but I'm wearing the same old yellow sundress I've had on all day.

I can already see the glow from the bonfire on the beach as it rises in a swirl of smoke over the pine trees. The hotel has one every Friday night in summer, which means I've been to *loads* of bonfires. But they never cease to be magical. It's a gift, I realize as I walk down the path to the lake. To have so much beauty in my life is a gift.

The thought makes me smile, but it's not the only reason I'm smiling. Tonight everything is going to come together in the most wonderful way to ensure this is the best summer ever.

That's a lot of "most" and "best" type superlatives, but there's a prickling excitement to everything right now, as if sparks could fly from my fingertips and no one would even blink an eye because they know this summer is magical, too.

I step out of the clearing and see JR standing off to the side, staring up at the colors of the dusk with his eyes blown wide and a look of complete awe on his face. The bonfire is huge, the orange glow of it lights up the whole side of JR that faces it, while throwing the rest of him into shadowy relief. It feels as if it's a metaphor for his personality, though I'd never say that to him.

Or maybe I would if I wanted to annoy him. Although, to be honest, he already looks pretty annoyed as he sees me approach him.

"You're late."

"I'm always late," I remind him. "I don't know why you still bother showing up on time."

A distinct frown forms on his face as he finally looks down from the sky and at me. "Or you could *attempt* to be on time and do the responsible thing for once."

But this is the last thing I want to hear. "You sound like my dad," I complain. "He was even lecturing me on how much *more* responsible you are than I am tonight."

The whole scene plays out in my head, making my ears burn.

"Have you gone downstairs to ask about a job yet?" Dad asked. "Maybe you could walk down right now and get an application."

"Dad, I have plans tonight, and . . ."

"Linda's already got a job," he continued. "And I'd bet good money that JR's already looking for one even though he just arrived today."

My shoulders drooped because I knew he was right. JR refuses to work at the hotel, but last summer he walked around town as soon as he got here and applied for six jobs in a single day. He ended up working two part-time. I'm sure he'll end up doing the same this summer. And Linda . . . the minute school got out she started working in the hotel's café.

JR shoots me a surprised glance. "Your dad thinks I'm the responsible one? He doesn't even like me."

Like a knee-jerk reaction, I protest. "Yes he does!"

"No, your *mom* likes me," he says. "Your dad . . . tolerates me."

I want so badly to deny this—to chalk it up to JR just being grumpy and paranoid—but the more I think about it, the more an uncomfortable grain of truth gets lodged in my brain.

"You're not going to keep griping about my dad on this perfect night, are you?"

"Nope, I'm gonna gripe at *you* for being late, then move on to being my usual delightful self," he replies. "Ask anyone. They'll tell you all about my youthful joie de vivre."

I bump my arm into his. "Stop being a grump so we can go make s'mores, and let the happiness of the night seep into us until we can't bear it anymore."

When I open my arms to take in the beauty of everything around me, JR gives me a strange look. Not a griping one, or a mask of indifference, or even the reluctant smile he sometimes deigns to bestow upon me. This one I can't read at all.

"What?" I demand.

Before he can answer, though, the sounds of a guitar strum to life on the other side of the bonfire and a voice—a voice *like an angel* if the person it belongs to is to be believed—begins to sing. If the bonfire cast JR into light and shadow, it bathes Ryan Desmond in such a glow that he's his own little supernova. Truly. His blond hair glints in the firelight and he beams out this . . . this sparkling smile at everyone around him.

It's kind of annoying how good-looking he is.

Huffing out an irritated breath, I pull JR by the arm away from the bonfire. "Come on," I tell him. "There's someone I want you to meet."

His shoulders sag. "Wow . . . that's exactly what I want to do right now," he grumbles. "When I woke up this morning, I thought, *God I hope Emma has someone she wants to force me to talk to tonight!*"

I walk backward to face him so he can see just how much I mean this. "Wait and see," I insist. "You're going to want to be friends with her once you meet her."

A toss of his hair meets this assurance. "I don't need any more friends."

I elbow him in response. "Don't be a dolt," I reply. "The more friends the merrier." Then I grab his arm again. "Now let's make s'mores."

JR and I have always had different s'mores tactics. He meticulously toasts his marshmallow to a golden brown. It's the ideal—the ultimate achievement in marshmallow toasting every time. I, on the other, have burnt so many marshmallows over the years when I've stopped paying attention to what I'm doing that I actually like them charred now. So I make this one catch fire on purpose and then blow it out. He eats his so quickly it's as if he thinks someone's going to take it away from him, whereas I close my eyes and savor the hard graham cracker, the sweet, warm chocolate, and the char-encrusted gooey-ness of the marshmallow.

The deliciousness of it all is almost too much. I sink back into the sand and sigh.

"If you didn't have marshmallow on your chin, I'd have no idea if that's a happy sigh or a sad one," says a voice overhead. "But you're clearly blissed out on s'mores."

I open my eyes to find a tall girl standing over me, her uniform bow tie in her hand and the sleeves of her shirt rolled up. The fire makes her blond hair look like spun gold, though the scowl on her face looks anything but. I grin up at her.

"Linda, you look tired," I say, holding out a hand to her. "Come lie down and look at the stars with me."

Linda doesn't lie down but she does take my hand and plunks onto the grass next to me. She sits in silence for a moment or two before she says, "So are you going to introduce to me to JR or am I supposed to pretend he's not here all night?"

This makes me sit upright again. After all my talking this introduction up to both of them, I forgot to actually introduce them.

"Oh . . . of course!" I say. "Linda, this is JR. JR, Linda."

He stiffens on the other side of me. "My name's not really JR."

The coolest of once-overs meets this statement from Linda.

"Well, that's what she calls you," she tells him. "So that's the name I know you by."

I watch as they glance at each other with mutually unimpressed expressions on their faces and something inside me—some part of all my hopes for this night and for them becoming friends—flattens out just a little.

"Emma's told me a lot about you," Linda says in a dubious voice, even though I didn't say anything *that* bad about him.

With a look of indifference to beat all of his looks of indifference, JR tucks his hair behind his ear. "That's weird. She's never said a word about you," he replies. My jaw drops at how rude he's being—even for JR. Then I elbow him again.

JR pulls away from me. "That's the fourth time today that you've resorted to violence," he grumbles. "And I've only been here a few hours."

"Maybe you bring out the worst in her," Linda remarks.

"Maybe *she* brings out the worst in *me*," he argues.

I slump back onto the sand. This really isn't going the way I'd hoped. I guess I'd been hoping for too much? Or too soon? Or maybe there was no way this was going to go the way I'd imagined it would.

"Stop being a grump, JR." My voice sounds a little too pleading, even to me.

"Sure," he agrees. "As soon as you stop being a perky princess."

Linda's eyes light up with laughter. "Okay, I like him," Linda says to me. "I was on the fence till the *perky princess* thing, but now I'm sold."

I glance from one of them to the other—at Linda's smirk and JR's frown.

With a small sniff, I say, "I'm not sure I want you two to be friends anymore."

"Too late," Linda replies. "Now you're stuck with us."

"Besides, *you can never have too many friends*," JR echoes my words from earlier.

Linda nudges me with her foot. "And I got to be friends with you when I didn't think I would."

I stop breathing for a second. Then I sit up again so I can look directly at her and see if she was kidding. She doesn't look as if she was kidding.

"You didn't?"

But Linda leans into me. "No, I didn't," she admits. "But you're always so positive and I'm . . . not." She smiles. "Plus, who's going to come to my swim meets and cheer me on if you don't?"

I sigh. "Not Ryan."

"Or my dad," she agrees. "I rely on you to scream out my name."

"She can be pretty loud," JR interjects. When Linda smirks at him, he almost physically shrinks away. "Just don't get any ideas about me coming to swim meets, 'cause organized sports are *not* my thing."

Linda laughs as she leans into me more.

My eyes stray from him to her and then back again. A huge grin breaks out over my face. I'm smiling so hard that my cheeks hurt a little. "This is exactly how I'd hoped the night would go!"

This time JR sighs. Dramatically. "There's no way to dampen her spirits when she gets like this," he tells Linda.

My smile fades a little at his words. "Not that you'd ever want to?" I ask hopefully.

JR has that same unreadable expression on his face from before. "Not that I'd ever want to."

For a second or two, neither of us looks away. Then his eyes drop to the ground.

I squint my eyes at him, trying to figure him out.

"Hey, what'd I miss?" Linda's brother Ryan—having stopped his fireside singing—plops himself and his guitar down next to JR.

"I got off work, Emma's still got marshmallow on her chin, and the legendary JR turns out not to be as unbearable as I thought he'd be," Linda informs him.

Ryan ignores almost all of that and leans over JR. Right toward me. "Here, lemme see," he says. With the swipe of a single finger, he gets the marshmallow off my chin. My cheeks burn, but Ryan doesn't seem to notice as he licks the marshmallow off his finger and smiles at me. It's that smile—all his general pleasantness—that makes parents love him. At least mine do.

Ryan sits back down with the same smile and holds out his hand. "Hey, JR. I'm Ryan, by the way."

But JR's not looking at Ryan at all. He's still got his eyes on me, one brow raised.

"JR?" Ryan says.

Startled, JR turns to him. "Yeah, what?"

With a jovial little bounce of his shoulders, Ryan laughs. "Handshake?"

With a small shrug, JR says, "Okay. Whatever," before he shakes Ryan's hand.

"Great!" Ryan says cheerfully. "Nice to finally meet you."

"Um . . . you too?" JR says, decidedly *less* cheerfully.

There's a crease between his eyebrows now, and I know why. It's only his first night here and I've sprung too many people on him. For better and very often for worse, we always hang out just the two of us in summer. I just changed all the rules without even warning him about it. A little knot of worry forms in my stomach, but I have no idea how to make this better.

So I ask the first lame question that pops into my head. "So . . . um . . . what's our plan for tonight?"

No one says anything for a painfully long moment or two, so I just keep talking. "Does anyone want to go canoeing? Because that might be fun and . . ."

Linda's whole face lights up. "Wait, can we do that? I thought the canoes were only for daytime."

Okay, progress! I can work with this. "It's not like they're under lock and key," I tell her. "No one will notice if we take a couple out." Then I look at JR sideways. "And it's not like we haven't snuck one out before, right?"

This makes his shoulders droop. Dramatically. "Yeah, but you only like it because I do all the work."

With my shoulder, I nudge him again. "I like doing it because it's beautiful out on the lake when the stars are out." I pause for dramatic effect, just because I can. "And also because you do all the work."

"So, we're going canoeing?" Ryan says. He's on his feet already, like an eager puppy, bouncing up and down on his toes.

Relief washes over me like the cold lake water on a hot summer day. I smile at all three of them. "We're going canoeing."

Once we get to the canoes, though, I look around at the three of them. JR, who I spend every moment of every summer with. Linda, who I've spent every moment this past winter and spring with. And Ryan, who's . . . very excited about canoeing. The question is, who's going in which boat? I almost want to pick Ryan just so that I don't have to choose between Linda and JR.

Then JR sidles up to me. "You ready?"

"Oh . . . yeah, definitely."

My surprise must be visible on my face because he shakes his head at me.

"Then let's do this." He gestures to the canoe.

"Guess I'm stuck with you, then," Linda tells Ryan. "Try not to do anything to make me want to dump you out of the canoe."

He rushes to assure her that he won't as I climb into our canoe and lie down diagonally across it as I always do, dangling one foot over the lowest part of the side into the cool water. JR lumbers in after me. He's not a big person, but he still manages to rock the canoe as he sits down and picks up the oars.

"Wait . . . you don't help him row at all?" Linda says. Then she turns to JR. "I can't believe you just let her lie there."

JR slots the oars in place but doesn't respond. When we were younger, we use to fight about this all the time but I always won. I don't even think he's ever really cared if I help row or not. JR just likes to argue.

"I'm calling front of the boat like Emma!" Ryan says as he jumps onto the other canoe. "You can row me around like JR does."

This earns a glare from Linda. "You know I worked all day, right?" she demands. "And that you did absolutely nothing while I was working?"

An argument starts up between them. I close my eyes and attempt to stop listening.

JR pushes off with his oars. We cut through the water, gentle waves lapping at the side of the canoe and splashing up my leg. Linda and Ryan pull up beside us, Linda still grumbling that she got stuck rowing.

But then quiet falls at last. The stars twinkle in the evening sky and it's so beautiful that it almost hurts to look at. It's so beautiful that it's impossible not to want to paint it. And I will. Tonight. Then someday soon I'll stay up all night and paint watercolor after watercolor of the sky as it changes from dusk to dawn.

It sounds like heaven, actually.

"You good?" JR's voice is just above a whisper.

I nod. "You?"

He doesn't say a word, but since he'd be hurling complaints at me if he was not, in fact, good, I smile.

Just as quiet begins to fall again, Ryan strums at his guitar. His strong, clear baritone rises above the water—he really does have a beautiful voice—as he sings an old Simon & Garfunkel song they play in the breakfast room at the hotel sometimes.

"'Kathy,' I said as we boarded a Greyhound in Pittsburgh
'Michigan seems like a dream to me now.'"

We're in Michigan, or at least a tiny sliver of it, and it does seem like a dream right now. I close my eyes again, listening to the sound of his voice as the cool night air blows my hair over my face. And I wonder, for the first time ever in my life, if there can be anything better than this—a group of friends, or hopefully soon-to-be-friends, out together under the stars.

I'm inclined to think that there isn't.

CHAPTER 6

Lexi (Now)

By the time I get to the ferry terminal I've been in the car for so many hours that my legs ache. The GPS on my phone said it would take six and half hours to get here. Instead it took a little over nine. Nine whole hours.

Part of that was my own fault, of course. If I hadn't downed a huge iced coffee and most of my bottle of water, I wouldn't have had to go to the bathroom so many times. I'm now an expert on where to find public restrooms over approximately four hundred miles of Michigan.

I wish I was joking about this.

But I'm finally here, even though I almost turned around countless times.

My biggest moment of panic was at a gas station in Benton Harbor, Michigan, when my dad called to check in while I was fueling up. Not because he hassled me at all. But because every word out of my mouth was a lie.

All I kept thinking about was that when he finds out where I'm really going this week, it's not going to be pretty. My mind listed all the what-ifs: What if the credit card company calls him because the charge at the hotel is too big? I only put a deposit down. What if there isn't even enough on the card for more than a night or two?

It's not too late to go home, I reminded myself. *I can tell him I got homesick.* That I realized I really didn't want to do this by myself. Maybe I could even ask to see his spreadsheet of potential majors and colleges and actually *do* something about my future. Anything would be better than just waiting for him to find out where I was and what I was doing.

But Mom's chest, sitting in the passenger seat next to me, gave me the courage to press on. Now I'm here, though, and I can't move.

I know that I can't bring the car with me onto the island; leaving it behind still causes another pang of guilt to hit me hard in the chest. But even more than that, leaving Chloe's shitty old car, as she calls it, here in this parking lot means moving forward entirely on my own.

I take the keys out of the ignition but that's the only movement I make for a few minutes. Then I check my phone. I already missed the previous ferry. If I don't catch this one, I'll be late for my reservation at the hotel, too.

It's now or never.

This might be your only chance to find out more about her. Chloe's words echo in my brain.

I'm letting Dad down if I step on that ferry. I'm letting Mom down if I don't.

I've had years and years to disappoint Dad. Hopefully, I'll have lots more to come.

I have to do this for Mom. Shouldering the bag with Mom's mosaic chest in it, I step out of the car and into the late afternoon heat and humidity. Lists begin to form in my head of things I need to do right now. Get my suitcase? Check. Get my ticket ready on my phone? Check. Look at my hotel reservation and the cost of all of this one last time? Unfortunately, that's a check, too.

My feet take me, slowly at first, to the terminal entrance and then to the dock. As I see the ferry waiting there . . . as I see the people lined up to get on . . . a sudden excitement takes over me. An actual smile spreads across my face.

Because *this*. This is what I wanted. This must be a place Mom had been over and over again when she came here on vacation. And it's just the beginning. Soon I'll be able to walk where she walked, eat at places she might have eaten at. I'll be able to see all the places she wrote about and painted.

I hold my phone up so the ticket guy can scan it and then I walk over the gangplank and onto the boat. Within minutes, the horn blows. We're leaving. I stand at the railing of the ferry, looking out over the water. I can't see the island yet, but I'll be able to soon. So soon that it makes my palms sweat.

I'm almost there.

A giant plume of water shoots out behind us as the ferry races to Mackinac Island. Holding the bag with Mom's chest in it tighter, I move away from the water's spray. The closer I get to the front of the boat, the sooner I'll see the island anyway.

It doesn't take long. In the distance lies Mackinac, wooded and hilly with a pastel seashell of a town sitting on the edge of it like the lake washed it up or something. Flanking the town stand two huge hotels. The white wedding cake of the Grand Hotel on one side and the sky blue turrets of the Palais du Lac Hotel on the other. A bark of laughter escapes from me. Because I did it. I'm almost there. Even if Dad catches me tomorrow, I'll still have had this moment.

Though I really hope he doesn't catch me tomorrow.

I lean over the railing, trying to get a closer look as we pull into the dock, but everything erupts into chaos. People bustling around with their bags. Bikes everywhere. Workers on the dock tightening ropes and making sure we're secure before the lines of people waiting to pour off the boat can disembark.

It takes about ten minutes to walk back over the gangplank again. When I do, it's like walking into another world. A real horse-drawn carriage rumbles by. People cruise past me on bikes. One couple is even riding a bicycle built for two. I've only seen those in movies before. I didn't know they were a real thing.

"Oh my God," I breathe.

It's like the ferry dropped me off onto Main Street, USA, at Disney World. The buildings are painted in a blend of whites and pastels with pretty facades and old-fashioned awnings. Honestly, if Mickey Mouse or

Cinderella suddenly rounded a corner, it would not surprise me at all.

But instead of fictional characters, there are real people everywhere. Tourists walk and bike around the town, people work in the little shops. There are even a few guys around my age who joke with each other as they sweep up horse manure behind one of the carriages. Every single person I can see looks happy. Up to and including the horse manure guys.

I didn't know places like this really exist.

I can't believe my mother used to come here.

Someone calls out, "Carriage for Palais du Lac!" and I turn to find a fancy, enclosed carriage with the hotel's name emblazoned on it. It takes me a second to realize that this is my ride to the hotel. That I, Lexi Carter, will be traveling by horse and buggy.

The carriage takes me and two other guests up a tree-lined road. It's pretty, but it looks like almost any other tree-lined road. A tiny tendril of disappointment curls inside me that everything's not perfect and different here. That is until the trees give way and the hotel comes into view. As we pass through the gate, I look out the window to take in my home for the next few nights.

It's huge. I knew that from the pictures online, but am still not prepared for just how enormous the place is. It sits on the top of a small incline with a lawn leading up to it, all towering turrets, cobwebby balconies, and dramatic gables. The blue of the siding is set off by the white woodwork and even bright touches of spring green paint.

This is where my mother used to come. A weird fluttering feeling jumps up in my stomach. I can't believe that I'm really here. The carriage driver opens the door and I wait to let the couple who've been riding with me get out first. As soon as I step out, I stare up at the front of the hotel as it looms over me. Even the tallest building back home doesn't faze me anymore, but this . . . this isn't anything like a skyscraper or a tall apartment building. It's wide and old and gleaming in the afternoon sunshine. It's beautiful.

Tears form in my eyes just as a girl in a hotel uniform comes up and offers to take my bag for me. I swipe at my eyes as I glance down at the little suitcase I've had since I was seven. It's almost embarrassing to hand it over. Like I'm showing her, at least, that someone like me . . . with a bag like this . . . doesn't really belong here. But she stands there waiting for me to answer, so I hand over the suitcase and my name, keeping my backpack and the smaller bag holding the mosaic chest. Sweat drips down my back and into my bra strap. I blow a strand of hair out of my eyes. Even after driving to the ferry, worrying the entire time that the car would break down, I'm not sure I've ever wanted to get in a car and drive away as much as I do right in this moment.

Shouldering my backpack, I look up at the hotel again.

From up close, it's harder to tell just how large a scale it's been built on. As far as the eye can see, there's a long, wide verandah with rocking chairs on it. Walking up the stairs, I turn to see the view. The lawn stretches out before me, with a pool and tennis courts flanking it. Beyond that is a stand of trees . . . not quite big enough to be a forest or anything, but still enough to make up something more than an odd tree planted here and there. Besides, these are big trees. They look like they've been here for a while.

Then, between the trees, the lake shimmers in the afternoon sunshine. It's so pretty that it makes my chest ache at little at just how perfect it is. This is somewhere my mother loved. A place where she used to come, seemingly lots of time if the different sets of her handwriting are to be believed.

I have no idea how Mom could have afforded to stay here. Or even her parents. My dad and I have always had enough to get by on, but it's not like we've ever been swimming in cash. As it is, I'm basically going to have to hand over every penny I make for the next two years to my dad to pay for all of this. Yet she came here on vacations. She promised her mystery friend that she'd be waiting for him here, at their palace by the lake. I hug the bag holding the mosaic box to my chest, and think about what she wrote on that postcard. Her days here were the best of her life. She never thought anything would come between her and her friend. She wanted to see this person again, even if just in her memories.

It feels almost like something I'd write to her. That last part does, anyway. Yet she wrote them to someone in her life who was clearly important to her. Maybe I'll even find out who. And who her other friends were . . . the people who filled her life so much that she thought nothing could be any better. Mom had this whole life that's going to open up for me now. I'm going to drink it in and enjoy every minute I'm here and try to find out even more.

But first I have to check in.

I push through the French doors into the lobby and look up and down and . . . everywhere. It's so wide and tall, so cavernous in its dimensions, that it's almost like walking into a cathedral. Except this particular cathedral has soft white sofas and chairs, and pastel yellow walls that glow in the sunlight. Some kind of flowering tree stands in pots around the room, their scent permeating everything around me. I close my eyes and breathe in deep, wondering if there were trees like this in the lobby when Mom stayed here, and trying to memorize the smell for later.

When I open my eyes again, the whole lobby bustles with people. Hotel employees, guests . . . everyone's moving and talking and eating and drinking. The whole place throbs with excitement. Or maybe that's just me? My pulse seems like it's pounding through the veins in my wrists, my neck, which can't be a good thing.

A kind of desperation settles my brain. I have to stay here long enough to find out more about Mom. I've lied to my dad and Abby so many times. I spent their money without telling them. I snuck around . . . I'm still sneaking around . . . doing things I know would make Dad furious and Abby disappointed in me. And the only reason

I've done it is to feel closer to someone I barely remember, when all I know is that she's stayed here. That's all I have. And I don't know if that will be enough.

Will I feel her presence here? For some reason, I had this vision of walking up to the hotel and having her aura . . . a kind of ghost of her time here . . . wash over me. It hasn't happened yet, but maybe it still will. Maybe all the stuff in the mosaic box will make more sense now that I'm here. Maybe I'll feel her in a way I never have before.

God, I hope so. Because right now, I'm back to *A Chorus Line*, only this time I really do feel nothing. I'm just one of about a hundred people moving around a crowded space.

My palms sweat so much that they stick to the straps of my backpack as I hold on to them. I really need to check in and get my key. I'll feel better . . . I'll cool down and have a fresh perspective on all of this . . . when I get to my room.

After I check in with a man whose name tag says *Alain, East Lansing, MI*, a golden, mirrored elevator drops me off at the third floor and I walk down the carpeted hall to find room 315 . . . way down the hall on the inside of the building. By the time I get there, my hands shake and I fumble with the key, dropping it three times before I finally get the door unlocked.

Then I step inside. Eggshell-colored paint topped with gold scrolled wallpaper covers the wall, and a blue rug sprinkled with rosettes spreads across the floor. The double bed has a tiny canopy over it in the same color as the rug. There's a desk and a dresser, a tiny bathroom, and two windows. I walk over to them, curious what a non–lake view room will offer, and get my answer. It offers a view of fire escapes and the other side of the U-shaped building.

But that's okay. I didn't come here for the view. I could never have afforded one anyway. Lake view rooms cost more money than my whole family spends on a vacation. As irresponsible as I'm being, I couldn't quite bring myself to go that overboard.

Placing my stuff on the nearest bed, I gingerly take the mosaic box out of the bag I transported it in. Somehow the blue of the chest . . . the mosaics themselves . . . feel more at home here than they did at, well, home. They belong in this fancy summer palace, where Mom made the memories inside the box in the first place.

Light slants through the windows, illuminating the pale walls. It catches on the tiny pieces of glass in the greenhouse mosaic. I open the chest and take out the postcard again. *I never intended to hurt you, but I know I did.*

I wonder who she hurt and how. I wonder if they ever saw each other again.

Taking the postcard to the window, I gaze out over the rooftops of the other wings of the hotel. On the desk next to me lies the same hotel notepad Mom drew her scratchy pink dress on and wrote about her friends. It's enough to bring tears to my eyes, but it's also a good reminder of why I came and what I need to do.

Already I'm finding things that link back to her in this hotel room. And I know. I *know* that I'm going to find more.

CHAPTER 7
Emma (Then)

Why did I let you talk me into this?" Linda demands as she eats the last bite of chocolate croissant. She's flat on her back on the sloping lawn in front of the hotel, licking her fingers clean of melted chocolate.

"Because you love pastry and you love me, so it was worth getting up to watch the sunrise with me?"

She rolls over to look up at the morning sky, still rimmed with peach along the horizon even though the sky above us is clear blue. "Maybe," she sort of agrees. "Or maybe I just wanted to get out of our place before my dad woke up." Linda's eyes close in what I hope is chocolate-induced bliss. "Maybe it's a combination."

"Is everything okay with your dad?" I venture.

Her knees curl up as she tucks onto her side. "Nothing new," she says. "I keep trying to show him I should be the one to take over the business. But he's like a horse with those things on its head." Her lips purse together as she thinks. "What're those things that make a horse look straight ahead instead of at the grass on the side of the road?"

"Blinkers?"

She sits up and presses one fingers to her nose. "Ding, ding, ding, ding . . . that is the correct answer!" I laugh but stop when she sighs. "It's like the man has on blinkers. Except he doesn't see anything that *is* actually right in front of him. Only what he wants to see."

The idea of that gets stuck in my head. "Do you think it's easier or harder to go through life that way?" I ask. "I mean, in some ways, it would be easier, right? You just see the part of the world you want to, so everything's kind of . . . uncomplicated."

Linda stretches both arms over her head. "I guess," she replies. "But wouldn't you want to see everything around you?" She looks at me. "You're an artist. Would you want to only see some of the colors of the sunset or all of them?"

That's easy to answer. "All of them. Every color. Every slant of light."

Linda smiles. "See, this is why I like you," she tells me. "You want to see everything and experience everything."

A bitter little sigh escapes from me. "Except I don't," I reply. "I only see what's here. I've never gone anywhere else."

She turns to face me. "But you want to?"

My eyes stray out over the treetops and the pool house to the lake beyond. I love it here so much. It'll always be home. But . . .

"I want to."

Linda sits up. "So why don't you?"

I shake my head, not sure how to answer.

"No really, why don't you?" she persists.

"It's not that easy," I tell her. "My parents . . . they're relying on me to learn my dad's business. To carry it on."

Linda picks up her third chocolate croissant and takes a bite. "Maybe we should switch families," she says. "Then no one will ever give a damn what you do, and I can let your dad retire early."

I hold my out my pinkie to her. "Deal."

With her pinkie linked in mine, we shake on it. I try to smile at the bargain we've struck, but instead tears come to my eyes.

"Oh God, not another pinkie promise. I can't believe she talked you into that."

JR stands in front of us with his hands on his hips.

Linda gives him a withering glance. "Just because you're not reliable enough to keep a promise doesn't mean I'm not."

With a roll of his eyes, JR sits down next to me. As surreptitiously as I can, I wipe the corners of my eyes. JR gives me a quick glance before turning back to Linda. "I'm the most reliable person you know."

One corner of her mouth turns down while the other turns up to give her a lopsided smirk. "You're the most *ridiculous* person I know," she says. "And no, that's not a compliment."

"Didn't think it was." JR pulls the bakery box toward him and scoffs. "You just left me one croissant? That's the only reason I got up this early."

He lifts the last croissant out of the box and turns it over in his hand.

"The invitation I issued was for croissants at sunrise," I inform him. "And you're late. Aren't you supposed to be the punctual one?"

"Six a.m. on a Saturday doesn't count," he grouses. "It's unnatural to be up this early."

I look over and smile at him. "Even to spend a glorious morning with your friends?"

JR considers this. "Passable. But not good enough."

Linda pats her stomach. "I'd be insulted except I ate your other croissant."

He grunts as he digs into his lone pastry. While he eats, we watch the peach hues seep out of the sky, replaced by an intense blue. The hotel comes alive around us. Families head down to the beach. Guests take their coffee and pastries on the verandah. A group of kids have already organized themselves into a game of hide-and-seek. Even the tennis courts are filling up.

"Ugh . . . they're always so *busy*," Linda groans. "You'd think they'd want to relax a little on their vacations but they're like ants scurrying around for scraps of *anything* to do."

"Some people don't like to sit around on their vacations," I reply.

"People with empty minds who can't stand a moment of reflection," JR adds, gesturing at the gathering crowds.

"You mean not everyone's as deep as you, JR?" I tease.

Linda snorts. JR frowns. "That's not what I meant."

"It definitely *sounded* like that's what you meant," Linda says.

He pops the last bite of his croissant in his mouth. "You know, the pleasure of your company isn't as strong a draw as you think it is," he informs us. "If you two are gonna hassle me all morning, I have other stuff to do."

It's an opening too hard to resist. "You mean you like to keep busy?" I ask. "Like an ant scurrying around without a moment of reflection?"

JR collapses onto the grass. "This is fun," he grouses. "Really. I'm having a great time."

I push his shoulder. He elbows me back.

Just then, Ryan joins us. "So," he says. "I had the best idea ever of what we should do today!"

"Ant," Linda says under her breath.

"What?" Ryan looks so confused that I laugh out loud.

"It's nothing," I tell him. "What's your best idea ever today?"

I try to keep the sarcasm out of my voice—he really is a nice guy— but he gets all revved up about something different almost every day. And a lot of his best ideas fall flat.

"Okay, here it is." He's so excited, he's practically bouncing. "We're gonna go mountain biking! I already mapped out a route. All we need is to get bikes."

"Some of us don't find bike riding to our liking." JR nods in my direction.

Linda and Ryan turn and stare at me. His eyes are wide and hers are all scrunched up. The general effect of both is shock at what they just heard.

"For real?" Linda asks.

My cheeks burn up. I shrug, embarrassed—not wanting to talk about this.

Ryan looks at us. Rubs his hands together like an impatient little kid. "Does no one want to go biking with me?" His voice is just pleading enough that it makes me feel a little bad.

"I'll go," JR says.

My head whips back in surprise. "You will?"

He raises his eyebrows at me. "I told you I had other stuff I could do today. All you two are doing is teasing me." He turns to Ryan. "You gonna hassle me the whole time we're out?"

Ryan actually puts his hand over his heart as if he's pledging allegiance or something. "Wouldn't dream of it. Please consider me as an alternative to hassling."

JR gives him a squinty look as he gets to his feet. "Okay, whatever. Anything's better than this." If his hand gesture is to be believed, *this* means Linda and me.

Linda nudges me. "Do you . . . like . . . hate bikes, or would you just rather do other stuff if there's an option?"

My shoulders droop. "You want to go, too, don't you?"

"All I've been doing is working. I've hardly even had time to swim." She gives JR a sly glance. "And I ate three *delicious* chocolate croissants for breakfast this morning. "

JR lets out a groan and I let out a sigh. The problem is, I don't *hate* bikes exactly. It's just that something always seems to go wrong when I ride one. A chain breaks. I skid out in mud. Nothing horrible but . . . I kind of feel as if I'm cursed when it comes to bikes.

"Are you in Emma Land now or are you actually thinking about coming?" JR snarks.

The whole curse thing is all in my head, I remind myself. Besides, if they go without me, what will I do all day long? Probably get sucked into doing chores at our place. Or get hassled about applying for a job.

I take a deep breath. "I'm coming."

"Awesome!" Linda says. "It'll be good to get out of here and give my legs a workout."

"Terrific," I say half-heartedly.

. . .

Even when we're at the bike rental, Ryan won't tell us what route he planned. "It's a surprise!"

Linda grabs a bike. "Why does that make me nervous?"

"Because you doubt everything I do," Ryan says. "Pesky little sister."

I wouldn't know about that, as an only child. Neither would JR. We both keep quiet as Linda and Ryan bicker. My palms sweat as one of the activities staff bring around the last two bikes and hand them off to JR and me.

JR gets on his and looks at me. "Oh God . . . what's that face for?"

My head snaps back in surprise. "I'm not making a face!"

"Yeah, you are," he argues. "And it's a doozy."

When I don't say anything, he shakes his head at me. "Maybe you'll break the curse."

With a nod of my head, I say, "Maybe."

"And if not, I'll carry you to the medical center myself," JR continues.

I reach over and push his shoulder as hard as I can. "You're not helping, JR."

"To be fair, I'm not really trying to."

Before I can shove him again, Ryan wheels my bike over. "Your steed awaits," he says with a flourish of his right hand.

JR lets out a half laugh. "See, if it actually was a steed, she'd be *much* happier," he tells Ryan. "None of this newfangled transportation technology like bikes for Emma. She gets around the way nature intended. On the back of something else."

The sarcasm is entirely lost on Ryan. He turns to me wide-eyed. "You know how to ride a horse?"

"Um . . . yes?"

"That's so cool." He holds the bike steady so I can lift the bottom of my dress up and climb on. "I've never been on a horse before."

JR rolls his eyes before pedaling away from us.

"Oh . . . um . . . it's fun," I answer. "I mean, I don't ride much anymore, but I did when I was younger."

"So cool." Ryan grins at me. "You're so cool."

Then he shakes out his hair, all golden and shining in the sun, as if he's in a shampoo commercial. Honestly, he could be.

"Ryan, are you going to keep talking about how cool everything is, or are we actually going to leave at some point?" Linda calls.

He puts on his helmet. "Let's leave. The road awaits us!"

The two of them ride a little way ahead on the winding carriage road. I grip the handlebars of my bike as I watch them pass through the gate of the hotel. I know I can do this. I know how to make the bike go. The rest will just be pretty places in the woods. Besides, curses are *not* real. I will *not* need to be carried to the medical center.

For a second, a shiver passes down my spine, but I shake it off. If I can ride a horse, I can ride a bike. And so I start gliding down the road. Ryan leads us onto one of the bike paths and . . . it's okay. The wind whips my hair around my helmet. Trees whiz by. Every now and then the lake peeks through the trees for a glorious second or two. We stay on the same path for a half hour or so—it's smooth sailing.

Eventually we follow Ryan onto a smaller path. It's rougher here, bumpier. Linda and JR take off ahead of me, chatting peacefully for once. It takes a few minutes to get my bearings on the new terrain. I stand up in my seat as if I'm riding a horse instead of a bike so my butt doesn't keep bumping onto it. The light dapples through the dense trees and slants over the bike path. I breathe in deeply, filling my lungs with the kind of fresh air you can only find in the woods.

Another turnoff leads us up a steep incline. I have to pump hard now to keep the bike moving uphill. If Linda thinks she's out of shape, she'd be horrified if she knew how hard this is for me. Maybe I should exercise more, too? Build up my stamina and all that so it's a little . . .

Easier . . .

To . . . pedal.

When the ground levels out again, I say a silent thank-you to the fates or the gods of mountain biking or . . . whatever . . . that we're not going uphill anymore.

"Almost there!" Ryan calls back to us.

The gods of mountain biking must actually be listening.

Another fifteen, twenty minutes pass, then I hear it: the sound of water crashing down onto rocks. Up ahead, a thin waterfall streams from an overhanging limestone ledge. It's not huge or anything—just that one cascade coming from maybe thirty feet overhead—but it pours into a deep, dark swirl of a pool underneath.

I slip off my bike and lean it against a tree. How could I not know someplace like this existed on the island?

"How did you hear about this?" I ask Ryan.

"Oh, a biking blog," he says. "Little-known gem, it said."

I take in a deep breath. "That doesn't nearly do this justice."

They all put their bikes down, too, but I can't wait for them. I kick off my flip-flops and unclasp my helmet. Sweat rings the fabric of my dress under both arms—it mats my hair down where the helmet was just a second ago. The mist from the waterfall hits my face, cooling me off instantly. Everything about this place is magical.

Even the crunch in the rough gravel sounds almost musical as I walk toward the water. There's a rock at the edge of it that's covered in moss, as if the waterfall itself made a little cushion so I could sit in comfort to enjoy the view. I accept the waterfall's politeness and take a seat. For a second, I just close my eyes and let the sounds and the coolness envelop me.

I dip my toes into the dark water. It's cold and deep enough that it shimmers almost black in the middle of it, as if something spellbinding and mysterious must live in its dark depths.

"What do you think?" Ryan sits next to me and splashes his feet into the pool.

"It's beautiful," I murmur. "The kind of place a naiad would build as her own private sanctuary."

"Wow . . . that was *not* what I thought you'd say," Ryan tells me. "But I'm really glad you like it. I . . . um . . . was kinda hoping you would."

"I do. I love it."

JR and Linda sit a few feet away, both hissing at how cold the water is as they dip their feet in.

"Good surprise, right?" Ryan asks.

"Though it pains me to admit, this is nice," Linda says.

JR doesn't say a word. He just leans back on the heels of his hands and looks up into the trees swaying high above us.

Ryan grabs his backpack. "I have drinks." He takes out four water bottles. "And protein bars to fuel up for the ride home."

Linda grabs a water. "All right, it doesn't even pain me anymore," she tells him. "You did good."

Ryan breaks into huge smile, lighting up every corner of his face. There's something about his smile that's so unselfconscious—so completely honest and real—that it's hard to resist. The sunlight dapples on his hair and the greens and blues around us bring out the vivid color of his eyes. I wish I could paint him, just as he is right in this moment. Golden, glowing, happy. He may be goofy. And a little over-the-top. And seems to have a very short attention span sometimes. But there's no denying that he's nice to look at. That I like to look at him.

That realization hits me. Hard. *I like to look at him.*

Time to think about something else.

Like the protein bar he gave me. It's peanut-buttery and choco-latey. Very . . . chewy. I gulp down some water so I can actually swallow it. Keep my feet in the waterfall till they start to get numb. Then, finally, I'm ready to join the others when they get up to leave.

"The ride down's a little steep, but it looks super pretty," Ryan tells us.

Since I no longer doubt his ability to spot a pretty place, I get back on my bike eagerly. Our helmets back on, we take off down a different path. It's so narrow that we can only ride single file. "Stick right behind me," Ryan tells me. "The path can be a little wonky in places."

"I'll stay close by," I assure him.

And I do. I follow his lead, even down to how he sits in the seat of his bike and how he seems to shift his weight over rocky terrain.

"Do you do a lot of mountain biking?" I call up to him.

Ryan turns his head back to me for a second, flashing yet another smile. "Not a ton," he replies. "But I like it."

I nod as if he can somehow still see me, then we fall silent. I need to concentrate on the path in front of me anyway. It does get steep in places as we descend, though it's manageable enough. As my calf muscles start to ache, the trees thin out. Then, directly in front of us, is Mirror Rock. I've never seen it from this angle before—up higher, in a place where we can glimpse just how narrow it is as it faces out on the lake.

Ryan stops so I can pull up next to him. "Nice, right?"

I gaze out at the bright blue sky. The giant stone tower reaching up into it as if it wants to touch the clouds. "Really nice."

JR and Linda pull up beside us, but it's Ryan who's got my attention. He shakes both hands excitedly. "Ready for the best part of all?"

"The best part wasn't the waterfall?" JR asks. "'Cause it seemed like it was. You're just setting us up for disappointment by hyping whatever comes next."

As always, JR's sarcasm goes over Ryan's head. I can't tell if that makes me like him more or less.

"Nah, the best part's the way down from here," he says.

I want to believe him, but then the dirt path in question comes into sight. Ryan's right—the view's gorgeous. It feels as if we're on the tip-top of the island. The only problem lies with the steep hill down and the steep fall-off on the right side. But curses aren't real. I've just hit a couple of weird bumps when I've gone biking in the past. Everything about today has been wonderful so far.

Ryan puts his hand on my arm, startling me. "I'm going to head down first to show you the easiest way to navigate it," he tells me. "I'll be waiting for you down there, okay?"

I nod just once, but it's enough to make him smile at me again. Then he races downhill, the sound of his laughter trailing behind him.

"Here goes nothing." Linda dashes down after him.

JR stands next to me with his hands on his hips. "You sure you want to do this?" he asks. "Or is your desire to have me sit by your side in your hospital bed too hard to resist?"

I shake my head and grit my teeth. "You're *really* not helping."

For a second or two, he just stares at me. A crease forms between his eyebrows. "Emma, your knuckles are white. You don't have to do it. You should just walk the bike down."

I glance down at my grip on the handlebars and then back up again. My breath hitches in my throat. *Everything about today has been wonderful so far.* I square my shoulders. "It's okay. Curses aren't real, right?"

I can do this. I can let go of this irrational fear.

Before he can say anything else, I put both feet on the pedals and fly down the first bit of the hill. The wind is glorious. It feels as if I'm flying—as if I'm a bird and the sky is mine to explore. Laughter pours from me, my breath gets whipped out of my nose. I speed down the hill, till I realize I'm going a little too fast. All I have to do is slow down and . . .

I squeeze the brakes but nothing happens. I try them again. And again.

The bike hurtles down the hill.

"Hit the brakes!" JR yells from behind me. I try again, but nothing happens. Again. The bottom of the hill races toward me too fast. Too soon.

"Try to fall!" Linda calls.

But if I fall I'll get hurt. Scraped skin. Bloodied palms and knees. That moment before I hit the ground with a sickening thud. I know what it feels like. I can't do it. Not on purpose.

My chest heaves as a sob rips out of my lungs.

Ryan runs uphill, racing toward me. "Let go, Emma!" he shouts. "Hands and feet! Let go!"

He's so close now. I can see the fear in his eyes. "Let go! NOW!"

So I do. With one deep, frantic breath I lift my feet, my hands. My flip-flops fly off as I barrel toward him.

One of his arms hits my abdomen. The other reaches behind to try to keep my head from whipping backward.

The bike goes a few more feet before it crashes into a tree. I watch, stunned for a second, before something inside me explodes. I choke out a sob as Ryan's arms close around me. I cling to him, crying into his shoulder. "I've got you," he says. "It's okay."

Footsteps pound around us as both JR and Linda skid to a stop in front of me. Linda wraps her arms around me and Ryan as he holds me up.

"Are you okay?" she says. Her voice is too loud—too close to my ears.

I nod to keep her from asking again.

When I can finally look up, I see JR a few feet downhill from us. One hand clutches his stomach. The other covers his eyes. "Jesus Christ," he says under his breath. *"Jesus Christ."*

Ryan's hold on me loosens. I wobble on my feet for a second but Linda props me back up. The bike lies under a tree, its front wheel bent sideways. I could have crashed there along with it. I could have . . .

I turn to Ryan, whose whole face seems to have collapsed in worry. "Thank you."

"Nah, you don't . . ."

"Thank you," I say in a stronger voice, my eyes latching onto his. For a bit too long, maybe?

His nod breaks it. "Anything for you, Emma." Though it lacks his usual enthusiasm, Ryan sounds as if he actually means it. "You okay to walk?"

My neck aches. The insides of my ankles are bleeding.

"I'm fine."

Linda goes to get my ruined bike, leaving JR standing before me. Sweat drips down his face. His eyes are tense.

"Why didn't you *listen* to me?" he spits out. "I tried to stop you but you *never* listen."

He steps even closer to me, but I wince away from him to avoid the angry desperation in his eyes.

"You could have *died*." His voice comes out low—almost like a growl. "Did you think I was serious about the medical center? That I really want you to go there? Because I don't." He rubs his hand over his eyes again. "Jesus, Emma."

When I finally turn to look at him again, it's with tears in my eyes. I didn't mean to scare anyone. I just wanted to . . . to not be so afraid of something that no one else is. But I can't say any of that to him right now. I can't say anything at all.

JR turns to take my ruined bike from Linda and hefts it up on his shoulder. As soon as he and Linda go to get their own bikes, Ryan walks over to me.

I try to smile at him. "I might actually be cursed."

He shakes his head. "Nah, this was my fault," he says. "I knew you were nervous. I should've asked everyone how much biking they've done before we set out and . . ."

Reaching up, I lay my hand on his shoulder. "It wasn't your fault. You didn't make me get on the bike."

I try to laugh this off and make light of his apology, but one look at him and I know he's dead serious.

"It's okay, Ryan. I'm fine," I tell him. "I'm totally fine. And I promise I won't get on a bike ever again."

He smiles at me and it's like sunshine breaking through the clouds. "And I won't ask you do dangerous things ever again."

"Sounds good." I try to smile back, but I'm still shaking so much that I'm not sure I succeed.

Ryan puts his arm around me and leads me to where JR and Linda are waiting at the bottom of the hill. We all walk quietly home.

CHAPTER 8

Emma (Then)

Mom breezes into my room without so much as knocking. She's got an armful of files that she picked up at Dad's office and a huge smile on her face. "I bumped into Eliza Desmond this morning," Mom tells me before I can say a word.

I pause in the midst of the sketch I'd been making of the waterfall. There's got to be more to this story than that. "And?"

She sits down on my bed and rearranges the files in her arm. "Well . . . ," she says. "We were talking, and Eliza mentioned that Ryan wants to try out horseback riding."

The pencil I'd been holding drops from my hand. "Mom, you didn't!"

"I did!" she exclaims. "I told her you'd be happy to take him riding and show him the ropes."

My head rolls over my shoulder in defeat. "Why did you do this to me?" I say. "He's . . . he's so . . ."

"Nice?" she supplies. "Good-looking? Kind enough to rescue you last week?"

"You make it sound more dramatic than it was," I tell her, even though I know I'm not being honest.

Mom does, too. She tosses her hair back and just keeps talking. "It sounded pretty dramatic to me. Your neck hurt for days afterward. Thank God nothing worse happened." She pauses for effect. "Thank God he was there."

I pick up my pencil again and glance down at the sketch I'd been making . . . the one of the magical place Ryan was so excited to show me. "Okay, you're right, but——"

"And it's not as if you've filled out an application downstairs, as we've asked you to do. On multiple occasions," she cuts me off. "So you have plenty of time to take him riding today."

This walks the line between passive-aggressive and outright aggressive on Mom's part. It's not as if I don't know they want me to get a job in the hotel, it's just that . . .

"Two thirty," she tells me as she gets up and walks to my door. "Meet him in the lobby. I've already called the stable to let them know you're coming."

I let out a sigh.

"And who knows?" she continues. "Once he gets the hang of it, maybe you two could go trail riding all summer long."

The door closes behind her, but the plans she's made for me still loom ahead of me.

When the Desmonds first moved into the hotel's penthouse at the end of January, Mom and Dad both kept trying to force Linda and Ryan on me. It was . . . awkward.

Then one day, after I'd failed an AP US History test *and* dropped an entire tray of food in the middle of the cafeteria in a single afternoon, I fled the minute the bell rang and straight toward the hiking path in the middle of the woods. I sat on the only bench I could find and hid my face in my hands as if that could make my anger and embarrassment disappear.

And that's when Linda Desmond rounded the bend carrying her backpack. She stopped short when she saw me. The look she gave me was anything but friendly.

"What're *you* doing here?"

The hostility in her voice threw me for a loop. "Oh . . . um . . . it's just that . . . today was . . ."

Linda looked me up and down. "That good, huh?"

A long breath blew out of my lungs. "Pretty bad."

When she plunked down next to me, I physically jumped I was so startled.

"Don't worry," she said. "I don't bite."

My fingers clutched at my backpack even tighter. "Oh, no that's not . . . I mean . . ."

"Emma?"

"Yes?"

"Relax, okay? I'm not one of the assholes who made fun of you today."

The knowledge that Linda saw the whole junior class laugh and jeer at me made my face burn despite the cold.

"I may have also flunked a history test," I told her.

She let out a low whistle. "I may have had someone pretend they had to go to the bathroom so he could avoid being my lab partner."

"Jerks."

"Assholes."

"Fools."

"Idiots."

Wracking my brain for something—anything—to keep the conversation going, all I could come up with was "Noodlebrains."

Linda snorted out a laugh. "Noodlebrains? That's the best you can do?"

This made me laugh as well. "I have friend who used to tell me I acted like I had soft noodles for brains when we were little kids."

She raised her eyebrows. "Sounds like a great friend."

"You have no idea." For a few seconds Linda just looked at me— long enough to make me squirm. "You come here when your day sucks, too?"

There was a tinge of hope in her voice that it killed me to dash. "I've never been here before," I admitted. "I just found it today for the first time." Then I turned to her. "Why do *you* come here when you've had a bad day?"

With a shrug she said, "I like this bench. Viola seems like someone I'd be friends with."

I bit my lips in confusion. "Viola?"

Linda moved, revealing a plaque on the bench behind where she'd been sitting.

TO THE MEMORY OF VIOLA BENSON WHO LOVED THESE WOODS SO MUCH SHE WANTED TO SPEND ETERNITY IN THEM. MAY HER FIERCE SPIRIT WALK AMONG THE TREES IN DEATH AS IT DID IN LIFE.

Tears filled my eyes as I read the inscription. Right there, where we sat, the ashes of someone who loved this spot were probably scattered. "I think I would be friends with her, too."

I smiled at her. She smiled back.

We walked back to the hotel that afternoon together and sat in the café drinking hot chocolate while we did our homework. After that, we were inseparable.

Since Linda and I became friends, though, my mom has been a little too enthusiastic about me getting to know Ryan as well. And I know why. Not only have I had just one friend for as long as I can remember, but he doesn't live here year-round. Which means a lot of the time, I'm on my own.

I've always minded this much less than Mom does. Whereas I see it as having lots of time to make art, she sees it as me trying to fill my lonely hours. But for some reason, being alone with Ryan makes me . . . nervous. And I hate feeling nervous.

"And try to remember that it's opening night tonight, okay?" Mom says, breaking my thoughts.

"Um . . . yes! Of course," is my brilliant response. "I absolutely remembered that it's tonight."

She sighs. "You have to be home and ready to go by six at the latest."

I lean back in my chair. "Mom, I doubt Ryan's going to last nearly that long," I tell her. "Even if he does, I won't."

She frowns at me disapprovingly.

"Don't worry!" I say. "I'll be on my best behavior."

Mom walks out of my room calling back, "Two thirty in the lobby. Home and ready by six."

"I'll be here, all cleaned up and ready to go on time!"

"Emma, you're never on time."

I consider that for a second. Punctuality has never been my strong suit. "Maybe I'm turning over a new leaf!" I call back as the door closes behind her.

I'm not in the lobby by two thirty. It takes me so long to dig out my old riding boots and helmet, then I have to change clothes and find my keys. I tried to be on time—I really did. It just didn't quite work out.

Finally I get out the door and bolt down the stairs. Jackson swings onto them next to me on the second floor. He recently shaved all his hair off, so the dark skin on the top of his head reflects the sunlight streaming through the lobby windows. Pocket square and tie are firmly in place—he looks fantastic.

Of course, as I'm admiring his ensemble, he's taking in my outfit as well. "You're going riding?" he asks. "I thought you stopped lessons a while ago."

"My mom roped me into taking Ryan Desmond," I say. Then my breath hitches in my throat—someone might have heard me say that. *Ryan* might have.

But no one else is on the stairs. The coast is clear.

"I hate to ask this, but does Ryan actually know how to ride a horse?" Jackson asks. "Or are you just going to let him sink or swim, so to speak?"

"Bad mixed metaphors," I tell him with a grin. "And I'm apparently going to *teach* him how to ride."

Jackson shakes his head. Just as we reach the lobby, he says, "Go easy on him, okay?"

But before I can respond, my dad materializes seemingly out of nowhere. I brace myself for another round of questions, but he barely says hello to me before he's talking to Jackson about how he forgot something at our place and how glad he is to see him. Despite their age difference—Dad's a good fifteen years older than Jackson—Jackson's probably Dad's best friend. He's definitely one of the people he most trusts. I hope it never comes down to my dad having to choose between me and Jackson, because I'm honestly not sure who he'd go for if pressed.

I watch them walk off, then glance at the grandfather clock in the corner of the lobby. I'm already twenty minutes late, but Ryan's nowhere in sight. So I sit in one of the window seats and watch the sunlight slant across the patterns in the Turkish carpets, making the designs even more vivid than they already were. The jasmine trees that hover over the sofas and comfy chairs are just starting to bloom, and a hint of their scent wafts over to me. And, of course, there are the people. Some live here year-round like we do, some are here for the whole summer. Still others are just here for a few days or a week. They lounge around having afternoon drinks, or bustle about waiting to get bike rentals and carriage tours.

It's an enormous room, all pale yellow walls and grand window dressings. In winter it's empty. Almost severe. But in the summer, it bursts with life. I close my eyes for a second to take in the sounds and smells. A baby cries somewhere by the main restaurant, a burst of laughter rises and then disappears. Everything and everyone seems to be moving and shifting, as if I'm the only thing that's not in motion.

"Emma?"

I open my eyes to find Ryan standing before me. He's got on a pair of worn-in jeans and sneakers, which isn't ideal, but he smiles as if he's kitted out in the best riding gear that money can buy. I look at the clock again. He's thirty-five minutes late. I'm briefly annoyed, but who am I to judge—not to mention, I don't mind sharing a habit of tardiness with someone.

"You ready?" he asks.

"Absolutely."

We walk out the side door of the lobby onto the verandah. A carriage pulls up just as we hit the waiting area, and Ryan holds out his arm and bows low. "After you," he says in an overly courteous voice.

"Thanks," I return, not nearly matching his tone.

We sit down with several inches between us, then have to move closer as more people climb on board. Being this close to him makes the nerves prickling my skin intensify. With no Linda to act as buffer, a silence falls that makes me even more anxious. I wish I had something to do with my hands. Something to paint or carve or . . . *make*. But maybe if I'm feeling this way, he is too? Probably for a completely different reason, but still.

I force myself to talk. "Are you nervous about riding?"

Ryan shakes his head. "Nah, how hard can it be?"

I turn and take a good look at him, to see if he's just putting on a good front or if he's really not at all worried about his first time on a horse. He appears to be completely at ease.

"I can ride a bike," he continues. "How different can it be, right?"

"Well, seeing as how I can ride a horse and not a bike"—my cheeks redden—"as you probably remember, very different."

He smiles at me. "Are you nervous for me? 'Cause you don't need to be. I've got this!"

"Of course you do," I tease, wondering if he was born this secure or if it was something he developed over time. I envy it. "Why would any horse mess around with Ryan Desmond?"

"No horse would dare." He smiles. "It'll be like those old Westerns. Once I'm in the saddle, I'll show the horse who's boss."

"Or, you know, it'll show you who's boss."

"Probably!" he laughs. "But either way, it'll all be good. I'm ready to get my butt kicked if that's what the horse wants."

Ryan leans in so close to me that his breath rushes over the bare skin on my shoulder. "Will you rescue me if it does?"

A tiny shiver runs down my back. I try to hold it in—not to show any reaction at all—but I don't know if I succeed or not. He's very much in my personal space, hovering enough inches taller than me that I have to look up at him to reply. As soon as I do I regret it. He's so close that I lose track of what I was going to say. Or what he just said.

Horses. Rescue him. RESCUE him.

"Of course," I tell him, my voice just a teeny bit shaky. "I'll be your knight in shining armor."

Ryan clearly likes that idea because he laughs out loud. A group of ladies in their sixties turn around and smile at him.

"Maybe you can even ride a white horse today," he suggests. "Though it's a little too hot for armor."

"Who wants to wear metal on a warm June day?"

"Or ever?"

He smiles at me as the carriage comes to a stop at the stable and leans in even closer. "I think this is going to be my new favorite thing."

As Ryan talks in a happy, confident voice to Bullet, the horse he's going to ride, I begin to wonder if this really *is* going to be his new favorite thing.

"You're such a sweet, pretty girl," he tells her. "We're going to have so much fun today."

"Bullet's a boy," I tell him. "And I picked him on purpose so that you *would* have fun today."

"Because he's faster than a speeding bullet, like Superman?" He lifts his arm as if he's a superhero about to fly away.

"No, because he's ironically named and the slowest, calmest horse in the stable."

He grins at me. "I'm not offended you chose a slowpoke for me," he replies. "I'm all about taking the slow road in life, whether it's on a horse or not."

"Then you've come to the right place today."

I help him tack up and get Bullet ready to ride, showing him how to secure the saddle and get Bullet to take the bit into his mouth. All the while, Ryan is saying soft things to the horse like, "We're gonna walk so slow today, buddy," and "Look at those beautiful eyes! A guy could get lost in those eyes."

Though I hate to admit it, I find this kind of endearing.

He continues his ongoing conversation with Bullet as I tack up Tanner, the horse I'm going to ride. By the time I show Ryan how to mount the horse, it's like they're old friends.

"Okay, now take the reins in both your hands and hold them like this," I tell him, demonstrating how to hold your fingers and thumbs so you have a loose but steady hold on the reins. I look over to see what he's doing, and it seems okay. Then I explain how to hold his feet in the stirrups. For some reason, this seems to confuse him.

Ryan adjusts his feet, but he's still sticking his toes down too low with his heels too high in the air. I ride over to him and kick at his toes. "Pick them up," I tell him, "and try to balance your weight on the balls of your feet."

He sort of gets the hang of it but takes so long even Bullet gets impatient. The only thing keeping me from doing the same is Ryan's unfailing cheerfulness. He's still smiling. And . . . wow. He has a nice smile. I'm still not used to it.

"Okay, now you're going to very gently press on Bullet's sides with your feet and legs," I tell him. "With the emphasis on *gently*. You don't want to spook him, or he'll take off like . . ."

"A bullet?" Ryan suggests.

"Just do it gently," I remind him. "And ideally he'll slowly walk forward."

"Got it," Ryan says. With a low bow in my direction, he takes hold of the reins, clearly mouthing reminders to himself about how to hold them and how to steer and stop. It's getting harder and harder to stay annoyed with him when he's being this cute.

"Now I press gently," he says in an undertone. "And . . ."

Ryan seems to do what I tell him to, but nothing happens. Bullet stays stock-still.

So Ryan kicks him harder—once, then twice.

"No, not that hard!" I call.

But it's too late. Bullet jumps as if he's startled, then takes off like a shot. It's the fastest I've ever seen him move, and for a second I laugh out loud. Then I realize that Ryan's bouncing around in the saddle. He lists to one side as his feet slip in the stirrups.

He's going to fall off.

"Pull on the reins to get him to slow down!" I yell out to him, but it's too late. Bullet's gone rogue. He canters over to a jump and I groan out loud.

"Hold on to the saddle!" I shout. But it's a lost cause.

Bullet's airborne, and so is Ryan. It's just that Bullet makes it over the jump and Ryan lies flat on his back in the sandy riding ring. For a second, I freeze. Every muscle in my body tenses up. I have to physically shake myself to get moving again. Then I slide off Tanner and sprint to Ryan's side. It looks like Ryan has started to shake. A lump clogs up my throat. He's in shock. Oh God, he's in shock.

I drop to my knees by his side. "Ryan, are you okay?" I can't believe he fell. I can't believe I didn't teach him enough so he'd know what to do when Bullet took off. That any of this happened.

Only then do I realize that yes, he's shaking. But he's shaking with laughter. *"Inconceivable!"* he calls out.

I close my eyes for a second, trying to make sense of this. "Ryan!" I say. *"Are you okay?"*

"I'm fine," he gasps out. "Except for my bruised ego." He lets out another laugh. "I thought you said that horse was slow!"

"He is," I say, leaning farther down to adjust his helmet as he stays on his back. "You just . . . I mean, you just . . ."

"I stink at this?" he suggests. "And you actually did have to rescue me?"

For a second, I look at him in awe. Who laughs when they've been bucked off a horse? And their first time on one, no less. Yet here's Ryan cracking up as if something hilarious has happened because the slowest horse in the stable threw him off the saddle. This kind of positivity is . . . well, it's . . .

"Come on," he gasps out. "It's funny, right?"

My heart is still racing. He scared me to death. Now I know why JR launched into me for the biking accident. "Do you know how terrifying that was? How can you be laughing?"

Ryan continues shining his golden smile at me. "Ah, see. I knew you were nervous for me."

Nope, I realize. *I'll never get used to that smile.* I shake my head, trying to avoid the smile tugging at my own lips. "You're something else, Ryan Desmond."

His laughter dies down, his smile becomes eager. "Something good, though, right?"

Ryan still lies in the dusty sand of the riding ring, right in the middle of a pile of manure. He's probably going to have a nasty bruise on his tailbone. But he's still smiling at me like that and . . .

"Yes," I say. "Definitely something good."

I get to my feet and hold out my hand to him, which he takes, pulling himself to his feet as well. We're both covered with dust and sand now.

He holds on to my hand even after he's on solid ground again. "Now we've rescued each other. Which is kinda nice, right?"

When my eyes meet his again, he's not smiling anymore. Instead he's looking at me as if it's Christmas and he just got the one thing he wanted most as a gift. But that can't be. I can't be what he most wants. Or what he wants at all.

A warmth spreads over my cheeks and even down my neck. "It is pretty nice."

So we groom the horses, put the tack away, then begin the long walk back to the hotel since he can't get in a carriage in this state. Our hands brush as we walk. At first I think it's an accident, but then it happens again. And again. I can't tell if he's doing it on purpose or by accident—or even which of those two I hope it is. I take a step away from him to try to get myself together. But Ryan moves closer as we walk. His hand brushes against mine once more. I can feel his eyes on me and I want to look up. I really do. But I'm too anxious about what I'll see if I do.

By the time we get back to the hotel, we're already late for opening night. My parents are *not* going to be happy with me. But I'm feeling—oddly—happy enough for the three of us.

CHAPTER 9
Lexi (Now)

Breakfast is included with my room, so after a quick shower, I walk down a grand staircase with a deep burgundy carpet covering it. The banisters are a dark, shiny wood that I've never seen before. Framed art, some of which is by such famous artists that I *have* seen them before, hang on the walls of the staircase.

If I needed any proof that I don't belong here, just these stairs alone are enough to provide it. People in expensive-looking leisure wear and actual tennis outfits pass me going in both directions, making me tug at my *Little Shop of Horrors* T-shirt self-consciously. I bet these people saw the latest revival on Broadway. Or at least they could've if they'd wanted to. I wanted to but Dad said I'd have to wait till it came to Chicago . . . and pay for my own ticket.

Breakfast. I need breakfast.

As I descend the stairs, I step into the bright lobby. The morning sunshine casts the whole place in a different light. The pale yellow walls are more luminous. The flowers on the trees give off a stronger smell. The whole place seems to be glowing. Alive.

For a second, I stand there and just take it all in. Mom probably walked down these stairs. She probably sat in this lobby. Maybe under these same trees and in one of these same sofas. Or maybe not. It was a long time ago.

Giving myself a stern shake, I follow the signs to the dining room. When I step inside I stop short.

The walls are covered in pale blue-and-white wallpaper with a dainty pattern on it till it meets the ceiling in a burst of elaborate gold scrolls and curlicues. Immaculate tables, already set with stark white tablecloths and forest-green chairs, fill every corner of the room. It's . . . a lot.

"Can I help you?" a server asks.

For a second I just stare at her name tag—an emphatic *BONJOUR* with *Eden, Trenton, NJ*—instead of answering.

She looks at me expectantly. "Oh . . . um . . . of course," I stammer out. "I'd love to have breakfast."

Eden from Trenton, New Jersey, asks me to follow her and leads me to a tiny table set for two by a window. The view is pretty . . . all sunlight glinting off the lake . . . but as Eden takes away the second place setting, all I can think about is the fact that I am, in fact, all by myself.

Someone else comes by offering me coffee, which I gratefully take. Yet another hotel staff person pops by and introduces himself—Jacob, my server for the morning. I glance down at his name tag. *Marion, IL.* I look back up at him, suddenly excited. "I'm from Illinois, too!"

He smiles politely. "Where do you live?"

"Chicago. Just outside the Loop," I tell him.

Jacob laughs. "I'm jealous," he tells me. "My town's a *lot* less exciting than Chicago is. But I'm going to school there in the fall. University of Illinois."

"That's great!" I say. "You're going to love it."

He smiles again, but it's clear that he's just waiting to give me my menu so he can go help other people, so I let him.

The menu is . . . extensive. Which is a good thing for me since it's the only meal of the day I don't have to pay for.

When he comes back with a basket of pastries, I place my order: ham and cheese omelet, sides of potatoes and fresh berries, and orange juice.

"Always good to start the day with a healthy appetite!" Jacob jokes.

I try to smile, but now I'm feeling out of place again. I glance around nervously at the other people sitting near me. They're all in groups of at least two—sometimes up to six or seven. They're reading the paper or checking their phones or chatting and laughing with each other. Part of me wishes I could go over and introduce myself to someone . . . anyone . . . and ask if I could sit with them. But I know that wouldn't fly.

Before the loneliness starts to creep into my chest, I take out my phone and glance at the list I made of steps I needed to take once I got here.

1. Text Dad so he doesn't freak out.

2. Go to historical society and ask for help.

3. Library!

4. Possible residents who might remember Mom?

5. Hotel records?

6. Text Dad again. See above re: freaking out.

7. Wander aimlessly trying to feel Mom's presence like she's some kind of ghost and I'm one of those guys on TV who hunts them.

Okay, so the list kind of fell apart toward the end. But I do have real things I can do while I'm here to try to find out more about Mom. I just have to actually *do* them.

And first I have to eat the absolute feast of a breakfast that Jacob just laid out in front of me. The omelet is HUGE. The basket of pastries has croissants and scones and banana bread—far too much for one person to eat. Which means I'll have to figure out how to pop them in my pack to save them for lunch. Or something. Right now, all I want to do is eat.

After scanning the map of the island on my phone about four dozen times while I scarf down my omelet, I think I have a plan. Or at least the beginnings of one.

First things first: I shoot a text off to Dad.

Tour at 11:00, I write. Give Connor a hug for me.

Or in other words, *I'm still alive so please don't look too closely into where I am or what I'm doing.* For a few seconds I hold my breath and watch my phone to see what he texts back. Then I get a terse thumbs-up emoji. I guess he's not that concerned about where I am after all. My phone dings again, making me nearly jump out of my seat.

Let me know how it goes. Connor misses you. He keeps talking about the pirate chest you're going to make with him when you get home. Stay safe.

It's both more than I expected and not enough. I'm sure Connor misses me. I miss him, too. But Dad would never stoop to admit that he does. Maybe because he actually doesn't. I read the text again, looking for clues that he cares about me, but all I have to cling to is the *Stay safe* at the end of it. So I guess that's it. Later I'll feed him some lies about the school I'm supposed to be at from the list Chloe and Kiera put together.

As quickly as I can, I pop two of the scones and a croissant into a napkin and fold it over. One last furtive glance, to make sure no one is watching, and the whole thing's in my backpack. It's going to make a mess in my bag, but there's no helping that now. I'll run to the bathroom after this and get more paper towels to wrap everything up in.

And I'll have a free lunch later . . . even if it's not exactly a healthy one.

Out in the lobby, I look at the island map again. The historical society's not far away, but it's not close either. Besides, I can't afford to keep paying for carriage rides if they're not on the hotel's bill like the ride here was. An idea occurs to me. Hopefully a much cheaper idea.

Walking across the lobby, I head to the concierge desk and force myself to ask for help. "I need a bike," I tell the concierge. "Can you let me know where I could rent one, please?"

Eve, Lansing, MI smiles at me. "I can have one waiting for you downstairs in fifteen minutes."

"Oh, okay," I reply. "So I don't have to go into town or anything?"

"No, we have our own stable of bicycles here. All I need is your room number and I can get you one."

She types in my room and then looks down at her computer screen for a second. "Okay, you're all set!" Eve smiles up at me. "Going mountain biking? There are lots of good trails if you need some help choosing one."

"Oh . . . um . . . no," I stammer out. "Actually, I'm heading to the historical society right now, to be honest."

Eve's eyes widen. "Really?" she says. "The exhibits aren't huge, but there's a lot of information." She leans in as if she's sharing a secret. "The *Island in Winter* exhibit is the best, especially if you don't live here year-round like me."

I nod. Over and over and over. Like my head can't stop bopping up and down. "Okay, great!" My voice comes out a little too perky and loud. "I'll have to check it out." When I move to walk away, Eve calls me back.

"Let me give you a map," she says. She pulls out an actual paper map and puts an *X* to show me where to find the historical society. Then she draws the route there for me in bright neon-yellow highlighter so that it stands out on the colorful map. "And I'm going to mark a few other places for you, too, if you want to check them out, too. Mackinac's Greatest Hits."

I glance down at the map as she puts little *X*s next to Mirror Rock by the coast, a fort farther inland, a memorial for people in the fishing community lost on the lake, and a few other places.

"Here you go," she says with a smile. She's being relentlessly nice to me. Maybe because she's paid to? To me, it seems like a nightmare to have to talk to strangers all day, but she seems happy enough.

"This is really great," I tell her. I mean it, too. "Thank you so much."

She smiles again and wishes me a nice day.

With fifteen minutes to waste, I wander around the lobby and look at the pretty furniture and all the trees. Everything here seems perfect. The colors mesh well with each other, the trees are carefully tended to. There's a smell of fresh-baked cookies in the air. My mind strays back to my mom's list of places she'd rather be than here, and for the first time I wonder if her father might have been right—if maybe this hotel was as good a place to be as anywhere else in the world.

It feels like an eternity has passed, but when I check my phone it's only been five minutes. A man in a hotel uniform walks by and I check out his name tag: *Juan, Ann Arbor, MI*. An idea forms in my head for the first time and I start to watch every employee who passes by, hoping someone might be from around here—*Monique, Albany, NY*; *Thomas, Green Bay, WI*; *Teisha, Fort Wayne, IN*; *Kenji, Beaver, OH*. No one from Mackinac. Why is the whole staff from somewhere else? Why can't anyone be from this island?

I plunk down on one of the sofas and look at my phone again. Eight more minutes before I can pick up my bike. I could walk outside and wait there. At least it would kill a little time. Not eight minutes, but still. As I head to the French doors that lead onto the verandah, my eyes catch on someone walking in my direction. The guy looks like he's probably about my age, maybe a year or two older. He's tall, with short dark hair, light brown skin, and hazel eyes. His eyelashes are longer than mine, which is frustrating but also kind of . . . nice? His eyes are really beautiful. He's in a Palais du Lac uniform as he hurries out of the restaurant with a tray of drinks in his hands. But it's his name tag that gets my attention.

Casey, Mackinac Island, MI.

My eyes widen. He's from here! Which means I have to talk to this guy.

Of course, I don't usually just saunter up to strange guys and strike up conversations. To be honest, I'm not all that good at talking to guys I know, let alone cute ones with nice eyelashes who I've never met before. And who are walking right past me as I fret on this sofa.

Wow, I am seriously a mess right now.

Casey from Mackinac Island continues blissfully on his journey to wherever it is he's going without so much as looking my way. He'll be gone if I don't do something. Like right now. It's a big hotel and my time here is short. I might never find him again.

I suck in a deep breath. I have to do this.

"Um . . . hi?" I sputter out. I apparently sputtered too quietly, though, because he just keeps walking.

"Excuse me?" I say in a louder voice.

No reaction. Nothing.

Finally I just go for it.

"Casey!" I call out.

He turns abruptly and faces me. "Yeah, what's up?" Then he gets a good look at me. "Oh . . . sorry, I didn't . . ." He looks at me with knit eyebrows. "Do I know you?"

"Oh . . . um . . . that is . . ."

A look of confusion passes over his face, with a hint of annoyance lying just beneath it.

Okay, I have to do better than this.

"Um . . . so I saw that you're from Mackinac," I manage to get out. "And I just want to ask you a few questions about the island. I mean, if that's okay?"

"Yeah, of course," he says. "I have to drop these drinks off but if you can wait I'll be right back."

"Really?" I ask. "I mean, just like that you'll help me?"

He shoots me a condescending smile. "I work here," he reminds me. "I get paid to help you."

"Oh . . . sure," I blather on. "I forgot about that part."

Casey starts to walk away with his tray of drinks, but stops to give me a quick once-over. Probably to see if I'm for real.

"Just give me a few minutes to deliver this." He nods to the tray. The drinks on it are sweating in the afternoon heat. "I'll be right back."

"Um . . . yeah, sounds good," I stammer. "Sorry I interrupted you."

For the first time, he looks at me with curiosity in his eyes. The expression is gone in an instant . . . as is Casey. I watch him leave and delete ghost-hunting from my list and add on to a different entry:

7. Talk to local people who might have known Mom (or who might know people who might have known Mom).

In some alternative dimension, what I just wrote makes sense. In this one, well . . .

By the time Casey from Mackinac Island comes back . . . way past when I was supposed to pick up my bike . . . I've paced the lobby so much that I'm ready to explode.

"So . . . how can I help you?" he asks.

This is it. I just have to suck it up and ask the cute person who's from here pertinent questions that will lead to me learning more about my mom and when she stayed here.

"Do you know anyone who lived here twenty or thirty years ago, and if you do could you give me their phone numbers so I could call to ask them some questions?" It all comes out in one rambling sentence. Or, I guess, question. Either way, I was rambling.

Casey shakes his head like he's trying to clear it. "Wait . . . what?"

I physically lift my hands to my shoulders and then press them down slowly to try to center myself. "I need to talk to someone who's lived here for a long time." There, that came out much clearer and more straightforward.

"Are you a researcher?" he asks. "The historical society is about twenty minutes away by bike." He turns to point to the concierge station. "Eve could give you a map and—"

"No!" I freeze when I realize how loud that just came out. "No," I say again. My voice is at a completely normal decibel level now. "I'm not a researcher. And I already have a map. Eve even showed me how to get to the historical society."

"Okay," he says, dragging out the word. "Then you're all set."

I close my eyes for a second. This is why I don't ever talk to cute boys. I get tongue-tied and weird and nothing I say makes any sense. "I'm . . . my mom used to stay here." I try to focus on talking more slowly and actually making sense. It's harder than I thought it would be. "I'm trying to find out more about her, so I wanted to know if you have neighbors or even family members who you might be able to hook me up with who might remember her?"

Casey gives me a decidedly less enthusiastic smile than he did when we first started talking. "You want me to introduce you to my *family?*" He shakes his head. "Yeah, that's not exactly in my job description." He takes one step backward and then another. "If you need a lemonade or something, let me know. Otherwise . . ."

Just as he starts to walk away my panic sets in again.

So I do something I normally would never do. I reach out and grab his arm.

"Wait, Casey!"

Slowly—painfully slowly—Casey turns around again. His eyes drop down to where I'm holding on to him and then back up to meet my eyes. He does not look pleased. I move my hand off his arm so fast it's like it suddenly got burnt.

"Look . . . I'm happy to help you with anything hotel-related but that's it," he says. His voice is polite but full of disdain. I didn't know you could make your voice be both of those things at once.

"I just want to talk to you," I reply. "I'm looking for information about my mother. She used to stay here sometimes and I'm trying to find out more about her when she was younger and—"

"So ask your mom if you have questions about her past," he cuts me off. "It would make life a lot easier. For both of us."

"I would, but she . . ." My eyes drop to the floor. "She died when I was five."

For a split second, Casey stares at me with wide eyes. "God . . .

I'm really sorry," he says. "I wouldn't have said . . . I mean, at least I wouldn't have been so obnoxious about it." He tucks the tray farther under his arm. "But . . . but I'm still not sure how I can help you."

My eyes meet his again. "You can talk to me about the island!" I respond. "You can help me find someone who lived here when she used to come. Maybe who'd even met her."

With a resigned sigh, he shakes his head. "You *really* think you're going to find anyone who remembers a hotel guest?" Casey says. "'Cause you're not. If she'd lived here, that would be one thing. No one cares about the tourists."

With that, he pivots on his heels to leave. But he turns back for one more moment. "Sorry about your mom."

Then he starts to walk away again for real.

He can't just walk away. I won't let him.

"Casey, come on," I say as I trail behind him. "You must know someone I can talk to. An older relative or a neighbor? Anyone?"

Casey stops in his tracks and faces me again. "You know what? I have a job to do," he says. His voice is cold as ice now. "And you're keeping me from doing it. Unlike you, I can't afford to come someplace like this on vacation. I *work* here."

Heat rises in my cheeks. "I can't afford to stay here either!" I tell him. "I'm using the emergency credit card my dad gave me. He's going to kill me when he finds out where I am."

"Not my problem," Casey says. "I don't care how you pay for your hotel room and I . . . I *really* have to get back to work." There's an edge of desperation to his voice, and I feel terrible that I might be getting him in trouble.

"Oh God," I say. "I'm so sorry. Like . . . super, super sorry."

He looks at me incredulously for a second and then shakes his head and walks back into the restaurant without saying another word.

I sit down on the nearest sofa and close my eyes. Maybe Casey's right. I came all this way thinking that just by being here, I'd feel closer to her. As if a hotel or a historical society could give me back some missing piece of her and everything about Mom's past would slot into place like a jigsaw puzzle.

But that's probably not how it's going to work.

It sounds like she only visited here during the summer. Maybe not even every summer. So what possible record would there be of her? Historical societies don't keep track of who passes through, do they? I mean, why would they?

Oh God, why am I even here?

"Lexi?" Eve's voice cuts through my thoughts, startling me.

"Yeah?"

"Your bike's ready whenever you are," she tells me.

I nod and get back to my feet again. Historical society, here I come.

CHAPTER 10

Emma (Then)

The thing with the hotel's opening night is that it should be tedious and boring, but instead it's glorious. Well, at least it's glorious except for the glares my dad occasionally throws my way. And for the fact that JR refuses to come every year—as far as I can tell, out of plain old stubbornness because he knows I want him to. Tonight, he wouldn't even agree to meet me at the greenhouse afterward like we always do. But even the combined forces of my dad and JR are not going to bring me down tonight. The whole lawn in front of the hotel is lit up with strings of fairy lights and torches. Staked garden lights dot the pathways and lanterns hang from every imaginable surface. It's like something out of a dream—as if the whole hotel has slipped into some magical, fairy-tale gown for the first Saturday night of the summer and is determined to be the belle of the ball.

It doesn't hurt that the huge barbecue is already fired up by the time I reach the lawn, and the smells of grilled ribs and corn on the cob fill the air. If there's a person in this whole wide world who could resist the sights and smells of this, well . . . I feel sad for them.

When Linda joins me on the verandah, looking ready for summer adventure in a pale blue tank top and khaki shorts, though, even the fairyland before me can't help ward off my nerves.

She nods toward the lawn. "We're not actually going to have to play croquet, are we?"

I palm the bracelets I made in my pocket, willing myself to act normal. "Not unless you want to," I reply. "But I have to warn you that I swing a mean mallet, so you'll probably lose if we do."

She rolls her eyes at me. "That's very aristocratic of you, Emma. But I'd rather get some dinner and lemonade, if you don't mind."

"Me too."

"See, I knew I liked you," Linda tells me.

She grabs my arm and starts to pull me away, but I hold back. I am not going to chicken out of this. I'm not going to assume that she'll be like other girls I tried to be friends with who ended up scoffing at me for being different. She's already not like that. So I take a deep breath.

"Wait," I say, holding up one hand. "I have something for you."

Digging back into the pocket of my sundress, I bring out the two bracelets I finished this morning and hold them out to show her. "One for me and one for you."

Linda takes the bracelet nearest her and gives it a close inspection. "Did you make these?"

My head bobs up and down a little too vigorously. "I found some old rope washed up on the beach and took the fibers apart so I could reweave them."

I brace myself for some snarky reply from her, or some of her usual dry joking, but instead she quietly slips her bracelet onto her wrist, then looks up at me. "Okay," she says. "Thanks."

"I thought it would be nice to have something matching," I admit, a little sheepishly. I've never had a girl for a friend, at least not a real friend. It's a mortifying thing to admit, but it's true. Before the Desmonds moved here, I either had no friends at all, or I had JR when he was here. Or when he deigned to keep in touch when he wasn't.

"I've never had a friend like you," Linda says.

Tension tightens between my shoulders. "What's that supposed to mean?" I ask, almost dreading the answer but still needing to know it.

She gives me a once-over. "You're just so . . . you," she says at last. "Most of my friends in Detroit were either on my swim team or did debate with me. No flitty sundresses or arty outlooks."

"Oh" is all I say. I don't want it to hurt that she's reduced me to a sundress and being *arty* of all things. Not that I don't love my dresses or love making art. I do. I really do. It's just that I get reduced to things like this all the time. Outward things. Things that are part of me, but not all of me.

"Ugh . . . don't get all mopey," Linda says. "I meant it as a compliment. The world could use more arty outlook in it."

"And flitty dresses?" I venture hopefully.

She shrugs. "I wouldn't want to wear them, but they work for you," she says before she nudges me. "Now come on. Put on your damn bracelet and let's go grab some food."

That's an idea I can get behind. I slip mine on and hold my wrist up to hers. Linda wraps her pinkie around mine and a kind of . . . warmth courses through me. I've never had a friend like her either—male or female.

We walk across the lawn to the barbecue with our pinkies still linked and then break apart to make heaping plates of baby back ribs and grilled pineapple, corn bread and bottles of lemonade. We head right past the crowded picnic tables into the relative quiet of the grass by the tree line. It'll be buggier here, but it has a view of the rest of the proceedings to die for.

I spot my parents, making small talk with some of the summer people, and frown. My mom was so disappointed in me for being late. Again.

"It's just that you promised you'd be on time," she'd said when I finally got home. They were already dressed and walking out the door. I still needed to shower and change.

"I didn't actually *promise*," I'd replied. "I think I just said I'd be here, didn't I?"

But Mom wasn't having any of that. "You're not a child anymore, Emma," she'd told me. "I need you to start stepping up and acting like an adult. That means making good on your promises and commitments."

The conversation only went downhill from there.

I'm falling into a funk not even the fairy lights or the presence of Linda is helping. I have to think about something else. The crisp night air, maybe. Or the sounds of the little kids laughing at the magic show by the pool. Maybe even the afternoon spent with Ryan and how sweet he was to the horse that literally caused his downfall.

Just as I'm about to ask where Ryan is, I spot him walking away from the barbecue with two giant plates of food in his hands. We had so much fun this afternoon. He was so . . . so . . .

Then I see JR, right next to Ryan, deep in conversation.

My jaw hangs open. The sight of JR, on this night of all nights, is so bizarre that I actually do a double take. He wouldn't come here with me. He wouldn't even agree to meet up with me afterward in the greenhouse. But he came with Ryan?

"I can't believe it," I breathe out.

"What?" Linda asks. She looks over and rolls her eyes again when she sees her brother, too. "He could eat a whole football team under the table. Completely ruled by his stomach."

But that's not what I'm gawking at. "No, I mean JR," I explain. "I can't believe Ryan convinced him to come. I try to get him here every year, but he always says no. It's so weird that he actually showed up."

Linda doesn't say anything for a long few seconds, and when I turn to look at her, she's giving me this strange, questioning look.

"Are you mad he's here?" she asks. "'Cause we could avoid the two of them tonight if you want."

I look over at her, startled. "No, I . . . that's okay," I reply. "I don't *mind* that's he here, I'm just . . . surprised. That's all."

She studies me for a second to see if I really mean it. "Okay," she says at last. "But if you change your mind, I won't be broken up about leaving." She pauses. "I mean, after we have ribs. And dessert. Before that I'd mind a lot. But after . . ."

This makes me smile. "I thought your brother was the one ruled by his stomach in your family."

Yet another eye roll meets this statement. "I swam ten laps and then did sprints before this. I'm hungry." Linda gives me a side-eye. "Don't make me tell you you've got noodles for brains."

Laughter pours from me despite everything.

I've been friends with JR since we were both seven years old. And in those early years, *friends* would have been a bit of an overstatement. More like kids who constantly bickered but had no one else to play with, so they made do.

The memory of the two of us as kids makes me smile. JR was less grumpy then, but much, much more contrary. He wouldn't answer to JR for two whole years, during which time I, of course, refused to stop calling him that. Eventually I wore him down.

That makes me smile, too.

And now JR sits down across from me with Ryan by his side. One of them is actually rubbing his hands together in excitement while the other is . . . not. JR's eyes dart around, taking in the whole *scene* of opening night. His posture is uneasy—too upright. He wipes his hands on his shorts before looking over to find me staring at him.

"What?" The tone of his voice has a defensive edge.

It hits me all at once that maybe he doesn't come to stuff like this not because he doesn't want to, but because he doesn't feel comfortable at them. The very thought of this makes me melt a little. It must show on my face, because he blushes and turns away. His face settles back into his studied look of indifference.

"You even *look* like a perky princess tonight," JR says to me, the edge back in his voice.

I know what he's doing but I play along anyway to try to get him to relax. Nothing relaxes JR more than teasing me, after all. "You know, I'd already thought this night was magical, but Ryan must have worked some actual wizardry to convince you to grace us with your presence," I tell him. "Are you going to turn into a pumpkin at midnight?"

Ryan's face lights up. "Oooh . . . if he does, can I be one of the mice who turned into horses, like in the movie?" Ryan asks. "What were those guys' names?"

"Gus Gus and Jaq," JR tells him. I almost laugh out loud. So much for being tough and indifferent.

"Yeah!" Ryan says, his enthusiasm infectious. "I'll be those guys. Much more fun than turning into a pumpkin. No offense, JR."

"None taken," JR replies. "Cinderella doesn't turn into a pumpkin anyway. It's her coach. So all that'll happen to me is that I'll lose a shoe on my way home. Wouldn't be the first time."

I nearly snarf out a mouthful of lemonade. "I love that *you're* the perky princess in this scenario," I tell him. "And that you're not one but two different mice," I say to Ryan.

"What does that make me?" Linda asks.

"Evil stepsister for sure," Ryan replies. "Or maybe the mean cat?"

But there's no way I'm going to let that stand. "Linda *cannot* be the mean cat!" I tell him. "She has to be someone good. Like the fairy godmother or Prince Charming."

Now Linda is laughing. "I'll take the prince, thanks," she says to me. "Because you're clearly the only choice for fairy godmother."

"I can live with that," I reply with a smile. "I'll be the one who turns Ryan from a couple of mice to a couple of horses, and JR from the poor girl to a glorious princess."

They both look at each other and then back at me. "You just ruined everything," JR replies. "You know that, don't you?"

I take a big bite of ribs and then lick each of my fingers afterward. "I know," I say. "According to you, I often do."

Linda holds her hands up in two *L*s as if she's framing a picture. "Emma. Fairy godmother. Ruiner of everything."

But this time it's Ryan who won't let that stand. His eyes meet mine. "But Emma makes everything better."

It's a broad compliment. It means nothing, really. I know that. But my face burns up at it anyway. And at the way he's looking at me. "Um . . . thanks, Ryan."

Linda's watching me like I'm the one who's suddenly turned into a pumpkin or something. JR takes a bite of corn bread as his shoulders slump into a sulk. Everything suddenly seems off, but I don't know why.

We sit and eat and barely say another word until even Ryan has finished his dinner. Despite everyone's funk, Ryan seems full of good cheer. And good food. He gives his stomach a dramatic slap and says, "Now what're we going to do?"

Linda and I both say, "Dessert," at the same time.

Then JR says, "Dessert down by the dock? I wouldn't mind getting out of here."

For once, I completely agree with him. "There's no moon tonight, so the stars will all be out."

"Best idea I've heard all day," Ryan says. "Well, apart from the wonderful idea to teach me how to ride a horse. That one definitely has the number one spot." He gives me that same soft smile from this afternoon. In the fairy lights, with that smile on his face, Ryan could actually be a prince in a fairy tale. I can't take my eyes off him.

"You taught him how to ride a horse today?" JR's voice pierces the night, making me turn to look at him. "I didn't know that."

I clear my throat, and nod. "Well, I tried. He got tossed off the horse."

"That why it takes the top spot," Ryan counters. "Not everyone can say that the slowest horse on the island landed them on their butts."

"I'm sure you feel proud," Linda says to her brother. "Another great feat of athleticism on your part."

But Ryan is unfazed. "I've never wanted great feats of athleticism," he replies. "It's Dad who wants them for me."

"And as with everything, I deliver where you don't, but Dad couldn't care less," Linda says. The bitterness in her voice takes me by surprise.

Ryan frowns at her. "Count yourself lucky," he tells his sister. "There are lots of things Dad couldn't care less about, but none of them have to do with me."

I look across our little picnic at JR, and it's as if he can read my thoughts almost instantly. "So . . . . dessert?"

"Yes!" I agree. "Dessert's always the best part of opening night."

"Or of any meal," Linda says. It's clear she's trying not to dwell on her exchange with Ryan, but she still has a line between her eyebrows.

I slip my arm through hers and lead her away from the boys. "Thanks for the rescue," she says in a quiet voice. "I hate it when my dad comes between me and Ryan."

"I'm sure," I reply. "The one advantage to being an only child is that my parents can never pit me against anyone else." Then I frown as my parents come back into view across the lawn again. Mom's eyes meet mine but she quickly looks away. I really upset her tonight without even trying to. "I have to disappoint them all on my own."

Linda gives my arm a squeeze.

"You're really going to love dessert," I tell her. "And the dock on a dark, moonless night when it feels as if the stars are so close you can reach up and touch them."

"You sound like you're talking in poems," Linda laughs.

"Really?" I ask. The thought thrills me. "I would love to talk in poems!"

She squeezes my arm again as the guys catch up with us.

Ryan takes the lead as we head to the dessert table, with Linda following on his heels, clearly vying with him to get there first. JR falls into step with me but he doesn't say a word. We walk together in silence till I realize he's staring at me. This time I'm the one spitting out a defensive "What?"

He shakes his head, but there's no snarky comeback. No sarcasm about me or this night or anything. Instead a crease forms between his eyebrows as he turns to look over at where Ryan and Linda are already piling brownies and cookies and madeleines onto plates.

"Nothing," he says. "Nothing at all."

CHAPTER 11

Emma (Then)

There is never a time when the chefs at the hotel don't go the extra mile to make everything special, and tonight is no exception. One table brims with cookies and brownies and cupcakes with perfect little icing flowers on them—yellow roses and orange day lilies, even pale pink and magenta peonies. They're like tiny works of edible art. The other table is covered with miniature patisserie—meticulously created eclairs, macarons, mousse cakes, and chocolate truffles. The smells of chocolate and sugar and pastry cream fill the air. If there's a heaven, I think it would smell like this.

Linda actually moans when she gets to the pastry table.

"It's like this place doesn't want me to stay on my swim regimen anymore," she says. "It's conspiring against me. I swear my mother told the pastry chefs that the breaststroke is *unladylike* and they acted accordingly."

"I don't think it's personal," I tell her. "They're trying to ruin everyone's resolve to eat healthy."

"And . . . it's working!" Ryan adds cheerfully as he heaps mousse cakes onto a meal-sized plate.

I have no idea how he could possibly eat anything else tonight, but he's grinning ear to ear with a gleeful determination to give it a try. Ryan edges over to me, so close that his arm touches mine.

"What're your favorites, Emma?"

"Definitely the truffles," I reply. "Followed by the mousse cakes and brownies."

Before Ryan can respond, JR cuts in. "Basically, anything with chocolate," he says. "Never, ever go to a fudge shop with Emma, 'cause it's not pretty. No free-sample plate is safe from her."

I turn to him indignantly. "Or from you!" I reply. "Don't pin the raiding of fudge samples all on me, JR. You were as bad as I was when we were kids."

A tiny hint of a smile teases at his lips, but it's gone in an instant.

"What's this about free fudge samples?" Linda asks. "And why did no one tell me sooner?"

"Because the shops weren't open for the season yet," I say. "And now you know."

Both Ryan and JR open their mouths at the same time and say, "And knowing is half the battle!"

They look at each other. I look at Linda. "Did I miss something?"

"*GI Joe* cartoons," she tells me. "From the dark ages of animation."

But the guys aren't paying any attention at all.

"I can't believe you've seen that show!" Ryan exclaims.

"My dad has all the episodes," JR explains. "I used to watch them when I was a kid."

They keep talking about this cartoon as they toss desserts on their plates. I watch them, fascinated.

Linda walks up to me, her plate overflowing with treats. "It's not too late to ditch them, you know," she says in a low voice. "We could take all the dessert and visit Viola to eat in peace."

For a second, I don't know what to say or do. JR and Ryan are talking nonstop. I haven't seen JR so animated since . . . I don't even know when. He definitely never is with me. My eyes flit over to Ryan. He's drawing JR of all people out. He listens to something JR just said with every ounce of his attention. They're an unusual duo, but . . . it works?

A tiny twinge of jealousy hits me in the gut. My stomach tenses as if I'm about to be punched. But there's nothing to be jealous of. Not really. It's good that JR's making a new friend. And that Ryan is so interested in becoming his friend. Everything about this is good, yet . . . the twinge returns.

"Emma, you still with me?" Linda's voice interrupts my thoughts.

I glance up in surprise. "What?"

Her head falls back onto her shoulders in what I hope is mock frustration. "Do you want to go down to the dock or to the woods?"

But that's not as easy a question to answer as it should be. As the guys walk toward the wooded path that leads to the lake, JR turns back to make sure we're following. Our eyes meet, just for a moment, before he turns away again.

Do I follow JR to the dock to stargaze, or go with Linda to the woods? I'd be happy doing either, I guess. Both. But I feel as if whatever I choose, I'll end up disappointing one of them. Maybe even myself. It's as if there's a little rope pulling me in two different directions now that JR's back. I spent most of the spring with Linda. But summer . . . summer has always been about time with JR.

Plus, there's Ryan added into this baffling mix.

I look over at Linda, who's still waiting for me to respond. "Why don't we stargaze tonight and go visit Viola tomorrow night?"

"I work till ten tomorrow night," she reminds me.

Something inside me deflates. "Oh . . . then maybe Monday night?" I suggest. "That way we get to do both."

After a long pause, Linda finally nods. "We can do that," she agrees. "They've got half the dessert anyway, and I don't want only half the dessert."

I'm so happy—so relieved—that it feels as if I could float.

That happiness carries me past the lawn bowling and cornhole games, past the heated croquet match wrapping up at the last wicket, and the last vestige of the hotel's lights. Soon we're in the little wooded area where the nature path begins, then out of it again just as quickly. The whole world opens up when we get to the lake. The water stretches out before us in what feels like endless darkness, even though I know the shores of Michigan aren't all that far away. The sky is that deep, almost black shade of blue that can only happen before a new moon.

"Are you going to gawk at the sky all night or are you going to have dessert?" Linda asks.

"I'm going to gawk at the stars all night *and* have dessert," I tell her. "Neither would be quite as good without the other." This was the right decision. I know it was.

The four of us sit in the sand and we eat, sharing plates of everything that had been on offer back at the hotel.

Ryan sighs. "And to think I didn't want to move here."

"You were sooo pissed off about it," Linda agrees.

This stuns me. I've never seen Ryan angry about anything before. "Were you?" I ask, genuinely puzzled. "But this place is amazing!"

Ryan glances my way, and the expression in his eyes gets all soft and serious. "There are some amazing things about it."

A tiny chill runs down my spine. I have no idea what to say or how or even if I should say anything at all. Ryan looks beautiful under the lights of just the stars. He looks beautiful in the daylight, too. Or really any time of day. My cheeks burn at this revelation: he's just always beautiful. He holds my gaze for what feels like a second too long before dropping his eyes toward the sand.

"But I didn't know that when we first got here," he tells me. "It was really hard leaving my life back home. My parents only told us we were moving after they'd signed on the dotted line. Then we moved in the middle of junior year."

"It's always great when parents take our concerns and thoughts so seriously," JR says, his voice dripping with sarcasm.

"Wait, did you not want to come here either?" Ryan asks.

JR looks out over the water. He doesn't say anything for long enough that I wonder if he didn't hear the question. Then the muscles in his jaw start to tense and then twitch.

"I mostly live with my mom and her boyfriend on the mainland," he finally says. "Things are . . . less than ideal there."

His words lie between us for a while, no one quite sure what to say.

"Then why don't you move here with your dad?" Linda asks. "Does he not want you to?"

"No, he does," JR replies, but he pauses, giving me a quick glance. His hands reach out to pick up a nearby rock and he turns it around over and over again. I want to reach out and still his hand—to let him know that it's okay to tell them. That they'll understand. I give him the slightest of smiles and he nods back, just barely, before tossing his rock into the water.

"My dad was in jail," he says at last. "Drug charges. The kind of stuff that wouldn't even be a felony in our state anymore. But at the time there was a mandatory sentence for possession. I didn't see him for . . . a long time."

Ryan puts his hand on JR's shoulder. "That must have been horrible."

"It was," JR admits. "Even when he got out, my mom didn't want me to spend time with him. Once an addict, always an addict, she said."

"But you're here now," Linda says. "So what changed?"

JR takes a deep breath. "Dad got a job here," he says. "And my mom's boyfriend has never really wanted me around. So they worked out a deal. I get to visit for holidays and school vacations, then they get rid of me for the whole summer."

He grabs another rock and this time he throws it, hard, into the lake before grabbing another. Just as he's about to throw that one, Ryan gets to his feet and holds out his hand to JR.

"What're you doing?" JR demands.

"Just get up," Ryan says. So JR takes his hand and Ryan pulls him off the ground. "It's time to hug it out."

The expression on JR's face would be funny if he didn't look so genuinely shocked. "Yeah, I don't think so."

"Well, I do," Linda says as she gets up, too. "You're practically screaming *I need a hug* right now, and as your friends, we can't stand by and let you suffer for lack of one."

She turns and looks at me, the only person still sitting on the ground. "No group hug for you?" Linda asks me. "I would've thought this'd be right up your alley."

With one sad attempt at a laugh, I get to my feet, too. "I'm in."

When JR sees us all standing here ready to hug him, he takes a big step backward. "You really don't have to do this." He puts his hands up as if he's trying to physically hold us off. "Like *really*."

We do it anyway. All three of us throw our arms around him and hold him between us. I can feel the warmth of his bare arm under my fingertips and squeeze ever so gently.

When we finally break apart, JR no longer makes eye contact with anyone, but I can see both the embarrassment and happiness on his face.

"So . . . um . . . are we going to stargaze or what?" he asks.

"Stargazing sounds good to me," I reply, pushing him out onto the dock. Ryan follows close behind me, then Linda pulls up the rear. We all kick off our shoes and dip our feet into the chilly lake water. During the day—when it's warm out—the water temperature is passably swimmable. At night, when the air is chilly, the water has an edge to it. It cools down our feet and maybe even this whole situation.

I lie back and look up at the night sky, tracing out the constellations with my eyes—the Big and Little Dippers, Lyra, the big Summer Triangle. A satellite meanders across the sky.

"I see a shooting star!" Ryan says as he lies down next to me. "What's everyone's wish?"

Very gently I elbow him. "You can't say it out loud, or it won't come true."

"Or you can say it or not and it won't make any difference?" offers Linda.

"It always makes a difference," I reply. "If you keep the dream inside you, it'll always stay perfect, just as you wished it. If you tell other people, they can misinterpret it or try to affect whether or not it will happen."

"Besides, that was a satellite, not a shooting star," JR adds, making me smile. "You've got to wait for the real thing if you're gonna make a wish."

Linda lies down on the other side of Ryan, making JR the only one who's still sitting up and missing the full view. I tug at his sleeve to get him to lie down. "You'll never see a shooting star if you're not looking for one."

He shrugs. "Wishes aren't really my thing."

Linda laughs out loud. "You're ridiculous," she tells him. "What does that even mean?"

He shrugs again, even though she can't see him do it. "If you already know what you'd wish for isn't going to happen, there's no point wasting energy on it, right?"

Despite his words, JR lies down next to me and looks up at the night sky.

"Cynic," I say under my breath.

"Perky princess," he whispers.

I nudge him and he nudges me back, until finally our arms come to rest against each other's. I turn my head to try to catch his attention, but he's looking straight up at the sky and the stars. When Ryan shifts slightly, his left arm brushes against mine. For a second I can't move or even breathe. A distraction. I need a distraction.

I let my eyes focus on the Milky Way—at how our galaxy paints a swath of pale colors across the sky. Some night I'm going stay up till dawn and paint the sky. Maybe even some night soon. Maybe with my friends there to keep me company.

For now, though, I try to relax into the moment—let my arms ease into a more natural position against JR on one side and Ryan on the other. There's something wonderful and reassuring about being sandwiched between them—as if I couldn't be in a safer, happier place. But there's something . . . unsettling . . . about it, too. A star shoots across the sky.

"There's one!" Linda says, pointing her arm up as if we could follow it into the sky above. "Everybody makes a wish. Even you, JR."

I close my eyes to formulate the right wish, but mostly I wish I could make sense of how I'm feeling right now. I don't tell them that, though, even when Linda and Ryan ask repeatedly.

Some things are meant to be kept just for me.

CHAPTER 12

Lexi (Now)

My mind is filled with questions. Like . . . what're the rules for sharing the road with horse-drawn carriages? Is it the same as with cars? And what's the speed limit on this island? Is it just as fast as the carriages can go? Because other bikers are zipping past me way faster than the carriages can possibly go. Add in the tourists just walking out into the street to take pictures, and it's a biking nightmare.

I turn off Main Street and follow my GPS instructions down tree-lined streets with pastel houses on them. If there weren't people out watering their lawns and playing with their kids in shorts and T-shirts, I'd think I really had gone back in time.

As I glide past these people, I wonder if any of them might have known my mom. Then Casey's words echo in my mind. *If she lived here, that would be different. But no one pays attention to the tourists.* Which is why I'm going to the historical society, I guess.

The historical society is so small that I ride right past it the first time and then have to backtrack when the GPS tells me I've gone too far. As I finally glide to a stop in front of it, a tiny fear coils inside my stomach. The building looks like something out of a storybook. It's a pretty pastel pink that you'd never see anywhere near Chicago, with white woodwork that's carved in waves and carefully manicured topiaries in front of it. It's like the evil witch from "Hansel and Gretel" lives here but without any candy involved.

I would not have minded if there'd been candy involved.

Leaning my bike against the side of the building, I face the historical society head-on. There's a sign on the door that says *Come Right In!* I follow its instructions.

"Hello?" I call out.

No one answers.

The door opens into a tiny foyer that's lined with racks of brochures about things to do on the island. A little table on my right has a guest book for visitors to sign. I flip through it, skimming over the names and places of the people who've come here looking to learn more about the island. Just as I pick up the pen to sign my own name, that coil of fear slinks its way back into my stomach. It's probably better to leave as little evidence as possible that I was here. Dad's a lawyer, after all. He loves to examine evidence.

Putting the pen back down on the guest book, I walk into the next room and the first thing I see is a sign that says: *More Than Meets the STY: Farming on Mackinac*.

"Oh boy," I breathe out.

The room is filled with black-and-white photographs of farmers tending their land, some leading plows with oxen yoked to them . . . some riding on horse-drawn ones. There's old farm equipment, from shovels and hoes to ancient seed packets to a whole plow carriage . . . if that's a thing . . . from 1869.

It's fair to say that this is *not* what I expected. I thought it would be some musty place filled with old island records in file cabinets. Instead it's like a mini museum.

Through the door is another exhibit: *Holy CARP: A History of Island Fishing*. I groan out loud when I read the sign. Whoever put this all together had a terrible sense of humor. And a terrible sense of design. There are fish of all different shapes and sizes mounted on the wall. It's so jumbled together that it's hard to look at. One whole wall is covered with dioramas made by kids in the elementary school showing how fishing boats changed over the years. A glass cupboard containing fishing rods and nets rounds out the exhibit.

The *STIRRUP Some History: Island Transportation and the Role of the Horse* exhibit is in the next room. An old carriage has a *CLIMB ME!* sign on it, so I take its advice and climb into the driver's seat. Or whatever you call this.

Resting my head against the worn wood of the carriage, I finally face reality: I'm not going to find anything here. There's no curator or historian. The whole building is file cabinet–free. This is all interesting, I guess . . . or at least some of it is . . . but I don't have time to get a history lesson about the island. I sit here for God knows how long, trying to figure out what to do next. Finally I take out my phone and look at my to-do list again.

Library! is next on the list. I was excited enough about the library when I was still at home that I put an exclamation mark on it. Right now, it's hard to muster any kind of enthusiasm about it. But it has to be better than here.

Jumping down from the carriage, I walk into the final room of the historical society—the one Eve from the hotel said was the best. But as I look around, I can't quite register what I'm looking at anymore. Mom wasn't even here in the winter. I don't *need* any of this.

My frustration grows so strong that I have to squeeze my eyes shut to keep tears from streaming out. It's a good thing no one is here, or they'd think I'd lost my mind crying in the *Snow and Tell: The Island in Winter* room of the historical society.

There has to be somewhere else where the historical records are kept, right? Then I see it: a little sign by the exit that says *Want to learn more?* It lists someone named Rayla and a phone number. This is more like it! I take out my phone, but don't have any cell coverage here, so I plug the number in and head back outside in the warm sun.

In a desperate bid to get any bars on my phone, I walk the bike a few blocks so I can call Rayla the second they show up.

Just past the church, three glorious bars of cell coverage pop onto my screen. I dial up Rayla, thrilled to finally have a lead. Or a potential lead? At least it's something.

The phone rings on the other line once, twice, three times before it goes to voicemail. *"Hi, this is Rayla. If you have any questions about the history of the island, please leave me a message. If you have questions about the future, please find a time machine."* Rayla chuffs out a laugh into the phone. I guess I know who made all the exhibition signs now. *"But seriously, I'm at my desk on Saturdays and Sundays, so I'll return your call then!"*

"Um . . . my name is Lexi Carter and . . . um . . . I'm looking to find some information about my mother," I stammer into the phone. "So . . . um . . . give me a call back." I'm about to hang up when I realize I left out some key details. "Oh . . . my mom's name was Emma Roth," I manage to get out. Then I give her my number.

Smooth. Very smooth.

As soon as the phone's back in my pocket, though, other realizations set it. Like the fact that it's Monday and Rayla won't call me back until at least Saturday. If then. She's not what I would have thought a historian would be.

Then again, not much here has been.

Jumping on my bike, I pedal to a park I saw on the way here with a little white bandstand in the middle of it. As soon as I get there, I sit in the grass and take out the pastries I stole from breakfast. The croissant's smushed into oblivion . . . so bad that I have to dump crumbs out of my backpack. But the scones are mostly intact. I break off a piece and pop it in my mouth. Then I close my eyes because it's soooo good. Like, better than any scone I've ever eaten. I wash it down with a swig from my water bottle and let my eyes wander. There's a placard by the entrance to the park advertising a "Music of the Movies!" concert on Thursday night. Three little kids run around playing tag while their dad reads in the shade. A mom and her toddler play some kind of hopping game together. Both of them are laughing as if whatever they're doing is the most hilarious thing in the entire world. A pang of jealousy hits me again as I watch them. I probably did stuff like this with Mom when I was this kid's age. Mom might have even played in this very park . . . or gone to concerts . . . with her own mother. The one who just died. Who Mom and Dad never talked about. Who tried to take me away from Dad.

Okay, I've got to get out of here.

Standing up to stretch my legs, I grab my phone again and look up where the library is. It's only a few blocks from here, so I jump onto the bike and start pedaling. The historical society might not have anyone on duty to help, but there's got to be a librarian.

I pedal as hard as I can. So hard that I'm sweating by the time I get there and need to stop to catch my breath. That's not the only reason I stop, though. As I reach the building, I stand there with my bike and just stare at it. At home, libraries are made of brick or stone. Stern, old-fashioned designs in even sterner colors. This is . . . not that.

The outside is a pale turquoise that stands out in stark contrast to the deep greens of the trees surrounding it and tall white columns that line the front of the building. I look up at this place and wonder all over again if maybe Mom ever came here. What did she read if she did? Did she even like to read? Or was she more interested in making art?

Anger at my dad . . . at my grandmother . . . makes my cheeks burn. I should know this stuff. I should know all about her. And instead I'm chasing around this place looking for any tiny breadcrumbs I can find about her life.

I close my eyes. The library. I have to focus on what I'm doing right now and on the possibility that I'll find something here.

Pushing through the heavy front door, I stop short when I get inside. Deep mahogany bookshelves are lined up in neat rows throughout the room. There's a funky gold chandelier hanging from an ornate carving on the ceiling. The walls are a deep teal and a rug of the same color covers the floor. It's like stepping inside an emerald in here. It takes me a second to get my bearings, but I finally I walk to the front desk.

There's a man behind the counter who looks like he's about ten years older than my dad, maybe a little more. He's not tall, but he's sort of cute for a guy his age: pale, freckled cheeks, with dark hair and hazel eyes set off with librarian-chic wire-rimmed glasses. His hair is slightly gray around his temples. A nameplate on the desk says *Caleb Murray* on it.

"Hey!" he says when he sees me. "How're you doing?"

"Um . . . okay?"

"Great, that's great." It's then I notice that he's putting a water bottle and some books into a messenger bag.

"Is the library closing soon?" I ask in a trembling voice.

Caleb smiles at me. "Nope, we're open till five." He zips up the top of his bag. "But I'm personally closing shop for the day." He stands up and smiles at me again. "Is there something I can help you with before I go?"

This is it. A real person, even if he's running out the door. Real resources that I can use. All I have to do is find my voice and ask for what I need. I take a deep breath and pin my arms to my sides to hold myself together.

"I need to access your archives," I blurt out. "I'm hoping to find out more about my mother."

A smile crinkles the skin around his eyes. "Well, you've come to the right place," he replies. "Let me get Liza, and . . ." He looks up at me again. "I can't believe I've got to go right now! I'd *love* to help you with your research."

His enthusiasm is a little . . . overwhelming. But I still wish he could stay. I could use a little enthusiasm right about now.

"Liza!" he calls in a not at all quiet library voice.

A girl my age comes out from around a bookshelf. Her hair's dyed black with one neon-yellow streak behind her left ear. Her mouth is screwed up like a question mark. "What?"

Caleb leads her over to me and pats us both on the shoulder. "All you need to do is give Liza a little information and she can point you in the right direction," he tells me. Then he smiles at Liza. "She's the best assistant librarian on the island."

Liza frowns. "I'm the only assistant librarian on the island."

Honestly, I don't care if she's the only one for another hundred miles as long as she can help me.

Ignoring her snark completely, Caleb turns back to me. "So you're in good hands. Just give her your mom's name and date of birth, and you'll be good to go."

He takes out his phone and looks at the time. "Speaking of good to go, I'll be off. Good meeting you . . . ?"

"Lexi," I tell him.

"Good meeting you, Lexi!" With one last parting smile, Caleb's gone.

Liza sighs and shakes her head. "Sorry about that," she says. "He had to leave early because his hot husband just got home from a business trip."

I have no idea how to respond to that. "Oh . . . um . . . okay?"

"If you'd ever seen his husband, you'd understand why Caleb's in such a hurry."

A surprised laugh escapes from me. This library is . . . something. But Liza's already getting behind the front desk.

"So let's do this," she says. "Mother's name and date of birth?"

"Emma Roth," I tell her. "June fifteenth, 1986."

She writes all of this down, mouthing the details as she does. Even though she's my age, this girl exudes a confidence I don't have. Like at all. But at least I'm finally getting somewhere.

"And was she born here, or did she move here later?"

Maybe I'm not getting anywhere after all.

"Um . . . I'm not sure, to be honest," I admit. "I know she spent summers here. At the Palais du Lac. But I don't know what summers or how many."

Liza's mouth becomes a question mark again.

"So she didn't ever live on-island?"

"Um . . . probably not," I reply. "It seems like she just visited here in the summer."

The assistant librarian puts down her pen. "That makes things trickier," she says. "Have you done any research online about her? Do you have her birth certificate? Any idea where she might have lived during the rest of the year?"

A lump forms in my throat. Because it hurts that I don't know these things about her. It hurts that no one ever told me, and that I've never been able to find anything about her online. There are lots of Emma Roths out there. Just not mine. The whole reason I came here is to fill in the blanks I don't have the answers to.

"I've looked her up before, but I've never been able to find a birth certificate." With a painful swallow, I force myself to continue. To admit just how little I know about my own mother to a complete stranger. "I honestly have no idea where she's from originally."

Liza's eyes narrow. "Well, that must suck."

"It does." Another breath, another swallow. "I came here to try to find out more."

The frown that had been on this girl's face transforms into something even harder and more determined. "Okay then . . . let's see what we can dig up."

Three hours later, I've got nothing. I even looked up the address on Mom's postcard and all the internet would tell me is that it's residential. Whoever lives there worked hard to keep their information private.

"So, we didn't get very far," Liza helpfully tells me. "But . . . I mean . . . you could go up to the hotel and see what they could tell you." She looks at the front door and shakes her head. "Freaking Caleb has to take time off on the one day something's actually happening here."

Then she turns to me again. "See if you can get access to the archives up at the *palace*." The word drips off her tongue like it's covered in acid. "They might be able to tell you more. I'm pretty sure from stuff Caleb's said they keep their records for a long time."

Suddenly something shifts inside me. "The hotel!" I say. "Of course!" I jump up from the table and toss the bag over my shoulder.

My research helper winces at my sudden burst of energy, but I don't honestly care.

"Thanks for all of your help," I tell her. "I'll head up there right now."

Grabbing my backpack, I practically run toward the door. I have a lead now . . . and one that gets right to the heart of all of this. The hotel where Mom used to stay. Why didn't I think of this in the first place?

CHAPTER 13

Emma (Then)

JR has been proving strangely elusive in the three weeks he's been here, and not in his usual pretending-he's-a-hermit kind of way. It's a whole new world of weird-and-unlike-him elusive. We've never gone three weeks without going to the greenhouse. We've never even gone three whole days before. So I track him down in the rose garden with his dad and try to get him to commit to doing something—*anything*—with me.

"Tomorrow," I tell JR. "We'll spend the whole day at the beach tomorrow."

"I'm working tomorrow," he reminds me. "I can't just ditch my dad."

"I heard that," Terry calls from a few yards away. "And you can, in fact, ditch me if you have other plans. It's not like I'm paying you to help out today."

But JR just shakes his head. "It doesn't matter, Dad," he says. "You know you need the help, so I'm going to help you."

My eyes stray to Terry as he bends over one of the oldest rosebushes, deadheading it so that it will keep blooming. He's sweating. As in, sweating a lot. Much more than JR is, anyway.

"Are you okay, Terry?" I ask. "Do you need to hire someone else to help on the grounds, because you could—"

"I'm fine, Emma," he interrupts. "My son just has an overdeveloped sense of duty, that's all." Then he turns to JR. "You should be taking more hours at the jobs that actually pay you, kiddo. College money doesn't grow on trees."

"Neither do fathers," JR says in a quiet voice.

I glance from him to Terry and back again. "Do *you* want a job at the hotel?" I ask JR. An idea forms in my head for the first time—a way to appease my dad and spend more time with JR. "We could apply for something together and then—"

"Emma, drop it, okay?" JR cuts me off. "I'm not getting a job here. I already have two, remember? And since when are you getting a job? I don't see it happening any time soon."

The tone of his voice is so hard that I wince. I don't think he's ever spoken to me that way before. I have no idea what's wrong with him or what I did to make him not want to spend time with me, but I know I want to make this better.

"I would if you applied with me," I say in a low voice. "I've barely seen you this summer, JR, and I . . . I just . . ."

JR closes his eyes for a second. When he opens them again, he goes right back to deadheading roses.

"I know" is all he says. "It's been . . . things have been busy this summer."

I slide my hands into my pockets to keep from reaching out to him. Why doesn't he tease me or say horrible things about what a princess I am? Why won't he do something as simple as meet me in our old clubhouse?

My eyes catch his for just a second, but he looks away again. Back to work and back to ignoring me. He slips in and out of his mask of indifference, as if he can't quite hold it in place.

"JR, please can we talk?" I plead. "I don't know what I did to make you this angry at me, but . . ."

Finally he looks up again. "I'm not mad at you," he says. "I'm just busy. That's all."

"Which is code for, *I love spending time with you but I'm too much of a blockhead to admit it*," Terry says. "Isn't that right, kiddo?"

A grunt is JR's only response.

Wave after wave of disappointment and hurt wash over me.

"Maybe tomorrow then?" I ask a little desperately. I wish he'd just talk to me—that things could be the way they've been every other summer. "We could meet for lunch in the greenhouse if that's all you have time for. I . . . I could bring a couple of BLTs on the rye bread we like, and . . ."

"Emma, I can't do lunch tomorrow," he replies. "Maybe tomorrow night we could walk into town and grab a hot dog or something, okay?"

"Yes, okay." At least it's something, I guess. Not enough to make me feel any better, but . . . something.

We stand there staring at each other for a second, but I finally turn to leave. "See you then, I guess," I say over my shoulder.

But I don't hear JR's voice responding to me. I hear Terry's instead.

"You're going to have to come clean about what you've been up to at some point," he says. "You're hurting her feelings."

"She'll understand," I hear JR say, but then I run out of the rose garden so that I don't have to listen to another word.

Because I don't understand. I don't get any of this. Under any other circumstances I would be worried about him. He's been acting so strangely the last few days. JR teases me and answers half my questions with shrugs, but he's never seemed as if he wanted to get rid of me before—as if just having to spend time with me is a burden. Why should I worry about him when he could clearly care less about me?

I stop short in the tea garden, my need to catch my breath finally winning out over my need to get away from him. No one's here at this time of day anyway—teatime's still hours away. The peonies bloom as if they're giant pillows of white and pink and magenta in contrast to the dark green foliage. Even those colors don't do justice to what the flowers contain. There's magenta, yes, but also blues and purples, with hints of orange flaming to life at the curves and contours of each frilled petal. I could pick some—or even just one—to see what I could make with those petals. Doing that, however, would also mean a slow, painful death if anyone found out. The garden is sacred space in the hotel, and the last thing I need is to have anyone else upset with me.

Maybe my parents are right. Maybe I need a job, or something else to focus on. It's not even that I don't want to work, exactly. I just don't want to work *here*. And here is the only possibility my dad's willing to entertain at the moment. But the thought of living here and working here—of my entire world narrowing down to this one dot on the map—it's just a lot to wrap my head around.

And yet I would have done it if JR would've done it with me.

For a while, I wander aimlessly trying to get my mind in a better place and the walking does help. So does the beautiful day. The wild blueberries at the edge of the woods are ripe, so I stop in to pick a few handfuls in the shade, gobbling up the tiny bursts of flavor. They're warm and tangy and taste like late July. They still don't make me feel better, though. So I head back to the hotel to pick up some art supplies. Instead I find Tom, one of the waiters, hurrying through the lobby.

"If you're looking for Linda," he says, "she left in a snit because she had to polish silverware all morning."

"To be fair, that doesn't sound like a lot of fun," I reply.

"Then maybe you could do some of it so she'll be less unpleasant later on."

I look at him for a second, trying to figure out what to make of him. I'm in no mood to listen to someone insulting my friend.

"Or you could be kinder to her and maybe she'd like work a little bit more."

Tom opens his mouth to say something, but nothing comes out. Instead, his jaw just hangs there, all loose and shocked. He wipes the corners of his mouth and looks away. "Anyway," he says. "She's on her lunch break." Then he's gone.

JR won't talk to me. Linda's off God knows where on her break. And I know for a fact that Ryan's been roped into helping his dad on his campaign for U.S. Senate this morning, so he's not around either. I stand in the lobby at a complete loss for a few minutes. Only when I see Jackson coming toward me do I snap out of it.

"Your dad's meeting me here for lunch in about five minutes," he tells me. "So if you want to avoid being marched to the HR office to fill out an application, your time to escape is now."

I squeeze his hand in thanks, then make a run for it. As in, I actually run down the stairs of the verandah and out onto the road into town. I don't stop till I get to the docks and then it's only to catch my breath before I keep going. My pace slackens, though, as I realize I have absolutely no destination in mind. As well as no money. Or library card. Or anything.

So I keep moving. The hiking paths aren't far away, so I turn up a side street and through the small neighborhood that abuts the deeper woods of the island. I know where I want to go now, so I turn onto the right path and push myself to keep moving. Viola's bench is just around the bend and I won't stop till I reach it.

As I turn the corner, though, I stop in my tracks. Because there, on the bench, is Linda.

"Would you maybe want some company?" I ask. Normally I'd just assume she wanted my company, but normally I'd assume the same about JR, too.

Linda looks up, startled. "Company sounds good," she says. "As long as you're not going to bark orders at me."

I smile. "That's not really my style."

This makes her smile, too. "No, you're more of the charming-everyone-into-doing-your-bidding type," she tells me. "No need to bark orders."

"Talk to my parents," I say with a bitter laugh. "I think they'd dispute any claim I have to being *charming*."

"Your parents worship the ground you walk on," Linda counters.

"They want to give you literally everything in the world. There are worse things."

"I know it," I agree. "I'd never say I'm anything other than extremely lucky."

She hands me half her chicken salad sandwich. "Why are you way out here on your lunch break?" I ask. "Did something happen?"

Linda takes a bite of her sandwich and shrugs. "If I have to polish one more piece of silverware, I'm gonna lose my mind." She sighs. "And I have a *lot* more to polish when I go back, so it won't be pretty."

I want to laugh at her joke, but there's something so weary in her eyes right now. "I could help you, you know. Then you'd be done sooner."

She gives me an assessing glance. "I thought you didn't want to work at the hotel."

"I don't. But I do want to help you."

The sunlight slants through the trees around us, casting little pockets of light and shadow. There's something sort of . . . ethereal . . . about it. As if sprites or spirits might be hiding in those shadows till we leave and they have the woods to themselves again.

Or maybe I can feel Viola here today.

"Have you ever wondered what Viola was really like?" I ask Linda. "I mean, beyond having a fierce spirit and liking the woods."

Linda's quiet for a second. "I looked her up, actually," she admits. "She owned Benson's Landscaping when she was alive. Her obituary said she left behind three ex-husbands and a dog named Theodore. She hated the exes so much she left all her money to Theodore."

I mull that over. "That's even better than I could have ever dreamt up." I throw my head back and open my arms to the trees. "Viola Benson, we salute you!"

Linda smiles at me. "Why'd you come here today?" she asks me. "There's no way you could've known I'd be here."

I shake my head. "No, I . . . I wanted to avoid my dad and . . . and things with JR have been really . . . really kind of bad."

She nudges me. "You want to talk about it?"

"Would it be okay if I said no?"

Linda snorts. "It would be awesome," she tells me. "I hate listening to other people's problems."

I choke out a laugh. "That's what I like best about you. Your total disregard for other people's feelings."

"It's my best quality."

A silence falls between us for a while.

"I'm glad I found you even if I didn't know you'd be here," I admit.

"Yeah, me too," she says. Then she starts rummaging through her backpack. "Actually . . . um . . . I was going to drop this off at your place later on so that you could have it but I wouldn't have to witness your joy in receiving it. Might as well just give it to you now."

After much digging, she pulls what appears to be a crumpled-up piece of paper out of the pack. "Here you go."

I take it from her and slowly open up the paper till I see that there's something inside. Not just one thing, actually. Two.

Two bracelets with identical matching blue cords and lobster claw clasps. Hanging from both of them are tiny silver charms shaped like the island. I hold them in one hand while I smooth the paper out even more. On it, there's a message scribbled.

I really like the friendship bracelet you made me even if I was a little weird about it at the time. I'm weird about a lot of things. Bad habit, I know. Anyway, you and I both know I'd never be able to make one friendship bracelet, let alone two. And if I did, neither of us would want to wear them. So I did what any red-blooded American would do and bought these for us instead. What can I say? Capitalism runs through my veins.

L

I smile at what she wrote and then some more when I lift up the bracelets again to get a closer look. "Thanks, this . . ." I whisper. "It's . . . just thanks."

Linda looks away, as if she's embarrassed. "Well, it's not like I could let you get all the gift-giving glory, right?" she says. "Plus, I'm supporting the island's small local businesses, which in turn keeps the economy running."

"Which is always your first priority," I supply.

"Someone's gotta keep this place going," she jokes. One side of her mouth turns up while the other turns down. "You should put it on."

So I do. I hold my wrist up to admire the way the two bracelets look on it. "The colors of the rope and the cord work well together."

"Yeah, well, I'm all about adding to the aesthetics." Then she looks at her watch. "I'm also all about getting back to work on time. You staying here or coming with?"

"Definitely coming with."

Linda slings her backpack over her shoulder, then wrestles the new bracelet onto her own wrist before we start walking.

She's like Viola, I realize as we go. Fierce, protective of the people and things she loves. The kind of person who'd leave her money to a dog instead of to exes who don't deserve her. Just as I'm about to wax poetic in my own mind about my friend, she interrupts my thoughts.

"So I need you to level with me about something," she says.

I smile. "What's that?"

But Linda's not smiling. "My brother."

Suddenly I'm not feeling all that perky either.

"He's been acting like an idiot about you for months, but now it seems like you might be into him too, and I just . . . I'd rather know it's coming than be surprised afterward."

Something inside me freezes up. I do not want to have this conversation. Not with anyone, let alone with his *sister.* Even if she's my friend, too, Linda's still his sister.

"You do know that every single thought you have is written all over your face, right?" she asks. "So, let's just skip the whole *Oh no, he's your brother* BS and talk about it, okay?"

I nod. Then I nod again.

"Does that mean you're going to talk?" she says. "Or are you going to pretend you're a bobblehead all day?"

I glance up at her and our eyes meet. Despite her brusque tone, she looks worried. "I'm not sure what you want me to say."

"You can say whether or not you like him."

There's no easy answer to that question, though. "I don't know," I reply. Then I squeeze my eyes shut. "Would you be mad if I did?"

She scoffs at the question. "Would I be mad if my brother and my best friend were into each other?" Linda stops and grimaces. "I mean, maybe, yeah," she admits. "But I also wouldn't have a problem with it."

Despite myself, I smile at her. "That's probably the most contradictory thing I've ever heard you say."

"I'm one big enigma."

"Wrapped in a mystery?"

She smiles, just a little. "I get why you'd be on the fence. Ryan's a really good person but he's also a pain in the butt," she replies. "And before you respond, I know you could say the same thing about me."

I slip my arm through hers. "You could say that about me, too," I tell her. "And probably about just about anyone."

"I don't know," Linda says. "JR might just be a pain in the butt."

"That's just because you don't know him that well yet."

We walk out of the woods and back into the glare of the midday sun. "I could try to distract JR from now on if you want more time with Ryan," she offers.

A thought pops into my head that never occurred to me before. "Wait, do you like JR?"

"Um, no," Linda says, as if the very idea is distasteful to her.

Even as upset as I am with JR, I find myself jumping to his defense. "He's a good guy, you know."

"I know," she concedes. "He's just not my type."

This begs yet another question. Since we're being so honest today, I go ahead and ask. "So what is your type?"

"Well, taller, for one thing," she begins. And she has a point—JR is no giant specimen of humankind. "And significantly more athletic," she continues. "I like someone who can keep up with me." She doesn't say anything else for so long, that I start to worry.

"What's wrong?"

"The thing is," she says, "I've never told anyone this before but . . . I'm not really into just a single gender."

I'm both surprised and not surprised, and honored she trusts me with this all at the same time. "I'm glad you told me," I say. "At the next dance I'll look for tall guys *and* girls for you to dance with."

"You're already making me regret that I said anything," she sighs.

"Too late now," I tell her as we reach the hotel gate. "Now that I know, there's no *unknowing* it."

"So thanks to you, my life will be a whirlwind of romance now?"

"Whose life is gonna be a whirlwind of romance?"

Linda and I both turn in shock, to find Ryan standing in front of us, both probably thinking the same thing: How much did he hear?

"Yours is," Linda replies. The confused look on Ryan's face makes Linda roll her eyes. "What do you want, Ryan?"

Confusion gives way to a long, lazy grin. "I want to see if you two want to come with JR and me for a dinner hike tonight after work," he says. "I just bumped into him and Terry and we hatched a plan."

It's impossible not to feel hurt by this—not to have it sting that JR made plans with Ryan and not with me. Everything's changing. Even the things I don't want to change. Especially those. I don't much like it.

CHAPTER 14

Emma (Then)

The plan is simple: meet at six thirty and hike up to Box Hill. Since it doesn't get dark till about nine, we have plenty of time to eat and hike back home before night falls. And even if we do stay out later, who cares? As Ryan told me earlier in the day, "We'll do what feels right and stay out till we stay out."

The question is, what feels right? It's already about ten degrees cooler than it was earlier in the day, and the strappy sundress I have on isn't exactly practical for hiking, so I know I need to change. And maybe find my hiking boots. Where *are* my hiking boots? As I search around my closet for them, there's a soft knock at my bedroom door. The kind of knock that says *Mom* and definitely not *Dad*.

"Come in," I call, and the door just as softly opens.

"I can't remember the last time I saw you in jeans," Mom says. "Where are you off to now?"

"Box Hill," I tell her. "For a dinner hike."

"It seems a little late in the day for a picnic," she says. "And not very practical. The bugs are going to eat you alive." She sits on the edge of my bed. "Was this JR's idea?"

Finally I find my boots and sit next to her to put them on. "No, it was Ryan's," I tell her. "JR's never the architect of impractical schemes. It's not his way."

"I don't know," she says with a smile. "I seem to remember him luring you out at midnight so you could howl at the full moon like werewolves."

"Mom, we were twelve," I remind her. "And that was as much my idea as his."

She runs her hand over my bedspread as I keep getting ready. "Is that how you're going to wear your hair?" she asks, innocently enough. But then I look in the mirror and grin. My hair is sticking up all over my head, as if some unseen hand has teased it within an inch of its life over the course of the day.

"It's very . . . rustic," I comment, and she smiles.

"Which is a nice way of saying messy," she adds. Mom gestures to the stool by the vanity table they bought me when I was little. "Sit."

"I'm going to be late."

"You're always late," she replies. "Your friends must be used to it by now."

I think that over for a second. "Ryan will be late, too," I say. "Only Linda and JR will be on time."

She makes an absent-minded noise as she stands behind me and brushes out my hair. "Well, they can bond a little while they wait for you and Ryan."

It's like I'm a little girl again, with my mom brushing out my unruly tangles before she tries to smooth it into two French braids. My hair is just as uncooperative now as it was then, but without her to twist it into some kind of neatness, usually I just let it be at this point.

"You've been spending a lot of time with your friends this summer," Mom comments.

"Yes," I say. "It's been really nice." I pause, thinking about JR making plans with Ryan and not with me and how awful he was in the garden today. "Well, it mostly has been."

She smiles again as she puts in the hair tie at the end of one braid.

"I am glad you're having such a good time," she tells me. "Though I do wish you'd go down and fill out a job application."

I stiffen under her hands. "Why is it such a big deal that I get a job here?" I ask. "Is the hotel short-staffed this summer?"

"It's not about staffing issues." Mom pulls the other braid tight to my head. "You know that."

She's right—I do know that. I also know that continuing to talk about it is only going to make both of us unhappy. Finally she finishes the second braid and lays her hands on my shoulders. I glance up at her in the mirror and watch her for a second. Mom looks tired—much more tired than I ever remember seeing her before. Suddenly my mild annoyance with her turns to worry.

"Mom, are you okay?"

Her eyes widen in surprise. "Of course I am! What a funny question."

"It's just that . . ."

Her reflection beams back a halting smile, but there's something behind her eyes that I don't like.

"I'm fine, love," she says again. "Now go get some bug spray before you head out so that there's something left of you at the end of your hike."

"Yes," I say. "Sure."

"And say hello to your friends for me," she says as I pack up my bag. "I'm so glad you have such a nice group to spend your time with this summer."

She loves that there are four of us. I've only ever had JR up till now, which worries her. Not that she doesn't love JR—she definitely does. But most of the time, he's not here.

Mom kisses the top of my head as I stand to leave. "Be home at a reasonable hour, please."

I just nod and get out of there as fast as I can. I'm twenty-five minutes late already, and it isn't even my fault this time. Or least, it's only partially my fault.

As I spill out the front door of the hotel, it's clear that I'm the last one to arrive.

"You're late," JR says without even looking up.

"She's always late," Linda says.

"It's part of what makes Emma *Emma*," Ryan adds with a grin.

"Plus, it was worth the wait to see your hair like that. You look pretty."

My cheeks feel as if they're on fire, and I'm painfully aware that I'm blushing.

"Your hair does look good like that," Linda agrees.

All three of them are staring at me now, which makes me self-conscious. Which then makes me blush again. And shuffle my feet. And . . .

"So . . . are we going to head to Box Hill?" I ask.

"Let's do it," JR says.

We all spray ourselves with the insect repellent my mom made me take before we start to walk, all four of us side by side, to the path that leads up to Box Hill. We make a comical foursome. I have a small backpack with four bottles of water in it. Ryan only has his guitar, as if he cheerfully assumed the rest of the world would provide for him. Since Linda's carrying a cooler and JR has a huge, jam-packed backpack, it seems he's assumed correctly.

Once we're under the trees and on the path, we have to separate. JR leads the way, so I make sure to let Ryan and then Linda go before me to put a little distance between the two of us. While the hike's not long, it's steep in places and Linda and I take turns handing the cooler up to each other so we can both scramble up the rock face when we need to. Finally we reach the top just as the sun is starting to dip closer to the horizon. I've been up there a few times, but never at this time of night.

It's a pretty view in the daytime—the bright blue of the sky and the lake, with the fringe of trees on the hill and the tall turrets of the hotel shining in the sunlight. Right now, the sky has a full spectrum of colors and the light feels like a gossamer, wispy thing that could disappear at any moment. I let out a contented sigh. There's been an unsettled feeling in my stomach, my chest today. Everything just feels strange and complicated and *wrong*. But this? There's nothing complicated about this. It's just a view of the lake that goes on forever and colors that make my eyes water, they're so beautiful.

Thankfully, I brought my little travel watercolor case and some paper.

Everyone starts unpacking, but I go and sit at the edge of the cliff face and pour some water into the well of my watercolor case. I take yellow and cadmium red and a hint of manganese blue. I mix them with just enough water so that some of the original colors in their original forms remain. Then without looking down at the paper, I splash the colors onto it with one large brush, using even more water to wash them together. More blue, this time with a little ultramarine mixed with the other colors. I barely register my friends talking and laughing as I layer on color after color, never once stopping to see how it looks. Because it doesn't matter. All that matters is creating. Feeling the colors—feeling the *joy* of the paints and the brush and the rough paper.

I lean my head back and breathe in deeply, savoring the cool air up here on the hillside.

"It's really different from your other stuff," JR says, much closer to me than I'd realized he was. "But I like it."

I glance up at him. The hard expression in his eyes from earlier in the day has been replaced with a softer, more pensive one now. But at this point, I don't really care. I put one hand on my hip and look him squarely in those annoyingly soft eyes. "So you're being nice to me now?"

He cocks his head to one side. "Am I ever really *nice* to you?"

"You know what I mean, JR."

To my great surprise, he actually nods in agreement. "I know what you mean."

He tosses a folded-up piece of orange paper into my lap. "You should do this."

When I open it up, I find a flier for an art show at one of the local galleries. *LOOKING FOR LOCAL ARTISTS!* it says, followed by information about how to submit your work to the gallery.

"You'll definitely get in. Your stuff's so good." He nods at my painting. "That one's so good."

"Lemme see," Ryan calls, and then pushes past JR so he can lean over my shoulder to look at the painting. His whole face is so close to mine that we're almost touching. Every muscle in my body freezes up—mostly because I don't trust myself not to touch him right now.

"Really pretty," he says in my ear. "I can't believe you're such a good artist."

JR walks past us, right to the edge of the cliff, and looks out at the view.

"See, I told you being arty is a good thing," Linda adds. "Also, we could see the water bottles in your bag, so we all took one. And being excellent friends, we saved you some food since you were in an art-induced trance, and we didn't want to interrupt." She hands me a sandwich, which I unwrap to find a BLT on marbled rye with spicy mayo.

I smile at her and take a sniff at the sandwich before taking a bite. It's so delicious that I close my eyes and focus on how it tastes and smells.

"It must be good if she's blocking out her sense of sight to savor it," JR says as he walks back to us. "If she'd rather eat than paint, something's gone right."

He sounds more like himself again. I'm so relieved that he does that I smile at him over my shoulder. "What did you have?"

"Same as you," he says.

"Linda must have ESP."

"Actually, I heard you two talk about your BLTs once," she says. "So it's not like I had to read your minds." Then she takes a big brown bag from her cooler. "I did, however, use my special intuition when it came to ordering dessert."

"I'll eat faster," I tell her, making her laugh.

Out of the kindness of their hearts, they wait for me to finish dinner before they break out the cookies Linda stole from the kitchen—chocolate chip, snickerdoodles, along with melt-in-your-mouth butter cookies.

"I don't think this night can get any better," Linda mumbles with her mouth full of cookies.

"Well I think it can," Ryan counters. "Who wants some music?"

Linda and I both raise our hands as if we're in class. JR shrugs. That's all Ryan needs to break out the guitar. He strums aimlessly for a bit before the sounds begin to take shape into something like a song. It's an old Beatles tune I recognize from my dad's record collection. It's soft and sweet and his voice is as meltingly smooth as the butter cookies were before as he sings out lyrics about promising not to tell a secret.

I watch him, rapt. The moon is low in the dark sky. He sings in a quiet voice, looking all silvery and shadowy and beautiful. Maybe Linda's right. Maybe I do like him. If he dropped that guitar right this moment and kissed me, I wouldn't object. I wouldn't object at all.

Although now that I started thinking about kissing him, I can't stop thinking about it. Would he kiss as enthusiastically as he does everything else? Or would it be slower, more lingering? As if he wanted to savor the moment when his lips first touched mine.

Oh God, I have to stop thinking about this. I can't even look at him for fear that he'll know exactly what's running through my brain.

Ryan gives me a mysterious little smile as he stops playing and I wonder if maybe he's been thinking about the same thing I have. Then he says, "Anyone want to have even more fun?"

So I guess not.

We all murmur our assent, so he puts the guitar down and takes out a small bottle of vodka that he must have gotten the from the bar in the penthouse. "Any takers?"

JR stiffens next to me. He's never had a single drink or done any drugs because he's afraid of what having addiction in his family might mean for him. There's no way he's going to drink any of this.

"None for me, thanks," I say, giving him an easy out. "We still have to hike back down and I don't want to fall in the dark."

JR presses his knee into mine. He knows what I'm doing. "None for me either."

"And I know what Linda will say," Ryan adds, "so I raise a glass, or . . . um . . . a bottle to you, my friends and family!" With that, he takes one long swig, then shudders as he wipes his mouth with his wrist. "That's . . . um . . . powerful stuff."

After one more drawn-out drink, he caps the bottle and picks the guitar up again. "Come 'ere," he says to me, patting the spot next to him on the hill. A tiny, nervous laugh escapes from me as I move to his side. But now he's too close again and I actually look at his mouth for a second and wonder what it would be like to kiss him again and . . .

Ryan leans into me as he starts to play his guitar. First his shoulder, then his whole arm comes to rest against mine. I'm starting to lose my breath a little, and then it gets even worse when he turns to me and starts to sing again. It's almost dizzying being this close to him. I don't know if I want to get even closer or to push him away. I don't even know if he's only doing this because he had a couple of drinks or if he really does like me.

Somewhere to my left, I can hear Linda engaging JR in conversation about their jobs and college. It's small talk—nothing of great importance—but I know what she's doing. She's giving Ryan and me space. The question is, do I need space with him right now?

Then Ryan starts to sing "Brown Eyed Girl." Not to all of us. No, Ryan's singing to *me*. I close my eyes for a second to savor this but when I open them again, he's got this quiet smile on his face as he sings. The kind that makes me think he wouldn't rush our first kiss. It would be the kind that stays in your mind long after it happens. I shiver at the thought. He inches closer.

A silence falls when Ryan stops playing and singing. Linda and JR both stare at us—her with squinty eyes and him with . . . I don't even know what.

Linda sighs. "I guess that answers my question," she says, which definitely doesn't help right now.

Then JR gets up and stretches out his arms. "It's getting late. We should pack up."

Before anyone has time to agree or disagree, he hands out flash-lights that his dad let him borrow from the groundskeeping building. The walk back is a quiet one. JR just gives us a salute before he heads back to the staff housing. I watch him leave, palming the flier he gave me in my jeans pocket. Then turn to find Ryan watching me.

Linda rolls her eyes at us before taking us both by the arm and pulling us toward the hotel. My eyes meet Ryan's as we walk inside. He smiles. I suck in a deep breath as I smile back.

I guess that does answer this particular question.

CHAPTER 15

Emma (Then)

The notes from the orchestra float off the instruments like bubbles blown by a little kid on a sunny day. I know that everyone else my age listens to different music—music that was made more much recently—but this is what I love. The Gershwins and Duke Ellington, Cole Porter and John Coltrane. The music I grew up with, dancing and singing along in this very ballroom. I'd do the same right now if I didn't think my parents would practically faint from embarrassment. Even knowing that, I'm tempted.

The current batch of little kids in the ballroom don't have to worry about giving in to that temptation. They leap and dance around the room together. Sometimes I wish I was still that young, without a problem in the world my parents couldn't help me fix. This summer it feels more as if I'm constantly disappointing them. Either I take a job here and have my whole world shrink down even further than it already is, or I don't and upset them.

Even tonight is a thousand percent less fun than I hoped it would be. I thought I'd be swaying around the dance floor in Ryan's arms. Maybe even wrapped up in a haze of romance. Instead his dad whisked him off to meet some important person or other, and I'm standing here by myself.

When Linda comes and stands by my side, I almost sigh with relief. "Remember when you said you'd fix me up with tall athletes at this dance?"

"Of course I do."

"Well, I'm taking you up on the offer," she informs me. "Because if I have to spend another minute talking to either of my parents, I'm going to lose my shit. And you do not want to see me lose my shit."

I glance at her sideways. "Everything okay?"

"Just the usual," she replies. "Ryan, the laziest person on the planet, is their golden hope for the future of the business and I am an afterthought." She takes a swig of lemonade, then hands it to me to take a drink. "If I'm going to be an afterthought, I might as well have fun doing it, right?"

"Right," I agree. "Now the question is, who are you going to have fun with?" I look around the room until I see Tom, off duty tonight and looking pretty good in his suit. "Tom?"

"Tom can't stand me. He thinks I'm abrasive."

"Tom doesn't have a clue how amazing you are," I tell her. Then I glance around the room again. "What about June?" I nod in the direction of the daughter of Mr. and Dr. Lieu-Smith. "She's pretty and an all-state volleyball player."

The song changes and Linda takes her lemonade back, swigging it down in one long gulp. "I'm going in," she says. "Wish me luck."

"Good luck," I call.

I walk around the dance floor to find Ryan, but he's still caught up talking to his dad. As I near them, I hear Mr. Desmond say, "I wish you'd show even a little bit of initiative, Ryan. It's not as if you don't know what's at stake here."

Ryan's jaw tightens. "Dad, I don't know what you want from me."

"You know exactly what I want," Mr. Desmond says. "I've been very clear. You just don't want to hear it."

This whole conversation sounds too familiar for comfort. I know how Ryan's feeling right now—how horrible it is when we disappoint them. Seeing him look so defeated when he's usually so vibrant—so *him*—hurts something inside my chest. The day we went riding together, he asked me if I'd rescue him if he needed it. Right now, it looks as if he might.

So I take a deep breath and walk over to them. "Ryan, may I have this dance?"

He gives me an eager smile, but Mr. Desmond answers first. "I'm sure Ryan would love to, but we have some things we need to discuss, Emma," he says, not even pretending to be happy to see me. "He can come find you when we're finished here."

"I'll catch up with you in a little while," Ryan assures me in a deflated voice.

"Okay."

But it's not okay. Not really. As I walk away from them, I turn to look over my shoulder at Ryan again. His dad's still talking at him, but Ryan's eyes are on me. I wish I could have saved him from this. I wish he didn't look so miserable.

Mr. Desmond shakes Ryan's arm to get his attention. Ryan turns away from me.

All alone again, I wander around, but watching the older hotel guests pair off to waltz makes my eyes glaze over and my envy start to kick in. Everyone here seems to be in pairs or groups, dancing and talking and sipping on drinks. Everyone seems to *have* someone.

Everyone but me.

Even looking for my parents doesn't cheer me up. They're not dancing together—they never do. I can't even imagine them dancing, though I guess they must've some time or another. Maybe at their wedding? I'll have to look through their pictures again to see if there's any proof.

Whatever they did at their wedding, they're not dancing with each other now. Dad's in the corner, deep in conversation with a group of men around his age. They all wear suits and drink martinis like a bunch of slightly paunched James Bonds.

Then I see my mother. She's standing all by herself near the musicians watching them play. There's a longing in her eyes, and I know why. She'd been an aspiring concert violinist before she married Dad.

I've heard the story before—Mom had been auditioning for different orchestras and Dad somehow convinced her to marry him and help him carry on his family business instead of sticking with the violin.

It's not even like they're old enough that society expected her to just give up her own dreams when she got married. She did it willingly. I can't imagine ever wanting to give up your own life—your art.

The music changes, and our eyes meet. Mom smiles at me, then it fades into concern. I smile at her so she doesn't worry about whether or not I'm having fun, but she starts walking toward me anyway even more worry in her eyes. Before she can reach me Mrs. Flores, who also lives here year-round, approaches Mom to say hello.

I think that's my cue to get out of here.

Walking as slowly as I can so as not to arouse my parents' suspicion that I'm ditching the first official dance of the summer, I make my way to the glass-paneled doors that lead onto the verandah and slip into the night. When I'm out of view of the ballroom I kick off my shoes. Run my toes through the grass.

The music stops. There's a toast inside—a soft, magical tinkle of glasses, and laughter as everyone sips at their champagne. The band strikes up an old Frank Sinatra song—it's a slow one, lilting and romantic. *"You're lovely, with your smile so bright."* Even with no Ryan to dance with, at least there's this: beautiful music on a beautiful summer night.

I lift up the edges of my dress and dance in time to the music, pirouetting by myself in the dark. For two songs, maybe three, I sway and skip and run like I'm a little kid again. I throw my arms out in the wind as if I'm a bird about to take flight, and laugh as I twirl around in circles.

Finally I'm so dizzy I have to slow down. The world swirls around me even after I've stopped moving. Everything feels like a whirlwind in the best possible way.

I bend down and put my hands on my knees to catch my breath.

"Why're you dancing out here instead of in there?"

My whole body goes rigid for a second till I realize whose voice it is. Behind me, JR leans against a tree as if he'd collapse if it wasn't holding him up.

"Because I want to," I tell him. "And because no one was paying enough attention to tell me not to."

A deep frown pulls down his mouth. "Where's Ryan? Shouldn't you be dancing with him or something?"

"He's with his dad."

JR's eyes stray to the ballroom.

"What are *you* doing here?" I ask, looking around and behind him. "If someone's holding you hostage, you should quietly signal to me."

"And you'll rescue me?" he asks dubiously.

"Or at least contact the authorities," I reply. "Let them do the dirty work." Then I frown at him. "But really . . . what are you doing here?"

He shrugs. If I had a dollar for every time he's shrugged at me over the years, I'd have a *lot* of money.

"Ryan talked me into coming."

His words hit me like a ton of bricks. So many times I've asked him to come to these dances and he's always said no. At the beginning of the summer, I'd worried about him feeling as if I was replacing him with Linda. Now, as I stand here in the dark, I wonder if it's me who's been replaced. Part of me wants to be angry at him, but mostly I just feel sad.

And alone. Again.

JR pushes himself off the tree and starts walking toward me. Now that he's in the light, I get a better look at him, taking in his weird-fitting jacket and cuffed pants.

"Where'd you get the suit?" I ask at last.

JR looks down at himself. "It's my dad's," he says. "Hasn't worn it in years."

"It doesn't fit you."

A deep frown plays at the corners of his mouth. "Yeah, I know."

Something about the way he says those three words—dripping with snark—turns my sadness into anger for the first time since he got here.

"Then maybe you should take your ill-fitting suit and go into the ballroom," I declare. "Girls will be falling over themselves to dance with you."

"Or they'd be literally falling over 'cause I can't dance," he replies.

I stand up straight and look at him. "How did you let yourself get talked into this again?"

He huffs out something that might have been a laugh if he didn't still look so unhappy. "Honestly? I have no idea."

I thought I'd be with Ryan right now. JR apparently did, too. Instead we're standing out here together. "Do you want me to teach you how to dance? It's not that hard."

He steps away from me. "Um . . . that would be a no."

Now that I know the idea bothers him, though, I can't let go of it. "Come on, it'd be fun." I follow him. "I bet I'd be a great dance instructor!"

"Still a no."

I was kidding at first, but now . . . just once it would be nice if he weren't so stubborn. Just one single time.

"Then I guess you can go inside and sit on the sidelines all by yourself," I inform him. "Because I'm staying out here."

"Okay," he says, turning to walk toward the ballroom. For a second I think he's really going to go sit around gawking at hotel guests in their finery, but then he pivots back to me.

The band starts a Gershwin song, my favorite in the entire world. The singer's voice melts into the words *"Embrace me, my sweet embraceable you."* I close my eyes and wish I could somehow be transported back inside and that Ryan wouldn't be stuck with his dad and we'd be making our way around the dance floor right at this very moment.

As it is, all I have is myself. So I start to sway, just a little.

"You realize I can still see you, right?" JR asks.

"Don't ruin this for me, JR," I say in a soft voice. "I love this song."

He stops talking. I keep dancing. Swaying at first, yes, but then I twirl once, twice. Just as I start to spin away from him, JR catches my hand in his. Tugs me to an abrupt stop.

I start to move away from him. "What are you doing?"

JR gives me a squinty-eyed stare, which usually means that he's plotting something. Finally he pulls me even closer to him. "Taking you up on your lesson. I bet you'd be a *great* dance teacher."

My eyes widen in shock. "Are you asking me to dance?" I reach over and put my free hand on his forehead to check for a fever. "I mean, you seem okay, but something's wrong if you're asking me to dance."

He rolls his eyes but doesn't let go of my hand. "This is a limited-time offer."

There's not a doubt in my mind about that, so I move toward him.

"Like this," I tell him. I take the hand that's clasped in mine and place it on my side before resting my left hand on his shoulder. Then I hold his other hand in mine. His palm is sweaty. Mine feels ice-cold.

Never once in all the years we've been friends have we ever held hands. We just weren't the kind of kids who did. Even now, we stand here staring at each other for a few seconds. I wonder if we're ever really going to dance. I wonder what on earth he's thinking.

JR's eyes dart around, looking at everything but me. "Now what do we do?"

But I'm not sure what to do anymore. All of the dance skills I bragged about before seem to have escaped me.

"Move," I tell him. "Just move. You go forward, I go backward. Doesn't have to be anything fancy."

He nods. I do, too. Neither of us goes anywhere. JR's only a couple of inches taller than me so it's easy to look right into his eyes. There's a crease between them that makes me think he's nervous. Or at least overthinking this.

I slip my hand out of his and reach up to rub between his eyebrows.

The muscles in his shoulder tense under my left hand. "What're you doing?"

"Trying to get rid of the crease here."

He closes his eyes. "I think it's gonna take more than this to get rid of it."

When I don't stop, he opens his eyes. Catches my hand in his again. "Let's just dance, okay?"

My eyes meet his and something in my stomach . . . drops. "Okay."

I step backward and tug him with me, leading him into what I guess is a passable dance. He steps on my toes more than once. I squeeze his hand a little too hard to keep him moving.

JR really can't dance. He's awkward. Clumsy. I can feel the sweat from his hand through my dress. But he's trying.

I never, ever thought he'd try like this. Not at something like dancing. Not with me.

His hand slips from the side of my waist to my lower back. I have to stop myself from gasping out loud at the nearness of him. Then I have to do it again when I feel his breath on my bare shoulder.

We turn around and around, me trying to lead, him concentrating too hard.

The orchestra winds down the song with one last slow refrain. For a moment, there's no music at all, just some polite applause. Then a much faster Duke Ellington song fills the air. *"It don't mean a thing if it ain't got that swing."*

JR pulls us to a stop but we don't move apart. The crease between his eyebrows returns. I don't try to smooth it out this time. His eyes meet mine. Neither of us looks away.

Something feels as if it's swirling inside me. A storm brewing. I need some space so I can make it stop. I let go of him and step back, out of his arms.

JR's eyes drop to the ground. "You're not as bad a teacher as I thought you'd be."

I huff out an awkward laugh. "And you're not as bad a dancer as you claim to be."

He shakes his head, his eyes still firmly on the ground as if the grass there has suddenly become the most fascinating thing in the world. "I stepped on you. More than once."

Words come out before I can think them through. "I didn't mind."

JR looks up. He opens his mouth to say something, but Linda's voice cuts him off. "What're you guys doing out here?"

"Dancing." I force myself to look away from JR. "I gave him a dance lesson."

I sit down in the grass and Linda joins me. "For real? He let you teach him how to dance?" Her eyes slide to JR. "You feeling okay?" She nudges me. "Did you check for a fever?"

Another awkward laugh escapes from me. "I did, actually. He's fine."

"Well, Ryan's on his way. Want to ditch the dance? I just got blown off by the prettiest girl in the room, so I'm ready when you are."

JR finally joins us on the grass, but he sits next to Linda, not me. "Maybe you'll have better luck with the ladies next time."

It occurs to me only in this moment that he didn't know Linda isn't straight until now. I shoot Linda a worried glance, hoping she knows that I didn't tell him, but Linda's not even looking my way.

"Or with the gentlemen."

"Sure. Or that," JR agrees.

Linda gives him a piercing look. "You're all right, JR."

He shrugs. So Linda turns to me instead. "He's all right."

A blush warms my cheeks. "I know. He just pretends he's not."

"Hey, who wants to go skinny-dipping?" Ryan calls from up the hill, startling all of us.

"No one," the three of us say in unison.

"Oh . . . okay," Ryan says cheerfully. "Then maybe we could walk to the lake but everyone keeps their clothes on?"

"That sounds much better," Linda tells him as she gets up and starts heading down the path toward to the beach. "No matter how much you want to get Emma naked, I'm still your sister. Keeping your clothes on is *not* optional."

Ryan gives me a panicked look, blushing furiously. "I . . . I never said I was trying to get . . . She . . . she's just so . . ."

"Just so Linda?" I supply for him.

The smile returns to Ryan's face, lighting him up. He's glowing. Like he's made of the spun gold Rumpelstiltskin made out of straw. There's a softness in his eyes when he looks at me that burns me up from the inside.

I turn away from him, only to find JR staring at me, a crease between his eyebrows again. I try to smile at him—try to make everything seem completely normal between us. Because it is.

Ryan reaches out a hand to pull me up and I take it. I want to make everything seem completely normal with him, too. Instead, I do the exact opposite. "Don't worry," I tell him. "I know you weren't trying to get me naked."

The blush is back in full force but it quickly morphs into something else. Something less innocent. Ryan looks at me as if maybe he would like to get me naked after all.

This time I'm the one whose face is on fire.

"Um . . . I'm gonna go find Linda," JR says from behind us. "See you guys down there."

I turn to try to catch his eyes, but he's already walking away. I watch till he disappears into the trees. Until Ryan's fingers brush against mine. Looking up at him, I find him gazing at me with that same expression in his eyes. Soft but . . . not.

My own eyes widen. I don't know what to do right now or what to say. Ryan looks so beautiful in the starlight it makes my breath catch in my throat.

What is going on with me tonight?

Ryan holds his hand out to me again. It takes just a split second for me to slip mine into it. His smile deepens as he lifts my hand to his lips and places the softest of kisses on it.

Goose bumps rise on my arm.

His lips just barely brush against my hand again before he pulls me even closer to him and runs his fingertips over my cheek. My heart stops for a second.

We stand there, just looking at each other in the darkness for what feels like a long time.

When my hands start to shake, Ryan takes a step back from me and pulls me toward the path to the beach. "Come on. Let's go find Linda and JR."

Hand in hand, we walk down to the lake to do just that. Both JR and Linda glance down at our clasped hands. Neither of them says a word.

"Um . . . should we grab canoes or . . . ?" Linda says, breaking the ice.

But JR shakes his head. "I'm heading home to get out of this suit," he tells her. "If I have to spend another second in it I won't be responsible for my own actions."

"Unlike usual when you're in complete control of everything," she snarks.

JR doesn't smile or even laugh. He gives us that silent salute again. Then he's gone. I have to bite the inside of my mouth to keep myself from asking him to stay.

I let go of Ryan's hand so that it's not awkward for Linda, but she rolls her eyes at me anyway. I go through the motions of a fun night with my two friends. Laugh when someone says something funny. Uphold my end of the conversation. Every time Ryan touches me, my whole body feels ablaze.

For the first time tonight, I *want* to be alone. To run back to my room without arousing questions or having anyone offer to walk me back. I need some time to think about everything that's happened tonight. And I need some quiet to do that in.

CHAPTER 16

Lexi (Now)

asked Eve the concierge and then two other people just to cover my bases, but I got the same answer from all of them: they can't let me into the hotel archives. Everyone was very polite, but no one budged. Guest information must be protected at all costs . . . even if the guest stayed here decades ago.

Eve offered to call the hotel archivist, but the woman's only here one day a month, so I don't have much hope. I also don't have an indefinite amount of time here. If Dad catches me, even that will disappear.

I lie back on my hotel bed, wondering what the hell to do next.

Eat. That comes to mind right away. The scone I ate before I went to the library hasn't exactly held me over. Other than that . . . I come up empty.

I check the time on my phone and find three missed texts, none of which make me feel better. The oldest is from Dad. **When you don't respond I assume something is wrong. If you don't want me to think that please text back.**

I shoot him a quick text to assure him that I'm fine but cell reception is spotty. Then I read Chloe's text. **Have you found anything?** It hurts to admit that I have nothing new, so I don't reply. Instead I open the message from Abby. She's attached a drawing Connor made with two stick figures, labeled *you* and *me*. I appear to have on an eyepatch, so I'm assuming we're pirates. He drew a box in between the two of us and wrote *plees com home* at the bottom. This makes me laugh but also fills me with longing for home. I'm not sure how I'm going to get through college if I get this way after only a couple of days.

I'll be home in a few days, kiddo. Miss you! I write with lots of hearts.

For a minute, I lie back again and close my eyes. When I open them, I see the chest sitting at the edge of the bed and I open it up again, only to find a drawing of the Doors of Durin from *The Lord of the Rings*. Somehow finding out that Mom liked *The Lord of the Rings* doesn't make me feel any better. I mean, don't most people like those books? I need something solid. Something real.

As I pick up the postcard to her mystery friend, an idea forms in my head. I could mail it. Put my phone number on it, buy a stamp and just . . . pop it in the mail slot downstairs to see what happens. Maybe he'll respond. Maybe I'll find out who he was and he can tell me more about Mom. My shoulders collapse a little at the thought of losing this piece of her, especially if whoever it was written to doesn't live there anymore. Or doesn't want to respond. It definitely doesn't seem like they broke up on great terms. Even that would be good to know.

Shaking my head to clear my thoughts, I put the postcard aside till I can decide what to do. I'm too tired right now to make that big a decision. So instead I search through the box again looking for clues in the things I've already seen and then pushing beyond. There's a single sheet of notepaper underneath the Doors of Durin filled with tiny writing.

Today was like being a leopard in a cage at the zoo. Trapped. Nowhere to go.

Take Your Daughter to Work Day is the worst. Maybe if Dad was an astronaut or something, it would be good. But sitting around his office all day is NOT.

As soon as he got a call from one of his managers I broke free from my cage and ran like a leopard to Jackson's office. Then I hid away behind his comfiest chair. Somewhere Dad wouldn't find me and make me go with him again.

Jackson came back to his office and sat at his desk going through some papers.

Then he said, "Are you going to stay behind there all after-noon?"

So much for hiding. I crawled out and explained about being a leopard at the zoo.

"So what's your plan?" he asked.

I shrugged. "Run like the fastest animal on the planet and then eat raw meat?"

That made him laugh. "How about having some cookies and helping me out here?"

Then he called my dad to tell him where I was. Dad's going to be SO mad later. But I still got four cookies out of it. Best Take Your Daughter to Work Day ever.

I hold the notepaper to my chest and wish I was one tenth as bold as Mom seems to have been as a kid. Hell, I'm not that bold now and I'm seventeen. Though I guess I am here. And got here by myself. So that's something. Something kind of big, actually. Chloe's right. I'm not a little kid anymore. Just because it's lonely doesn't mean I can't handle it. My mind wanders to the time I went to see *Matilda* on a field trip in fourth grade. I cried when I first heard "When I Grow Up." Some of the boys in my class teased me for months about it. But now I *feel* the words to that song. *"I will be strong enough to carry all the heavy things."*

I wonder if this means I'm like Mom? I've never known enough about her to think I had much in common with her aside from the way I look. Even Dad has commented on that. But maybe just being here means that I'm more like her than I thought?

God, I hope so.

I pick up my last scone and take a bite. I can do this.

When I wake up in the morning, though, I'm less certain about it. For one thing, I'm lying flat on my stomach on an unmade bed with my mom's postcard stuck to my cheek. I still have my shoes on. I feel gross. And achy from sleeping that way.

And *hungry.*

Pushing myself off the bed, I force myself to take a shower. The hot water rushes over me, waking me up properly for the first time since I opened my eyes. The promise of breakfast—and grabbing much more food this time for the rest of the day—keeps me moving. In my mind, I formulate a plan:

1. Eat
2. Check about the archivist
3. Text Chloe
4. See if anybody will talk to me, at least about the time period when Mom stayed here.
5. Maybe mail the postcard? Or not?

I stuff my face at breakfast and use paper towels from the bathroom for my pastry basket. I even manage to snag an apple in the lobby. In the middle of this huge space I stop short. My hand goes almost instinctually into my bag and feels for Mom's postcard. I might just do it.

I'm probably going to.

Maybe.

Then I read through it again. *I miss you and hope to see you again, even if only in my memories.* I have to find out who Mom wrote those words to.

Rummaging through my bag again, I finally find a pen. Then I do something I never thought I'd do: I write on Mom's postcard.

This is Emma's daughter, Lexi. I'm staying here in room 315 and I need to talk to you. I add my cell number, then turn and walk to the front desk. I have to do this now or I'll lose my nerve.

"One postcard stamp, please."

The woman behind the counter takes my money. I place the stamp on the postcard.

"I can put that in the mail slot for you," the woman says.

And without another word, I hand it over.

For better or worse, my mom's postcard is now in the hands of the U.S. Postal Service. It's on its way to the friend she said she'd be waiting for here so many years ago. Now that it's gone, something like a sob rises in my throat. The postcard has now become one more thing of Mom's that I don't have, and I just hope I made the right decision.

I back away from the front desk, putting some distance between myself and what I just did, one step at a time.

And back right into someone.

"Oh my God . . . I'm so sorry," I say, turning around.

And there I find Casey from Mackinac Island. There must be hundreds of guests and staff in this hotel right now. *Hundreds* of complete strangers I could have knocked into. Instead it's him.

"Are you kidding me?" he says. "I told you I can't help you."

Then his eyes widen and he looks around . . . I'm guessing to make sure no one heard him be so rude on the job. He exhales deeply and says, "I mean . . . if I can get you something from the kitchen, just let me know, Miss . . . ?"

"Lexi!" I blurt out. "My name is Lexi Carter." My mind flutters to the mental list I made this morning. *See if anybody will talk to me, at least about the time period when Mom stayed here.* Casey probably could help me. He just doesn't want to.

"If you really want to help me," I reply, "you could introduce me to someone who might've lived on the island when my mom used to come here."

Casey sighs. Like, pretty dramatically. Deflated chest, closed eyes. It's a whole thing.

"You've gotta stop doing this," he informs me. "I have a room service order to pick up right now. I don't have time to have this conversation again."

With that, he walks away from me and heads toward the kitchen.

I have no idea what's come over me, but I follow him. "Do you take a service elevator with the food?"

"Yeah, there's one right back . . ." He looks in the direction where the elevator must be and seems to realize what he's done the moment that I do.

"Okay. I'll meet you there once you get your order," I tell him.

"No, that's—"

"And then we can keep talking."

He stops in his tracks for a second. "Are you always like this?"

Even though I have no idea what he means, I know there's only one answer. "No."

Usually I'm quiet and do what I'm supposed to do. Usually I'd rather die than follow a cute guy around, even if he didn't make it so clear that he wanted nothing to do with me.

Casey walks away from me and disappears behind a discreet door. I find the service elevator.

The disappointment on his face when he sees me is almost like a cartoon character's it's so exaggerated. His mouth droops. His eyes turn down at the corners. On a normal day, having someone react like this to my mere presence would send me crying into a dark corner. But I have nothing left to lose here.

I jump in the elevator after him. "Just one person," I tell him. "Just one person I can talk to and I'll leave you alone."

He doesn't answer me. He doesn't even look at me. The elevator dings and he rolls his cart off it, with me on his heels.

"Casey, come on," I say. "You have to help me."

"You're right," he agrees. "I have to help you carry your bags or get an ice-cold beverage for you. Nowhere in my job description does it say I have to play Nancy Drew with you or invite you into my personal life."

I jump in front of him so that he either has to stop short or bump his cart into me. "Casey, please," I say. "You're the only person I know who grew up here. You have to be able to introduce me to someone I could talk to."

"You don't know me!" he spits out. "And I don't *have* to do anything. Not for you, not for anyone else." He pushes past me. "Two more months and I'll be out of here. Living in a dorm, not having to deal with rich people telling me what to do every second of every day."

Rushing to catch up with him again, I keep talking. "I already told you, I'm not rich! My dad's going to annihilate me when he finds out I'm here."

My eyes sting. My chest hurts. Desperation is beginning to set in and I'm not even sure why. I just know I have to do something—anything—concrete before I get caught. All I have now are maybes. Maybe I'll hear from Rayla at the historical society. Maybe the archivist will come this week. Maybe the postcard will reach the right person and he'll call. But finding someone to talk to is something I could do with no maybes attached.

"Casey, I'm begging you to help, okay?" My voice cracks and I don't even care. "You have to know someone I can ask about my mom."

Finally he stops walking and turns to look at me. I must look bad, because he says, "Jesus, Lexi. Calm down."

My head drops back on my shoulders. "I can't calm down!" I insist. "All I want to do is find out more about my own mother. Is that really so much to ask of the universe?"

When Casey doesn't answer, I crash backward into the wall and slide down.

A hand appears in front of my face. Casey's hand, which he's holding out to me. For a second, I'm so confused that I can't move a single muscle.

"Are you going to get up or what?" he says.

I shove his hand away. "Just go away, Casey," I tell him. "Go do your job and pretend I never asked, okay? I'll figure it out on my own."

He rolls his eyes and holds his hand out again. "Look . . . there's no way I'm introducing you to my family, but I do know someone you might be able to talk to," he says. "Someone in the hotel who grew up here and who's lived here off and on."

Our eyes meet, and I try to read his to see if he really means it or if he's just trying to get rid of me. But he doesn't look like he's joking or lying.

"You'll introduce me to them?" I ask in a quiet voice.

"Yeah," he says. "But only if you come right now."

That gets me right on my feet. "Okay," I say. Deep breath in. Deep breath out. "Okay, let's do this."

Casey leads me through the hotel to drop off his tray of food, warning me to keep out of sight as he delivers it.

So I stay down the hall as he knocks and then enters one of the swankier suites.

"Took you long enough," says the man inside the room. His voice is loud, sharp. "I thought I was going to have to go pick the damn food up myself, so don't think you're getting a tip for lousy service."

"Understood, sir," Casey tells him. "My sincere apologies for the delay."

Casey walks back out the door without the tray. Closes it quietly behind him.

His eyes flit to mine for the briefest of seconds before he looks away again and starts walking his cart back down the corridor.

"I'm sorry, Casey," I tell him. When he doesn't reply, I just keep talking. "I didn't mean to make you late and miss out on a tip, and I just—"

"Lexi." He holds his hand out to stop me. "Let it go. Okay?"

"Okay."

I follow him into the service elevator and up to the fourth floor. Together, we walk down yet another hallway. The door we stop at has no room number. Instead it has a little plaque that says *La Suite du Lac—The Lake Suite*. Casey knocks on the door.

I close my eyes and shake my hands to try to calm myself down.

The door opens, and an elderly woman stands before us. "Casey," she says. "Did I order something?"

"No, but I'd be happy to get you some tea and cake if you'd like."

She pats him fondly on the arm. "That would be lovely, thank you," she says as she walks into the room.

Casey holds out his arm, beckoning me to follow her inside. The room is all done up in soothing colors. Sky-blue walls. Tan-colored sofas and chairs. White curtains and throw pillows. Accents of deep blue here and there. A pot holding a bouquet of flowers . . . a blanket thrown over an armchair. When my eyes stray to the open window I realize that they're the same colors of the lake and sand, the sky and clouds. This is not a normal hotel room. There are frames filled with black-and-white and color photographs all over the place, and a tall bookshelf against one wall. It's homey. I turn back to smile at Casey, but my eyes settle on something else altogether. On the mantel, just over the fireplace, sit three Tony Awards. As in, three *actual* Tony Awards with the comedy and tragedy masks. Not the kind you'd buy for someone as a joke with "Best Actress in the Role of a Friend."

For the first time, I focus in on the woman whose suite I'm in. She looks old, older than even Abby's mom, and she's in her seventies. This woman leans on a cane but not the kind you get from a hospital. This is burnished wood with a carved handle. I look back at the woman holding it again. Her dark skin is set off by puffs of short white hair that wave around her face like a halo. It's her eyes that get me, though. They're dark, with deep crow's feet and a shrewd expression in them.

"Do I know you?" she asks me.

I take a deep breath. "No, but I know you." At least I know who she is: Clara VanHill. Broadway star. The first African American Eliza Doolittle. And Auntie Mame. And Annie Oakley.

Good Lord, she's a legend. I am standing in the hotel room of an actual legend. I let out a nervous laugh and then clamp my hand over my mouth to stop myself. But it's *Clara VanHill*. My chest starts to shake a little. I can't let myself laugh again. That's too weird . . . too . . .

"Is she quite well?" Ms. VanHill's voice cuts through my panic.

"Not that I've been able to tell so far," Casey responds.

Rude. So rude. And I don't even care. I am standing in *Clara Van-Hill*'s suite!

"I've . . . I've listened to you sing," I stammer out. "So many times. And I . . . I always wished I could have seen you on Broadway."

Ms. VanHill smiles at me, deepening the creases around her eyes. "I wish you could have, too," she nods. "I was something."

Casey smiles at her. "You still are, Ms. VanHill," he tells her. You can tell he means it. While I'm a thorn in his side, it's pretty clear from the look on his face that he adores her.

"Are you planning to introduce me to your friend?" Ms. VanHill asks as she gestures my way.

"Oh, of course!" Casey replies. "Ms. VanHill, this is Lexi Carter. Lexi, this is Clara VanHill."

"It's so nice to meet you!" I gush. "I mean, I can't believe I'm actually meeting you, and that you're staying right here in the same hotel as me, and . . ."

Ms. VanHill gestures at the nearest chair. "You're obviously overwhelmed," she says. "Why don't you sit for a minute?"

I follow her instructions, almost collapsing into it.

She gives me a strange look. "That wasn't exactly what I'd intended when I said to sit, but you're there now, I suppose." Ms. VanHill turns to Casey. "Is there any way we could get some tea? You know what I like."

"I'm on it," Casey replies as he heads toward the door.

"If you have a break coming up, bring enough for three," Ms. VanHill instructs him.

He gives her a salute before closing the door behind him.

"Now," she says, turning her eyes on me. "Why did Casey bring you here? Other than to provide me some much-needed admiration." She sits on the sofa across the coffee table from me. "It's been days since anyone's given me any real adulation."

I can't tell if she's kidding or not. Also, I can't speak. I just sit here staring at her.

"Hm . . . I can see that're you're still overly awed by meeting me," Ms. VanHill says. "So why don't we start with some preliminary questions. What was your name again?"

Okay, this one's easy to answer. "My name's Lexi. Lexi Carter."

Ms. VanHill nods. "And where do you come from, Lexi Carter?"

"Chicago."

She wrinkles her nose. "Dreadful climate. I don't know how anyone lives there."

"Oh . . . um . . . it's not really that bad when you—"

"And you're here on vacation?" Ms. VanHill cuts me off.

This one's much harder to answer than my name and where I'm from. "No, I . . . I came to Mackinac to find out more about my mother."

"Your mother?" she says. "Who was your mother?"

"Emma Carter," I reply. "Though she would have been Emma Roth when she stayed here." I pause and think that through. "Do you . . . Casey said I could talk to you about her."

Ms. VanHill tents her fingers over her chin and goes quiet for a minute. "The name isn't familiar at all," she says. "But I've met so many people over the years. Why don't you show me a picture of her so I can see if I remember her?"

My heart breaks a little. More than a little. "I don't have one. I . . ."

For a few seconds, she gives me a searching look. "Well, then what do you know about her?"

"Not as much as I'd like" is all I say at first. But once I get going everything spills from me. Losing her. My dad never talking about her. The mosaic chest that came in the mail and everything I've found inside.

"Hm . . . ," she says. "And you brought the box with you?"

I nod.

"Why don't you go get it and bring it back here. I'll order us some tea. Maybe even some cake. Good sleuthing deserves good cake."

I stare at her for a second, puzzled, and then a realization hits me: she doesn't remember that Casey's already getting the tea for her. How is she ever going to remember if she met my mom or not if she can't even remember that Casey's already getting tea? Where will that leave me?

A burst of heat spreads over my face. What kind of person am I that I'm more concerned about myself than the fact that Ms. VanHill doesn't remember something that happened five minutes ago? Not a good one.

"I'll take care of ordering the tea," I tell her in a gentle voice. Then I pause, not sure what to do . . . not wanting to be a horrible, selfish person who only thinks about myself. "Um . . . do you still want to see my mom's stuff? Because if not, I . . ."

She waves me away. "Bring it here with the tea."

I nod at her. "Okay, I will."

As I walk to the door, her eyes stray out the window toward the lake. For a few seconds, I just watch her. *Clara VanHill.* I still can't believe I got to meet Clara VanHill. And I'm going to have tea with her. And cake. Maybe even talk about my mom with her.

This trip is not turning out the way I expected it to at all.

CHAPTER 17

Emma (Then)

The flier for the art gallery has been sitting in my drawer for days. I've taken it out and put it back in more times than I can count and still don't know what to do. Part of me is so afraid the gallery will reject my work that I don't even want to submit anything. The rest of me wants this so badly it almost hurts.

I take out my big leather portfolio and start looking through my old paintings and drawings. There are sketches and watercolors of so many places around the island. Of Mom and Dad, Jackson, Linda and Ryan. Tiny corners of the hotel that I blew up into large-scale paintings. The flier says to submit two pieces, which shouldn't be difficult but . . . well.

I give myself a shake. This is a good opportunity and since when do I shy away from something like this? From anything?

Thoughts flash through the back of my mind—times I did, in fact, shy away from something hard. Times I did just recently. Admitting out loud that I like Ryan. Telling my dad I don't want a job at the hotel.

A sigh escapes from me and I go back to the task at hand. I *will* submit something, even if I have to make something new. My eyes catch on a painting I made last winter after a snowstorm. It's nearly black-and-white—all light and shadow under the dock at low tide— but there are undertones of purple and blue, hints of green and even yellow layered in to make the shadows pop more. I have no idea if this is what the gallery wants—it's definitely *local art*, just not the pretty landscapes tourists buy up. I set this one aside.

There are paintings tucked into the back of the portfolio that I made when I was little. Weird abstract ones and ones trying so desperately to be like a "real" artist's that they're almost painful to look at. I loved the old art classes I took, though. I so badly wanted to learn how to be a better artist.

My fingers trace over a particularly vibrant watercolor painting of a rock that I did in class. My teacher at the time was trying to get us to see that even gray rocks had many other colors in them and I took that advice a little too much to heart.

I sit up straighter in my chair, an idea forming in my mind.

I could teach art classes. Here at the hotel. Dad would get what he wants, and I'd feel less trapped working here if I could carve out my own kind of work. I open up my old journal and start brainstorming ideas.

What ages would the classes be for? What kinds of mediums? How many days a week? For how long? I scribble out answers and new ideas, thrilled to have thought of this. Dad'll be so happy if I finally have a job here. This is going to be so—

"Emma, if you show up late to dinner, I'm going to . . . to . . . ," my dad calls through my bedroom door. "Well, I don't know what I'm going to do, but I won't be happy about it."

I swing my door open to reveal myself, already dressed and ready to go. Dad jumps back as if he's seen a ghost. The look on his face is worth having had to set my alarm to remind myself to get it together much earlier than I had to.

"I definitely don't want to make you unhappy," I tell him as I stand on my toes to kiss his cheek. "Besides, it looks as if *you're* not ready this time," I continue. My eyes stray to the clock on the mantel. "Better get moving, Dad. If you show up late to dinner, I don't know what I'm going to do!"

He shakes his head at me. "You can tease all you want, but *I'm* late because of work," he reminds me. "You're always late because . . . why *are* you late all the time, actually?"

This time I rumple his hair and push him gently toward his room. "Punctuality is for the small-minded."

"Or the highly responsible," he counters.

"Richard, are you still not ready?" my mom asks as she breezes into the room. "We have to be downstairs in five minutes."

Dad is always on time, but often by the skin of his teeth. Mom, on the other hand, is always on time without any fuss, *and* always impeccably dressed to boot. I guess it's not just the musical genes that I didn't inherit from her. I watch as she puts in her earrings.

"Mom, I had an idea," I begin as I walk up behind her and lean my chin on her shoulder.

"About what?"

I take a deep breath. "It's just that I've been thinking a lot about—"

"Okay, let's go," my dad says as he bursts back into the room. "We don't want to keep the Desmonds waiting."

Mom squeezes my shoulder. "We'll talk later," she says to me before taking my dad's arm. I follow them out the door and downstairs to the lobby. The whole Desmond family is waiting for us by one of the jasmine trees. The setting sun casts them into a glowing light that in no way reflects the faces of the four of them. Mr. Desmond looks at his watch impatiently while talking steadily to Ryan. Linda scowls as Mrs. Desmond straightens out the dress she's clearly been forced to wear for the evening. Every one of them looks unhappy in a completely different way. That is, until they see us.

"There you are!" Mrs. Desmond calls out. "I'm so glad we're doing this, aren't you?"

"Of course, Eliza," Mom answers. "I've been looking forward to it all week!"

The two of them stream off toward the door, leaving the rest of us to follow.

"I was about to ask to have the reservation pushed back," Mr. Desmond tells my dad, even though we're only about three minutes late.

"Sorry for the delay," Dad replies. "I had to take a call. You know how it is when you run a business. There's always something."

There's an edge to Dad's voice that I know all too well because he's used it on me so many times over the course of my seventeen years of existence. The *I'm not going to make a scene, but oh am I annoyed* tone. I'm just surprised he's using it on Mr. Desmond.

Mr. Desmond is, too. "I understand, Richard," he says with the same constrained annoyance in his voice. "Business before pleasure."

"And it's a pleasure to see you, as always," Dad replies.

As they walk away, Linda, Ryan, and I trail behind them. "What's up with them tonight?"

"You mean, what's up with our dad?" Linda clarifies. "Because nothing seemed wrong with yours."

I give her a half laugh as I slip my arms into both of theirs and we make our way to the little pavilion where we're having a barbecue tonight. By the time we get there, our parents are all talking business and new opportunities and Tom already has the grill going. I watch him get everything ready to cook. I've never been to a real barbecue—the kind you read about in stories where parents grill up meat and everyone sits at a picnic table. Our barbecues have always been exactly like this. With someone on the hotel staff doing the cooking and everyone sitting around a wrought-iron garden table. I think I'd like to do the normal kind someday. Maybe when I'm in college? Or afterward? I don't know when I'd have a chance to, but . . .

"Emma?" my father's voice cuts through the fog of my thoughts.

"Yes, Dad?"

"Are you still with us?" he asks.

"Of course!" I lie. For a few seconds, I listen in to see where the conversation has gone without me. College, it turns out. And our futures. Without doubt, one of my least favorite subjects.

"Ryan's hoping to go to University of Michigan," his mom tells my parents. "And following his father's footsteps."

"That's wonderful," my mom replies. "It's so nice to have a sense of family history, even when it comes to planning the future."

"It is," Mrs. Desmond says. She looks over at Ryan with shining eyes and reaches across Linda to give his arm a squeeze. "We couldn't be prouder of him."

"Unless he decided to join ROTC, too," Mr. Desmond adds.

Ryan tenses up. "Dad, we talked about this," he says. "I don't think the military's for me."

Mr. Desmond turns to my dad. "What could be more important than serving your country?" he asks. "That's the whole reason I'm running for Senate. You've got to use the gifts God's given you to serve, right, Richard?"

My dad, a dyed-in-the-wool atheist, adjusts his collar. "The world wouldn't run properly if some folks weren't called to serve." God, he's so good at this. "And you know we're supporting your campaign one hundred percent, Jack."

Mr. Desmond slaps Dad on the back hard enough that Dad's shoulders hunch up. "I appreciate that," he tells Dad. "You know I'm counting on you." Mr. Desmond looks around at our surroundings. "Nothing says old-fashioned ideals and traditional values about hard work like this island does."

Linda visibly bristles across from me, and I stretch out my leg to touch hers under the table. She gives me a weak smile as our parents keep talking.

"I tell Emma all the time that she's got to get more serious about the future," Dad says.

This time Linda presses her leg against mine.

"Richard, she's still got time," Mom says. "She'll figure it out this year, won't you, Emma?"

I don't know where to turn or how to respond. It's like I'm a bug being pinned down for close examination. Nowhere to run. No way to escape.

"I don't know," Mr. Desmond says before I can reply. "No time like the present, right? The more you plan ahead, the less guesswork there'll be when the time comes to apply to colleges." Then he turns to me. "What are you going to major in?"

"Oh . . . I'm not sure yet," I stammer.

"See, this is what I mean!" he barks out. "The first line of attack when it comes to colleges is knowing what you want to pursue. And you've got a family business to step into down the road." He smiles at my dad. "Much further down the road, I hope. Right, Richard?"

Dad takes a swig from his wineglass.

Suddenly Linda sits up straighter in her seat. "And planning so that you can take over your family business is the most important thing, right, Dad?" Her voice has an edge to it.

Her father completely ignores her. Before he can get another word in, Linda cuts him off. "That's why I'm laying the groundwork for college and even afterward."

Her mom reaches over and touches her shoulder. "Honey," she soothes.

But Linda shrugs her off. "No, I mean, isn't that what you want Ryan to do, Dad?" she persists. "Get a business degree and take over when you retire? Be just like dear old Dad?"

Ryan's practically shrinking beside me. But she's not even looking Ryan's way. Her eyes are trained on her dad.

"Except he doesn't care about any of it, and I do."

"Linda, we've been over this before," Mr. Desmond says in a calm, measured voice. "You're free to make whatever choices you want."

I wince at the look on Linda's face. Can he possibly not realize he's making the situation even worse?

"Sure, Dad," she spits out. "As long as I don't choose running Desmond Automotive. That's strictly a patriarchy all the way, right?"

A silence falls over our group, interrupted only by the sounds of Tom setting out dinner on a buffet table. A fly buzzes around the food. Something rustles in the azalea bushes nearby.

"Tom, that looks great!" my dad says, breaking the ice. "Smells delicious, too. I can't wait to dig in."

"Everything's all set whenever you're ready," Tom replies with a forced smile.

We all file up to grab grilled chicken and pork chops slathered in barbecue sauce. Everything smells good, but I don't really have an appetite anymore. Everyone else is picking at their food as well. Things have gotten very quiet again.

Mom, always hostess extraordinaire, decides to jump-start the conversation again. "Linda, I hear only good things about how hard you've been working at the hotel this summer."

"Thanks," she says in a subdued voice. "I'm trying to save up some money for college."

Her dad throws his napkin onto the table. "Now you know there's no reason to . . ."

"Jack," Mrs. Desmond says. "We can talk about all of that later, don't you think?"

Mom shoots Linda an apologetic look but seems momentarily at a loss as to what to say next. Everyone does.

Maybe I can take the spotlight off Linda and Ryan. One glance at my dad shows me that he's feeling ill at ease, too. So I gulp down a sip of water. I change the subject.

"Dad, I came up with an idea for some work I could do at the hotel this summer."

A hopeful smile spreads across his face. "You did?" he replies. "What is it?"

He looks so happy that I know this is the right thing to do. For both of us. And once I tell him about the art classes, I can tell him about the gallery show. Everything will start to fall into place.

"I'm going to see if I can start teaching kids' art classes here at the hotel," I tell him. "A quieter activity for families looking for something different."

The smile on Dad's face slowly fades away until there's no trace of it left.

"You . . . you want to teach art?"

I nod but my confidence about this plan has already started fading like Dad's smile. "That way I'll be helping out here and doing something I love."

For a second or two, Dad doesn't say anything. I keep hoping he'll smile again—that he'll see this is the perfect solution to me working at the hotel.

"That . . . that wasn't quite what I had in mind," he tells me.

Mom puts her hand on his. "I think it's a great idea, Richard," she intercedes. "She'll get hands-on experience managing people under . . . trying circumstances." Mom turns to Mrs. Desmond for support. "Because what's more trying than a group of small children?"

"Nothing that I can think of!" Mrs. Desmond laughs as if she hasn't picked up at all on any of the tension at this table. "If Emma can wrangle a bunch of little ones into sitting and doing something quiet, she has my admiration!"

"Mine too," Ryan pipes up. He wraps his arm around me and pulls me just a little bit closer to him. "But I know she can do it. Emma's an amazing artist. The kids'll love her."

Our mothers exchange a look before they start talking about what handfuls we all were as little kids. Apparently, Linda used to swing from the ceiling beams in their old town house in Detroit and only stopped after she fell and dislocated her shoulder. Nothing about that is surprising except the fact that Linda let it stop her from doing it again.

Ryan gets up to get some lemonade and ends up bringing a glass back for me as well. He crouches down by my side. "Want to take a walk?"

I lay my hand on his shoulder and whisper, "The sooner the better."

After pressing his hand to mine for just a second, he sits down again and turns to his mother. "Emma and Linda and I are going to take dessert for the road, Mom," he says. "We've got plans tonight."

Before Mr. Desmond can say a word, his wife replies, "That sounds nice. We'll finish up here, sweetheart." She smiles at him and then at me. "Have a good time."

I glance at my parents to make sure they're okay with this, but Mom's smiling so hard there's no doubt about how she feels. Even my dad looks at me as if for once I've done something right.

But then Ryan holds his hand out to me and I don't care quite so much what my parents think about this or about anything. I slip my hand into his and then reach out to take Linda's as well. I want to saunter through the warm night air and find JR and try not to think about my dad's reaction to my plan to teach art classes. Someday I'm going to have to tell him about the gallery. About the fact that I don't want to run his business.

I think about the black-and-white painting on my desk. The flier folded up in my desk drawer. I just need to prove to my parents that art can be my future and I know they'll understand. Maybe this art show could be the first step in doing that.

For now, though, I squeeze both of my friends' hands.

For now, I'll eat the dessert we brought with us. Later I'll talk them into getting some ice cream. Drowning our worries with sugar doesn't seem like such a bad idea, really.

CHAPTER 18

Emma (Then)

The problem with curing stress with dessert is that I wake up this morning with a serious sugar hangover and headache. A huge, shuddering yawn comes over me. I stretch out in bed, letting my fingers and toes dig into the softness of the sheets. My bed is pure comfort—plush yellow quilt and soft cotton sheets. Even the pillows are just the right balance of too firm and too cushiony. White lace curtains I picked out myself drape over the windows, art, and little treasures I've collected from all over the island fill every space. I love this room—I love everything about this place I get to call home.

I just wish I had a little less of a headache.

Then I roll over and see what time it is. Ten thirty. My parents are going to kill me if they find out that I stayed in bed this late on a Thursday morning. With a sigh, I drag myself out of bed and swing open my bedroom door. Thankfully, neither of my parents is home, though this isn't such a great surprise. Dad's always off to work early, and Mom's got her own stuff to deal with. So they'll never know about this.

"It's ten thirty-four, Emma." My mom walks into the living room. "Well past time to be up."

My shoulders slump. "I know, Mom."

"The whole island has already been going about its business for almost two hours," she reminds me.

"Mom, I'm sorry, I just—"

"And you have a meeting with Clarice at eleven thirty to discuss your idea to teach art classes," she interrupts.

This makes me pull up short. "You made me an appointment with Clarice?"

"I did."

"Even though Dad doesn't think it's a good idea?"

"Even though," she says. Mom straightens out her blouse and turns to look at me. "I don't see why this wouldn't serve as a first attempt at working here as well as anything else."

And I can't help myself. I really can't. I throw myself at her, laughing and hugging her. "Mom, you're the best!" I tell her. "This is going to be *spectacular!*"

"If Clarice says yes," Mom reminds me.

"Yes, if that," I reply. But I know Clarice will say yes. I've known her since I was nine years old when she took over as the hotel's activities director. She won't say no when I explain what I want to do. I hope.

"So maybe you should shower and get ready," Mom suggests. "You *cannot* be late for this appointment, Emma."

"I won't be, Mom!" I assure her. "I promise."

Just as I start to run to my bathroom, my mom says, "Oh, and this arrived for you this morning." She hands me a note that's been written on plain notebook paper, folded and taped shut, with the torn edges still on it. My name's scrawled on the front in JR's messy handwriting.

"Read it *after* you shower!" Mom calls as I run into my room.

I call back saying that I will, but then immediately break my own word, as my curiosity is going to kill me if I don't see what's inside. Ripping it open, I find just three words inside.

Greenhouse at 7:30?

I stand there staring at it not knowing what to think or do. JR's been so weird about the greenhouse this summer. Every single time I've asked him to meet me there, he's said no and now—now he wants to go? It's great that's he found a time to squeeze me in, but maybe tonight won't end up working for me. Part of me *wants* to be the one who says no this time. Just out of spite. I want him to see how it feels to have your friend reject your invitation.

Except I don't really want to do any of this. I just . . . I wish he'd wanted to meet up sooner. That everything could go back to the way it used to be.

I drop his note in my mosaic box. I don't have the energy to deal with him right now—not when I need to take a shower so I won't be late for my appointment at eleven thirty. I really want this to work.

"So, your mom told me you have an idea for a new activity?" Clarice says.

My hair's still dripping down the back of my sundress into my bra, making me shiver in Clarice's air-conditioned office. I shiver again—this time because I'm suddenly nervous about all of this—then break out in goose bumps. What if she says no after all? What if my dad's right and this isn't a good idea? I was so sure it was, but now . . .

"Emma?"

"Oh, sorry!" I tell her. "Just thinking."

"Is it about your plan?" she asks. "Because if it is, maybe you could share your thoughts with me?"

I nod a little too vigorously. I can do this. It'll be good.

"I was wondering if maybe the kids who stay at the hotel would want art classes," I begin. "Well, really more like crafts classes. But we wouldn't call them classes, because then none of them would want to come because it would sound too much like school, and they're on vacation, so we'd have to call it something else if you—"

"Emma," Clarice says again, this time with a smile. "Take a deep breath and tell me, slowly, what your idea is."

With another nod, I breathe in and out and start over. "Yes . . . yes, of course." I try to gather my thoughts so I can be a little more coherent. "There are so many activities, but most of them are sports or more summer-campy stuff. And don't get me wrong, the archery lessons are amazing!" I tell her. The last thing I want to do is complain about the activities to the *activities director*. "But there's nothing for the kids who need something quieter."

"So, you want to start offering art lessons?" she says, supplying the words I didn't manage to find.

"I would," I reply. "We could do different activities on different days. Painting, drawing, working with clay, making collages, or even things like making sand art." I pause for a second, because this means so much more to me than just being a way to appease my dad with a hotel job. It's something I really want to do. And it's a good idea. I just need to be confident enough to convince Clarice it's a good idea, too.

"For lots of kids, having some quiet time to work on a project can be a really good thing," I continue. "Even kids who loves sports love to make stuff, but . . ." My voice falters just a little. "But for a lot of kids, it's hard to find the time or space to do it. Especially on vacation when there's so much going on."

"I see what you're saying," Clarice replies. "So what's your proposal?"

Probably I should have brought all my notes with me. But they're sitting on my desk and I'm sitting in Clarice's office, which means I'm going to have to wing it.

"Well, we wouldn't want to meet every day because people are busy," I begin. I wrack my brain for where to go from there. "And we wouldn't want to interfere with meals or people going to the beach or anything."

"That's true," Clarice agrees. "It would have to be in later in the afternoon. Maybe three o'clock?"

"Yes! That would be perfect!" I agree. "And maybe Tuesdays and Thursdays to start?"

Clarice types up notes on her computer, so I just keep going. "We need to talk about supplies, too," I add. "We can start simple enough just to get going. Some colored pencils and drawing paper. And it wouldn't cost a lot of money to buy some cheap watercolor sets and brushes. If you tell me who to talk to, I can ask for old magazines that the hotel is going to recycle for collages. Which would also mean—"

"Why don't you put a list together for me of everything you'll need?" Clarice says. "Get it to me by tomorrow and I'll put in an initial order so we can get this on the weekly schedule."

I stare at her not sure if I heard her correctly. "You mean . . . we're going to do it?"

"Yes, we're going to do it, Emma," she laughs. "Once I get the logistics from you, we'll get the ball rolling. It's a good idea. I'm glad you came to me with it."

Neither of us says anything for a second or two. Me because I'm stunned that this is actually going to happen, and Clarice probably because she's waiting for me to leave.

"Oh, okay, well, I'll get to work and get the list to you and . . ."

"Sounds like a plan, Emma."

She looks down at her computer. I'm clearly being dismissed. Which means I should go. And get to work . . . and . . .

And actually walk out the door. "Thanks so much, Clarice," I say as I finally leave.

Then I'm out of her office and into the hallway. I know I should go straight upstairs and work on this plan, but I can't be inside right now. So I practically float through the lobby, the smell of the jasmine trees tickling my nostrils and the yellow of the walls cheering my mood even more than it already is. The gleaming wood, the sunlight through the huge windows—every single detail of it is perfect. I want to paint the lobby—just as it is in this light—but I'm not sure I could sit still long enough to do it right now.

So outside I go, sweating in the sun. By the time I reach the cool of the woods, I immediately break out in goose bumps. Not that I mind. The warm, the cool, my skin's reaction to both—it all just means that I'm alive on this glorious day.

I'm going to get to teach art classes. And make at least one of my parents happy. And myself, too.

I trip over a pinecone as I reach the beach and stoop to pick it up. It's huge, with perfectly formed scales. The inside is almost rust colored—the tips a deep, warm brown. The delicate petal-like formations on the bottom and the tight whirl of pine seeds at the top. The pinecone prickles my hand when I close my fingers around it. An idea forms in my head. I take in a shaky breath and practically laugh it back out.

Picking up more cones, I lift the edge of my dress up to hold them. Some twigs join them there, followed by leaves and pine needles. I keep foraging till I have everything I need and then rush home.

Candles. I'm going to need candles, I realize as I walk through the doors. And a strong canvas or piece of wood. Other than that I'm just going to need time to layer the wax and the 3D objects—to paint and layer on even more wax. I've never made anything encaustic before but I've seen pictures of what you can do with wax.

Running up the stairs, I burst into our place. Mom doesn't seem to be here, so I dump everything I gathered onto my desk and rummage through the kitchen for our emergency candles and some matches. No one will notice if one or two of them is missing. The lights never go out in the hotel anyway.

Besides, this is an art emergency! I can't wait for Mom to get back home to make sure she doesn't mind if I take these.

A canvas, some pencils, watercolors and oils—I collect everything I need to do to get started. Then I sketch idea after idea, revising as I go.

I need one more piece so that I can submit my work to the gallery. One more piece to help show my dad what I really want and how I could achieve it. And this is going to be it.

CHAPTER 19

Emma (Then)

After spending the whole afternoon working on my plan for Clarice, I scarf down dinner with my parents so I can meet JR. When I'm done, though, I find I'm not in such a big rush after all. His note said to meet at seven thirty at the greenhouse, but by the time I get there it's a teeny bit past eight. Half an hour is not tragically behind schedule anyway. Far from it. Any normal person wouldn't think twice about it.

But JR is not a normal person.

"You're late," he says as I walk into the greenhouse. "By like half an hour." He's sitting up against the far wall—the one that faces the hillside—with a book on his lap.

Normally, his constant reminders that I'm late roll off me. I *am* late. A lot. And he does wait around for me. A lot.

Tonight it makes my hackles rise when he says this.

"*You're* late," I tell him. "By like four weeks. So don't lecture me about a few minutes."

His mouth turns into a deep frown. "If I had a dollar for every minute of my life that I've spent waiting for you, then I'd be . . . "

"Then you'd be what?" I cross my arms over my chest.

He shrugs and looks away. "I'd be as rich as a perky princess like you."

I squeeze my arms to keep myself from shoving him. Because the urge to shove him is so hard to resist right now. "JR, are you trying to start a fight with me?" I ask. "Because I'm not really up for it tonight."

His eyes meet mine, a sudden spark of worry in them. "Why, what's wrong?" he says. "Another argument with your dad?"

"No," I tell him. "I'm in a fantastic mood, JR. I'm *thrilled* to finally be here with you." Then I realize he's still frowning. Some of the fire goes out of me. "Did *you* get into an argument with your dad?"

Another shrug. God, I wish he'd just talk to me for once. Why does this have to be so hard?

"Are you just going to keep shrugging or are we going to have an actual conversation?"

JR shrugs yet again, but a sly smile creeps up on his lips as he does.

"Wow . . . you're so hilarious," I say, making him smile even more. "I can barely contain my laughter."

The smile fades quickly enough. JR turns to look out the window. He runs his fingers down one of the panes. As I watch him, I start to worry, too.

"What's going on with your dad? *Are* you in a fight?"

JR rolls his head back over one shoulder and then the other. "We're not in a fight. Me and him . . . we don't argue, exactly," he says at last. "We discuss. We very. Calmly. Discuss."

"What did you discuss?"

"The importance of never putting myself in the way of establishing addiction," JR replies. "All the ways I could fall into it anyway. It was really inspirational. Someone could put it in one of those Chicken Soup books."

I walk over to the overgrown lime tree near where he's sitting. "I keep getting told how flighty I am. Even when I try to do the right thing, it never is."

"Sounds fun," he says as he runs his hand over his eyes.

"Are you okay?"

JR doesn't say anything right away, as if he's thinking it over. "I'm fine."

I watch his face as frustration and sadness play over it before he tries to make it go neutral. But I've known JR long enough to be able to read even that particular facial expression.

"You're allowed to not be fine sometimes." Then in a lower voice, I say, "You can talk to me when you're not."

"Jesus, Emma, I didn't ask you to meet me here tonight for a therapy session," he says, his voice edging on annoyance.

But now I'm annoyed, too. "We haven't come here all summer long because you didn't want to, and now you're going to act like *this*?"

Anger flashes in his dark eyes. "Like what?"

"Like . . . like . . ." I stop, trying to clear my mind enough to find something to actually say.

"Emma," he says, finally getting to his feet. His voice sounds weary. Defeated. "I don't want to fight with you, okay? I'm just . . . I'm tired, that's all. I had hours at the dock and at the market today, then had to help my dad with a few things and listen to him lecture me. And it's getting dark and I want to show you something before you can't see it anymore."

A light bursts to life inside me. "You have a surprise for me?"

JR's eyebrows—his whole face—blow back as if he's startled by my enthusiasm. But that's nothing new. What is new is that he won't meet my eyes.

"I was kidding, JR," I assure him. "I know you don't have a surprise for me."

He walks over to where I'm standing. The rosy light of the sunset shines in his dark hair, over the contours of his face. It makes him look . . . softer. Younger. When he looks up at me again, he's biting his lower lip.

"It is a surprise, though," he says. "Kind of. But I don't know if you're gonna like it or not." He tips his head down, letting his hair fall over his eyes. "You might not, actually."

"Okaaaay," I reply, drawing out the syllable. "Then what is it?"

"Look down."

So I do. I look down at my feet. Even in the darkening greenhouse

I can see what he means, but I need to get a closer look. Dropping to my knees I run my fingers over the tiles on the floor.

"JR," I almost whisper. "When did you . . . how did you?"

He squats next to me. This time it's JR running his fingers over the tiles. "I've been working on it since I got here," he says. "My dad showed me how to do the grouting. I finished it last night while you guys were having dinner with your parents but then it had to harden up."

When I don't say anything, JR—shockingly—fills the silence.

"Look, I know we said we wouldn't come here without each other, but I thought you'd like it," he tells me. "I hope I didn't mess up your art and . . ."

His voice trails off, but he doesn't need to say anything more. We found this place years ago—overgrown, broken down—and we started to fix it up. JR borrowed tools and old gardening stuff from his dad. We repotted plants and boarded up the broken windows. Then, last summer, we tore up the tiles that had lain in shards here, and JR helped me break them up even further so that I could make a mosaic out of them.

Now the swirls of paisley I painstakingly put together over the course of last summer are a permanent fixture of the greenhouse. I have to blink my eyes a few times to make sure what I'm seeing is real.

"I can't believe you did this," I breathe. I glance up at him. "It must've taken forever."

He looks down, his fingers pulling tightly at the loose strings of a hole in his jeans. If he keeps doing that, his whole knee is going to be bare soon. "Not as long as I thought it would."

But there's no possible way that could be true. How could he have done all this work in just a few weeks? He works all the time. He must have come here almost every night. Every day off. Then I remember our conversation in the rose garden. *She'll understand,* he told Terry. Even then he was working on it.

"I can't believe you did this," I whisper.

I run my fingers over the tiles again. The pale grout stands out against the terra-cotta paisley patterns in a way that makes the whole design pop more than it did before. It's beautiful. The floor looks beautiful. I crawl around, eager to examine every inch I can before we lose the last lingering bits of light.

Only when I get to the door do I stop and sit down. My knees hurt from the rough edges of the mosaic tiles but it's hard to find it in me to care. After years of saying he couldn't make art, JR has made some.

I look up at him to find that he's standing a few feet away, watching me closely. His eyes shine in the darkened greenhouse.

"So . . . do you like it?" His voice sounds unsure, as if he's still in doubt about my reaction.

I'm on my feet in an instant. It only takes two steps to reach him and throw my arms around him. "I love it so much, JR," I tell him. "I'm so happy you made it permanent. Something that will always be here."

JR freezes for a second before giving me a tentative, one-handed pat on the back. I pull away from him. Level him with a glare. "Are you *seriously* not going to hug me back?" I demand. "What's wrong with you?"

He shrugs. "I don't really do hugs."

"God, you're the most frustrating, grumpy . . ." I step right in front of him again and his eyes widen. "How long have we known each other?"

"Since we were little."

"And how many times have I tried to hug you? Never."

"Um . . . there was that group hug with Ryan and Linda," he says. "That counts."

I let out an exasperated huff. "JR! Can you *please* humor me just this once?"

Try as I might to keep my tone light, even I can hear that that I'm not succeeding. I sound as if I'm pleading with him. I sound desperate.

I have no idea why this means so much to me—why it stings so much that he can't bring himself to do something as simple as hug me—but it does. For a second, he looks at me with this odd expression in his eyes. Then he wraps his arms around me.

This time it's me who hesitates, my arms limp at my sides, not sure how to react. It's so new—so strange—to be this close to him. But then I slip my arms around him, too.

My chest feels as if it's expanding—bigger and wider till something inside me might explode. It feels so good to hug him that I can't figure out why we haven't done this before. Or all the time. JR isn't a big person. We're practically the same height. But he's strong. He works so hard all the time that it shouldn't surprise me, but it does. His back, his shoulders feel solid under my hands. The urge to dig deeper into his muscles—the urge surprises me.

He smells like grass. Like lake water and salty sweat. I have to keep myself from leaning in even more. Taking in deep breaths of him. JR's hand slides down to my lower back, pressing us closer together.

Our faces touch. Our cheeks. I tilt my head down to avoid being quite so close to him, but even then . . . even then he fills my senses. My nose in the softness of his hairline. My chin against the bare skin of his neck. He's so warm. I'm so warm.

Tears gather in my eyes and I can't do anything to stop them. Wiping them away would mean letting go of him. I can't let go of him.

My breath shudders—rattles—in my chest. He can feel it. I know he can. Then he reaches his other hand up to the back of my neck and into my hair and I stop breathing altogether.

My eyes open wide. My whole body stiffens.

I draw back—take a couple of steps away from him. Swipe at my eyes as I do, not wanting him to see. But he turns away, rubbing the side of his neck where I'd just been pressed against him.

My eyes flutter shut. "I've been really mad at you."

He lets out a sad laugh. "I know."

One step back from him, then another. I let my feet put more distance between us, nodding my head so fast—so much—that my neck starts to ache.

"I'm not mad anymore."

JR blows out a long breath. "That's good, I guess."

Our eyes finally meet. His eyes are too bright. Too shining. There's too much . . . something . . . in them. Something I don't want. My chest aches with how much I don't want it. I have to look away again.

"So . . . um . . . Linda and Ryan are going downtown for . . . um . . . ice cream," I manage to stammer out.

He looks at me across the darkened greenhouse. "You want to go meet them?"

I have to squeeze my eyes shut to get out any more words. Then they spill from me as if I have too many and they all need to get out at once. "It'd probably be fun, right?" My voice sounds pleading again. "Then we can come back here in the daylight so I can see your handiwork for real. Maybe even invite Linda and Ryan to come. I mean, I know it's our clubhouse, but it's not like we're little kids anymore, and . . ."

"Emma?"

"Yes, JR?" I look at him expectantly. Fear coils in my stomach. I have no idea what he's going to say.

He rubs his neck again. "Let's go find Ryan and Linda," he tells me. "I could use some ice cream."

I nod like a fool again. "Oh . . . okay . . . yes," I sputter. "That would be really good."

He grabs his book. Holds the door open for me as I pass through it into the warm evening air. We walk over the lawn and down to town to find our friends. The whole time, neither of us says a word. The whole time I stay far enough away from him so that our hands won't touch—so that no part of us will. I glance at him sideways but he's looking down at the road.

Tears fill my eyes again. I don't even know why anymore.

"Thank you for this," I say at last. "The greenhouse, I mean."

He nods.

The lights of Main Street glow up ahead. We'll find Ryan and Linda. We'll have some ice cream. And everything will be just like normal.

The way it should be.

CHAPTER 20

Lexi (Now)

Chloe texts again as I stop in my room to get the mosaic chest. That sound you hear is the impatient tap of my foot as I wait to hear from you, she wrote. I smile just a little as I write back about the historical society and the library, Ms. VanHill, and Casey.

What's Casey's deal? How old is he? Is he cute?

I shake my head. You're skipping over the important stuff, I tell her. And I'm not answering that question.

Three dots dance before her message pops up. That means he's cute. Don't do anything I wouldn't do.

I write back almost immediately. You don't even like guys. EVERYTHING with a guy is something you wouldn't do.

Rereading my last text I realize what I walked right into.

Does that mean you LIKE him? That you WANT to do things with him I wouldn't???

My cheeks burn, but there's no way I'm digging myself in deeper when there's nothing to dig deeper about. Instead, I put my phone in my pocket and head back to Ms. VanHill's suite.

By the time I get there, though, I'm out of breath and a little bit sweaty. When Casey opens the door all I can think about is Chloe's text. My face burns even hotter than before.

"You okay?" he asks, shooting a concerned look my way.

I force a smile. "Yeah, I'm good! Everything's great!"

He shakes his head as he holds the door open for me.

At a little table by a wide window, Ms. VanHill pours tea into three teacups.

"Are you on break?" I ask Casey. He wouldn't even talk to me because work was so important and now . . . what? He's sitting down for tea?

"I always take my break if Ms. VanHill wants some company," he replies, making the older woman smile.

"He's one of my favorite people," Ms. VanHill admits. "Such a lovely young man. A good listener. They don't make them like Casey anymore." She raises one eyebrow. "Come to think of it, they never did. We're in rare company."

Okay, maybe I'd drop everything to have tea with Ms. VanHill, too. Especially if she said stuff like that about me. Hell, if she said *anything* nice about me, someone would have to pick me up off the ground afterward.

As Casey sits down next to her, she pats his cheek in such a grand-motherly way it stops me cold. Something about them makes me tear up. It's hard to imagine what it would be like to have a grandmother. I never met either of mine and my grandfathers both died when I was really little. A twinge of longing lodges under my ribs. What would it be like to have a grandmother? Or even someone who acted like one? I guess it would be like what they have.

I wish I had something like they have.

Ms. VanHill loudly clears her throat. "Are you joining us, Lexi? Or will we have to eat with you hovering over us like an insect?"

Wow, she's *really* not saying nice things about me. Ms. VanHill glares at me expectantly, spurring me to action.

"Yes, of course I'm joining you!" I sit at the table.

Not only is there tea, but a plate of chocolate truffles, a tiny iced cake, and some scones.

"Lemon cake or truffles?" Ms. VanHill asks. "There are scones, too, as Casey has a bizarre obsession with what foods should be consumed at what time of day." She sniffs indignantly. "As if I care when I eat truffles or why."

A soft laugh chuffs out of Casey. It's the first time I've heard him laugh and it's . . . quiet. Not that he's loud in general. Except when he's annoyed with me.

"My mom's a nutritionist," he tells her. "I can't help it. She ruined me at an early age."

With another soft pat on his cheek, Ms. VanHill turns to me. "So what will it be?"

My mind wanders to the scones I ate yesterday and the ones I'll eat again later today. "Some lemon cake, please."

An approving nod from Ms. VanHill makes me sit up straighter.

Casey cuts me a slice while Ms. VanHill closes her eyes to savor a truffle. "There's nothing like Mischka's truffles. The man is an underappreciated genius."

"So you haven't been able to get him a raise yet?" Casey grins at her. He looks . . . good . . . with that particular expression on his face. Really good, actually.

Time to focus back in on Ms. VanHill telling Casey she's still campaigning for Mischka the truffle maker's giant raise and promotion. "It's only a matter of time before I wear down the *management*." Her voice drips with disdain. "That man wouldn't know a good chocolatier if one hit him over the head."

Casey chokes out a laugh at this dig at the person who, presumably, is his boss. "Maybe you can lobby for a raise for me, too."

"Done!" she declares. Her eyes settle on me and she grimaces. "What are you clinging to so fervently, Lexi?"

My shoulders stiffen. I hug my mom's mosaic chest even closer to me. I have no idea if she still wants to hear about it, or if Ms. VanHill only asked earlier to be polite. And I know Casey's interest is nonexistent.

"Um . . . it's my mom's stuff," I reply. "That I told you about before."

For a second, Ms. VanHill looks confused, but it passes. "Remind me of her name?"

"Emma," I tell her. "She was Emma Roth when she used to come here."

She grimaces. "Doesn't ring a bell. But then, I'm much older than your mother is."

I gulp down a mouthful of tea. "Was," I tell her. "She died twelve years ago."

For a second or two, Ms. VanHill just stares at me. Then her whole face softens. "I'm so sorry. Nothing is worse than losing someone you love."

Ms. VanHill's eyes stray to the coffee table by the sofa before she closes them. I follow her gaze, only to find a picture of her as a much younger woman with her arm around a white woman with pale hair and a beaming smile.

I have no idea who this woman is but it's clearly a painful memory.

But then Ms. VanHill opens her eyes again and focuses in on me.

"Show me what's in the box."

Slipping aside the slice of cake I still haven't touched, I put the chest on the tea table. "It's all old stories she jotted down, notes to one of her friends, drawings." I start laying the things I've already looked through on the table. Ms. VanHill and Casey take them up, one by one. As I wait for them to look through everything, I have to sit on my hands to keep from tearing through more of the mosaic chest.

Finally I can't help myself. I take out another little hotel notepad filled with my mom's writing from when she was younger. Ms. Van-Hill looks up at me. She's holding the napkin with the fudge smeared on it between her fingertips like it's the most distasteful thing she's ever had to touch. "*This* is one of your mother's treasures?"

"I mean, that's . . . it's just one of the things in there," I begin. I look down at what's in my hand. "There's lots more. This one is . . . it's . . ."

She drops the napkin back into the chest with a shudder. "Perhaps you could read that to us so we can judge for ourselves, since you seem at a loss for words?"

"Oh . . . of course," I tell Ms. VanHill. Then I start reading.

Today I:

1. Had tea with a bunch of ladies who talked my ear off about my future.

2. Got mad when they assumed my future equaled getting married to one of their sons and not having any kind of career of my own.

3. Got a lecture from Mom about how rude I was. (Apparently saying, "But 50% of marriages end in divorce, so I'll need a job when your son leaves me" doesn't qualify as polite.)

4. Ranted to JR about how much I hate being polite even though he says I'm never polite.

I sit back in my chair and smile. I mean, Mom is too much telling a bunch of stuffy women off when they assumed they could marry her off to their sons.

"Your mother sounds like you," Casey tells me.

"What?" No one's ever said anything like that to me before. Like, ever.

He blinks in surprise at my reaction. "I mean, the whole stubborn streak," he clarifies. "It must run in the family."

"Thanks," I say, even though I'm not sure if he meant it as a compliment. The idea of being like her warms something inside me. Plus, I don't mind if he thinks I'm stubborn. I could say the same about him, to be honest.

I flip to the next page, but the writing doesn't stop there. It's one long note that Mom wrote over lots of pages. I read it to Ms. VanHill and Casey.

I told JR I was polite ALL THE TIME even if I wasn't to him. "I need a secret identity as a supervillain so I can be as bad as I want."

JR shook his head at me. Big surprise.

"You could never pull off being a supervillain," he said. "You're way too nice."

The way he said "nice"—like it was an insult—aggravated me.

"It's a full moon tonight," he said. "Maybe you could turn into a werewolf."

"A werewolf?"

"Yeah. You know, once a month, you run around and do stuff you shouldn't," he told me. "Howl at the moon. Then go back to being your usual annoying self."

At first I thought he was trying to help. I should have known better.

"I'm going to do it," I said, mostly to shock him. It worked.

"You can't actually be a werewolf, you know," he informed me. "I was kidding."

But there's no way I was going to let JR of all people tell me what to do. "Well, I'm not kidding. I'm going to sneak out at midnight and be a werewolf."

"You're gonna get caught."

I lifted up one shoulder. A whole shrug was too much effort for a supervillain werewolf like me. And I knew he'd end up coming with me. I was just waiting for him to think it was his idea.

"I should probably come with you," he said. "To make sure you don't do anything dumb."

"Whatever. I don't care if you come or not."

JR can never resist doing what I don't want him to do.

For a second I stare at the page, not sure what else to do.

"Is that it?" Ms. VanHill demands. "She didn't finish the story?" She *tsk*s at me. "Incomplete storytelling would never have been acceptable when I was onstage." Then she stops to consider this. "Though nowadays, anything seems to go. Unsubtle sexed-up songs. Musicals about bodily fluids." She waves her hand dismissively. "It's absurd what gets produced."

My eyes move from her to the notepad and back again. I'm at a complete loss for words.

Ms. VanHill sighs. "Well, is there any more to the story or not?"

"Oh . . . I . . ." I turn to the next page, worried that Mom actually got into trouble for sneaking out and being a werewolf. And also worried that Ms. VanHill will lose interest. "There's more."

She raises her cane at me in a *Go on then, foolish girl* kind of way. I clear my throat. I keep reading.

We got caught. But only because we actually howled at the moon. If we'd kept our mouths shut, no one would have known we were there.

I snort out a nervous laugh and keep going.

Thankfully, we only got caught by JR's dad, who went from "What do you two think you're doing?" to laughing till he had tears in his eyes when we told him.

"Why don't you werewolves keep it down," he said. "Then you can keep doing . . . whatever it is werewolves do."

I couldn't believe he wasn't going to make us both go home.

"And try not to bite anyone," he called as he walked back to the staff housing. "I don't need more werewolves on my hands every full moon."

We agreed to stop howling much faster than we ever agree on anything. Then we went down to the lake and skipped stones and talked until the sun started to come up.

We really aren't such great werewolves.

A tiny watercolor of the full moon reflecting off the lake fills the last page of the notepad. I run my fingers over it before handing it to Ms. VanHill, who then passes it to Casey.

"So, your mother was an artist," Ms. VanHill says. "And, as Casey stated, rather stubborn."

"Don't forget a really bad werewolf," Casey adds. He turns the pages of the notepad over, rereading what she wrote. "Who's JR?"

"I have no idea," I admit.

"Maybe you could Google him?" Casey persists.

"I don't know his full name."

"But what about . . . ?"

I squeeze my eyes shut and rub my temples. "Casey, I don't know anything about him except that they were friends. Okay?"

He nods, a sheepish expression on his face. "Sorry. I was just trying to help."

"I know, but . . . ," I tell him. "But it's a dead end. Everything is a dead end."

Some part of me wonders if that's really true, though. I know JR was her friend. Maybe he was even the person she wrote the postcard to. Maybe he'll get it and call me?

Ms. VanHill is clearly thinking along at least some of the same lines. "*Nothing* is a dead end in this day and age," she informs me. "You young people should know that. You just don't have enough information yet to proceed."

The thing is, I haven't just started looking into this. I've been Googling Mom for ages.

Ms. VanHill touches my arm. She actually touches my arm. Like we're friends or something. A jolt of excitement goes through me.

"Someone I used to know said that despair is the refuge of small minds." She pauses. Rubs her jaw. "Though he turned out to have a pea-sized brain himself, so I suppose we can disregard his pithy saying."

Casey lets out another one of his quiet little laughs. I grin.

In return we get a majestic smile, which turns into something . . . else. For a split second she looks at me with confused eyes. "What were we talking about?"

"My mom?" I say. "Her friend JR?"

A regal nod meets my words. "We'll keep looking into it. I was *famous* for the research I did for every role when I was younger. I'll help you."

But just because Ms. VanHill thinks I'll find out more anything doesn't mean it will happen. The thought of looking into it together is a comfort, though.

"Yes," I tell her. "Let's do that."

For a few seconds, Ms. VanHill's eyes go soft, like she's still thinking about her research for old stage roles. Then, just as suddenly, she turns a sharp eye on me.

"What else is in the box?" she asks. "You shouldn't keep an old woman waiting like this."

My head spins ever so slightly, but I jump to attention anyway. Ms. VanHill doesn't seem like someone who likes waiting for what she wants.

"Well?" she persists, proving me right. "Read whatever's next."

Following her command, I look inside the mosaic chest to find something to read aloud to her and Casey. My fingers brush against a swatch of pale blue silky fabric. Then I see one diamond stud earring stuck into a piece of paper with At least I didn't lose both? scribbled on it.

Ms. VanHill shows zero interest in the jewelry, instead taking up the fabric. "Pure silk," she says. "Too high quality to waste on a stage costume." She pauses and looks out the window. "Award-show gown material. Or a wedding perhaps."

She pauses like she's deep in thought. "Did your mother ever get married? What's your father's name?"

"My mom and dad were married," I tell her. "His name's Matthew Carter."

"That doesn't a ring a bell either," she replies.

"He's from Saginaw," I tell her. "And from what he's said about when he was young, his family *definitely* didn't have enough money to come here. They met in college."

"Hm." Ms. VanHill strains her neck to peek into the chest. "What is that?" she asks, pointing to what now lies on top of the pile inside of it.

"Um . . ." I put the paper with the single earring aside to look at what's underneath.

It's a picture of two people standing close together, both with their backs to the photographer. The woman's dark updo is coming undone in unruly masses. I know that hair. I have it myself. *Mom.* It's got to be Mom. She wears a full-length dress. Maybe it's blue silk? It's hard to tell because they're outside in the dark on the verandah.

On the verandah of this hotel.

For a second, it's hard to breathe.

I mean, I knew she'd been here. Not just on the island, at this hotel. But knowing it and *seeing* it are completely different things. All I can do is stare at the picture. At her. Then I look at the guy next to her, his hand draped so low on her back it's almost inappropriate.

"Is this your mom?" Casey asks.

"I think it is," I almost whisper.

"You think?" Casey's eyebrows join over his nose in a unibrow of concern. Like the idea that I don't know for certain is unimaginable. And it should be. In a perfect world . . . hell, even in a not-perfect world . . . I'd have tons of pictures of her. I would've already known all about her summers here. But I don't.

"It's the hair," I continue, trying to make the situation less horrible. "My dad told me once that I had the same hair as her. Wild and unmanageable. So I'm pretty sure it's her." I pick up the picture again and look at the guy with her. "But that's *definitely* not my dad."

This guy's super tall, for one thing, and I would never, ever describe Dad as broad-shouldered. Besides, the guy in the picture both slouches and holds on to Mom in a lazing, sloping way. Like it had been too much effort to raise his arm onto her shoulders. Dad does not tolerate laziness. It's not a thing in our house.

So maybe it's JR? A fudge-stealing werewolf might be someone who looked this relaxed. Or it could be a random guy who she went to a formal dance with. It could literally be anyone.

"Was your mother married before she met your father?" is Ms. VanHill's next astonishing question.

My jaw drops.

"Oh, don't look so shocked," she says. "People remarry all the time. When I first knew Elizabeth Taylor, she'd already gotten hitched to husband number four." It's hard to process the words I'm hearing. Ms. VanHill knew Elizabeth Taylor. I mean, of course she did. She's Clara VanHill. But . . . wow.

Ms. VanHill, on the other hand, rolls her eyes at the very thought of the woman. "When she told me she planned to marry Dick Burton a second time, I sat her down with an extra-dry martini and tried to talk some sense into her. But would Liz listen?"

Casey and I look at each other. Neither of us knows the answer to this question.

"Um . . . no?" I venture.

"Of course not," Ms. VanHill says with a wave of her hand. "She never did. But hopefully your mother had more sense than that."

It takes me a second to think that over. "She and my dad had me when they were really young," I tell her. "They got married a year after I was born. I don't think she would've had time to get married before that."

"Hm . . . that's probably for the best," she says. "Remind me of your mother's name again?"

"Emma Roth," I tell her. "She changed it to Emma Carter after she married my dad."

"Yes, yes," Ms. VanHill says. "You told me that."

Without another word, Ms. VanHill pulls the chest toward her and peeks inside. "Oh my." She pulls out a small pile of postcards tied with a green ribbon. Then a strip of condoms.

"Oh my," echoes Casey, his face flushing.

Somehow this makes me laugh. "My mom was . . . something. "

"Well, at least she was responsible," Ms. VanHill informs me. "You should always practice safe sex." She points a stern finger first at me and then at Casey.

If he'd been embarrassed before, Casey's actually cringing now.

"Don't look so mortified, young man," Ms. VanHill tells him. "I had too many friends die during the AIDS epidemic. Too many gifted, beautiful people in the theatre gone before we even knew what the disease was or how to prevent it. Using protection is of the utmost importance."

It's like Casey and I both have whiplash.

"I . . . I'm so sorry, Ms. VanHill," he stammers out. "I didn't mean to make light of . . ."

She pats his arm again. "No, I know you didn't," she says. "But you really should use condoms when you have sex. And perhaps have a supply at the ready so that you're not caught unprepared should the occasion *arise*, so to speak."

"Okaaaayyyy," Casey says, getting to his feet. "Well . . . I've gotta get back to work."

"Take the tray with you," Ms. VanHill says. "Please."

Then she turns to me. "You should go along as well," she says. "Let an old woman get some rest." She slowly rises from her chair. When I put out a hand to help her, she bats me away.

So I collect my mom's stuff and head to the door.

"But you may come visit again tomorrow," Ms. VanHill says, like she's the queen granting permission for an audience. "Both of you. Bring the box, Lexi."

As Casey and I walk to the service elevator something inside me breaks. "Thank you, thank you, thank you." I throw my free arm around him.

"Um . . . you're welcome?" Casey pulls away from me. "I'm not sure what you're thanking me for anyway. She didn't know your mom."

"No," I agree. "But she does know just about everything else. She gave me so much to think about. Plus, she's *Clara VanHill*!"

Casey pushes his cart toward the elevator. "Glad it helped," he says quietly. "Maybe if you keep showing her stuff something will ring a bell."

But it already helped. I know JR's dad lived in staff housing. Mom and her date were at a formal here.

I open my phone and look at Chloe's latest text. **WHAT'S HAP-PENING????**

I have so much to tell you, I punch in. Call you later.

Today, I'll do more Googling. Tomorrow I'll go see Ms. VanHill again. And I'll keep trying not to have a small mind that despairs.

CHAPTER 21

Emma (Then)

I t took four days to get the supplies Clarice ordered in. During that time, I had a whole slew of things that needed to be done. For the first time in my entire life, I hit the hotel's business center. It's small—the hotel does everything it can to discourage working and using technology while you're here—but packed with computers and printers and even a fax machine. I'd hoped it would be empty so I could really focus all my attention on making fliers, but instead I found a man at a computer frantically typing up written notes and a woman pacing the room in frustration as she talked to someone she works with. I turned on a computer as far away from either of them as possible, not wanting their negative energy to curse my class preparation. Then I got to work. I had fliers to make, after all. Big type so kids and parents would notice it. Key details. Even some clip art of paintbrushes and artist's easels.

All of this gets printed up on brightly colored paper—yellow and orange, pink and blue—so that they'll stand out. I still have to post the fliers all over the hotel and grounds, remind Clarice to put the art classes on the activities schedule, and organize the supplies into bins.

By the time I walk down to where my little class will meet—arms full of markers and paper, plastic tablecloths and smocks—I'm practically tripping with excitement.

Two picnic tables sit in the shady part of the lawn. I chose the spot myself, one that not only has shade but contains every imaginable color green. It's so beautiful that it's impossible *not* to want to create art when you're sitting here.

At least I hope it will be.

After spreading the tablecloths over the two tables, it's time to set up the art supplies. Three sets of markers on both tables. Tablets of paper. A smock on every chair. Between the green grass and trees, white tablecloths, blue and yellow smocks, and a rainbow of markers, this little outdoor classroom looks like a work of art all by itself.

I stand back to admire it—wishing that the hotel had had something like this when I was a kid. Hopefully the little ones here now will enjoy it. Or at least a few of them? I glance down at my watch. 2:55. Class starts in five minutes. Then my eyes scan around the lawn. No one seems to be coming in this direction.

But I'm always late for everything, I remind myself. And everyone here's on vacation—they're in no rush to be anywhere, let alone a hotel activity. I sit at one the tables. After a few seconds, I get back up again. The markers look like they should be rearranged by color families, so I do that. Straighten the smocks. Make sure the tablecloths are even.

I look at my watch again. 2:59.

I tap my fingers on the table. Oh God, what if nobody comes at all? What if I have to go home and admit to my dad that my perfect idea for working at the hotel fell flat? I wipe the sweat away from the back of my neck before it drips down my back.

This is fine. The people in the business center didn't curse my art class. Curses aren't even real.

"Is this where art is?" A little girl who's maybe seven tugs at my dress.

I gulp in a deep breath. "Yes, this is where art is!" I tell her. "You can sit wherever you want and put on a smock."

She waves to her parents before getting down to business. Smock on, markers out. She couldn't care less that no one else is here. She didn't come to play.

I could learn something from this kid.

Twin boys show up, their pale skin burnt red from the sun. Their mom looking harried as she drops them off. Three girls who must be around ten show up together with no parents in sight—clearly too big to need supervision on their way to art class.

A little boy with dark skin and eyes and sand in his hair introduces himself as Devon Burgess the third and formally shakes my hand.

In the end there are ten kids, who look as if they range between ages five and ten.

I take a minute to introduce myself and to have them do the same. The kids go around and tell me their names and how old they are. One of the twins crosses his arms and says, "I hate art. I'm only here because *he* wanted to come," pointing to his brother, "and Mom made me come with him."

I smile at him, too. "That's fine," I reply. "You can just doodle if you want."

He narrows his eyes at me. "You can't doodle in class."

"Good thing this isn't school then," I tell him.

He still doesn't look convinced, but his brother is already digging in.

It takes everyone else all of three minutes to sort out who's using which markers and to start making their drawings.

If this little tableau—the colorful tables and the shady green and *everything*—was beautiful before, it's so much more so now. But as I move from kid to kid talking to them about their art, it all gets even better.

Tobias from Des Moines draws what looks like a floating futuristic city in the clouds. "On Jupiter," he tells me. "It's a gas planet so it can't be on the ground."

I look at it for a second. "I'd live there."

He holds it up, looking at it with a critical eye. "Me too."

The three older girls—Anais, Ivy, and Camila—are drawing on paper and all over each other's arms.

Then Devon Burgess the third pulls at my hand. "Do you think my sister Jeannie will like the picture I made of her?"

I squint at the drawing in question. The face looks as if it could possibly be his sister. I mean, she's clearly not another *species*. But he's filled her face, arms, and legs in bright red. There are horns involved, as well as a long tail with an arrow at the end of it.

"Well . . . you made her into a devil," I tell him.

He grins at me. "Looks just like her."

The twin who wanted to come today has drawn a scene with snow-capped mountains and a cloudy sky with a rainbow cutting through it. But it's his brother—the one who didn't want to be here—whose work catches my eye. He's filled nearly every inch of the white paper with doodles in bright magenta—birds, dragons, candles, tents. There are even places where he's made words in a style that looks like graffiti.

"It's really interesting," I tell him. "If you want to take paper with you when you leave, you should."

His magenta marker stills on the page for a second. Then he goes back to his work again without another word. I move on to give him space to create.

By the end of class, everything is a complete mess.

Devon's dad comes to retrieve him, little sister in hand. After he explains what he's drawn, his dad gasps out an "Oh boy."

Devon shows the drawing to his little sister. "Now you know what you really look like."

She seems confused. "I have a tail?"

I try not to laugh as their dad ushers them away, calling out his thanks to me as they go.

By the time all of their parents come to collect them, I'm exhausted but also . . . not? Is that possible? It was only an hour, but they kind of wore me out. They were also funny, creative, and honest. *I like this,* I realize. I liked this class. And working with them all. Dropping onto a picnic bench, I breathe a sigh of relief. One class down, and . . . it went well. The doodling twin even snuck a small pile of drawing paper away when he thought I wasn't looking.

For the first time ever, the thought that I could teach art pops into my head. Not just for the summer. I could it do it for a job—go to art school and teach and create my own work.

I'm almost looking forward to telling my parents about it tonight. Dad especially. Maybe he could come to a class someday. Then he could see what I want to do before I tell him. He could see that I'm good with the kids.

For now, though, I have to clean up this mess and get everything back to the activities office before I get down to the other work I need to do today: finish my final piece to submit to the gallery.

Mom's at a dinner meeting right now and Dad's eating with Jackson, so I have the whole kitchen to myself. I don't have a lot of time to work with, though, so I set a timer on the stove to make sure I don't get caught.

Gathering the supplies I needed to work on this piece has taken a village. Linda got me a wide foil pan from the kitchen so I can keep the wax soft on the stove. JR got me a scraper as well as the piece of wood that I'm making it on. Even Ryan's helped—though his help has mainly taken the form of stopping by while I'm working to massage my shoulders and talk to me. It's more distracting than actually helpful. I can't bring myself to mind.

The piece I'm making is nearly done, lying rigid on the top of my closet when I'm not working on it since I don't want my parents to see it till the night of the gallery show. If the gallery takes my pieces. Which it might not. It might be one more thing that I'm cursed about.

No, I'm not going to do this to myself. Class went well today, this will, too.

I tie my hair back—wax in this mop is *not* fun to deal with—and put on an old apron.

Wax melted. Pigment and paint added. Time to do this.

I've been layering the wax and 3D elements—not just the ones I gathered at the beach, but ribbons and twine, sand and soil—on top of each other in such a way that they're rising off the wood like a carving in relief. More wax, more whittling away to make shapes and surfaces. Another layer of the blue ribbon from my old hair tie with a spattering of green paint and clear wax over it. Pine scales painted white and others a deep rust color.

As one layer of wax dries I add another, scraping away at what I don't need to form ridges and lines. Peaks and valleys emerge on the wood. I've never done this before, but I'm definitely going to do it again.

After a while, I stand back and look at what I've made, a rush of pride warming me from the inside out. I love this piece. I've loved every minute I've worked on it. But it's a risk—I know that. The gallery's probably looking for polite landscapes and architectural renderings. Not the chaos I've created.

I want them to take it so desperately I can almost taste it. Or maybe that's the smell of the hot pigment and wax finally getting to me? Either way, I want this. I need something concrete to show my dad—something that will let him finally understand why I need to carve out my own path.

I smudge one last edge in the upper righthand corner and try to look at it objectively, but I'm not sure I can anymore. A knock at the front door startles me enough that I clasp my chest and drop a waxy paintbrush on the floor.

Then I panic. No one's supposed to be here till seven. At least. I thought I had more time to clean up and to get my piece safely back in the closet till I can bring it to the gallery in the morning.

Another knock.

Okay, it can't be my parents because they have keys. I wipe my hands on my apron. This is not a big deal. I peek through the hole in the door to discover Linda standing outside of it, still wearing her work uniform, and nearly collapse from relief.

Swinging the door open, I grab her arm. "Come in quick."

She lets me drag her into the kitchen and then stops short. "What's that smell?" She scrunches up her whole face in distaste. "It smells like something died in here."

I point to the mess on the table. "It's the wax and the pigment. And the paint." I run my hands through my ponytail. "It's all of it, I guess."

Linda twists up her mouth. "Have you eaten dinner yet?"

I shake my head.

"Have you finished your work yet?"

Once more I tug her by the arm, this time to show her what I've made. Linda's eyes widen, but she doesn't say a word. A knot forms in my stomach as I wait for her to say something—anything—about my work.

Finally she rubs her chin. Puts her hand over her mouth. Then she shakes her head and starts to laugh.

"Oh, Linda . . . please don't," I plead. "Even if you don't like it, please don't make fun of me, I . . ."

She gives me a shove. "Shut up," she says. "I'm not making fun of you. It's just . . . I can't believe you actually made this. It's . . ."

My hands clasp over my stomach and I squeeze myself, hard.

"It's just . . . different," she says.

Well, she's not making fun of it, I guess, but this isn't much better really. Slowly, carefully, I start to clean up the mess I've made. Putting everything back where it belongs is so much more depressing than taking it all out to work with, but it has to be done. Now.

When I turn around, Linda's still standing there with her hand over her mouth. After a few seconds, she looks up. "Come here," she says. "Right now."

I hold up a full trash bag. "Um . . . I have to throw this away, so . . ."

She holds up both hands as if she's so frustrated with me she can't even handle it. "Right now!"

A jolt of worry hits me in the gut as I walk over to her.

Linda throws her arms around me and practically tackles me into a hug. "You're so damn talented," she says into the side of my head. "I can't even believe I'm friends with you sometimes."

I pull away from her, needing to see if she really means it. Linda's shaking her head again. "I don't know how you even *did* this"—she gestures to my art—"it's so good."

Tears sting at my eyes. I have to tent my fingers over my mouth, my nose, to keep myself from crying. "You like it?"

"Oh my God, really?" she says. "Do I have to rent a plane and have it written across the sky in smoke for you or something?"

I shake my head over and over again. "No . . . I . . . I'm just so worried they won't take it and . . ."

Suddenly she tackles me again. "You're gonna be a famous artist," she says. "And when I'm rich and have my own business, I'm going to buy up all your art and hang it around my mansion."

I'm laughing and crying at the same time. "I'll give you art. You won't have to buy it."

Linda steps back from me. "Nah, I'm a capitalist, remember? I pay for the goods I consume."

This makes me laugh outright. "Then pay me all the money. I won't complain!"

She looks at the piece I made again and whistles before looking back at me. "Go clean up," she says. "And put that thing away." She nods to my art. "I'm going to make cookies so this place will smell like chocolate and not like dead possum."

My whole face lights up. "We're having cookies for dinner?"

"I already ate," she informs me. "*You're* having cookies for dinner. Now go clean up!"

I take her advice. Tossing the trash down the chute at the end of the hall. Stowing all my supplies away in my desk. And finally—finally—carrying my piece back into my bedroom. I look at it one last time and cross my fingers.

Tomorrow it goes to the gallery. Tomorrow it's out of my hands.

CHAPTER 22

Emma (Then)

The poster on the marquee outside the gallery says, *Exhibition Opening: Island Illuminated—Local Art by Local Artists*. As soon as I see it, my heart takes a little dive into what feels like the lower cavities of my stomach.

The day Mathilde, the gallery owner, called to tell me my work got accepted into the show was one of the best days of my life. I was so shocked at first that I couldn't even speak. She thought we'd been disconnected, I hadn't said anything for so long. Then I ran to find Ryan and he spun me around in his arms till I got dizzy. We found Linda and JR after work. We ate ice cream and fudge till we were so stuffed we had to hop a carriage ride home.

And now it's all happening. We're here. I dig my hands into the pockets of my sundress and cross my fingers. I even cross my toes over the divider of my flip-flops. I need all the luck I can get tonight.

My mom slips her hand through my arm, and I glance over at her to find her smiling her widest, rarest smile. "This is lovely," she says as we walk up to the door. "What a nice idea to showcase local artists." She gives my arm a squeeze. "I'm so glad you invited us tonight. We never do anything just the three of us anymore."

Something inside me crumbles at her words. Because I didn't just invite them so we could spend time together. Not even close.

"Mmm," I get out, but that's all I can manage.

The minute we step inside the gallery, I cross my fingers again. I want them to like what I've done. I want them to be proud of me. But more than anything, I want them to see that this is what I want to do with my life. There's so much riding on the two pieces of art hanging on the far wall of the gallery that I worry I'm going to puke up the heart I've just recently swallowed.

"Should we do the full tour around?" Dad suggests.

"Let's do it!" Mom replies.

She leads the way to the first part of the exhibition, a group of sculptures made from raw materials found on the island. As my parents discuss the driftwood and stone creations, my eyes stray to the corner of the gallery where my own work hangs on a stark white wall. There I see JR and Terry. Terry's saying something, but JR's just staring at the encaustic as if he's actually pondering my work.

"Terry!" I hear my mother call across the room.

JR's dad turns and smiles at her before he and JR walk over to join us. Terry's dressed for the occasion—a button-down shirt and khakis. JR, on the other hand, is in old ripped jeans and a sweatshirt. If I had any energy to get annoyed with him I would.

"Nice to see you, Jessica," Terry says, leaning in to give her a quick half hug. "You too, Richard."

Dad smiles as Mom puts her hand on Terry's shoulder. "I've barely seen you lately, but the lilies are beyond gorgeous this summer. I don't know what you're doing to make them blossom the way they are, but it's working."

My mom and Terry light into a conversation about the landscaping at the hotel as Dad follows them to the next artist's work.

"Do they know yet?" JR asks in a low voice.

I shake my head. "I'm going to let them walk around and find it on their own. Then *surprise!*"

He takes a good look at me. "Are you okay?" he asks. "'Cause you look a little green."

"Not tonight, JR," I say through gritted teeth. "I can't do this tonight."

For a long moment or two, he doesn't say another word. Then

he nods toward my stuff. "It came out great," he says. "I kinda can't believe what you made with a few candles and some sticks."

I glare at him, ready for a fight, but he's not being sarcastic. "You . . . you like it?"

He gives me a sideward glance. Our eyes meet. "I think it's the best thing you've ever made."

Air rushes out of my lungs, and with it just a tiny bit of my anxiety does, too. "Thank you," I whisper.

Then I see my parents and Terry standing in front of my work. I can just hear Terry's voice over the crowd saying, "This is some talented artist. Best in the whole gallery," to Mom. Dad turns to me with a perplexed look on his face. Before I have time to respond, his expression changes again—this time to a forced smile as he glances past me. I turn to find the entire Desmond family coming into the gallery.

Dad's jaw tightens. He straightens his shoulders as if he's going into battle.

Grabbing JR by the arm I say, "If my dad tries to kill me tonight, you'll stop him, right?"

"Your dad's not going to kill you," he assures me.

"No, but really," I tell him. "Promise me you won't let him."

JR's eyebrows knit together but he nods solemnly. "I promise I won't let anyone murder you," he says. "Including your dad."

The potential murderer in question crosses the room, just barely glancing at JR and me before going to shake hands with Mr. Desmond and give Mrs. Desmond a peck on the cheek. Ryan and Linda escape to find us almost immediately.

"Do they know yet?" Linda asks.

"Yes."

Someone touches my shoulder, and I find my mother standing there. "I had no idea your art was in this show," she says to me. Then her eyes take in my friends, all gathered around me. "Though apparently I'm in the minority about that."

I have to gulp down a breath—and then some bile that's risen up in my throat.

"I wanted to surprise you," I try to explain. "I wanted to you to see the kind of work I've been doing so that you could—"

"Here's the artist now!" Mrs. Desmond says. She gives me a big hug. "I can't wait to see your paintings. Where are they, Emma?"

With a shuddery breath, I point her in the direction of my stuff.

"You must be so proud," she says to my mother. "Emma's so talented. Linda's always talking about the things she makes."

Their voices fade as they move away, my mom giving me one last confused glance as they go.

"You good?" JR asks.

When I shake my head no, Ryan takes my hand and gives it a squeeze while Linda grabs the other. She pulls me from the spot I've been frozen to.

"Let's walk around and see all the other art."

I nod just once and start to follow her when Terry walks up to us. "I'm taking off," he says to JR. "But I want to congratulate the artist before I do." He gives me a big hug. "Your stuff is beautiful," he says in my ear. "Glad the garden tools helped."

"Thank you," I reply, my voice barely a whisper.

Then he's gone. Ryan and Linda, with a little help from JR, keep up a running commentary on the other art in the gallery, but I can't really listen. On the other side of the room, my mom is standing by herself in front of my work, staring at it.

"Give me a second," I tell the others.

"What do you think?" I ask as I approach her. My hands shake so hard I have to clasp them together.

"I think they're lovely," she tells me. "I've always known what a talented artist you are."

"But?" I venture.

"But nothing," she replies. "The painting is very pretty. And this one"—she points to the encaustic—"is far beyond just being pretty."

"Thanks, Mom," I exhale.

Her eyes are already back on my gallery entries again. "Why didn't you tell us about this, Emma?"

It's a good question. A fair one. My friends and even their parents knew ahead of time.

"I really did want to surprise you," I tell her. "I wanted you both to see my work with other artists' and in a real gallery and I . . ." I have to wrap my arms around my stomach to keep myself together. "I wanted you to understand how much this means to me."

Mom slips her arm into mine again and I lean into her. "I think I understand," she replies. "And I can see why you'd tell your friends, even if you wanted to surprise us." Mom's eyes move to take in Dad and Mr. Desmond as they talk nearby. "Dad's a little shaken, though. Especially since all your friends' parents clearly knew about it."

"I know."

Mom pulls me along with her as she moves to the next artist's work. "I'm well aware of what it's like to want to follow your heart, love," she begins. "But you—"

"Emma?" my father's voice cuts through Mom's, interrupting her. He holds his arm out, gesturing for me to go with him, so I do.

But once we're alone, Dad doesn't seem to have a whole lot to say. His eyes move around the gallery, snagging now and then on my friends.

"Um . . . are you enjoying the show?" I ask tentatively.

He nods and glances around the room. "There are a lot of . . . interesting . . . pieces."

It's hard to swallow down my fear and my pride to ask the next question on my lips. "What do you think of mine?"

Dad meets my eyes at last. "They're wonderful," he replies. "You've always been creative. I'm not surprised they wanted your work in here."

I watch him for any sign that he's upset or angry, but he just keeps looking around the gallery.

"It's just that I thought you wanted to spend time with us," he explains in an undertone. "I didn't realize that . . . that this was why."

"Dad, I always want to spend time with you guys!" I protest. "And wanting to share my art with you . . . that's not a bad thing. I wanted to surprise you."

"You did."

Those two words fall heavy between us.

Using my forearm, I wipe the sweat off my forehead. I dab at my cheeks. It's so hot in this room. I need some air.

Then I realize that Dad maybe could use some, too. For some reason, he looks suddenly old to me. Maybe it's the white light of the gallery or how hard he's been working lately, but he seems . . . weary.

"I heard from Clarice that your art classes are going well," he says at last. "And now you're in a gallery exhibit."

This is my chance—my chance to tell him what I've been thinking about teaching and being an artist. All of it. I rub my hands together. All I have to do is tell him.

"Dad, this is what I want to do," I force myself to say. I put my hand on his arm. "I . . . I love teaching. I love the kids. And if I got a job as an art teacher, I would have time when I'm not working to make my own art."

For so long—an eternity it feels like—Dad doesn't say a word. We just stand here, facing each other. His eyes on the ground. Mine pleading with him to look up and talk to me.

"You know I want you to be happy," he says at last. "And we've tried to give you every opportunity to be creative and to . . ." He rubs his hand over his eyes. "But this isn't realistic, Emma," he says. "You have to think about the future. Yours and Mom's and mine. Who's going to run the business when we're gone?"

I step away from him, feeling sick again. I didn't want to have to come out and say the actual words. In the back of my mind, I'd hoped he'd understand without me having to spell it all out. To say the one thing I know he doesn't want to hear.

But there's no other choice. As much as I wish we didn't, we *have* to talk about this. "Dad?"

With a shake of his head, he looks over at me. His eyes are creased with worry. If he looked old before, now he . . . he's wrecked.

"Dad, I don't want to run the business."

He closes his eyes. This is his worst nightmare. I know it is. I know I'm the worst daughter in the world for doing this to him, but I can't live someone else's life.

"I . . . I know what I want to do," I keep going. "I'm so, so sorry."

A bitter laugh bursts from him. "And how do you expect to pay for your life when you're making pennies as an art teacher?"

"I'll be fine!" I argue. "I don't need you to pay for my life!"

His nostrils flare. "I already pay for your life," he reminds me. "Who do you think pays for your art supplies and all these dresses?" He gestures to my pale lilac sundress. "Your shelter and food? Where do you think all that money comes from?"

His voice rises with each word he says. People around us are starting to stare.

"Dad, we—"

"It's through hard work, Emma," he cuts in. "*My* hard work. And sometimes even that's not enough. When business is slow, when we're having a hard time keeping things afloat, what do you do to help? Not a damn thing." He takes a deep breath and forces it out through his mouth. "So don't tell me that art is your life's work, because it's not. It can't be."

I step back, a sob growing in my throat. "I can't talk to you about this right now."

But he follows me.

"Then when are we going to talk about it?" he presses. "When's a good time for you? Let me know and I'll schedule it in like I did our little family outing tonight." The bitterness in his voice is more than I can bear. He's never spoken to me like this before. Ever. Even when I did fresh things when I was little. Even when I'd clearly disappointed him in the past.

Dad points his finger down at the floor. "We need to talk about this now," he insists, "so that we're both clear about how we're going to move forward."

"Dad, we're in the middle of the gallery!" I say in a low voice. "Do you really want to talk about how useless art is here?"

He glances around the room. Mom still stands by my artwork, her hand covering her mouth. The Desmonds exchange glances in another corner of the room. Linda's looking at me with so much sympathy in her eyes that I start to tear up again. JR's mouth is a grim line. Both of Ryan's hands are balled up in fists. All of the other artists—their families and friends—they all stare at us. Dad's not only ruined my big night, he's ruined theirs, too.

Taking me by the elbow, he leads me to the gallery's door. "Then let's go outside." Just before he pulls me out the door, Ryan steps in front of us.

"Emma, are you ready to go?" he asks me, not even looking at my dad.

"She's not going anywhere tonight, Ryan," Dad says. "You two can make plans another time. Emma wants to spend time with family tonight." His voice drips with such irony that it actually gives me a chill.

"Ryan, can you come with me?" his father interrupts. "I need to have a word."

His eyes flash at his dad. "Not now, Dad."

"It'll only take a minute," Mr. Desmond says, taking Ryan by the arm. "And Richard and Emma look like they're busy anyway."

He starts to tug Ryan away, but Ryan pulls back. "You know what, Dad? No," he says. "I'm not your puppet. You can't just tug at my strings and expect me to do whatever you want."

A blood vessel in Mr. Desmond's temple pulsates. "Can we not have this same conversation again?"

"That sounds really good to me," Ryan tells him. Then he turns to me, holding out his hand. "Let's get out of here, Emma."

Dad tries to hold me back, but I shake free of him. The hurt in his eyes—the hurt I've caused him—makes me hiccup out a sob.

"I'm sorry," I say.

Then I take Ryan's hand and I'm gone. As soon as we get outside of town, everything I've been holding back all night bursts from me.

Without a word, Ryan pulls me into his arms. I can't look at him. I can barely stop choking on my own sobs. I hide my face in his shoulder and cry until my eyes are swollen, stinging.

"Sorry," I whisper as I wipe my eyes on his shirt.

"You don't have to apologize to me."

But I do have to apologize to so many other people. My dad, my mom, Mathilde for causing a scene at her event. Ryan puts his arm around me and leads me toward the hotel. But we don't go through the gate or up to the hotel itself. We walk across the lawn till he pulls me to a stop.

"Are you okay?"

I shake my head. "Not really."

He smooths back my hair. "I'm really sorry that happened. I thought this was going to be your night of triumph."

I let my head fall back onto his arm. "Not so much."

"You were the best artist there," he tells me. "Nothing else even came close."

"Ryan, you don't have to . . ."

Leaning in toward me, Ryan presses the gentlest of kisses on my forehead. I close my eyes and let out a shaky breath. He takes my face in his hands and kisses my temple this time. My cheek.

When I open my eyes again, I find him looking down at me as if I'm some special gift he's been given.

"Nothing else even came close," he whispers before leaning in to hug me again.

But I reach up and stop him. I feel jagged—as if someone's cut me open and left me to bleed out every horrible thought and emotion I've had tonight. My eyes are swollen. I'm a mess.

"There's no one like you, Emma," he says. "Not anywhere in the whole world."

Even if I'm a mess, he's not. He never is. His hair almost glows in the moonlight. His eyes shine with a soft light and with . . . with . . .

I take both his hands and wrap them around me. "I need to kiss you," I tell him. "Would you . . . would that maybe be something you want to do?"

Instead of answering my question, he enfolds me in his strong arms and brushes his lips against mine, once, twice—the softest of touches—and I kiss him back. Ryan tangles his fingers in my hair and pulls me into a hug. As I lean my head on his shoulder, I open my eyes to look out at this beautiful night.

Then I see him. JR stands about twenty feet away from us, staring like he's seen a ghost. For a long second or two, neither of us looks away. I keep thinking he's going to keep walking—past us, down the path, and to his dad's place. But he turns around and disappears into the trees instead.

I have to swallow down a sob that rises in my throat.

Ryan holds me even closer. "I like you so much," he says in a low voice. "I've wanted this to happen for so long."

I pull away from him and look up into his eyes. He smiles at me in a way that reflects what he just told me in words.

"I like you, too," I tell him.

The smile on his face blooms into something so big—so glowing—that it makes my face, my neck burn up.

"So at least there's that, right?" he says hopefully.

I turn my head, glancing back at town and then through the trees where JR disappeared, before looking up at Ryan again.

"At least there's that."

CHAPTER 23

Emma (Then)

The next morning, Linda calls in sick and drags me down to Viola's bench so that I'm not sitting around the hotel all day. There's a cool wind whistling through the trees—one that I couldn't feel at all back at the hotel. I close my eyes and lift my face to it, letting it blow my hair around my neck and evaporate the sweat under my arms and down my back.

"I brought cookies," Linda says, pulling a brown bag out of her backpack. "And water."

This pulls me up short. "Wait . . . you called in sick but still went down to the kitchen to steal cookies?"

She shrugs. "I'm pretty stealthy. I don't think anyone saw me."

When my jaw drops, she rolls her eyes. "Who cares if anyone saw me?" she says. "I only took the job to show my dad what a great work ethic I have in comparison with my dear brother. And he didn't care at all." She leans back on the bench, pulling her knees up under her.

I lean against her. "So you stole cookies?"

"My dad did say recently that I was free to do whatever I want."

But that brings up another big question—one that I want to know the answer to. "So what are you going to do?"

Linda rummages through the bag instead of answering. She hands me a double chocolate cookie and then takes one out for herself. "I'm going to go to college," she says. "Figure out what kind of business I want to run. Then start it up." After a tiny nibble on her cookie she sighs. "The idea of starting up a rival car company has occurred to me. Just to be spiteful after Ryan runs the company into the ground."

I laugh out loud. "Poor Ryan. He has no idea what's coming for him."

Her elbow nudges mine and I push back into her. "You can't start defending Ryan now that you're making out with him," she informs me. "Bros before hoes, Emma."

My jaw drops again. "I can't *believe* you just said that!"

She lets out a low laugh. "It's true, though!"

I sigh and let out a weary laugh, too. "What are we going to do?"

A long silence meets my question. Finally I look over at her.

Linda sits up. "Since we're sitting on Viola's bench, I think the real question is, what would *Viola* do. And I think we both know the answer to that."

I think that over for a second. "She'd become an art teacher and world-famous artist."

"And start her own business and be *wildly* successful."

The wind picks up, blowing Linda's hair into her mouth—forcing her to spit it back out again. This makes me laugh out loud for some reason.

"And get a really kickass dog to leave all the money she made to," Linda adds.

"Because who else would you leave your elementary school teacher's fortune to?"

Linda takes another bite of cookie. "So that's what we should do. Right down to the kick-ass dog."

I breathe in through my nose and let it out in a long whoosh through my mouth. "We have a plan then."

"And our dads can go straight to hell if they don't like it," she replies.

The only problem with this plan is that Linda *can* forge her own path. Her dad wants her to so Ryan can run the business. She can start over with something else. And she'll be incredible. But if I don't take over for Dad, things will just . . . fall apart.

I take a bite of my cookie but can't really enjoy it anymore.

Linda nudges me. "You look like your imaginary dog just died," she says. "What's going on?"

But I can't honestly tell her what's going through my head—I don't want to diminish what she's dealing with in any way. "Nothing new," I reply. "Just thinking."

Linda grabs a new cookie from the bag. "Well stop thinking," she replies. "And start enjoying the wonders of my company."

I snort out a little laugh. "Wonders?"

She jumps up from the bench and spreads her arms at her sides, a cookie still in one hand. The wind blows her light hair around her face in a swirl. She'd look like something out of a Renaissance painting right now—like Aphrodite emerging from her shell—if she wasn't wearing jeans and a debate team shirt from her old school that says *In Pursuit of Dispute*.

"Yes, wonders," she tells me. "Stand in awe of me and the friendship I provide you with, Emma!"

I double over, laughter pouring from me. "I'm in awe!"

She sits down next to me. "As you should be," she says, straightening her T-shirt. "I brought you cookies, didn't I?"

"Ones you had to risk your job to obtain," I concede.

Linda looks at me for a second, then holds her cookie up, touching it to mine. "To our dads," she says. "Who don't deserve a cookie toast and definitely don't deserve us."

"To our dads," I repeat, laughing just a little. It's quickly followed by a sigh. "What are we going to do, Linda? I mean, really, what are we going to do?"

"Well," she says. "I'm going to go home and take a nap to sleep off all these cookies. You're going to teach little monsters how to make art." She glances sideways at me. "And rumor has it you're going out with Ryan later."

"I am," I agree. "He's meeting me right after my class to whisk me off to destinations unknown."

"I know where you're going, and it's definitely someplace you know," she replies. "But it's also kind of sweet."

I nearly drop my cookie. "Wait . . . are you complimenting Ryan?"

"Only because he's trying to be good to you," Linda admits. "Mostly he's an annoying dolt, but he has his moments."

Linda gets up and pulls me into a one-armed hug. "Have fun with Ryan," she says. "And try to relax a little, okay?"

"Okay, I promise."

By the time I reach the picnic tables eighteen kids already there. *Eighteen.* The most kids who've shown up so far. For a second or two I blink at them, clutching my stomach in worry.

"Oh . . . wow . . . ," I say. "We're a nice, big crowd today!"

"Good luck," says one of the moms. "I'll be at the bar if anything comes up."

It doesn't sound as if she really means it.

I watch this enormous group, crowded at the two tables, who look to range in age from about five to about twelve, and sigh. I'm not sure I'm up for this today. Though I'm pretty positive I don't have much choice in the matter.

"Okay," I call out in a loud voice. "Who's ready to make some sculptures?"

The kids all cheer as I hand out the clay they're going to use. For the first fifteen minutes, I wander back and forth, helping whoever needs help as they work quietly. Shortly afterward, things begin to dissolve. And I know—I know the minute the first piece of clay flies from one table to the next—that there's going to be no salvaging this. There's going to be a clay fight and their parents who are off drinking or having spa treatments are going to be furious when they pick up their kids all covered in gunk.

A blotch of clay hits my face. The heat rises in my cheeks. Can nothing go right anymore? Can I just have this one thing not be a fiasco?

Then I hear it above the chaos.

"LISTEN UP!"

The kids all stop and look in the direction of Ryan Desmond, standing at the edge of the picnic area with his hands on his hips. I've never been so relieved to see him in my entire life.

"What's going on here?" he asks them. "Clay's not for throwing, is it, Emma?"

"No, it's *definitely* not."

"Then keep the clay on the tables," he tells them. "And out of each other's hair. Got it?"

They all look at him as if he's a superhero or something. To be fair, with the windswept blond hair, broad shoulders, and sparkling blue eyes he kind of *looks* like a superhero.

"Got it," they all say in unison.

One little girl tugs at his shirt, leaving a clayey handprint in her wake. "You gonna make a sculpture, too?" she asks. "'Cause I can squeeze in if you want to sit next to me."

Ryan smiles his very widest, most heartrending smile. "I'd be happy to sit next to you."

For the next half hour, he chats with the kids and makes arguably the worst statue I've ever seen. His sculpture bulges and clumps in kind of distressing ways. It even looks disturbingly like someone chewed up one side of it.

"What's that supposed to be?" the girl asks.

"It's Emma," he says. "Can't you tell?"

The girl's eyes widen in shock at she looks from the mangled clay to me. "Is Emma your *girlfriend*?"

He looks at me and smiles. "She is, actually."

A tiny thrill runs down my spine. He's never called me that before. We haven't even talked about anything like that. But here he is, telling this little girl I'm his girlfriend.

The girl picks up the statue he made and give it a dubious look.

"Do you think she'll still like you after she sees this?" she whispers.

Ryan scratches his chin as if he's considering the question seriously. "I hope so," he says. "Though I guess I can't guarantee anything."

The girl agrees that his art's so bad it could go either way, making Ryan laugh.

As class winds down, parents—mostly moms—come to pick up their kids. Many of them bat their eyelashes and try to flirt with Ryan. He is, after all, gorgeous. And with the wind rifling through his hair and his sun-kissed cheeks, he's . . . well, he's a lot to take in. He's also very pleasant while maintaining a polite distance from some of the more hands-on moms.

After the last of the kids is gone, I collapse onto a picnic bench. "You are my hero," I sigh. "I was losing it when you showed up."

Ryan sits next to me. "I could tell. When we have kids, let's hire a nanny."

"Ryan!" I blurt out. My shoulders recoil away from him in shock.

"What?" he protests. "I didn't say we should have kids tomorrow. I said *when*. Like, in the future."

As if that makes a difference. We seriously haven't even talked about the boyfriend/girlfriend thing. The fact that he's already thinking that far into the future makes my palms clam up. Ryan doesn't seem to notice, though, which makes me feel even worse.

"Anyway . . . I brought some stuff to cheer you up 'cause you've seemed kind of down lately," he tells me as he plunks his backpack down on the table and reaches inside. "First, there's fudge. Chocolate for you and peanut butter for me, but I'm willing to share if you are."

I grab the box of chocolate fudge from him. "Only if you're very nice to me."

He grins at me. "Wait till you see!" he says. "Next up we have a mix CD that I made for you featuring the most relaxing music I could think of." He hands me that, too. The song list is all sixties and seventies rock—heavy on the Rolling Stones and Beatles—which is Ryan's kind of music, not really mine. Still, it's a sweet gesture.

"Um . . . ," he says as he digs through the bag. "Oh, there's caramel popcorn," he tells me. "Some bug spray for tonight . . . two bottles of lemonade."

"That's quite a list of stuff," I reply. "Can I ask what we're doing?"

"Not yet!" Ryan keeps feeling around the bag. "There's one more thing I . . . here it is!"

He triumphantly lifts a blue award ribbon that says *I Survived Mackinac Island* on it. I look at it for a second and then do something I absolutely did not expect to do—I shake with laughter.

"It feels that way sometimes," I gasp out.

The grin on his face is a mile wide. "I've been hoping you'd get a good laugh 'cause of this," he admits. "I went rummaging through the shops till I found just the right thing to give you."

"And we will survive this island," I say.

Ryan reaches out and takes my hand. "We're gonna be great."

"Are we?" I wish I had his conviction and optimism about that.

Things definitely haven't seemed fine with my dad since the gallery opening. He's barely spoken to me the last few days, and when he has . . . well, he's been polite. Lots of *Please pass the butter*, and *Don't forget dinner is at six*. Nothing more than that, though. Every now and then I catch him looking at me with this heavy expression of disappointment pulling down the corners of his eyes. Just the thought of it makes my chest ache.

"Hey," Ryan says, squeezing my hand.

I look over at him and he smiles again, a much quieter smile this time.

"We're gonna be totally fine," he assures me. "Our parents can't tell us how to live our lives, right? Before you know it, we'll be going to college and doing what we want."

"With their money," I remind him, my dad's words from the night of the art show still fresh in my mind. "They'll still be paying for college and our lives while we're there. They'll still want a return on the investment."

I feel tired all of a sudden—as if the last few days are finally catching up with me and I'm not sure how I'll be able to get through tonight, let alone college and what comes after.

With a shake of his head, he takes both my hands in his. "We really will be fine," he tells me. "You can be an artist and I can be . . . something. I have no idea what yet. I'll figure it out as I go. As long as it's not a CEO of a company, it'll all be good. "

I try to smile up at him. I used to always feel as optimistic as he does, but it's slipping away from me.

Ryan's eyebrows knit together as he watches me. "Emma, come with me and we'll try to forget about everything for a little while, okay?"

Forget about everything. I don't know how he even thinks that's possible, but I guess I'm willing to give it a try. When I look at him, at the hope in his eyes that he can barely contain—that I wouldn't ever want him to contain—I finally smile again. How could I not? His optimism, his hope . . . he's like a bonfire on a chilly night, warming me up and letting me feel something like hope, too.

"Yes, let's go." I let him pull me to my feet.

"We're gonna survive the heck out of this island tonight," Ryan tells me.

"I don't doubt it one bit."

It turns out, Ryan's way of surviving the island involves eating our way through it. After a long walk, we have dinner on the deck of a tiny restaurant overlooking the lake as the sun dips lower in the sky. We follow that with ice cream as we stroll down Main Street looking in shop windows at all the clothes and candies and souvenirs. When I tell him I want to sit for a while, he leads me to the village green where the island band is setting up for a concert in the little white gazebo.

This last stop was obviously part of the plan, as Ryan pulls a blanket out of his backpack and lays it out in the grass.

"So we're going to take in some music tonight?" I ask.

This secret little smile plays at the corners of his mouth. "It's Gershwin night," he replies. "And I know someone who really loves that music."

I touch his arm, overwhelmed that he'd been paying enough attention to know this without my ever having to tell him. My eyes get watery.

He must see it, because he lifts my hand off his arm and raises it to his lips. A tiny thrill goes through me as he places the gentlest of kisses on it. "I want to help you relax."

Nervous laughter escapes from me. "You're doing a really good job."

A bewitching smile meets that statement.

"Can I be super practical for a second?" he asks. Before I can answer, he passes me the bug spray. "Can't relax if you're someone's dinner."

"Agreed."

After we both douse ourselves in a cloud of the stuff, he plops down on the blanket and pats the spot next to him. As he unpacks the lemonades and fudge, I think about all the effort he put into tonight.

I take his hand and kiss his this time. Ryan's whole face lights up. His eyes are actually glowing right now. "You're the best," he whispers as he slips that hand into my hair.

"So are you."

He kisses me so softly, so tenderly that I let out a nervous giggle. Ryan pulls back and gives me a questioning look.

"No . . . don't stop. I just . . ." I close my eyes and breathe in deeply. "I've just been such a mess lately, and you . . ."

That hopeful look is back in his eyes again. The sunset casts him in a pink-and-orange glow. He's so beautiful. But it's more than that. He's sweet and enthusiastic—he's like sunshine.

"I just like you," I explain. "A lot."

He grins. "Me too."

After one last kiss, he turns toward the bandstand where the conductor is getting the show started. The band strikes into a bouncing rendition of "I Got Rhythm." They play song after song—music that I've loved since I was a little girl—as the lights strung around the bandstand twinkle like stars in the darkness.

"And now, for our last song, we invite you all to get up and dance!" the conductor says, gesturing to the small area around the bandstand that had previously been cordoned off.

Ryan gets up and bows low with his hand on his stomach. "May I have this dance?"

"Of course." Scrambling to my feet, I take his hand so we can walk to the makeshift dance floor while the band starts playing "I've Got a Crush on You." Ryan steps up close to me and raises one hand while he puts the other on my waist. Then, as we sway to the music, he hums along with the singer to the words he doesn't know. But I know them. *"I've got a crush on you, sweetie pie."*

I pull away from him so I can look him in the eyes. "Thank you for this."

Ryan holds me even closer. "Any time."

As we dance around the bandstand, I think about the award ribbon he got me. About this lovely, thoughtful, whirlwind of a night. If tonight is any indication at all, I might just survive this island—and everything that goes with it—after all. Fingers crossed, anyway.

CHAPTER 24

Emma (Then)

t's one of those perfect evenings where the temperature hangs in the balance between too warm and too cool without a hint of humidity to be found. On the verandah, folks rock gently in the chairs there. A grandfather reads *The Little Engine That Could* to a tiny girl on his lap, while next to them the grandmother sips tea with one hand and holds the girl's hand with the other. It's a lovely little scene, and if I had the patience or equipment, I'd ask to paint them just as they are.

But I don't have either right now.

What I do have is relief at having escaped dinner with my parents and Ryan's that's too strong for me to focus on any one thing right now. His mom seems sweet, but has to be one of the most clueless people in the universe. She asked me to paint something for her in front of both my parents—causing one to smile tensely and the other to shrivel up into himself and stop speaking. But it gave me this chance to escape to "scout" for a landscape for her instead of endlessly sitting in the dining room under the heavy weight of Dad's disappointment.

Now that I'm outside, it feels as if someone just took some of that weight off my chest and I can breathe again. At least for a little while.

I head down the stairs and kick off my flip-flops on the lush green lawn. Then I sprint away. The wind whips through my hair and dashes the bottom of my sundress around my ankles. I stop short and throw my arms out, trying to let it sweep away all of the things I've been worrying about. No amount of wind could ever truly do that, but it does make me feel better.

After a few deeps breaths, I run down to the lake. But it's still packed with afternoon beachgoers and folks just coming back from early evening canoeing. There're too many people here—too much chattering and kids yelling and *noise* when all I want is some quiet.

So I take off again, this time just to feel the ground hard underneath my feet. By the time I reach the hill near the staff housing, I'm out of breath and sweaty despite the nice weather.

"Emma!"

I turn to find JR's dad walking toward me with a small cooler in his hand.

"Hey, Terry."

"You going to get my son? Because he's been in a *mood* the last couple of days," Terry says. Then he takes a good look at me and laughs. "Even if you weren't, you should come get a cold drink. You look like you just ran a race."

"I kind of did."

Terry nods toward the staff housing. I freeze up. On the one hand, I am thirsty from running all over. On the other, JR's been avoiding me since the art show. He works, he does stuff with Ryan—he has time for everything but me. It's making me tired. And the kind of hurt and angry that burns up my insides.

I sigh and follow Terry anyway because it would be rude not to and because Terry's great even if his son's not.

JR's bad mood is on display the minute we open the door. He takes one look at me and says, "What're you doing here?"

The burning returns—along with anger and disappointment so deep it hurts.

Terry cuffs him on the shoulder. "Be a little more polite to your guest, okay?"

JR rolls his eyes. "Sure, Dad," he says. "How lovely to see you, Emma. Might I invite you in for a spot of tea?"

With a shake of his head and another cuff on his shoulder, Terry says, "Or, *I'm really glad to see you, Emma.*"

I walk past JR and into their place literally for the first time in all the years I've known JR. He's never once invited me here, which seems weird until I remember that he never comes to our place in the hotel either. Though in that case, it's because Dad's always kind of stiff when JR is around. Terry's not like that with me at all, though, so I don't know what the problem is. Honestly, I don't know what his problem is half the time. Or right now.

"Come sit," Terry tells me. "I'll grab you a glass of water."

He gestures to a worn blue sofa against a wood-paneled wall. There are mismatched pillows on it, and even one of those poofy pillow pets in the shape of a purple unicorn. I walk over and pick up the unicorn. "Dare I ask what this is?"

JR's face tenses with annoyance. "It was a gift."

I raise my eyebrows. Maybe I shouldn't poke the beast—Terry said he's been in a bad mood—but I can't help myself. I want to poke him. I want to make him as angry as I am at him.

"Very cute. Very perky princess."

JR swipes the unicorn back from me. "Yeah, yeah," he says. "You're hilarious. But you can blame my dad for this one."

I do a double take at this revelation. "Terry gave you a purple unicorn?"

JR puts the pillow pet back on the sofa and looks down at his hands. "I used to send him jokes when he was . . ." He stops and balls his hands at his sides. "I used to write to him and I had this book with jokes about magical creatures. I'd send them to him to cheer him up."

Some of my anger vanishes in an instant because the whole situation is so unfair that it hurts to even think about—tiny JR sending unicorn jokes to a dad he barely knew because he'd been locked away so long.

I finally sit down and he does, too. "No more making fun of the unicorn, I promise," I say. "I'll even pinkie promise if you want."

JR lets his head fall onto the back of the sofa and huffs out an annoyed breath. "You know I hate pinkie promising. I actually thought you were trying to be nice for a second."

The kind thing to do would be to leave this alone and move on. Yet I don't.

"Am I ever really *nice* to you," I counter. "Besides, I'm nice to lots of other people. You just don't always recognize how delightful I am."

JR's about to get up from the sofa to get away from me. My eyes follow him and I see it. "You have a TV?" I say in awe. "How do you watch anything on it?"

It seems like it wouldn't be possible for JR's whole face to scrunch up in confusion, but he's sitting right next to me doing just that. "What're you talking about?"

"There's no cable," I remind him. "Do you have a satellite dish or something?"

Terry walks back into the room with my water. "There's no cable in the hotel," he clarifies. "To preserve the old-timey image. But you can definitely get cable on island."

I watch the TV for a second open-mouthed in shock as a man and a giant furry creature fly off in a spaceship. "What *is* this?"

A disgusted sound comes from somewhere deep down in JR's chest. "You spend way too much time cooped up in that hotel," JR says. "Star Wars? *The Empire Strikes Back?*"

I ignore the irritated tone of his voice and just shake my head. "I've never seen the Star Wars movies," I admit. "Are they good?"

JR and Terry stare at each other in disbelief before they both turn to me with matching expressions of horror on their faces—even down to the same crease between their eyebrows.

This visit is . . . not going the way I thought it would.

"Um . . . the movies are amazing." JR pauses. "Well . . . most of them are."

Terry rubs his chin. "Some of them are. The oldest ones."

I think I've lost track of this conversation. Either that or they've contradicted themselves so much that there's no way to keep track.

"So . . . they're . . . not good?"

This makes Terry laugh and JR frown. As in dramatically frown.

"Next time they're on TV, your friend here will have to invite you over to watch them all in the right order," Terry says. "I'll make popcorn and everything."

"That would be amazing!" I reply. Sometimes it's hard to believe JR and Terry are actually related. This is one of those times. "I never get to watch TV." There's no theater on island, so I never get to see any movies either.

Then I notice JR shaking his head at me, the edges of his mouth still turned down. "You've got perky princess written all over you right now."

"And you're being a grump again." I cross my arms over my chest and glare at him. "I got distracted by the TV from the fact that I'm angry at you right now."

"Let's keep it on then, Dad," JR says.

That's all it takes for Terry to switch off the TV and say, "I'm going for a walk, so you just relax and make yourself at home."

"I *am* at home," JR reminds him.

Terry rolls his eyes the exact same way JR does. "I meant Emma, you fool of a Took."

JR rolls his eyes back, but whatever that meant went right over my head. A lot of this conversation has, which is even less fun than my usual conversations with JR. I turn to Terry. "What's a Took?"

JR and his dad exchange another shocked glance before Terry looks back at me with pity in his eyes. "*Lord of the Rings?*" he says. "You've never read the books?"

I shake my head. "Never."

Terry turns to JR. "We have to aid this shieldmaiden."

"You have my bow," JR offers.

"And my axe."

For some reason Terry bursts out laughing. Even JR smiles this time. He seems lighter than I've seen him in a while. His whole face looks different—softer—than it usually does. Maybe this is why he's never invited me here before. He doesn't want me to see him relaxed and happy.

As Terry walks over to a small bookshelf, one leg drags a bit. How did I not notice that before? I open my mouth to ask if he's okay, but he's already handing me a battered paperback.

"Here's *The Fellowship of the Ring*," he tells me. "First book in the trilogy. Come back for the next one when you finish."

"How do you know I'll finish it?" I ask.

He cocks his head to one side as if he's deeply considering me. "You seem like you have good common sense," Terry replies, as if that explains something.

"I've read the whole trilogy six times," JR admits.

My head whips over in his direction. "Wait, what?"

He looks away, that completely *irritating* mask of indifference on his face.

"Okay, I'll bite," I tell Terry. "JR doesn't like anything that much."

His dad's eyes shoot over to JR for a second before he smiles at me. "I can think of other things he likes that much," he tells me. "But these books are definitely top ten."

Terry has always been super nice to me, ever since I was little and he first came to work here. I never could figure out how someone who'd been in jail could be such a kind person—in all the stories I'd ever read it was terrible, villainous people who got thrown in jail. That's when I asked my dad about it and found out that Terry probably just would have gotten a stint in rehab if he'd been arrested today, which seemed horribly unfair to me. "Sometimes life's unfair, Emma" was my dad's comforting response.

"Are you gonna rejoin reality, or I am just gonna sit here all night watching you in Emma Land?"

The question startles me, but I answer right away. "I'm going to rejoin reality."

Then I look around the room and realize Terry's gone. "Did your dad leave?"

I get the eye roll again. "Wow, you really were zoned out, weren't you?"

"Shut up, JR."

"Make me, Emma."

There's only one way to respond to that, so I pick up the stuffed unicorn and hurl it across the couch at him. JR doesn't even attempt to block it—he just tucks it under his arm so I can't throw it at him again. He turns, just for a second, to glance my way. His eyes . . . I'd say he looks grumpy again, but this is far beyond that.

The TV screen is blank except for the reflected lights of their living room but JR stares at it intently, like it's the most interesting thing in the world. Now that Terry's gone, we seem to have run out of things to say. So I ask the question I've been aching to ask.

"Where've you been the last few days?"

He fiddles with the Velcro holding the pillow pet together. Fiddles with the hem of his T-shirt. Looks out the window. What he doesn't do is answer.

"Are you in JR Land now?"

He picks up the remote. "Want to watch some TV?"

"Seriously?" I blurt out. "That's how you're going to answer my question?"

"Emma . . . ," he begins, but then doesn't say anything else.

"*Fine,*" I spit out. "Let's watch TV." I let myself sink farther into the couch, my arms over my chest.

"Fine." He turns the TV back on. There are robots walking into a dark, cavernous place. I don't want to be interested. I don't want to care. But after a few minutes I'm very confused.

"What is this?"

"*Return of the Jedi*," he says. "Last of the original Star Wars movies."

That gets my attention. "So I can see one right now?"

He shakes his head at me. "You won't understand any of it."

"Then you'll have to explain it to me."

He sighs and leans back into the couch. "You're going to hassle me with questions through the whole movie, aren't you?"

There's only one way to answer this. "Absolutely."

Our eyes meet for a second. There's a frown on JR's face, but despite his turned-down mouth, his eyes are kind of . . . shining? That can only mean one thing—he's going to cave. "Fine. Let's watch it."

I smile in satisfaction at this tiny win. "Now tell me who the robots are."

He sighs again. "This is gonna be a long night."

As I rearrange myself on his couch, I nudge him with my foot. "But isn't it nice that you get to share something you really love with me?"

Our eyes meet for a second but he looks away again quickly.

"It is."

This tiny concession gives me some hope that everything will be okay between us. I settle into the couch and rest my feet on the tops of his legs. Not because I want to annoy him or anything, just because I want to get comfortable. And maybe annoy him just a teeny bit.

It works.

"I'm not your footstool, you know." His voice is aggrieved, tired.

"Don't look now, JR, because it appears that you are."

JR leans his head back on the couch again in defeat as he begins to explain who the robots are and what they're doing with the giant blob creature on the TV screen.

We talk—me asking questions, him answering them all with surprising patience—for about an hour. He shifts on the couch, moving my feet along with him as he turns a bit more sideways toward me. Then his hand comes to rest on my ankle. I freeze. I don't even breathe for a few seconds. At first I think he did it on purpose, which would be . . . weird. But that can't be. JR can't seem to take his eyes off his hand. My ankle.

Then he looks up at me. There's a crease between his eyebrows—almost a question in them, but I don't know what he's asking. The movie plays on in the background. Neither of us watches it. Instead we watch each other. I don't know what's happening here. Not that it isn't nice. Not that I mind him doing something as simple as laying his hand on my ankle. It's just . . . new. Something he's never done before.

I turn back to the TV. I can't look at him anymore.

He still doesn't move his hand. I can still feel his eyes on me, so I glance at him sideways.

"You good?" he asks.

"I'm good."

We sit like this—frozen in one place—till I realize I've been holding myself tense and need to move into a different position. So I turn the angle of my shoulders and ease into the couch a bit more. His fingers glide over my bare skin as I move, settling farther down my foot. For a second, we both freeze again. Then he gives my foot the gentlest of squeezes. My mind zeroes in on the exact place where his hand lies now—the part of my foot where he and I meet. I'm not paying enough attention to the movie anymore to ask any other questions.

A tiny storm swirls in my stomach. I press my hand into it and try to focus back in.

In my mind, I hear JR saying my name through what feels as if it's a dense fog. His voice is closer this time when he says my name. Something touches my shoulder. His hand.

"JR . . . ?"

I lean into the back of his hand. Press it to my cheek.

"Emma," he says. "Emma . . . you gotta wake up. It's getting late."

I let out an exasperated grunt. "What . . . what do you mean?"

"You slept through the end of the movie," he says, his voice so soft I want to lean into that, too.

"Oh no!" My eyes fly open. "But you were sharing something you love with me! I wanted to . . ."

"It's all good," he tells me. "We can watch it another time."

"No, JR, I . . ."

His hand glides over the thin strap of my sundress, down my arm. "We can watch it another time, Emma," he says again. "I promise."

I nod but it's hard to find my voice with his hand on my bare skin. My eyes meet his and hold them for a second. JR drops his hand too suddenly.

"I'll walk you home," he says.

"You don't have to."

"I want to make sure you get home safe."

We stare at each other for another moment or two. Maybe even longer. I have no idea.

"Next time the movies are on TV, we'll watch them all," he says.

"Okay."

I pull my feet off his lap and unfold myself from where I've been lying on the couch. I stand up. JR won't look at me, but he gets up, too. It all happens like clockwork from there. I slip my flip-flops back on. He holds the door open for me. We walk back to the hotel.

"Sorry I haven't been around much," he says. "I didn't mean to . . . well . . ." JR's eyes meet mine. "You busy tomorrow?"

Something in his voice makes my eyes tear up.

"Tomorrow sounds good."

We walk for a while in silence.

"Noon outside the market?" he says.

"I'll bring lunch."

"You don't—"

"JR, I'll bring lunch."

He nods and I do, too.

The fire in his eyes—in the way he's looking at me—churns up the storm inside my stomach again.

"I've got to get home," I tell him.

He nods again before turning to walk away.

I watch him till he's gone around the side of the hotel on his way back to his dad's before I head inside to face the weight of disappointing my parents again.

CHAPTER 25

Lexi (Now)

Ms. VanHill seems surprised to see me the next day. "Did you bring tea?" she asks. "And what have you done with Casey?"

This may actually be the last question I was expecting her to ask. "I haven't done anything with Casey!" I reply. "I'm not even sure if he's working today or not."

She lets out a *psshhht*, and holds the door open for me. "That boy is *always* working," she tells me. "He's got big dreams and no way to fund them so he works himself to the bone." She walks to the hotel phone and dials three numbers. "Yes, yes, it's me again," she says irritably. "Is Casey working right now?" There's a pause before she continues. "Excellent. Ask him to bring me up a tray of my usual afternoon fare, please." She listens again for a moment. "No, I suppose I can wait until he's free. But send him just as soon as he's available. Tea and cake for three." She pauses again. "Casey is well aware what to bring, thank you very much. Just give him my message."

I don't mind saying that Ms. VanHill can be a little intimidating.

"Now, what were we talking about?" she demands.

"Casey. I think?"

She lets out a hearty laugh. "Yes, he's always working. He is today. . . ." Her voice trails off. "We should ask him to bring us some tea."

I watch her, trying to figure this out. I haven't really ever been around older people. My dad's parents both died pretty young and obviously I never knew my mom's. We see Abby's mom twice a year on holidays, but I don't know her all that well. Also, she's not nearly as old as Ms. VanHill is. Abby's mom is in her seventies and lives in Florida with all of her girlfriends like they're the Golden Girls in that old TV show. Ms. VanHill is ninety-seven. I have no experience with ninety-seven or with short-term memory issues.

"Um . . . I found some new postcards in my mom's mosaic chest," I tell her. "You know, from yesterday? I . . . I could read them to you if you like?"

For a second or two, she stares at me blankly, but then she says, "Of course I do." The imperiousness is back, to my relief. "You never leave your audience hanging. Incomplete performances are the worst thing imaginable." She taps her finger to her lips as if she's deep in thought. "Though I suppose I can think of nine or ten things just off the top of my mind which are worse, so there you have it."

It's impossible not to smile at her, so I don't even try. "Do I want to know?"

A majestic wave of her hand meets this question. "Not all of my stories are for general audiences."

This time I do laugh out loud. "Then maybe we should stick to the postcards?"

"That seems wise."

I take out the stack of postcards and flip through them, wondering if they're in order, but there's no way to find out because they're not dated.

There are no addresses on any of them, but they're all to the same person.

JR,

Sometimes I try really hard to understand all of this, and sometimes I'm still so furious at you that I don't want to understand anything more. I don't want to be consumed by this, but I am. I really am. Maybe someday I'll be able to forgive you. But it's not going to be today.

E

Silence falls in the room. I flip the postcard over and find the same picture that was on the one I mailed just a couple of days ago. Does that mean they actually were both written to JR? If he's the mystery guy she'd always have this palace by the lake with, why didn't she mail either of the postcards she wrote him?

"I don't understand," I whisper.

"Nor do I," Ms. VanHill says. "Perhaps if you read the other postcards, they might shed some light?"

It's a good suggestion aside from being the only thing that makes sense.

"Okay," I agree, and pick up the next postcard. This one has a lighthouse on it.

JR,

There are repair crews here around the clock trying to get everything back in order, and it's got to be costing a fortune. Not that you care. It's just a land of make-believe, right? Everyone here just lives on the backs of other people. But I was here when it happened, JR. Maybe you forgot about that? Or did you just not care? God, I wish I could talk to you.

E

"Well, it seems as if trouble was brewing in paradise," Ms. VanHill comments.

I read through the postcard again, not sure what to make of it. "What happened to the hotel?" I ask. "Do you remember?"

Ms. VanHill stops to think. "I wouldn't have been living here at the time," she says. "I was still tripping the light fantastic, you know."

I smile at her. "I do know," I remind her. "I have original Broadway recordings of you singing. Your 'Before the Parade Passes By' made me cry the first time I heard it."

Her eyes close and she smiles sadly. "I'd lost someone very dear to me right before that run of *Hello, Dolly!* began," she says. "That role meant a lot to me, even aside from showing the world I could play her. I needed to have something to throw myself into, heart and soul."

I've read so much about her career, but this is something I've never heard about before. "I'm so sorry," I reply. "Did you lose your husband or . . . ?"

My question is met with a short bark of a laugh. "I've never been married, Lexi," she tells me. "To a man or a woman. Marriage is for fools and romantics." She pauses and wags her finger at me. "And mark my words, there's a lot of overlap in those two groups."

I think that over for a second. "Then who . . . ?"

"Would you be so kind as to walk over and retrieve the photograph on that table?" She points in the direction I should go in.

I nod and jump up to get it for her.

"This is Frances Marley," Ms. VanHill says, running her finger over the woman in the photo with her. "The love of my life."

My eyes pore over the picture in more detail than before. Frances Marley was shorter than Ms. VanHill. Even in the black-and-white picture, it looks like she had pale white skin and blond hair. They have their arms around each other, smiling at something just off camera. They look . . . happy. Like really happy.

"Oh," I say, my eyes widening. "I had no idea!"

"Yes, well, we couldn't exactly publicize it, now could we?" she says in a tart voice. "Times were different then. People had to hide who they were. *We* had to hide who we were."

I try to wait for her to say more but can't help but ask, "When did she die?"

"Die?" Ms. VanHill visibly startles at this question. "She's still alive, kicking around in an old folks' home in San Diego. I haven't heard from her in . . . oh, a long time, I think." She puts the picture down. "Her daughter promised to let me know if anything . . . changes, though. When she loses Fran, I mean. I made my godson promise to do the same if my time comes first."

A shiver goes down my spine. I haven't even known Ms. VanHill long, but the thought of losing her—of having her not in this world anymore—still upsets me.

"But what happened?" I ask. "With you and Frances, I mean?"

With a shrug, she says, "Life happened. Work happened. We risked it for a while, but then her management found out and that was that." She shrugs again. "We had our careers to think about. We couldn't keep seeing each other."

I let that sink in for a second. Ms. VanHill and Frances Marley were in love. They were together. Then because society was so awful, they had to break up.

"But you said you still hear from her sometimes!" I say. "Maybe now you two can—"

"Lexi, I am ninety-seven years old," she cuts me off. "Fran is ninety-four and her health is poor." Her eyes stray to the window and fixate on the lake outside. "Even if she weren't, that ship sailed long ago." Ms. VanHill lifts her chin defiantly. "Besides, you don't think I led a lonely life, do you? I never wanted for companionship. I *always* got my needs taken care of, if you know what I mean."

I choke on my own breath and cough in surprise. "Um, it would be hard to miss your meaning here, Ms. VanHill."

She looks my way suddenly and points at me. "There's a moral to this story," she informs me. "And it's not just that times change and things can get better, though both are true enough. It's that the very idea that love will last forever is a myth. Love comes and goes and dies and withers away."

Ms. VanHill waves her hand at the postcards on my lap. "Look at your mother and that friend of hers," she continues. "They seemed close, but it didn't last. Nothing does. That might sound cynical, but it's the honest truth and there's no point in sugarcoating it."

It does sound cynical. The strange thing is that she doesn't even sound upset or bitter about it. This is just a fact of life for her.

"So you have to seize love when you have it," Ms. VanHill tells me.

"You can't waste it. Because you end up like your mother and the boy in the postcards."

"JR," I say in a low voice.

"Just so. JR. Do you have any idea who he is?"

"I still have no idea," I tell her again.

She shakes her head. "Because he went away," she goes on. "And he didn't just go away. It seems as if it was a traumatic break. Something terrible happened and he disappeared from your mother's life. There's no happily ever after. There's just happy for the time you have."

Neither of us says anything for what feels like a long time.

Maybe Ms. VanHill is right. Even if he was just her friend, Mom lost JR. Dad lost Mom. If you love someone, you're still going to lose them eventually. Or they'll lose you. So what's the point of even trying?

I'm not sure how Mom *could* keep trying. Or how Dad could after he lost her. But he and Abby—they're good together. I know she had to ask him out a few times before he said yes, but in the end he did say yes. He found a way to move forward. Not in a way that helped me at all, but that made him happy at least.

Ms. VanHill pokes me with her cane and nods at the two postcards still in my hands.

"Are you going to read those to me or do I to have to guess at their contents?"

I move out of range of her cane and take a deep breath. "Of course I am."

The next postcard is a black-and-white illustration of the Detroit skyline of all things.

JR,

I went to Detroit for a long weekend with Ryan and Linda for the campaign and thought about coming to visit you. I even called a taxi company to see how much it would cost to get there. It's so strange to be in the same city as you right now but not to be able to see you. I'm still not sure I'd want to even if I could.

Except that I do, JR. I want to see you and ask you a million questions and force you to give me answers. I want things to go back to the way they were. But I guess that's not possible, is it?

E

"JR lived in Detroit?" I say out loud. "I thought he lived here."

"Hm . . . ," Ms. VanHill murmurs. "Maybe he just came in the summer like your mother."

"But she said he lived in staff housing before. Wouldn't staff live here year-round?" I look over the card again, lost in thought. "I wonder who Ryan and Linda were. And what campaign she was talking about."

For a long few seconds, Ms. VanHill doesn't say anything. "Something about the campaign sounds familiar," she tells me. "But I can't put my finger on what." She looks up at me. "Read the next card. Let's see if it jogs this old brain of mine."

So I do.

JR,

The work's finished on the hotel. It looks like nothing ever happened. Except, of course, it did. I keep thinking I should mail this postcard—or mail any of the ones I already wrote to you—but I know there's no point. It's not like you ever wrote back to me before this. Why would you start now?

I just. . .I hope you're okay. I hope you're taking care of yourself. No matter what happened, I still want you to be okay. Honestly, I have no idea why.

E

After I read it aloud, I read it two more times through to myself. It's starting to feel like each piece of this jigsaw puzzle only makes the central image more blurry. There are all these people swirling around Mom's world, and I have no idea who any of them are or how they fit together.

Every time I think I might have found something, it turns out I haven't.

I Googled all three of her friends over and over again today, but their first names don't tell me anything. There were lots of people named Linda and Ryan, and I'm not even sure if JR was his real name or just his initials. I know Ms. VanHill thinks there's no such thing as a dead end in this day and age, but Mom keeps proving that wrong over and over again.

A knock sounds at the door. When I open it, Casey comes in with tea for three. He smiles at me, but then his smile fades for some reason.

"Everything okay?" he asks.

"Yes, Casey, I'm quite well, as always," Ms. VanHill declares. "We were just talking about my performance in *Hello, Dolly!* back in the day."

His smile returns in full force as he brings the tea tray over to where she's sitting. "One of your best, of course," he replies.

"Of course," she agrees. "But then, every role I took I made my best in the end."

Ms. VanHill pours tea out for the three of us, but midway through cutting a slice of lemon cake, she stops short.

"A fire!" she exclaims. "There was a fire."

My mind tries to find a way into what she's saying and what part of her past it's from but I come up empty. "What do you mean, Ms. VanHill?"

"At the hotel," she tells me. "I remember my friend Milly telling me about it. A local boy caused a fire there, but thank God no one got hurt. There was quite a lot of damage, though, if I recall."

"Oh my God," I gasp out.

Picking up the postcards I've already read, I skim through them again. The repair crews. The fortune to fix everything. There had been a fire at the hotel. And JR didn't care that it burned. My brain snags on that for a long second or two. Sure, it seemed like they teased each other a lot, but he and Mom were clearly friends. So what's the deal with the postcards?

Then it occurs to me: if there was a fire at the hotel, maybe I'll be able to find something in an old newspaper article. Maybe I'll find the answers I've been looking for.

Or even just one or two, really.

I run my fingers over the bumpy edges of Mom's mosaic chest. Something's still not adding up. There are pieces to the story that I can't quite place. I just need to find out what they are and how to fit them together.

CHAPTER 26

Emma (Then)

This night has been in the works for so many years, months, weeks, days that it seems almost impossible that it's really here. One hundred years. The hotel has existed for a whole hundred years. I look around my bedroom and wonder who used to live here. Was it always a suite, or did it used to be a group of individual rooms that got transformed into this later on? I know the bathrooms got added in later, but what else has changed? I walk over to my window. The lawn is relatively quiet now as the heat sets in and people get ready for tonight, but usually there are young families out there playing frisbee and cornhole. Down near the pool, there's a beach volleyball court that clearly didn't exist a hundred years ago.

But the carriages, the horses, the bikes, the paddle boats—formal dinners in the dining room and dances in the ballroom—all of that probably hasn't changed much except for the clothes the people wear and the styles of the bikes.

Outside my room, I can my hear dad banging around in our living room and talking in a too-tense voice while my mom tries to soothe him. They may not be all warm and fuzzy like some couples are, but they're a team nonetheless.

A knock sounds at my door and my mom peeks in. "Emma, are you getting ready yet?"

When she sees that I'm still in my bathrobe, she hurries into the room in her full-length lavender dress. "This is not the night to be late, love," she tells me. "Dad had a rough day and he's already on edge tonight. Please don't make it worse."

She hurries to my closet where my dress—custom-tailored to fit me perfectly—hangs. Mom pulls out the dress and smooths it out on my bed as I stand there watching her.

"Emma, come on," she pleads. "You have to get ready!"

I nod and promise, "I already showered. It'll only take a few minutes to change into the dress."

"Good," she says. "Then I'll be back to help with your hair in five minutes."

So I head to the bathroom and then wash my hands and face. As I brush my teeth, I look at myself in the mirror. My hair's a mess, but that's nothing new. It never lies smooth and pretty like Mom's does. Not much about me is as smooth and pretty as she wants it to be. I both wish I was more like her and dread becoming her at the same time.

I slip out of my clothes and into my dress. At least this is pretty. Ice blue, with a delicate white lace overlay, it's fitted to the waist and then drops in an A-line from there. It has straps that go over my shoulders so that I don't have to keep worrying about my dress falling down all night. Even though in the blue and lace I look like the hotel tonight, Mom's happy with the way it looks and I'm happy that it's comfortable. Of course, right now, she's not happy at all.

Mom comes in to see what progress I've made and stops short.

"Oh, you look beautiful," she says in a low voice. "Here, let me do up the back of the dress."

I turn so she can zip me up and then sit in my chair at my old vanity table so she can do my hair in some elaborate style she found in a magazine. As she starts to work with the first section of my hair, she says, "You really do look beautiful, Emma. If he's not already smitten with you, he will be tonight."

My hands stiffen on the desk. "Mom . . . what are you talking about?"

"Ryan, of course," Mom replies. "You're not dating anyone else, are you?"

"No, of course not, but . . ." The last thing I want to do is discuss my dating life with her. Ever. But especially not when I'm stuck in this chair with her literally holding my hair hostage. She pulls another section of my hair into her hands and begins working on it. There's no way out of this. I readjust in my seat, trying to find a way to be comfortable right now.

"The music should be interesting tonight, right?" I say, trying to change the subject to something that might distract her. "I can't wait to hear the orchestra play the stuff from when the hotel first opened."

Mom looks at me in the mirror, her hand paused over my head with a piece of my hair it—her mouth a thin line, her eyes with a knowing look in them.

"You don't want to talk about you and Ryan?"

"No, I don't," I inform her. "We haven't even been together that long."

"Obviously," Mom replies as she tugs the next section of my hair into a coil. "But the Desmonds are thinking about making a pretty big investment in Dad's new plans."

My stomach drops to my knees. I have a sudden need to throw up.

Mom adjusts my head to keep it steadily in the same place while she works. "I'm guessing that Ryan's relationship with you isn't going to hurt the prospects of their investment."

It's as if I'm back in the gallery again with my dad spelling out how my life is going to be, except this time it's worse. This time it's Mom—and we're not talking about college majors anymore. They're trying to arrange every aspect of my life so there's nothing left for me to want or choose. She's even tarnishing my relationship with Ryan, making it feel . . . useful. As if we exist just to smooth things over between our parents.

I close my eyes and try to breathe in through my nose and out through my mouth to keep myself from vomiting all over my dress. But she's hovering over me so close that even the deep breaths aren't helping. My palms sweat so much I have to keep myself from wiping them on my dress.

As soon as she pins the last bit of my hair, I jump out of the chair and turn to face her.

"You can't arrange my life, you know." The words spill from my mouth, as if they've been bottled up for too long and I've only now gotten the courage to let them out. "It's *my* life, not yours. Not Dad's. You guys made your choices, now I get to make mine."

I will her to understand, beg her with my stare. Can't she tell how suffocating this all is? My heart hammers in my chest as I hear her let out the deepest sigh.

No, I remind myself. *She doesn't have a clue.* With her perfectly manicured hands, Mom reaches over to tuck away a stray hair that's already escaped from her handiwork. The touch is gentle, but I still flinch back from her. I try to ignore the hurt expression in her eyes.

"Your life is connected to ours, though. The choices you make are, too," Mom says in a patient voice. "You're our only child, Emma." Pausing, she takes a deep breath. "I love you so much. I want you to be happy."

There's a giant *but* after that statement. I know it—she knows it. She lets it hang in the air as she gives me a hopeful smile, her eyes finding mine in the mirror.

She wants me to smile back—to reassure her that everything will be okay and her faith in me isn't misplaced. I can't do it, though. They're putting all these . . . these walls around me and then watching contentedly as they close around me. Assuming that I won't ever try to knock them down because I'm their daughter.

The closer the walls get, the more I want to break free of them. My eyes drop. I can't look at her anymore, even the reflection of her in the mirror.

A knock sounds at the front door, then another when no one answers it.

"Dad went down early to meet Jackson and some other folks for a drink." Mom pats her already perfect hair in the mirror to make sure nothing's out of place. "I'll go let Ryan in."

"No, I will," I say, pushing past her into the living room.

Ryan stands outside the door wearing a slim black tux perfectly tailored to accentuate his broad shoulders and thin waist. The deep teal paisley of his vest and tie brings out the color in his eyes. My breath catches in my throat. For a second, I just stand there staring at him. Maybe he should dress like this more often. Or every day.

Then I think about what my mom just hinted at in my room and my cheeks burn.

"Hey," he says in a quiet voice. "You look incredible."

"You do, too."

There's just a tinge of a smile on his face. Not the usual *blind you with its glory* smile at all. I give him a questioning look, but his eyes shift behind me and I realize that my mom's standing there.

"Hi, Jessica," he says. "I like your dress."

When I turn, she's beaming at him. "Thank you, Ryan!"

I freeze where I'm standing, not sure who to look at or what to think. Finally he holds his arm out to me. "You ready?"

I slip my hand through his arm and look back at my mom. Unsurprisingly, she's still grinning ear to ear. Equally unsurprisingly, it makes my heart race again.

"Yes," I tell him. "I'm definitely ready to leave."

"I'll see you two down there in a minute," Mom calls out to us. Neither of us responds.

We don't seem to have much to say to each other tonight. Ryan is surprisingly quiet, but I'm all in my head, too. At least until we walk to the main staircase and the whole . . . scene . . . of tonight unfolds in front of us.

Walking down the stairs feels a little as if we're walking into the past. Floral garlands line the banisters and the whole lobby glows with tea lights and candelabra with tall taper candles in them. There's an odd mixture of guests and residents in formalwear and folks who look as if they've just returned from a day on the lake. It's both strange and kind of charming to see the two groups mingling together.

We walk through an arch of roses into a transformed ballroom. Candles flicker, satiny gold streamers sweep up into rosettes every few feet. Everywhere I look, there are flowers—everywhere I turn, a different scent rises up to meet me. The ballroom's pretty grand on a regular day. Tonight it looks like something out of a fairy tale.

"Wow," I breathe.

Ryan nods.

Everyone is dressed as if it's a fairy tale, too—in full-length gowns and tuxedos. Linda's standing in the corner in a stunning red column dress, her hair cascading over her shoulders in golden waves as she argues with Tom, who didn't manage to get the night off and is not only in uniform, but is carrying an empty hors d'oeuvres tray. I wish I could take a picture of the expression on Tom's face right at this moment, which is half annoyance, half lust as he gazes at her.

I spot Dad standing near the bar talking to the Lieu-Smiths. He's dressed to the nines, too, but something about his posture makes me think he's on edge even though he *loves* Mr. and Dr. Lieu-Smith (he runs a hedge fund, she's a paleobotanist—they're like his power couple heroes). He keeps switching his weight from one foot to the other, tugging at his tie.

Then I realize Ryan's doing the same thing. His hair shines in the candlelight as if he's a prince in a fairy tale, but his fingers tug at his collar as if it's too tight. He can't quite stand still. He hasn't said a word since we left my place.

One of the extra servers hired for tonight passes by carrying champagne glasses on a tray. "You want one?" Ryan asks.

I shake my head. "No, thanks."

"Well, I do," he says, grabbing one of the glasses. He downs the champagne in a single gulp, then deposits the glass on a nearby table and rubs his hands together.

I reach up and touch his arm, trying to catch his eyes. Trying to do anything to tamp down my own worry right now.

"Are you okay?"

"Yeah, of course," he reassures me. "Just thirsty."

He still won't look down at me. His eyes roam around the room as if he's searching for someone. The corners of his mouth are tense—turned downward. He definitely doesn't seem okay.

"You don't seem yourself tonight," I say in a gentle voice. "Are you sure you're all right?"

When he looks over at me, heat flashes in his eyes taking me by surprise. "Just a fight with my dad," he hisses. "Everything's fine."

But then he takes a second glass of champagne from another waiter and is about to down this one, too, until I slip my hand into his. "Talk to me, Ryan."

"There's nothing to say," he says. "Nothing ever changes. No matter what I say or do, he keeps . . ."

He blows out a long breath. "Look, I don't really want to think about it right now." I watch as he gulps down the champagne in his hand and holds his arm out to me again. "I just want to dance with the prettiest girl in the room, okay?"

At least he *sounds* more like himself now. But even the compliment kind of falls flat. Hopefully, after a few dances, a few songs, he'll feel more himself. Hopefully, I will, too.

"Okay," I tell him, letting him lead me out onto the dance floor.

While I can't say that I love the manic dizziness of waltzing, I do like dancing with Ryan. It's not even just that he knows how to waltz and glides us around the room with the ease of an old Hollywood star. Being this close to him makes my pulse race. It makes me want to get even closer.

He wraps his arm farther around my waist so that we're almost flush against each other and I have to force myself to breathe for a second. *This*, I remind myself. *This is what's real. What matters.* How I feel when I'm close to him. The way he looks at me. How much fun I have with him. I try to reassure myself of what I already know to be true: I'm not with him because my parents want me to be with him. I *want* to be with him.

Ryan leans down, brushing his lips against my ear. "You look so gorgeous in that dress," he says. "All I want to do is get you alone later."

My eyes widen. "I . . . I don't know where we could go to be alone tonight . . . like that, I mean."

His teeth pull at my earlobe, making goose bumps rise up on the skin of my neck. "Ryan!" I gasp, as his lips move down my neck. "You can't do that right now," I remind him, putting a little distance between us as I do. "Our parents are here!"

A shaky sigh blows into my ear. "They always are," he says. "Always around to make sure we don't get to do the stuff we want to do."

I'm not sure what to say to that, even though I know he's right. About both of our parents he's right. So I just pull him closer and lay my head on his shoulder. This doesn't help either as his hands begin to wander downward. "Ryan!" I say again. "Parents. In the room with us. Remember?"

To my surprise, Ryan lets out an angry laugh. "And we wouldn't want to piss off our parents, would we?"

I step away a little so I can look him in the eyes. I've never once heard him talk so . . . so bitterly before. "Are you sure you're okay?"

"As okay as I'm gonna be," he says. But then he reaches for another glass of champagne from a passing server at the edge of the dancing. "As long as I'm with you, I'm always okay, right?"

It's a fairy-tale romance kind of thing to say in a fairy-tale kind of setting and I feel as if I should be swooning. He wipes his mouth with the back of his hand as he puts the glass on a nearby table, then straightens up as we start to dance again. And I don't know . . . we're all dressed up in this beautiful room where everything is golden and shining and perfect, and yet . . . yet I'm worried about him. I'm worried about me, too. I feel as if I need *something* but I have no idea what. Someday, everything will fall into place for both of us. It just doesn't seem as if it's going to be tonight.

CHAPTER 27

Emma (Then)

By the end of the night, any trace of a fairy tale has slipped away entirely. Linda's making out with Tom in full display of her parents and all their staring coworkers. Mom's beautiful lavender dress got trampled by one of the dancing little kids about an hour ago, and now drags behind her like some ghostly appendage. Dad's in the midst of a heated discussion with Mr. Desmond.

And Ryan's reaching for yet another glass of champagne.

"Ryan, come on." I lead him toward a nearby table. "You need to sit and have some water."

Ryan pulls away from me, though. "I'm fine," he tells me. "I wanna keep dancing!"

"You're not fine," I insist. "You need to drink some water or you're going to be really sick tomorrow."

Once again, he moves away from me, this time pushing my hands away as I try to tug at him. "You gonna start telling me what to do, too?" he blurts out. "'Cause I've had it up to here with that tonight." He raises his hand as far over his head as he can reach.

I step away from him in shock. Close my eyes and rub my temples. I have to figure out a way to get him off his feet and get something nonalcoholic in him.

"Ryan, I'm really tired and thirsty," I say at last. "We've been dancing for hours. I think I need a break."

His whole faces softens. "Ooohhh . . . you should've told me," he says. "I'd've gotten some water ages ago. C'mon. Let's sit."

With a sigh of relief, I do just that. Now all I need is to get him hydrated and up to his place before his parents realize he's drunk. I look around the room again for Linda, but she and Tom have stopped kissing and are arguing again. I watch as she storms into one of the small function rooms just off the ballroom and Tom rubs his eyes in dismay. So that's one ally down. JR wouldn't come tonight even though he'd said he would—and even after Ryan tried everything he could to convince him. So that's two allies I could have used right about now who aren't here.

Finally I see Jackson coming this way—looking better than anyone has any right to in his dark blue tux—and manage to catch his eye. He nods at Ryan. "He looks a little worse for the wear."

"I'm great!" Ryan says defensively.

Jackson raises one eyebrow. "Yes, I can see that," he replies. "Maybe some water would help?"

"Thanks, Jackson," I breathe. "That would be amazing."

"Yeah, Emma's parched," Ryan tells him. "S'all the dancing."

After looking from me to Ryan and back again, Jackson says, "Okay . . . I'll be back in a second. Don't let him wander off."

"I'll try."

Before Jackson returns with water, Mr. Desmond finds us. Ryan's whole body tenses the second he sees him.

"What's going on here?" Mr. Desmond asks.

Ryan shrugs dramatically. "Just takin' a rest," he says. "Emma's sooooo tired."

Mr. Desmond watches Ryan with narrowed eyes before turning to me. "How much has he had to drink?"

For the second time tonight, it feels as if my stomach has dropped to my knees. I take a deep breath—the last thing I want is to get Ryan in trouble. "I don't know. Not much?"

The wrath of Jack Desmond turns on poor Ryan anyway. "You know what place we occupy in the world right now," he says in a threatening whisper. "You know the image we need to put forth for the campaign." Mr. Desmond lets out an exasperated grunt. "*How could you make such a fool of yourself in public?*"

"I'm not in public," Ryan argues. "I'm in the hotel. We live here, remember? Had to move so you could look all *I'm from the past, you should vote for me.* Which means . . . I'm home?" He turns to me with his eyebrows all bunched up. "It's home, right?"

"It is to me," I admit. "So maybe we should go up and—"

"You're in a space occupied by other people." Mr. Desmond steps right up in Ryan's face. "Which means you're in public."

I slip my arm around Ryan, trying to do something—anything— to show him that I'm here for him, but he shakes me off. I shrink back from him, stung.

"You're the one who made us move 'ere," he tells his dad. "This is on *yoouuu.*"

"Jack, I think we should have this discussion somewhere a little more private," Mrs. Desmond says as she comes up behind her husband. "Why don't we go upstairs and have some dessert sent up? Or maybe get some coffee in one of the rooms down here?" she adds, giving Ryan a worried glance. "Wouldn't that be nice? Emma, you'd like that, wouldn't you?"

I'm not sure what the right thing to do here is anymore. All I want to do is get Ryan away from them—to protect him from this. But he won't even let me.

"Leave Emma outta this," Ryan tells his mom. Then he turns angry eyes onto his dad. "She wasn't the one screaming at me before. She's not the one trying to run my life for me."

Mr. Desmond's face flushes a livid red. I'm not sure I've ever seen anyone this color before. Ryan's dad is terrifying right now.

"Someone has to!" Mr. Desmond spits out. "You're not doing a great job of it yourself." He takes a deep breath and tugs at the hem of his suit jacket, straightening himself out. "Now you are going to march out of this room and you are going to drink the damn coffee your mother gives you so you can sober up. Do you understand me?"

Ryan seems to shrink in his seat next to me. "Fiiiine," he slurs. "I'll leave. But I've gotta few things I wanna say to you, Dad."

Mr. Desmond takes Ryan by the arm and yanks him out of his seat, knocking me aside as he does. I sit there watching them go, too shocked to even say good night. Ryan's shoulders slump down. He trips once as his dad tugs on him, then yanks his arm out of his dad's hold. He doesn't turn back once to say good night. He's just . . . gone. For a few seconds all I can do is stare at the door he just passed through and wish with all my might that he's okay right now.

"Emma."

Mrs. Desmond's voice cuts through my thoughts. I'd forgotten she was still there. Which means we still can meet up with them. I can make sure Ryan's okay.

"Normally, you know we'd love to have you join us," she begins, and my hope sags. I know where this is going. "But under the circumstances . . ."

My eyes stray back to where Ryan and his dad just left the ballroom. I feel as if I'm abandoning him. Walking away and leaving him to the wolves, even though I'm not sure what else I can do right now as his mom disinvites me.

"No, of course. I understand," I reply. "Just tell Ryan . . ." I squeeze my eyes shut. Try to figure out what to say—and fall back on an inadequate "Tell him I hope he's okay."

She lays her hand on my shoulder and gives me a gentle squeeze. "I will, Emma."

Then she's gone. Before I can get up, Jackson sits down next to me with three glasses of water in his hands. "You look like you could use this."

"I could," I say in a low voice. "This . . . hasn't been a great night."

"Anniversaries, weddings," he begins. "Things can kind of get out of control sometimes when the alcohol flows too freely." He takes a swig of water. "I've been to weddings where . . . well . . . it's not worth repeating."

I take a sip of water. "That good?"

"You have no idea," he laughs. "All I'm saying is that big events like this can bring out the best and worst in people sometimes."

My eyes roam around the room. Some people are still laughing and dancing. Others talk in voices so loud they must be drunk. Every now and then, someone looks so miserable that my heart aches for them.

"Too bad it's so many extremes," I say.

"Sometimes," he agrees. "But sometimes they're just fun nights to celebrate happy events."

I think of how tense my dad was earlier. About Linda's angry face and Ryan shaking me off. "Did you have fun?" I ask dubiously.

He laughs. "I did, actually," he tells me. "I'm not sure what it says about me that I had such a good time when the band played 'Meet Me in St. Louis' three times, but I've decided not to examine it too closely."

I hold my glass and Jackson clinks his against it. "To parties that bring out the best in people," I offer.

A warm smile spreads across his face. "I'll drink to that."

"Jackson, would you mind if I steal Emma for a few minutes?" Looking up I see my mom standing over us, her dress even more battered than before.

"Of course, Jessica," he says as he gets up. Then he smiles at me. "Take care, okay?"

"You too."

Mom waits till Jackson's well across the ballroom before she continues. "Let's go somewhere we can talk."

Dad joins us at the stairs but he doesn't say a word. Neither of them does. He hasn't exactly been chatty with me lately. But Mom not saying anything? She must be really upset. God, will this night never end?

I just need to get through whatever talk they have planned about not drinking alcohol and learning from Ryan's mistake. Then I can go to my room and close the door on this night. I think of Ryan, upstairs with his dad, and something twists in my chest. Even with Mr. Desmond being so awful, I'd still rather be with Ryan—helping him however I could—than dealing with my parents.

The door closes in our suite. Dad turns to me. Jaw tense, mouth a grim line. My stomach clenches. This is not going to go well.

"I have to get back downstairs soon," he tells me in a voice of forced calm. "I was in the middle of a conversation with a potential investor."

Mom stands by his side. "Which means your timing could not have been worse."

I look at them both, genuinely confused. "My timing?" I ask. "What did I do?"

"You made a scene in the middle of the party," Dad replies. "Which is unacceptable."

Heat courses through me. I can't even believe what I'm hearing. "Then maybe you should talk to your good friend Jack Desmond, because he's the one who made a scene," I tell him. "Ryan and I were sitting peacefully at a table till he showed up."

Mom puts her arm on Dad's shoulder to keep him from saying whatever angry thing might have been on his lips. "Jack Desmond's on the cusp of officially announcing his campaign," she tells me. "He's under a lot of stress right now."

I throw both arms up in the air. "So he's allowed to make a scene, but you're yelling at *me*?" I spit out. "*I* didn't do anything. And I know you can't squeeze any investment money out of me, but that doesn't mean you get to accuse me of something I didn't even do!"

When I'm finished—when I have nothing left to say—something inside me breaks. Air heaves in and out of my lungs. My hands tremble. It's all I can do to keep standing on my own two feet.

A chilling silence falls in our living room. The ticking clock over the mantel almost echoes off the walls. The gentle whir of the air conditioner roars in my eyes.

"Sit down, Emma." Dad's voice is barely a whisper. "Now."

A vein pulses in his temple. Mom comes up behind him and puts her hand on his shoulder. "You heard your father."

But I don't have to do this. I don't have to keep talking to them.

Dad grabs my arm as I move to leave. "Listen to me," he says. "I know you're upset and it's clear that you don't understand what's at stake here. We have a family business that we need to keep sustainable. Which means we need investors." His grip tightens on my arm. "And I need someone who'll take the helm when I can't steer the ship anymore. I'm relying on you."

Tears sting my eyes, but I don't know what's left to say. I'm responsible for getting them an investor. For carrying on the business. For being everything they want me to be.

"I'm only seventeen, Dad," I remind him.

"I know that, Emma," he replies. His voice is softer now. The edge has gone out of it. "But that means you're not a little girl anymore. It's well past time for you to let go of this delusion that you're going to become an artist, and start learning the business from the bottom up the way I did. All you're doing is putting off the inevitable." Dad finally lets go of my arm. "It's time for you to grow up."

I stand there, still as a statue for what feels like an eternity. *It's time for you to grow up.* But doesn't being an adult mean being responsible for myself? That I should make decisions on my own? I silently plead with him for something he's never going to give. At least not willingly. Not as long as he doesn't have to.

The walls feel as if they're slowly closing in on me again.

"I'm going for a walk," I tell them. "And before you say anything, I know it's late and I know it's not *proper* for a young lady to walk around by herself at night. But you know what? As part of being all grown up, when I need some space I'm going to take it."

I let my parents watch me walk away and slam the door behind me.

My blood boils under my skin. My whole body itches red hot. I need to cool down. So I walk. Let my feet move one in front of the other, not caring where I go or how long I stay there. It's so humid that it's hard to breathe, though. There's no relief, even out here.

I turn, just once, to look up at the hotel. One of Strauss's waltzes is still audible in the distance. The lights from the ballroom shine through the dark of the night like a beacon, but I can't let myself follow it. I glance up at the penthouse, where Ryan is probably still getting yelled at. The livid red face of his dad jumps into my head and I shudder. I want to go back inside and up to the penthouse and save him from his own family.

Then I remember his hand pushing me away. His arms shaking me off. Even if I could go up to the penthouse, he probably wouldn't want me there. Tears sting at my eyes again. *Keep walking*, I tell myself. *Just keep moving and everything will be okay.*

I go to the greenhouse first but being there alone at night makes my skin crawl, so I keep moving. Around the grounds. Over to the playground. By the pool area, and even the rose garden. Then I look up and see the full moon overhead. Memories of the time JR and I snuck to the beach and howled at the moon like werewolves pop into my head. Terry thought it was hilarious when he caught us. My parents did not. Just the thought of it makes the anger churn inside of me again, and I don't want that. I don't want to feel this way.

The beach. I need to go to the beach. The water and the sand and the wind will cool me down. Then I'll feel better.

Just as I'm about to leave the tree line to get to the lake, I see him. He sits with his back to me in the exact spot where the pine trees end and the sand begins. Under his breath—in a low tenor—he sings my favorite Gershwin song, "Embraceable You." I've never heard him sing before. For a second or two, I listen. Mesmerized.

"What're you doing here?"

The sudden sound of his voice startles me. "How did you know it was me?"

JR turns and shrugs. "I always know when it's you."

"What's that supposed to mean?"

He shrugs again instead of answering. I try not to let it bother me. He always knows when it's me. That's what matters. It's the only thing that matters. Well . . . and getting myself back under control right now.

I focus on what I can. The breeze off the water, cutting through the humidity. The sound of the frogs in the nearby rushes. The fact that even though he's not currently speaking, just having JR nearby makes me feel better. So I walk over and sit next to him.

He looks me up and down. "You going to tell me why you're out so late all by yourself in that dress?"

"I had to escape," I tell him.

"Me too."

"Your dad?"

He nods. "Yours?"

He throws a stone in the water as I rake my fingers through the pine needles. JR understands. We have similar problems with our parents but completely different ones at the same time. Besides, I don't want to think about my parents right now. A restless energy simmers under my skin. I want to run or jump or . . . or make something. I pick up a handful of pine needles and start weaving them together, one thin green needle at a time until they form a tiny basket.

"What's that?" he asks.

"A gift." I hand it to him. "For you."

JR flips it around to take a closer look. "Only you can make something out of nothing like this," he says in a quiet voice. His fingers close around the little basket. "Thanks for this. I'll keep it with me. Always."

Always. He'll keep it always. He always knows when it's me. I have no idea how to respond to any of it so I don't say anything at all.

Something swirls and churns inside me as if a storm is about to break. I turn and watch him in the darkness, but it only makes the hurricane grow stronger. I want to step out of the storm. To let whatever it is that's been building up inside me out—to let it explode into a million pieces and see what happens afterward.

But I know what happens after big explosions. I've seen pictures in history books at school. Shrapnel. Burnt edges. Fallout.

A fear lurks inside my brain that the explosion will be less like fireworks and more like a nuclear bomb if I ever let it happen.

I want this and don't want it, all at the same time.

I look over at JR again. His hair's tucked behind his ears and he's wearing his favorite jeans with the holes in the knees. The moon sparkles in the water giving him a kind of halo. It shines in his eyes as he watches me.

He understands. He knows. The bare skin of his arm presses against mine but I don't move away. Instead I lean into the solid warmth of him even more. Our skin sticks together in the humid air. His knee touches mine. I lean into that, too.

The explosion feels so close now, so huge, that I have to do something to make it go away.

So I do it. I reach up to touch his cheek. I kiss him.

JR freezes. He doesn't kiss me back. He stares at me, a crease between his eyebrows, and I know. *I know* I've screwed everything up. I let my hand fall away, but he catches it in his. Presses it to his cheek again.

The storm roars inside me, stronger and stronger with every second that passes. Our eyes meet. I close the distance between us again. This time he kisses me back. But this isn't a soft brush of lips or tentative touch. My hands grasp onto him, hard. His hands are everywhere. Our teeth knock. Our tongues clash. He bites at my lower lip making me gasp out loud. I need him like I'd need water or oxygen that's been kept from me too long.

Desperately, frantically.

JR slips his arm under my knees and he lifts me onto his lap. His hands skim down my dress, over my backside. My fingers dig into his shoulders, tug at his hair.

It's an explosion—we are an explosion—just as I thought we would be.

That is, until it ends. We break apart, both gasping for breath as we cling to each other.

"Why'd you do that?" he whispers.

"Because I wanted to. I needed to."

He looks at me, but he's so close it's hard to meet his eyes. "You broke up with Ryan?"

The hope in his voice is so raw it startles me.

"What?" I say. "No . . . I haven't even talked to Ryan since . . ."

Since he left the ballroom drunk. Since I fought with my parents. Since I found JR.

I lean in to kiss him again, but he holds me back. "What the hell is this then?" he says. "You're still with your boyfriend, but you come out here and kiss me?"

"No, I . . . I don't even know," I try to explain. "I just need you."

JR slides me off his lap, then gets up to walk toward the water. I get up, too, but I'm unsteady on my feet, as if the earth is moving under them. Once I feel grounded again, I walk over to him.

"What's wrong?" I ask, my voice quivering.

"What's wrong?" he barks out. "I'll tell you what's wrong. My oldest friend just cheated with me on her boyfriend . . . who's also my friend, by the way." He rubs his eyes. "And it's not because she doesn't want to be with her boyfriend anymore, it's just . . . what, Emma?"

I blink my eyes to try to clear my head, but I can't make sense of what he's saying. I can't make sense of any of this. I don't know what he needs to hear or how to say it to make him stop talking like this.

"I need you," I whisper. It's not enough. I know it's not. "I always need you."

"You need me?" he repeats. "Then get rid of Ryan. Because you can't have both of us."

"I don't want both of you!" I protest. I don't know why this is so hard—why he won't give me any time to *think*. If he'd just give me a little time. A little space. I could find a way to answer him. I could make him understand.

But JR just throws his hands up in the air. "No, you want *him*," he practically yells. "You say you need me, but it's only when no one is around. Only if you don't have to deal with the fallout of it."

My shoulders shake with anger, fear . . . with too many emotions at one time. "What's that supposed to mean?" I practically spit out the words.

"It means this," he says. He walks right up to me, so close that I can feel the warmth of his skin even before he touches me.

Then he does it. He touches me. His mouth is on mine and his hands tangled in my hair—his breath's hot on my face. Every atom of my body wants this to never stop.

But of course it does. JR pulls away again, taking a few steps back. Leaving me with a gnawing emptiness in my chest. I want to him come back and touch me again so badly I ache with it.

"Is that what you want, Emma?" he demands. "To fool around with me behind Ryan's back?"

"No . . . that's not what I said!" I cry out. "That's not what I . . . I just don't know what I want . . . and . . ."

Why can't I make him understand? Why can't I find the words to say to him to make this right? I'm as frustrated and angry with myself as I am at him. I need him to *listen* but I'm not even sure what to say.

"I know what I want, though," he tells me. He comes up and stands right in front of me, right in my space again. But the look in his eyes—the angry, betrayed look in his eyes—makes me almost afraid of him.

I want to make that look go away. To explain everything in a way that will make sense. I *ache* for him. He's so close that it would be easy to kiss him again. To just touch my lips to his and see what happens. I want to do that more than I've wanted almost anything in my life before. But it would only make everything worse. I've never seen him like this before and I never want to again.

"JR, I . . ."

"I know," he says. His voice has an almost desperate edge to it. "I *know*, Emma. What I want isn't really what you want. And it was okay until tonight. It was okay until you made it not okay."

Tears stream down my face. I wipe them away with shaking fingers. "I have no idea what I'm supposed to say right now," I tell him. "I don't know how to make this better."

His eyes are brittle, as if he could shatter at any moment. Something inside of me feels as if I already have—that I'm hollowed out. Empty.

"You can't," he finally says. My hands drop weightless to my sides. He's angry. I'm lost.

Without another word, he walks away, leaving me here all alone. I watch as he makes his way toward town—as he picks up a rock and hurls it into the lake.

The swirling, churning feeling inside me has died down, leaving me feeling numb—leaving me to deal with tattered ruins of what I used to have.

CHAPTER 28

Emma (Then)

A fire alarm blares to life, startling me awake. A bitter laugh spills out of me. Of course the fire alarm has to go off tonight. I lie back in my bed and wrap the pillow around my head. The alarm's gone off dozens of times over the years and it's never been anything but literal false alarms. I can't really see the need to go stand outside at . . . I look at my clock . . . two o'clock in the morning in my pajamas right now to make this night any worse.

This night is cursed. I'm convinced of it.

A breeze comes through my open windows, bringing a whiff of smoky air with it. I sit bolt upright in my bed just as Mom flings my door open.

"Emma, get up! We have to go!"

Her hair's tangled—her eyes frantic. She's trying to pull on a robe and get to me at the same time and ends up tripping. I've never seen her such a mess in my entire life. She'd never be seen in public with her bathrobe on. With her hair like that. It's takes me a few seconds to process what's happening.

The smell of smoke gets stronger.

"Come on!" she cries out, pulling at my arm. "Please! We've got to out of here. Now."

I jump out of bed and follow her into the hallway outside our place. Aside from the smell of smoke in the air there's no other sign anything's wrong. The air is clear, the hall empty. But the alarm blares in my ears as Mom tugs me toward the stairs and something in me snaps into reality. This isn't a safety drill.

The hotel is on fire.

"Where's Dad?" I cry. "Is he already outside?"

She shakes her head. "He'll get out there as soon as he can."

I stop short, my eyes frantically scanning the ends of the hall for fire. For any sign of my dad. Mom grabs me with both hands this time, her fingers digging into me. "Emma, for God's sake, you have to *move*." Our eyes meet and I see the panic in hers. I nod. We keep going.

Only when we reach the stairs does the magnitude of what's happening hit me. Hotel guests crowd the staircase, each trying to barge their way past everyone else and get outside as fast as they can. I take Mom's hand in mine and she gives me a squeeze. "Come on," she says again, but her voice shakes this time. Her hand shakes, too.

I take a deep breath and we enter the fray.

A man shoves us out of his way as he pushes down the stairs. He knocks a little girl over, forcing his way through the crowd.

"HEY!" I shout out, but the girl's mother has already started screaming at him as the dad swoops the girl up and holds her close.

"Oh God," Mom says under her breath. "Oh my God."

The look in her eyes terrifies me. Wide with a fear—a grief—that makes my heart hurt. "Let's keep going, Mom."

She holds my hand even tighter and nods.

A woman starts yelling from somewhere above us on the stairs and it sets off some chain reaction of anger and panic. Another person screams back and then another shouts at them. A toddler in her dad's arms wails and bunches her fists into his T-shirt as he sings her the song from *Sesame Street* in a cracked voice.

Then I see Dad, wading through the sea of people moving down the stairs, as he makes his way to us. Tears fill my eyes. Relief floods over me. He's okay. He's going to make sure we're okay. Suddenly it's like I'm a little girl again, looking to my parents to make sure everything will be all right.

He pulls both of us into his arms for just a split second and holds us close. "Keep going," he tells us. "Get outside. I'll meet you by the big oak tree when I can."

I swallow down a sob. "Aren't you coming?"

Dad shakes his head almost frantically. "I can't." His eyes move all around us, taking in the chaos. Then he kisses my forehead. "Now go. I'll see you soon."

Just like that, he's gone again. I turn back to watch him, but someone bumps into me from behind. Almost topples me over. Mom grabs my arm and keeps me from falling.

"Where's Dad going?" I yell at her. "Why's he going back up there?"

"He's going room to room." She looks up the stairs to where Dad just disappeared. "They have to make sure everyone gets out of their rooms."

I choke on my own breath. "But what if . . . "

"Emma!" Mom takes me by the shoulders and shakes me. "We don't have time. I have to get you out of here." A sob passes over her face, but she shakes herself and swallows it down. "I promised him I'd get you out no matter what."

The sea of people keeps flowing around us until she takes me by the hand again and helps me move forward. Slowly, one step at a time, we keep going till we reach the lobby. There, we meet a whole other kind of chaos. Smoke fills the air. People throw themselves at the doors, knocking anyone in their path aside. Everyone's trying to push through, out onto the verandah.

Someone's going to get trampled.

I tug Mom to a stop. "This way," I tell her. "Come this way."

We struggle to the kitchen door together, knowing the staff entrance lies just beyond it.

When we finally get there, I turn back and yell out. "There's another way out. Come this way!"

The crush of people returns, their arms, legs press against us, pushing Mom and me forward even as we sprint toward the staff door. There's a squeeze through it. I can feel Mom's hand slipping out of mine as she pushes forward. Oh God, I'm going to lose her.

She looks back at me over the heads of everyone else with grim determination in her eyes. And I know. I know in that moment that there's no way she's going anywhere without me. Mom steps backward through the door, shoving a tall man out of her way. She takes my arm and hurls me through the door, pushing me from behind as she presses against me.

Then we're out. The air is heavy with smoke and humidity. People huddle on the lawn. Families cling to each other in the dark. I look around, limp and numb at what I see. But Mom doesn't stop for a single second. Her arms snake around me and she pushes us forward. We race toward the oak tree till a burst of smoke curls through the air.

I turn to see where it's coming from just as the fire department arrives. Sirens blare. Police struggle on their bikes to make their way through the crowd. There are people everywhere. In pajamas and underwear. Shouting, frantic. Crying. Finally I see why.

Flames lick out of the side of the hotel by the ballroom. It bursts through a window on the first floor, smoke pouring out afterward like some kind of nightmarish bonfire. My eyes scan the crowd. There's no sign of Dad. No sign of Ryan or Linda. Their parents. Jackson.

My feet start to move before my brain even tells them to. One step at a time, I move toward the hotel. Dad's still in there. They all might be. I break into a run.

A pair of hands grabs me, pulling me to a stop. I shake my arms, frantic to get them off me but they're stronger than me. They hold me fast. Only when I stop struggling do the hands on me loosen. Only then do I realize it's Tom who's still holding on to me.

"I can't let you go in there, Emma."

"But my dad!" I plead, tears coming again whether I want them to or not. "I don't know where Linda and Ryan are!"

"I know. I *know*. But you need to stay out here." He's practically shaking me now, trying to get me to understand. "Promise me you'll stay here." I look over his shoulder at the hotel. The firefighters have their hoses out. They're dousing the flames.

"Promise me, Emma," Tom pleads.

I can't bring myself look at him, but I force the words out anyway. "I promise."

He nods, then runs back toward the building. I watch him disappear into the chaos just as someone else takes shape before me. Jackson. He's walking this way, holding two tiny kids in his arms. Their parents have two bigger kids on their backs, piggybacking them out to safety.

He puts them down, talks to the parents for a second. Then he looks up and sees me standing here.

"Are you okay?" he calls.

"Are you?"

He shakes his head and turns to look at the hotel for a second before Clarice finds him and they both head back into the hotel together. Then they're gone.

Firefighters pour into the building. Police try to set up barriers, urging everyone to move back toward the lake. Some people follow their instructions. Others yell at the officers, gesturing toward the hotel. And it hits me: they probably have someone still in the building, too. They're probably trying to get back in.

I drop to my knees for a second, my legs giving out from underneath me.

Then I realize that it's not just Dad I can't find. It's Mom.

Back on my feet, I sprint toward the oak tree. Mom's standing there, comforting an older woman. When she sees me, her eyes blaze. She grabs my arm. Yanks me toward her. "Do *not* run off again, do you hear me?" she yells. "Stay *right* here till Dad comes."

New sirens blare as an ambulance comes up the driveway. Every single vehicle on the island is here. I start to move toward the hotel again, but Mom holds on tight. "Stay. Right. Here."

I stand by her side watching as our home gets swallowed up in smoke from the fire and water from the hoses. The crowd has thinned. I can't see flames anymore. Everything feels as if it's finally slowing down. As if maybe everyone's finally out and the fire is contained.

The police part the remaining crowd so the EMTs can get out of the building with a stretcher held between them. I strain to see who they're carrying, to make sure it's not Dad. Then my stomach lurches. Laid out on the stretcher with an oxygen mask over her mouth and nose is Linda.

"NO!" I scream. Mom grabs me again wrapping her around me. Holding me close.

"She'll be okay, love," she tells me. "I can see her moving on the stretcher. It looks like she's talking to the EMTs."

I pull out of her arms to see for myself, and there she is, being loaded into the ambulance with an angry look on her face and hands gesturing wildly. I'd laugh, just from relief, if I had any energy left to. Instead, I watch Mr. and Mrs. Desmond follow her into the ambulance.

"Come on, Dad," I whisper. Mom and I stand together, watching for any sign of him. Mom takes faltering breaths beside me. She's starting to panic. Then she cries out, her hand over her mouth. I follow her eyes, fear welling up in my chest.

Finally. *Finally*. Out of the smoke and haze, I see Dad and Jackson. Dad stands with his back to us, watching the last vestiges of the fire get stamped out. He puts his hand on Jackson's shoulder. Steadies himself. Then he leans in and says something to Jackson. Whatever it is, Jackson puts his arms around Dad. They hold on to each other for a long second or two. Then Jackson walks away, leaving Dad alone.

I try to break free from Mom, but she holds me fast. "Give him a minute," she says, her eyes never straying from Dad. "He knows where to find us. He'll come when he's ready."

My mouth opens to protest, but I never get the words out.

Because somehow, standing in front of me, is Ryan. I throw myself into his arms, rubbing my hands over his back, his arms, trying to make sure he's okay. I count to twenty, fifty, one hundred, trying to center myself. To get ready for what's to come. Ryan rubs his hand over my hair, smoothing it back. It shakes as it passes over the back of my head.

"I've gotta get to the medical center," he says in my ear. "But I needed to make sure you're okay."

I step back, just far enough to look in his eyes. "I'm *fine*," I tell him. "But Linda? They . . . they took her away on a stretcher, Ryan."

He closes his eyes and gulps in one deep breath. Then another. "She's fine," he assures me. "Dad says she's fine. She fell asleep in a room near the fire. They just want to keep overnight for observation."

A flash lights up the darkness, momentarily blinding me.

Mom's on the photographer in an instant, taking him away by the arm. Demanding that he leave the premises or she'll call the police over. As she argues with him, I realize that Ryan's holding his forehead. He's shaking in my arms. A cold sensation settles my stomach. "You said she's okay," I tell him. "You said they just want to keep her for observation!"

Startled eyes meet mine. "No . . . no . . . she's really fine!" he says frantically. "Dad said . . . he promised everything would be okay. That there's no reason to worry."

I nod again and again, wanting to believe him.

He looks back to the hotel and shudders. "Everything will be okay."

Ryan leans down to kiss me. He smells like smoke and stale alcohol. I kiss him anyway. "I've gotta go," he says again. "But I'll see you as soon as I can, okay?"

I nod one last time before he leaves.

For a few minutes, all I can do is breathe. In and out. Through my nose and out my mouth. Linda's fine. Dad's fine. Ryan, Jackson . . . everyone's okay. Mom touches my arms and nods toward Dad. He's standing on the lawn, watching the two of us, but he doesn't take a single step toward us.

Instead, we go to him. Slowly at first, but faster and faster as we get closer, Mom and I finally run into his arms. He holds us close, his arm tight around me. He kisses my hair, Mom's, breathing so hard I worry he's going to collapse.

"It's all going to be okay, Richard," Mom tells him. "Nobody got hurt."

Dad shakes in my arms. Hot tears run into my hair. "Jess, I . . ."

She pulls him away from me and cradles him in her arms. "It'll be okay, Richard," she says over and over again. "I promise you it will."

Dad wipes his hand over his eyes and shakes his head. "Emma?"

I'm by his side in a flash. "What is it, Dad?"

He holds out his hand to me and I take it. "Can you head down to the lake? Make sure everyone there's okay? I . . . I've been worried about them and . . ." His voice falters. It physically hurts to see him like this.

"Of course, Dad," I reassure him. "I'll head down there right now."

He squeezes my hand before letting go and turning back to Mom. I watch them walk, their arms around each other, back toward the hotel. Then I make my way down to the lake.

The farther I get from the hotel, the more everything seems as it always is. As it should be. The pool glints in the moonlight. The volleyball net waves in the wind. The trees stand exactly where they've always been. It all seems so . . . normal. Everyday. As if nothing has changed at all.

That feeling goes away as soon as I reach the beach.

There are people everywhere. EMTs hand out silver blankets. Even though it's so warm, everyone takes one, eager to have some sense of comfort. A woman walks around handing out bottles of water. Another passes around boxes of granola bars. I have no idea who either of them is. They don't live at the hotel or work there. They just came down to help.

Tears bite at my eyes as I watch them. As I watch how gratefully—how quietly and with what grace—the same people who pushed past each other in the hotel are now greeting the help of strangers.

Two police officers come down and talk quietly with the EMTs for a while before the one who's clearly in charge switches on a megaphone.

"I've got a few updates for you," she says, her voice echoing off the trees behind us. "The fire department has the fire out."

A cheer goes up in the crowd. People start talking, laughing even, at the news. The police officer holds up her hand.

"The fire's out, but it's still under investigation and we still have to determine how much damage that side of the building has sustained." A hush falls around her as reality sets back in. "So we're going to ask you all to stay calm . . ."

Voices rise all around me. A baby starts crying. Then another.

"LISTEN!" the policer officer yells into the megaphone. "I have updates for you but you have to listen carefully."

Only when the noise dies down does she begin again. "You're not going to be able to go back to the hotel tonight." A roar of protest rises, making me flinch. "BUT," she continues. "We have folks from all over the island who've volunteered to house you for the night."

"And what about after tonight?" someone yells. "We saved up for two years for this trip!"

I look at the people near me. They're smoky and dirty. Exhausted. They came here to relax and have fun, and this is what they got. I feel as if I should say something—*do* something—but I have no idea what. I know even less than the police officer does.

The hollowed out, empty feeling returns so I make my way through the crowd again and start walking back to the hotel. At least I can tell my parents what's happening at the beach and do something useful. In the distance I can see emergency lights trained on the building, lighting it up like a lantern in the dark of the night.

Only as I come out of the trees can I see the full extent of the damage to the hotel. A burnt-out hole mars the side of the hotel where the fire started. There are charred markings all the way up to the third floor, though I'm not sure the fire reached anywhere near that high. Police and firefighters are still roaming around, working to assess damage and to cordon off the hotel so no one can enter it. I walk toward the verandah, looking for Mom and Dad.

"Hey!" someone calls out. "You can't go over there!"

I turn to find a young police officer—probably not many years older than I am—coming my way. "This area's off limits."

"But I live here," I try to explain.

He gives me a curt once-over. "Yeah, I know who you are," he tells me. "Doesn't mean you can just waltz into a crime scene."

I stare at him, not sure I understood what he just said—how anything related to tonight could be considered a crime. "What did you just say?" The words come out of me slowly. Carefully. I need to really listen this time when he speaks again so I know. So I can understand.

"Your father and Jack Desmond fingered a suspect," he tells me. "They're giving their statements right now." He looks toward the hotel. Shakes his head. "So you can't go up there."

I sit with that for a second. "A suspect . . . for what?" I stammer out. "What's going on here?"

"Arson," the officer tells me. "Someone caused the fire."

I take a step back from him. "That's not possible," I assure him. "It's an old hotel. It was probably electrical . . . or something with the gas."

He gives me a hard glare. "You going to tell me how to do my job?" he says. When I don't reply, he keeps going. "They have a suspect already. It doesn't matter what you think happened."

He's trying to be rude but I couldn't care less. All that matters is the hotel. Home. The burnt-out hole by the ballroom.

A cold, numb feeling settles in my stomach. It rises, up through my chest, and down my arms into my fingertips. "Who . . . who do they think caused the fire?" I force myself to ask the question even though I'm not sure I want the answer.

The officer leans in closer, speaking in a quieter voice. "They thought it was the groundskeeper," he tells me. "Guy's already got a record, so it wasn't much of a stretch."

I shake my head. "No," I say. "*No.* Terry would never. It . . . it doesn't make any sense. I know Terry, he . . . he would never do this."

The man shrugs. "I guess not. Because they're questioning someone else now."

Something I've never felt before takes hold of me. It's not fear or panic. It's not anything in the universe I could name. I look up at the hotel, trying to make sense of this. My parents are up there, though. They'll explain everything and then I'll know.

I glance at the officer one last time. Then I take off at a run toward the hotel.

"Hey, get back here!" he yells behind me, but I just run faster.

The whole world feels as if it's spinning around me again—a swirling, massive tornado of a storm this time. The fear of what I'll find when the spinning stops terrifies me so much that I almost have to stop running. But I can't.

I spot my mom and hurry to her side, but she holds one finger up to her lips to shush me.

From somewhere behind her, JR's voice fills the early morning air and every cavity of my body until it feels as if I'm going to explode again.

"I already told you," he says. "I don't know what else you want from me."

A police officer starts asking him questions about what he was doing in the hotel at that hour of night and what he threw that knocked the candelabra over. JR just sits there still as a stone.

Then he looks away from the officer and sees me standing here. Our eyes meet. His cheeks turn a painful shade of red, as if someone just slapped him.

He closes his eyes for a second. When he opens them, he looks depressed. Defeated.

JR turns away from me. "It's my fault," he tells the officer. "Isn't that all you need to hear?"

CHAPTER 29

Lexi (Now)

C aleb!" I call as I sprint into the library. But instead of the adorkable librarian, the girl who helped me the other day is sitting there, her nose deep in a book. Liza, I think?

"It's Caleb's day off," she says.

It takes a second for me to catch my breath. The girl at the desk is completely unfazed by this. She doesn't even look up from her book.

"I'm having kind of a research emergency," I tell her at last.

"You know where the computers are." She points to the left. "Yell if you need help with anything."

I stand there, staring at her for a second. Is this girl for real? "Um . . . uh . . . can I just tell you what I need help with *without* having to yell?"

Liza finally looks up at me over the book she's been reading. "Not yelling works, too."

I guess that's progress. And I really do need her help. "Okay . . . so I need to research a fire that happened at the Palais du Lac. Maybe about twenty years ago?"

She nods. "Look up the *Island Crier* in the library database," she replies. For the first time since I got here, she closes her book. "And it actually happened nineteen years ago, not twenty. Year before I was born." She writes it down for me on a sticky note.

The girl points to the computers again. "It was during the summer," she says. "But I don't know when exactly. Just start in, like, May of that year and go from there. That rag of a paper only comes out once a week, so it's not like it's an extensive archive."

"Oh . . . okay," I say. "Thanks."

Despite the nonchalant attitude, she's being remarkably helpful.

So I sit down and open the library's database and take a deep breath. This might finally lead to something. Or at least it might if I actually looked at the newspaper archives.

The *Island Crier* isn't hard to find, and it's easier to navigate than I thought a small island paper would be. Beginning with May 1, I start sifting through the papers.

There's everything under the sun: articles about fighting hunger on-island, tidbits of gossip, Little League stats, pictures from the high school graduation, even an advice column called Ask Mack. For a paper that only comes out on Thursdays, it covers a surprising amount of ground.

That's just in the first two issues. I open up the next one. And the next. And the next.

Finally in June I find a piece about the hotel. The picture that goes with the article is bigger than the article itself. It shows a petite Black woman standing in front of the hotel. The caption reads, *Clarice Bello plans the party of the century at the Palais du Lac.* As I read through the article, though, disappointment sets in.

PALAIS DU LAC CELEBRATES 100TH ANNIVERSARY

June 6

The Palais du Lac first opened its door one hundred years ago this summer, and is going to be marking the occasion in style. "While every summer is filled with activities at the Palais du Lac, we're planning some special events to celebrate the one hundredth anniversary of the hotel," says Activities Director Clarice Bello.

Those events include a number of casual anniversary barbecues on the property for guests and residents of the hotel alike and will culminate in a formal ball in August. "We'll be opening up the ballroom in nineteenth-century style for the gala," Bello says. "So we can celebrate the hotel in a way that honors its origins."

To learn more about the hotel's anniversary celebration and its history, visit its website. Or just visit the hotel for tours and information about its centennial.

For a brief second or two I just stare at the screen. "That wasn't helpful at all," I say under my breath. Then I sit up straighter. Open a new tab. Maybe Clarice Bello's still at the hotel. Maybe I could talk to her. I search for the activities director on the hotel's website, but it's listed as someone named Finn Calahan. Okay, or not. But that doesn't mean I won't find her.

Clarice Bello, I type into Google. The very article I just read and others from the *Island Crier* about hotel activities over a few summers before the fire pop up. There's a wedding announcement that might be hers, but there's no picture. Then a few articles from a newspaper in Lyons, France, that are written in French. When I translate them, I discover that she worked at a hotel there for a few years, but then left—there's a piece about her retirement party.

I can't find anything after that.

Which means I'm sitting here just staring at the screen again. I fold my hands in front of me and try to . . . I don't know . . . center myself? Give myself any kind of motivation to go on?

But I'm only in June. There's still a whole summer's worth of small-town news to sift through.

I shake my head and close up my Clarice Bello tab. Back to the *Island Crier*. There's another article at the end of June about the hotel's one hundredth anniversary party. The party of the century, the article called it. Like that was a funny joke or something. Though thinking back to the names of the rooms at the historical society, it's hilarious by comparison.

It has nothing new. Just a reiteration of the fact that the hotel was going to have a huge party in August. On to July, I guess.

By the time I get to the end of July my eyes start to glaze over. Maybe library girl had the wrong summer in mind? Maybe the fire hadn't actually taken place the year before she was born? She seemed pretty sure. But then I seemed pretty sure this trip had been a good idea, too, and I don't really know anything more than what I've found in the mosaic box. And I could've just looked through that at home without the prospect of spending my entire senior year grounded. I'm going to kill Chloe if nothing comes of this trip. Right before Dad kills me.

I force myself to keep going.

Boy Scout jamborees. Bake sales. Church fairs. Milestone birthdays. It's all here in the pages of the *Crier*. If I was looking for a snapshot of a small town in America, this would be it. Except for the no-car thing, I guess.

My head is starting to throb.

Then, right in the middle of August, I see it.

Under the masthead is a huge picture from the night of the fire. In it, clear as day, is my mother. She's standing outside in the dark, her arms around a tall blond guy who's kind of gorgeous. It looks like Mom's wearing pajamas even though the guy with her has a tux on. It's such a discordant combination that I get stuck on it for a while.

Then it hits me: this is the guy in the picture on the verandah. Same blond hair, same tux, same huge hands touching her. Was he her boyfriend? Or just her date for the night? I have no idea who he is or what his name is but he looks lost in this picture after the fire.

Mom's lips are a tight slit of worry, her eyes devastatingly sad. In the few pictures I've seen of her, she's always been with Dad or me, smiling as if she couldn't be happier. This is the first time I've seen her look like *this*. Would it have been an expression I already knew if she'd lived? Something she'd pull out when I'd done something wrong? Or did it only come out when something horrible happened? Like when the hotel she was staying at went up in flames?

There are other people in the picture, all looking lost or anxious or just plain angry. But I don't know who any of them are and the caption doesn't give anyone's names. Not even Mom's.

As I scroll down the story unfolds in front of my eyes.

FIRE AT THE PALAIS DU LAC

August 15

Investigators are working to determine the cause of the fire at the Palais du Lac Hotel that broke out late on Saturday night. No one got seriously hurt in the blaze but one person was taken to the medical center for smoke inhalation.

Hotel owner Richard Wolfe could not be reached for comment, but the *Island Crier* has been informed that there will be a press briefing on Tuesday, August 19, at nine thirty a.m. out on the hotel lawn.

This is a developing story.

The next story in the archives is about a big blackout in Ontario, then there's one about the island's Girl Scout troop holding a beach clean-up day. There's nothing about my mom or anything else about what happened that night. There's just this picture and more questions.

I open up the next issue. Splashed on the front page is a huge picture of the aftermath of the fire at the hotel. It looks as if someone took a giant match and burned a hole in the side of the first floor of the building.

SUSPECT IN CUSTODY IN HOTEL FIRE

August 22

A seventeen-year-old boy is now in custody for destruction of property after a small function room on the first floor of the Palais du Lac Hotel went up in flames last week. Not a year-round resident of the island, he is nonetheless a regular summer resident staying with his father, an employee at the hotel.

"We feel deeply betrayed and confused by his actions," Richard Wolfe said during a press conference. "He's the son of an employee, one whom we hired despite him having a checkered past, and we're disappointed that our trust was so misplaced. This young man has hurt my family and many other people in so many ways."

The charges against the minor only include destruction of property, as the fire was accidental and the Wolfe family declined to press other charges.

Construction crews are working around the clock at the hotel to repair the damage, and part of the hotel is closed to visitors and the public until further notice.

The son of a hotel employee caused the fire. The article doesn't even say he *allegedly* did it, like reporters do when they're not sure what happened. Which means they were sure.

I sit back in the hard wooden chair. Even though the room is air-conditioned, even though there's no one but me and Liza here, it feels like something's pressing down on me. Squeezing me into this space, this chair. Making it hard to breathe. I rub my eyes, but the article . . . the picture . . . still glow on the screen in stark black and white.

Everything is falling into place, but not in a place I ever thought it would go. The fire, the angry postcards Mom never sent. The falling-out they had.

Mom had been staying in the hotel.

And JR caused the fire.

CHAPTER 30

Emma (Then)

hear the words. I know JR said them. But I don't believe it.

"Why are you saying that?" I say in a pleading voice. "You were with me tonight. You didn't do this."

The police officers exchange a glance, then turn to Dad and Mr. Desmond.

"Emma was upstairs asleep when the fire started," Dad tells them. "Whenever she saw this young man, it was earlier in the evening."

My eyes flash at him. "Dad, what are you *doing?*"

"I'm trying to get this matter settled," he says with a forced calm. "Go with your mother and we'll talk later this morning."

"No, I'm not leaving until—"

"NOW," he yells. Then in a quieter voice, "You're leaving now."

But I'm not. I can't. I'm not going to abandon JR like that. Not now, not ever. I need them to see that JR would never do something like this. I need him to defend himself. If I could just make him do . . . *something*. I pull myself up to the railing of the verandah so he can see me better.

"JR, tell them the truth," I beg. "Tell them it wasn't you."

He looks away from me, a grim expression on his face. He doesn't say a word. Not one single word. A silence falls in the group gathered outside the hotel, and it hits me for the first time. He's not defending himself and no one else is coming to his rescue. The only person defending JR is me.

"JR, *please*," I cry. "Please tell them."

Dad grabs me by the arms and drags me toward my mother. "Get her out of here. Now," he says to her. He lets go of me abruptly and heads back to the police. Back to JR.

"Mom . . ."

She takes a deep breath, her eyes on the ground. "Come with me, love," she says, her voice subdued. "It's all going to be okay. Just come with me."

Numb from everything that's happened tonight, I let her lead me away.

"We need to get some things together before we have to leave the hotel for a few nights," she tells me.

"But where we will we go?" My eyes scan the hotel grounds frantically. Everything is dark. Empty. I think of everyone down at the beach. The people all around the island taking them in. Will we go to a stranger's house, too?

I look at Mom, waiting for her to answer.

"We'll talk about it later," she says. "The . . . fire department will only let us in for a few minutes," her voice cracks. "They wouldn't have even let us do that except that our suite is on the opposite side of . . ." She rubs her hand over her mouth. "We have to move quickly."

Quiet tears form in my eyes. I wipe them away before they can fall, hoping Mom doesn't notice. She stops, though, just before she opens the door to the side entrance of the hotel and looks over at me. Her whole face crumples.

"Emma . . . oh love," she cries. Mom hugs me and I cling to her, trying to take some comfort in her arms. "Everything will be okay," she says as she strokes the back of my head. "It'll all be back to normal before you know it, I promise."

I let her talk—let her make promises and try to reassure me with soothing words. But I know none of it is true. Nothing will ever be normal again. The hotel will need repairs. Big ones. We might not be able to move back in for months, and even then . . . even then, JR will still be . . .

I pull away from her. "Let's just get this over with," I say. "I need this night to be over."

Mom nods and leads me inside. We trudge through the lobby, its walls dripping with water, and toward the smaller staircase on the opposite side of the hotel from the ballroom. The smell of smoke is so powerful in the lobby I can taste it. It gets less and less strong with each step upward we take. By the time we get to our floor there's just a hint of it still lingering. Everything looks . . . normal. Like Mom said it would be.

"Do you need help?" Mom asks.

I shake my head. I don't want anyone's help. I go into my room and pack up the things I need—bras, underwear, some dresses, shoes, sweaters. Then I get my toiletries together and toss them in my bag. With no idea how long we'll actually be gone, I'm not sure what to pack—how much or how little—so I just toss whatever I can find in there. My eye catches on my mosaic chest, and I almost leave it behind. There's too much JR in that chest for me to want it right now, and yet . . . all my other memories are in there, too.

Besides, there has to be an explanation. It must have been some horrible accident or . . . or maybe he was taking a new medication . . . or . . . or something I didn't even know about and he wasn't himself. *Something* must have happened. JR would never do anything so terrible—so dangerous. I know he wouldn't. I just have to find out what happened and then everything will be okay.

Zipping up my bag, I heft it onto my shoulder and grab my mosaic chest with the other arm. Mom's already in the living room all packed. "Let's go."

Downstairs, Dad waits for us so we can walk to the inn we're apparently going to be staying at. I look around the front of the hotel, the verandah, but the police are gone. So are Mr. Desmond and JR.

"Where is everyone?" I ask. "Where's JR?"

"Your friend is staying with his father for the rest of the night," Dad says. "Until the mainland police can come to collect him tomorrow morning."

That word makes me flinch. *Collect*. The police are going to *collect* him like he's a piece of garbage. I want to point this out to Dad, to tell him how wrong all of this is, but I just numbly walk with them to the inn and through its tiny lobby. Finally we're in our separate rooms.

I only wait ten minutes until I rush out the door again.

Town is quiet at this hour of the day—stores closed and dark, no sounds of tourists chattering and horses clip-clopping down the road. Down on the docks I can see the fishing teams already getting ready to leave for the day, but here it feels as if the whole world has gone silent.

The hotel looms eerily in the predawn light—water-logged and empty—with that burnt-out hole on the side of the first floor. I hurry past until I crest the hill and see it: the greenhouse. For a second, I just stand there and stare at it, looking like a little oasis in this otherwise upside-down world. But after a few deep breaths, I force myself through the door. Hear it bang against the wall.

"You're late." JR's voice sticks my feet to the ground.

It would be funny. Except that it's not. It's not at all.

JR slumps against the wall on the opposite side of the greenhouse, his eyes trained downward at the mosaic floor we made together. He hugs both arms around his abdomen. One of his legs jitters up and down too quickly. He looks as if he might crumple in on himself—as if he'd fall apart right now if he didn't physically hold himself together. I've never seen him like this before, I . . . I have no idea what to do. I need him to look at me. To talk to me. But he doesn't.

He doesn't even look up until I sit down facing him.

"Are you okay?" he asks, his voice softer than it was just a second ago.

I close my eyes, trying not to let the anger and hurt well up and get the better of me. But after . . . after what he did tonight, I don't know how to take that question seriously.

"Do you really care how I am?" The words hurt to ask. Even at our worst—even when we fought all the time as kids—I didn't ever think I'd have to ask that question.

JR lets out a frustrated breath. "I just want to make sure you . . . you didn't get hurt. I . . ." His voice cracks. Something inside me does, too.

"Are *you* okay?" I ask.

He lets out a quivery breath. "I've been better."

"And your dad?"

JR pulls his knees to his chest but doesn't say a word.

I watch him in the darkness, willing myself not to feel bad for him. Trying to harden myself to him so that I don't feel this aching despair every time I look at him. So I focus on what will ground me. Steady me.

"Linda's fine, by the way," I inform him.

JR fists his hand in his hair. "I know," he says. "I was so worried about her. I kept asking how she was until finally . . ."

This has to be the strangest, most awkward conversation I've ever had in my entire life, yet we have to keep pushing forward. There's no way we can turn back anymore.

"JR . . . ," I begin.

He passes his hand over his eyes. "Look, we should just get this over with, right?" he says. "Rip off the Band-Aid instead of . . . instead of this . . ."

His voice cracks again. I want to move closer to him, to reach out and touch him and make him realize that I'm still here for him. That everything will be okay, just like my mom said it would be. But I don't honestly know anymore if it will be, so I don't move.

"Let's do this then," he says. "I was mad at you. At everything. And I did something stupid. End of story."

My eyes flash at his, furious that this is what he thinks is an explanation.

"End of story?" I scoff. "That's barely even the beginning." I lean forward, facing him head-on. "What. Happened?"

JR looks down at his knees. He picks at the holes in his jeans. "I don't know what else I can say."

"But I know what you can say!" My anger is a seething, living thing now, taking on a life of its own. I can feel it in my fingertips, in my toes. "You can tell me the truth. I want to know what happened."

A bitter laugh escapes from him. "No, you don't," he tells me, his voice sharp-edged and angry. "You don't want to hear anything that will burst the little bubble you live in. You never have."

I turn away from him on the greenhouse floor, cringing back from his words.

"Stop it, JR," I almost whisper.

But he doesn't listen to me. He doesn't stop.

"All you want is to stay in that bubble, pretend everything is perfect there, and assume it's the same way for everyone else, too," he rants on. "That's all any of you want. To keep your heads up your asses and exist in a land of . . . of make-believe."

Every word he says tears my heart into pieces. I don't understand this. I don't understand *him* anymore. "Why are you doing this?" I cry.

He puts his head in his hands and huffs out a breath. "Doing what, Emma?" he demands. "Telling you the truth? Maybe you actually need to hear the truth." JR gets to his feet, startling me. He paces the greenhouse. "So here it is. You and every other person you know live on the backs of people like me and my dad. You take advantage of us, you use us. You pretend everything's all rosy and equal but you know it's not. It never can be."

I pull myself up and grab him by the arms. Shaking him. "JR, what are you talking about?" I almost yell. "I've never tried to use you!"

"No?" he snaps, shaking me off him. "Then what were you doing tonight at the beach, huh?"

I close my eyes to try to keep the tears from seeping out but it doesn't work. They stream down my face anyway, leaving me to wipe them away. "I just wanted to be close to you," I cry. "All I ever want is to be close to you. You're the most important person in the world to me."

JR lets out an unsteady breath. "No, *you're* the most important person in the world to you, Emma." He scrubs his hands over his eyes. "Otherwise you wouldn't have kissed me tonight when you knew you were never going to break up with him. You wouldn't have taken advantage of my feelings for you like that." He leans his head against the glass of the greenhouse. "You wouldn't have done that to me."

I don't even try to hide my tears anymore. The ache inside me has grown too strong to ignore or hold back. It feels as if I've already lost something so enormous that there'll always be a gaping hole in me where it used to be.

"I never meant to hurt you," I choke out.

He lays one hand on the glass and sighs deeply. "I know you didn't, Emma," he says in a softer voice. "But you did. Over and over again you hurt me without even knowing. Till tonight. When you did it on purpose."

My legs shake. Whatever adrenaline I'd been running on earlier in the night is gone. I can barely stand anymore. Before my legs give out underneath me, I slide down the glass and sit with my knees tucked to my chest.

"So that's it," I say. "That's why you did it?"

His head falls back and he lets out another sigh. "Not *did you do it*. There's no question in your mind about whether or not I caused the fire," he says in a low voice. "All you can ask is why."

My anger flares up again, filling the empty void I'd felt just seconds ago. "You told the police you did!" I yell at him. "You just told me you did, too! What am I supposed to question, when you keep laying it all out for me?" Hot, angry tears stream down my face again. "You put Linda in the hospital. You put all of us in danger." I suck in a breath before I say the part that hurts the most. "You put *me* in danger." I have to gulp down a sob. "I had no idea you hated me this much, JR."

"I don't hate you," he says, his voice cracking again. "I couldn't. You're . . ." He kneels in front of me. "I could never hate you. Emma, I . . . I . . ."

JR cups my cheek in his hand so tenderly I can barely breathe. Despite myself—despite everything that's happened—I lean into his touch. As desperately as I want everything else to disappear right now, I want him to stay even more.

"It doesn't matter," he says. "No matter how I feel about you, it's not going to change anything. People like your parents and the Desmonds will always be there to make sure of that."

I push his hand away, cringing back from him. "I don't think I can listen to any more of this."

Getting to my feet, I stagger toward the door.

Something rustles behind me. I want it to be the sound of JR's feet coming after me. Or his arm lifting toward me to stop me. But he doesn't reach for me. All he does is sigh.

"Take care of yourself, Emma," he says, his voice low and defeated. Broken.

My footsteps falter for a second. I think about turning around but then I picture Linda on the stretcher being loaded into the ambulance. My mother's face as she watched the hotel burn. Then I keep moving. A few steps bring me to the door of the greenhouse. A few more take me out into the early morning light. I won't look back. If he wants to say anything else—if he wants to apologize—he can come after me.

But he never comes.

CHAPTER 31

Emma (Then)

A kind of numbness settled into my chest earlier this morning. First it felt like pain—deep and throbbing—as I ran away from the greenhouse. Then it morphed into a dull, mundane ache. The pajamas that still smelled like smoke. The blisters that blossomed on my toes and heels last night. The spasms in my calves and thighs. It was all there, too *present* to ignore. And it distracted me. At least a little bit. It helped me focus on something else. Even blisters were better than everything that had happened during the night.

Now though . . . now the blisters have been bandaged. The pajamas lie in a heap in the corner of the room replaced by a soft cotton shirt and my one pair of shorts. Pain medicine has eased my muscles.

Now there's nothing left to distract me from the numbness, the emptiness.

I wish so much I could go back to the muscle spasms and blisters. They're so easy to deal with. They heal so quickly.

Slowly, painstakingly, I walk down to the water's edge. The morning is warm. The sky clear blue. Sunlight dapples and dances on the water. It's too beautiful. It's almost mocking in how beautiful it is on such an ugly day. I close my eyes but even that's not enough to shut it all out. The sun still radiates brightly through my eyelids. The sound of the lake water still splashes against the pier. The same pier where the police took JR away this morning.

I have to get away from here.

I turn and open my eyes. And I see Ryan.

He's standing farther back than I am, his eyes strained out over the water. I don't move, I don't make a sound. I just wait for him to notice me. When he does—when our eyes meet—all I can see in his is pain. Ryan and JR were friends, too. He's hurting, too. I take a single step forward and he moves instantly to meet me. Then I'm enveloped in his strong arms.

I let him hold me, comfort me, until a snake of guilt coils in my stomach, making me feel sick. He's too good to me and I don't deserve it. Last night when he was facing down his parents I . . . I was . . .

The feeling of JR's hands in my hair, of my fingers digging into his shoulders, of his lips, his breath . . . how much I wanted him. It all rushes back again. Even after everything that happened—after everything JR said and did—it still all rushes back.

I step away and hold him at arm's length. "There's something I need to tell you."

He waits, watching me, in silence.

"Last night," I begin. But where do I go from there? How do I tell him something that will hurt him when he's already hurting? How can I not? "Last night," I say again. "After you left with your parents—"

"Maybe we don't have to think so much about last night," Ryan interrupts me. "Would that be okay?" He forces a smile, but it's not a real one—it's not the one that sparkles.

His eyes drift out over the water. He seems . . . calm. Distant. As if he's far away from where we're standing right now. For the first time, I wonder if he already knows what happened.

Ryan clears his throat.

"Last night was . . . ," he says at last. "It felt like everything was all wrong. All of it." He finally meets my eyes again. "*I* was all wrong. And I need you to know that I . . . I'm sorry." He looks away again. "I'm really sorry."

"Ryan, you had too much to drink. It's okay," I tell him. "I'm the one who should be apologizing."

He shakes his head. "I did stuff I wish I hadn't last night," he says. "You did, too."

Oh God, he knows. He saw. I close my eyes and inhale deeply. Ryan reaches over to touch my shoulder. "And you know what I want now?"

I look up at him. "Honestly, I have no idea."

"I want to forget last night ever happened. I want us to . . . to move on like nothing ever went wrong," his words rush from him. "Then everything can be the same again, right? I just want everything to go back to the way it was."

For a second I'm not sure what to say. How can we just go back to the way things were? Linda's still in the hospital, JR's gone, and the two of us are standing here doing . . . I don't even know what.

"Can we do that, Emma?" he presses. "I'm just so . . . so crazy about you. You're all that matters to me anymore. I don't care that you kissed him." My jaw clenches at Ryan stating it out loud like that. "It was like . . . like the heat of the moment . . . after a rough night. When I was being a jerk, right?"

Every part of me just wants to say yes. To agree with him and do what he's asking me to do—just move on. His eyes are so pleading. Almost as if they're begging me to make him and even myself feel better by pretending it's all okay. And I don't want him to look like this. I don't want him to *feel* like this. I want the smile back on his face. The real one, that makes his eyes glow as if he's lit from within.

"Right, Emma?" His voice sounds so hopeful that I don't have the heart to hurt him any more than I already have.

I take a deep breath and nod. "Right," I whisper. "It's all a blur. I can hardly remember what happened."

How can that one statement feel as if it's a betrayal of both Ryan and JR? My chest heaves at the sound of my own voice saying it.

"And he's gone now," Ryan says. "It's all over and . . . and you do still like me, right?"

This question is easier to answer. "Of course I do," I reply. "But we can't just pretend that last night never happened."

His eyebrows furrow for a second. "Okay," he says. "Then how 'bout this? How 'bout we start over again? Like we're rewinding and doing it all over. Would . . . would you want that?" Ryan lets out an anxious breath. *"Please* want that, Emma."

I look out over the water—to the place on the horizon where the ferry and the police and JR disappeared. Kissing him may have come back to me in a rush before, but now all I can think about are the things he said to me. The accusations and the anger he hurled at me. The fact that he never once said he was sorry.

Last night I did things I wish I hadn't.

My eyes meet Ryan's again. He's watching me with such eagerness, such worry. He's waiting so patiently for me to answer.

"I do want that," I tell him.

Once again, he wraps me in his arms and holds on tight. "Everything's going to be okay," he whispers in my ear. "I promise."

I lean into his chest and listen to his heartbeat. The rhythm is steady, comforting, as if it's the one thing tethering me to this spot— to my whole life on this island. As Ryan hugs me, I look out over his shoulder toward the lake again. Somewhere on the mainland, JR's being taken to a police station. He's going somewhere I never thought he'd go, somewhere I'll never be able to follow him.

We all did things we wish we hadn't last night.

CHAPTER 32

Lexi (Now)

The sound of someone else's voice startles me so much that I jump out of my chair. "What? What did you say?"

The girl from the front desk stands beside me looking alarmed. "I asked if you're okay," she tells me. "You're breathing funny."

When I don't respond in any way, she points to one of the couches in the quiet nooks of the library. "Sit over there," she says. "I'm going to get you some water."

I nod and she disappears. Only then I do realize that she's right: I am breathing funny. Too fast, too shallow. I've never been so shocked in my entire life. How could he have done something so awful, knowing that she was staying in the hotel? How could he have put her at risk like that, let alone everyone else there? What possible justification could he have had?

I'm hurt and angry on my mom's behalf. JR had been her friend. Her fellow werewolf. One of the people in all of her stories.

And he caused the fire at the hotel.

"Here you go," the girl says, holding out a glass of water for me. "Drink this."

I take the glass and murmur a quiet thank-you.

"Are you gonna pass out?" the girl says. "Medical stuff isn't exactly my thing, so I can call someone if you are."

"I'm not going to pass out," I assure her. "I'll be fine."

She cocks her head to one side for a second before nodding and heading back to her desk.

I watch her for a few seconds and then take out my phone and type out a text.

What would you say if I told you my mom's friend JR might have caused a fire at the hotel? I press send and hope Chloe can text back to me soon as I desperately need her right now.

The three dots start moving right away.

That seems . . . weird? Especially if she was staying there?

I write back. **She was asleep in the hotel at the time. I don't know what to think.**

Three dots start dancing on my screen again. **Are you sure you've got it right? Wouldn't be the first time you were wrong about something.**

I huff out a frustrated breath. Now? She has to tease me right now? What's even more annoying is that she's right. So far, I just have what Dad would describe as circumstantial evidence. If he was defending me in court, he'd tear this all apart in about two minutes.

I'm going to do more research just to be sure, I text back.

Can you talk right now?

I'm in the library freaking out.

Cool, Chloe texts. **Call me when you're done.**

This makes me laugh, just a little. Only my stepsister would react to the news that I'm freaking out with *cool*. The laughter fades quickly enough, though. I need to keep looking through the paper. I need to see what else I can find.

Two hours later, I walk up to the Palais du Lac just as Casey walks down the driveway back into town. He gives me one of those wide, happy smiles of his and I freak out a little more. I mean, he's smiling at me. Which is new. And . . . weird? Not bad weird. Good weird. My cheeks burn up as I attempt to smile back.

Maybe I should mention this to Chloe when I talk to her later, too? Or maybe I won't. I'm not sure I want to hear her thoughts on this particular subject.

But right now, I have to talk to Casey. I grab his arm and pull him to a stop. The smile on his face instantly fades.

"What're you doing?" he asks.

I drop his arm . . . why do I keep grabbing him? . . . and take a step backward. "Um . . . I just wanted to make sure you'd stop."

He looks at me for a second like he's not sure if I've lost my mind, or if I'm joking. "You didn't think I'd stop to say hi?"

This is not going well. "No, I'm just . . . I've got a lot on my mind right now and I guess I'm not thinking straight so . . ." I scrunch my nose in embarrassment. "Sorry?" I offer. "And I promise I won't keep touching you?"

Casey crosses his arms over his chest and sighs. "I don't mind if you touch me," he says. "It's not a big deal. But the grabbing . . . that could go."

"Yeah." I nod vigorously. "No more grabbing. Only touching you in other ways and . . ." I stop for a second and realize what I just said. I never talk to him without Ms. VanHill there. Maybe this is why. Because I make a fool out of myself and I have so many things I need to tell him and now I've derailed everything.

"Lexi?"

My shoulders droop. "Yeah?"

"What's going on?"

It's a simple question that doesn't have a simple answer. Or maybe it does, just not one I want to deal with. I rub at my chin with the heel of my hand. Must. Get. Myself. Together.

"I . . . I found some stuff in old issues of the *Island Crier*," I tell him. "Not good stuff, to be honest."

With a tilt of his head, Casey seems to be closely considering me. Or at least his options. And maybe his options for getting away from me because I'm acting all . . . weird?

"You want to talk about it, or . . . ?"

Or maybe he's not trying to get away from me after all. I breathe a sigh of relief as he stares at me, waiting for me to answer.

"Are you going somewhere right now?" I ask him, then realize what a dumb question that is. He's leaving work for the day. Of course he's going somewhere. "I mean, other than home?"

He smiles at me again. It really is a very nice smile. "Home had been, in fact, my wild plan for the night," he says. "Why?"

"It's just that I found out some stuff and want to talk to you and Ms. VanHill about it, but I don't want to interrupt your night, especially since you only just got off work."

He puts his hands on my shoulders and I stop breathing. "You okay?" I just nod.

In a sure sign that my friendship with Casey has come a long way in just a few short days, he says, "Let me text my mom and let her know I won't be home for dinner. Then we can head up to the Lake Suite."

When Ms. VanHill opens the door, she seems completely unsurprised to see us this late in the day. Though we've probably been coming often enough that she just expects us to show up at all hours? At least she doesn't seem *sorry* to see us.

"You must both have ESP," Ms. VanHill says. "I just finished dinner and was wondering if anyone might join me for some lemon cake."

I take the dessert tray we brought while Casey moves her dinner tray out into the hall. I'll have to help him deal with both of them later on. After we all talk. And eat. And . . .

"Lexi, you wanted to talk, right?" he says.

"Yes!" I agree, a little too strenuously. But now that there's a cup of tea in front of me and a generous slice of lemon cake, I'm finding it hard to get any words out.

"Look at the poor girl. She's tongue-tied," Ms. VanHill states. "It's happened to fans when they're in my presence for years now. It'll pass," she tells Casey.

He grins at her and then at me. "You do have that effect on people."

Finally I take out the printouts of the newspaper articles and lay them on the table in front of Casey and Ms. VanHill. Casey immediately starts reading one of the articles, but Ms. VanHill lingers on the picture of my mother with a crease between her eyes.

"Well, there she is, isn't she?" she says to me. "Finally a picture of your mother."

Casey drops the piece of paper he's holding and cranes his neck to see Mom. "She looks just like you," he says in almost a whisper.

He's right. She does. I don't look anything like my dad, but Mom . . . from what little I've seen of her, we do look so much alike. And it's not just the hair. It's the shape of our dark eyes, the cut of our chins. It's strange and somehow . . . wonderful . . . that even after she's gone, part of her still lingers in me. Just the thought of it . . . the thought that I share these things with her . . . makes my eyes mist over.

"Hm . . . ," Ms. VanHill says. "Other than the fact that she looks like you, she doesn't look at all familiar. But that young man with her." She points down at the blond guy with Mom. "I recognize him from somewhere. I think I've seen that face before, I'm just not sure where."

She taps her chin as she sits in silence. If she does know who the blond guy is, maybe we could track him down and ask him questions about Mom and . . .

"Did I ever tell you about the time I sang for President Carter?" Ms. VanHill asks.

It takes me a second to realize that we've moved on from the boy in the picture.

Whereas Casey just rolls with it. "No, you didn't," he replies. "But we'd love to hear about it."

Ms. VanHill smiles at him, warmth radiating off her. "What a lovely man," she begins. "One of the only politicians I ever met who genuinely cared more about other people than himself. His wife, Rosalynn, just the same. We're about the same age, he and I. Did you know that?"

"I didn't," Casey says, "but it makes sense."

"I've met five presidents," Ms. VanHill tells us. "Some fool in the press office of a president who shall remain nameless asked me once if I'd sing to the man like I was Marilyn Monroe and he was Jack Kennedy." She makes a derisive, snorting sound. "I set the woman straight soon enough. Catch me making a fool of myself flirting with a married man. Or any man at all, for that matter." She pauses in thought. "I told her if the president wanted to hear me sing, he could come to one of my performances, the same as anybody else." She sniffs indignantly. "Besides, Norma confided in me later that she regretted doing it." Ms. VanHill looks at me and then Casey. "That was her real name, you know. She didn't always make the wisest decisions, but she was beautiful. And gentlemen aren't the only ones who prefer blondes."

Casey snarfs out a mouthful of his tea. Then we both start talking at the same time.

"You knew Marilyn Monroe?" I demand.

"You had a thing for Marilyn Monroe?" Casey spurts out.

A haughty rise of Ms. VanHill's chin meets that statement. "I have eyes, do I not?" she scoffs. "How did you expect me to react to the woman?"

Casey's eyes meet mine and I can tell he's trying not to laugh, which makes me laugh. Despite every single thing that's happened today, I still can't hold it back. I'm laughing so hard that tears start to form in my eyes and I'm crying laughing.

Then I'm just crying.

Ms. VanHill reaches out her hand to me and I take it. "I know this is hard," she tells me. "But you will find answers. Everything will make more sense in time, Lexi."

I want to believe her. I really do.

"You don't know that," I say, trying to calm my breathing. "I might just go home with more questions than I came with and my dad will ground me for the rest of my life for coming here and spending all this money and it'll all have been for nothing."

Another sob rises out of me. "What am I going to do?"

Ms. VanHill squeezes my hand and Casey does something I honestly did not see coming. He wraps his arm around me. Warmth floods through me—unexpected, unlooked-for warmth.

It's not just that these two people have been so good to me this week.

It's also that I feel closer to my mom, who—no matter what happened later on and how awful things got—came here for summers and made friends who meant the world to her. Maybe I'm starting to do the same. I hold on to Ms. VanHill and lean into Casey. I haven't even known these people long, but I would be lost without them right now.

We make a promise to regroup in the morning but there's no way I'm leaving Casey, who's already off duty for the night, to bring two room service trays down by himself.

"You're a guest," he tells me. "I can't let you carry this downstairs for me."

"And I can't let you take two trips to the kitchen when I can help," I reply.

This elicits an eye roll, but I don't care. "Casey, you've done so much to help me since I got here. Let me do this one very tiny thing for you."

A crease forms between his eyebrows, as if he's thinking it over a little too hard. "Okay," he agrees. "But you can't come anywhere *near* the kitchen, and you have to get back up to where you belong as fast as possible so no one sees you."

"Deal," I say.

Ms. VanHill clears her throat audibly. "If you two are quite done," she says. "Perhaps you could leave the newspaper articles with me? I really do think that young man in the photograph with your mother looks familiar."

"Of course, Ms. VanHill," I say. Laying everything on the table in front of her, I'm overtaken with emotion once again. "Thank you so much."

"I haven't done anything, Lexi," she replies.

"You have, though," I say. "You've done so much." There's no way I'm leaving this room without giving her a hug. It's just not a thing that can happen.

She seems startled when I actually do it, though.

"What was that for?" she asks.

I laugh out loud. "For being you."

I'm not sure how I thought she'd respond to that, but she gives me a regal nod. "It's an appropriate response," Ms. VanHill states. "You're not the first to be inspired to do so."

Laughter pours from me again. I work hard not to start crying again when it does.

Riding in the service elevator is starting to feel normal to me, even if it still makes Casey edgy.

"No coming in the kitchen," he tells me for the third time since we got in the elevator. "You just leave the tray outside the elevator door and get going, okay?"

"Got it, Casey," I reply. Then I nudge him, very, very gently. "Want to synchronize our watches and make a rendezvous point outside the hotel, too?"

He shoots me a glare. "See, you're joking, but I'm serious," he says. "I'll get in so much trouble if anyone sees you with a hotel tray."

"I don't actually want to get you in trouble, you know," I reassure him.

"I do know," he replies. "But the rules are pretty strict here, and as much as I hate this job, I need the money."

One sideways glance at him shows me how serious he is about this. I press the two button on the elevator. "I'll get off here so there's no chance anyone will see me by the kitchen, okay? Then I'll meet you by the front gate."

He nods just as the elevator opens. Then his jaw drops.

"Oh God," he groans.

Standing on the other side of the door is probably the best-looking, best-dressed person I've ever seen. This man is at least six inches taller than me, broad-shouldered, and wearing an impeccable midnight-blue three-piece suit with a yellow and teal pocket square and tie. His head is shaved, revealing the dark brown skin on his head, and he's got a full beard.

He's also looking at me as if he's seen a ghost.

"I . . . you . . ." At first that's all he says, but Casey jumps into action.

"I'm so sorry, sir," he spits out. "I know she's a guest, and . . ."

But the man just shakes his head. He's not even looking at Casey.

He hasn't taken his eyes off me.

After blinking his eyes a few times like he's trying to clear his mind, he reaches his hand out to me.

"My name is Jackson Murray," he says. "And you must be Emma's daughter."

CHAPTER 33

Lexi (Now)

A t first I have no idea what to say. I'm not sure I *could* say anything even if I wanted to. The good news is that Jackson Murray keeps talking.

"When did you arrive?" he asks.

"Um . . . a few days ago," I finally manage to get out. "And I'm leaving in two days." I somehow have the presence of mind not to mention that it could be sooner if Dad figures out where I really am.

"Then I'm so pleased I got back in time to meet you," he continues. "Emma was always one of my favorite people."

"How . . . how did you know her?" I stammer out. "When did you know her?"

"I started working here when she was around ten," is his next astounding statement.

"And now you're a guest, too?"

A slow grin spreads across his face. "No, I live here," he tells me. "I own the hotel."

Something akin to a shock hits me. For a long moment or two, I can't even speak. All I can do is stare at him, trying to put the pieces of what I know together. Then suddenly something falls into place.

"Jackson who gave her too many cookies when she was younger!" I exclaim. "You saved her on Take Your Daughter to Work Day!"

This time it's Jackson who looks shocked. "She told you about that?"

"Oh, well, no," I reply. "I have this chest covered in mosaics that she made and . . ."

He closes his eyes for a second. "Oh my God," Jackson says in a quiet voice. "I can't believe that's still around. She left it here when she went to college but then . . ."

I wait for him, eagerly, to finish that sentence but he never does. Jackson Murray squares his shoulders and looks at Casey as if he's seeing him for the first time. "Do I want to know why a guest of the hotel is carrying a tray to the kitchen with you?"

All of Casey seems to droop at once. His chin, the corners of his mouth. Even his shoulders. We tried so hard to be careful. I can't believe I got him in trouble after all.

"Oh . . . well . . . ," he stammers. "We were up with Ms. VanHill, and . . ."

Jackson shakes his head. "And of course she had you both doing her bidding," he says. "I understand now."

I honestly have no idea what's going on anymore. It's starting to feel like I've been spinning again and the room is just going to keep turning around me endlessly without stopping.

"I gather you two know each other?" Jackson continues, as he looks from Casey to me.

Casey pipes up immediately. "Yes . . . well . . . we've been . . ."

"We're friends," I tell Jackson, and Casey sputters to a stop next to me.

His face relaxes out of its determined frown. "We're friends," he agrees.

Jackson raises an eyebrow at us. "Well, then why don't I accompany you downstairs so we can get rid of these trays, and then you and I can go to my office?" Jackson says, turning to me. "I have a feeling we have a lot to talk about."

Within three minutes, Casey's on his way home and I'm sitting in a leather chair across a wide desk from Jackson Murray. The room is a creamy tan color with bookshelves lining the wall behind him. His desk is huge, made of some deep brown wood and covered in files and two laptops. There's a framed painting of the hotel hanging between the windows and a file cabinet by the door. It's such a weird mix of formal, fancy furniture and messy workspace that I'm not sure what to make of it. It does *not* look like the kind of place I'd go to hide to avoid my dad. Or at this point, maybe I would.

Jackson pushes some of the files aside and closes the laptop immediately in front of him. "I want to offer my condolences about the passing of your grandmother."

This is . . . not what I'd hoped he want to talk about. But I guess it's a start?

"Oh . . . thanks," I say. "I didn't really know her, but her nursing home sent me word." I pause for a second. "That's how I got the mosaic chest."

He shakes his head. "I can't believe Jessica kept it all these years," Jackson says. "But it makes sense, I guess."

Maybe to him it does, but not to me. "Does it?" I ask. "Why?"

"Your grandfather . . ." He turns to me and gives me a sad smile. "He never once mentioned your mom's name, in my hearing at least, after Emma left. It always seemed like he tried his hardest to cut himself off from the loss," Jackson tells me. "But Jessica was never the same again after."

None of this makes any sense. He's talking and I'm hearing the words, but they're impossible to process.

"What do you mean . . . after my mother left?"

A deep sadness comes over his face, making him suddenly look older. "After she went to college," he tells me. "They'd all had a falling-out the summer before she left. She barely spoke to them anymore. But then she went to Chicago and just . . ."

His eyes drift to the window. He tents his fingers under his chin. "She kept in touch me with for a while," he continues. "I'd get a postcard here and there to let me know she was okay. But then . . . then it just stopped."

"Mom stopped writing to you?" I clarify.

He nods, but he's still got his eyes fixed on the window. "She stopped writing. She stopped calling," he says with a smile. "Then one day I called her and her number had been disconnected." He lets out a sad laugh. "I even called the school to make sure she was okay, but they wouldn't give me a phone number or an address since I wasn't family." He pauses and finally looks at me again. "But I figured if they were protecting her personal details, she must still be a student there. It . . . it made me worry less, anyway."

He gives himself a shake. "But someone must have gotten in touch with your grandparents when she died," he goes on. "Because they knew she was gone." His voice falters. "They knew about you. In fact, I expect you'll be hearing from the estate about your share in the hotel."

Suddenly I find myself gripping the arms of the chair I'm sitting in. "What are you talking about?" I push myself up and start pacing the room. "None of this makes any sense."

Jackson pulls at his beard, but doesn't say anything for what feels like an eternity as he watches me pace.

"Why don't you sit back down, Lexi," he says in a calm voice. "I'm getting the impression that there's a lot you don't know about."

I have no idea what else to do, so I follow his advice and sit back down again.

"Now, where to begin?" He clears his throat. "Your grandfather had been having financial problems for a while. Shortly after your mom left, his biggest investor pulled out." He pauses and gives me a worried look. "It was . . . not a coincidence that both happened at the same time."

I shake my head at him. "I still don't understand."

He clasps his hands on the desk again and stares down at them. "Your grandfather was about to declare bankruptcy, so he came to me," Jackson continued. "He told me he'd sell me the hotel for as low a price as he could. He'd taken me under his wing, given me a chance to learn the business from the ground up, and I studied hotel management in college."

Jackson looks up at me with a sad expression in his eyes. "He didn't always make great decisions," he says. "But he was a good mentor. A good friend. I scrambled to get the money together, and we struck a deal that allowed him and your grandmother to keep a thirty percent stake in the business so they'd still have something to live on."

He pauses and flicks a pen that's been lying on his desk around in his hand. I watch the movement of the silver pen, not knowing what to do or say. "Now that they're both gone, that share of the hotel will certainly pass to you."

The spinning feeling is back, worse than it was before. Something's building up inside me. Pressure or . . . confusion or . . . I feel like I'm going to explode.

"I think there's been a misunderstanding," I tell him, struggling to keep my voice calm. "My grandparents didn't own this hotel. Whoever you knew, it couldn't have been my mother."

He starts clicking the pen again. "Then let's clarify," he says. "Your mother, Emma Wolfe . . ."

"No, my mother's name was Emma Roth before she got married," I blurt out.

Jackson stops moving mid-click of his pen. His eyes do that blinking thing again like he's trying to process something that isn't quite computing. My frustration that he's not saying anything—not even making sense anymore—is *this close* to boiling over. I grip my chair again, not sure what to do as he sits there lost in thought.

"I . . ." He shakes his head. "I guess that makes sense," he says, almost to himself. "They were together before she left, but I had no idea they'd . . ." He looks up at me like he's seeing me for the first time.

"Jackson?" I venture. "Can you *please* tell me what you're talking about?"

He nods again. "Yes. Yes, of course," he says. "Your mother's name might have been Emma Roth *after* she got married," he replies. "But she was born Emma Wolfe, the heir to this hotel."

I shake my head almost frantically. "No. That's not true," I say. "We're not talking about the same person!"

Jackson rises from his chair and walks around to the other side of the desk to sit in the chair next to me. "This is clearly coming as a shock to you," he says. "But I can give you proof of what I'm saying." He pauses. "Or at least I think I can."

He gets up again and holds his arm out to me. "If you'll come with me, we can settle this once and for all."

I want to settle this so badly I ache with it. So I get to my feet. I take his arm and let him lead me like a puppy out of his office. We walk through what looks like a modern library before we get to a room that's decorated in a completely different way from the rest of the hotel. Deep burgundy walls, heavy drapes on the windows. Dark, elaborate woodwork.

"This is the archival room," Jackson informs me. "I renovated the entire hotel after I bought it, but kept this room exactly the way it always has been."

My eyes wander, taking in the dark leather furniture and the deep red wall panels.

"The history of the hotel and its owners has always been maintained here," he continues. "It's kind of a time capsule of the hotel's past."

There's an old portrait of a stern white guy over the fireplace, flanked by two equally stern white women on either side of him.

"That's Henri Aurieux, who built the hotel," Jackson tells me. "And both of the women he married over time. He came to Mackinac from Paris by way of New Orleans."

Jackson stares up at the portraits for a second. "His family owned the hotel until they went bankrupt," he continues. "It changed hands two more times before your grandfather, Ellison Wolfe, bought the place."

I shake my head trying to clear it, but it's no use. It's like Jackson set out to only say the most outrageous possible things and then ran with it. My grandfather didn't buy this hotel. Mom's parents didn't own it.

"And here," Jackson says, "is your mother."

He takes a large framed picture off a nearby table and hands it to me. There, in the frame, is a picture of my mom. She's wearing an ice-blue formal dress and has her hair swept into an unruly updo. Standing by her side, a lazy smile on his face, is the tall blond guy from the fire.

It's as if someone took the picture of Mom and this guy from the chest and captured the exact same moment, but from the front.

All I can do is stare at it for a long time. Mom looked . . . beautiful. Really beautiful. And it's not just the dress or the way her hair's done up. It's just . . . it's her. Everything about her. I run my finger down the picture. She looked like she was my age now.

"When was this taken?" I whisper.

"At the hotel's one hundredth anniversary party," Jackson says.

It's her. I know it's her . . . I can see it with my own eyes. But it doesn't make any sense.

"But . . . but she wasn't rich enough to own this place!" I argue. "We've never had money like this," I say, waving my arm to take in the whole room. "How can any of this be possible?"

He sits down and gives me another sad smile. "I told you," he says. "She left. She didn't want any part of it anymore and she walked away." He clasps his hands over his knees. "And if the Roth last name is true, she married JR afterward."

My knees give out from underneath me. I crash down in the nearest chair. "What did you just say?" My voice sounds far away. Like I'm talking from the end of a long tunnel and can't hear myself well anymore. "She . . . she left the island . . . with JR?"

Jackson shakes his head. "Oh no!" he tells me. "She left to go to college. I dropped her off at school in Chicago myself. And JR . . . he left, too, but to go to Michigan State." He pauses and reaches out a hand to me. I don't take it. "They both left. But they didn't leave *together.*"

I'm still clinging to the picture of my mother. I'm trying so hard to process all of this, but my brain feels like it's hiccuping. "But . . . they got married?"

He gives me this soft, sympathetic smile. I have to look away before I start to lose it. "You said her last name was Roth, right? So they must have."

There's a cold dread settling in my stomach. "But he caused the fire," I argue. "She would never have . . ."

"They had a complicated relationship," Jackson concedes. "But unless she met someone else with the same last name . . ." He looks at me for a second, confusion settling in his eyes. "Wait, is Roth not your last name?"

I shake my head.

"Your father's name *isn't* Jason Roth?"

Jason Roth. JR. Her friend and fellow werewolf. The person she wanted to travel the world with . . . who was her friend till he ruined her world. She married Jason Roth and never came back here again.

A cold, numb feeling creeps into my chest.

"I'd never heard the name Jason Roth till you said it just now."

"Oh." That's all he says. *Oh.*

"I know this is a lot to take in," Jackson continues. "But whatever happened after she left Mackinac, do you at least believe me now that your mother's name was Emma Wolfe?"

"Yeah," I answer mechanically. "I guess there's no way not to anymore."

Neither of us says anything for a long time. I can feel him looking at me but I can't take my eyes off the picture in my hands. I hold it up to him.

"Is . . . is this JR?" I ask at last.

"That," Jackson says in a stiff voice, "is Ryan Desmond."

CHAPTER 34

Lexi (Now)

Thinking back, it's weird that I ever thought being dizzy was a good thing. Because right now my head is spinning and not in a good way. And I'm so terrified that even when my head stops, the rest of the world will just keep whirring around me—so terrified, I feel ill.

Jackson, with heaps of apologies and promises to talk more as soon as he can, got called away by the general manager. And I got left here, in this tomb of a room, all by myself. Ten minutes pass. Twenty. More. I still sit in this same chair in this same room.

There are more pictures of Mom that I can see even from here. Her as a baby in my grandmother's arms. A formal portrait of them together when she was about five. My grandparents are smiling politely at the camera. Mom, on the other hand, has a mischievous fire in her young eyes. She looks like she was plotting her escape. I've never seen baby pictures of her before. I've never seen pictures of my grandparents. I didn't even remember what they looked like from that one day in court. It's like they're there . . . in my memory . . . but the colors have run out of the picture, making everything blurry.

It's the same way with Mom.

I get up and gather all the pictures of her together and pull them down in the chair with me. One by one, I pore over them. Over this treasure trove of pictures that her parents had and I didn't. I don't know why she stopped speaking to them, but I do know they didn't deserve to have all these memories of her anymore. And Dad . . . Dad who kept her from me all these years. He doesn't deserve her either.

None of them did. They all got to have some of her and me . . . I got nothing. Nothing at all.

Anger surges through me. I want to throw something or *wreck* something but it can't be these pictures and it can't be the history of people who might have been okay. Who might have deserved to have her if they'd known her. All these people who aren't *me*.

A small scream escapes from me. I cover my face with my hands, pressing my fingertips into my eyes. It's not fair. None of this is fair.

All these secrets. Dad must know about them. Her parents clearly did.

I shake my head and put the pictures of her down on a low table. There must be more. Maybe some with JR. Or with Ryan Desmond. Or even with Dad. There's got to be more pieces to the puzzle that I'm just not seeing yet. I run around the room, picking up pictures and looking at everything I can find.

But there's nothing. Nothing more of Mom. Nothing of the rest of them. I collapse onto a sofa and take out my phone. There are no pictures of JR here, but there must be some online. I punch his name into Google and . . . and find this whole world of Jason Roths. Some Mom's age. Some older. Some younger. There are one hundred and seven of them living in Detroit alone.

I toss my phone aside and squeeze my eyes shut. But then it dings. Twice.

Two texts are waiting for me. One from Chloe. The other from Casey.

Chloe's feels like she's screaming at me over text.

WHAT'S HAPPENING? WHY WOULD YOU KEEP ME IN THE DARK LIKE THIS? Call me when you can, ok? And by that I mean SOON.

Then I open Casey's. He's had my number for two days, but this is the first time he's used it. **Everything ok?**

Somehow the thought of talking to Chloe right now . . . of having someone who knows me so well know *this* about my mom and my family is just . . . it's more than I can handle right now.

So I text Casey instead. **Not really.**

Because nothing is okay and I don't know if it'll ever be okay again and . . .

Meet me at the hotel beach? Will be there in ten minutes, he writes back.

If he'd asked me to meet up with him yesterday, or even this morning, my stomach would probably have been doing somersaults. Now, I don't even know what to text back.

You still there? Casey writes. **You're making me worry.**

I take a deep breath and let it out. **See you there in ten minutes.**

I get a thumbs-up emoji in response and then shut off my phone. All the photos of Mom are still lying on the table in front of me. If I leave now, I could take them. All of them. What do I care about the archival room and my family's history? All I care about is her.

So I do it. I steal from the history room of the hotel. Fill my arms with the framed pictures and get to the elevator as quickly as I can. As soon as I'm safely in my room, I hide them as best I can in my suitcase so the housekeeper won't see them. I am turning into a thief. Nothing good is happening right now.

I look at my phone one last time and then run to the stairs and down through the lobby. There are signs on the lawn pointing out paths to different hotel amenities. I follow the one to the beach through a bunch of trees. It's starting to get dark and the woods here are creepy. *Just keep moving*, I tell myself. And I do. Faster and faster I do. By the time the trees open up and the lake unfolds in front of me, I'm out of breath. Sweaty.

Casey's already there, staring out at the water. He turns when he hears my footsteps. Or my heavy breathing. God only knows. As soon as he sees me, his eyes crinkle with worry.

"You okay?"

I shake my head but I can't say a single word. It's like my voice has up and left me.

"You can talk to me," he tells me. "But if you don't want to talk, that's okay, too."

A croaking sound escapes from me at first. But then I clear my throat. "I don't know what to say."

"Come sit," he says, gesturing toward a couple of Adirondack chairs in the sand. "We can just hang out for a while."

I nod and follow him to the chairs. The water's pretty. So I guess there's that. I try so hard to focus on that and not on . . . everything else . . . but it doesn't work. I clear my throat again.

"So, Jackson knew my mom," I say.

Casey nods. "I caught that," he replies. "Did he say how he knew her?"

I nod and I breathe. And then I tell him. About my grandparents. My mom's real last name. About how they owned the hotel. How she left home and never came back. Only when I get to the part about Mom maybe having married JR does my voice falter. I can't even say the words out loud.

"So . . . that's a lot," Casey says, even though he doesn't know the half of it. "Have you . . . have you thought about talking to your dad about all of this?"

And just like that, my stomach drops into my hips. Down my thighs. It keeps falling till it slams down in the sand under my feet. "I don't know if that's such a good idea."

A sound pierces the air . . . one I haven't heard since I got on the island. A running engine. Then a siren.

Casey gets to his feet immediately. "Something's happened," he says. "Let's go see."

He starts to walk away, but turns and waits for me. The last thing I want to do is go see what the emergency is. Enough bad stuff has already happened today just to me. I don't need to think about other people's bad stuff, too. But I also don't want him to leave me by myself down here. So I get up. I walk with him back through the creepy trees and out onto the lawn of the hotel.

In the distance, an ambulance pulls up to the hotel . . . the first car or truck of anything like that I've seen on the island. The EMTs rush inside, taking a stretcher with them. My mind wanders to when it was Mom on the stretcher. When I was five years old and she was still alive.

A sudden wave of nausea hits me.

Casey just keeps walking closer and closer to the hotel and the ambulance. When I don't follow him, he turns back and says, "Lexi?"

He frowns at me. "Why are you making that face?"

A shrug and a short shake of my head are all I can muster.

"If you don't want to go, we can stay here," he says in a quiet voice. "We don't have do to anything you don't want to, okay?"

This time I nod, but I still don't say anything to him in response.

He holds out his hand to me. This is the second time he's done that, and the second time I've put my hand in his. When he first did it, he was annoyed but begrudgingly helping me out. Now . . . it seems like he's just doing it to be comforting. Which it is. His fingers slot between mine and he gives my hand a squeeze.

"Why don't we walk back to the lake?" he says. "Whatever's happening, it'll be okay."

I want to believe him, but there's a sinking feeling in my stomach. No one would drive a vehicle here unless it was a serious emergency. I look at Casey and then my eyes stray to the hotel entrance. The EMTs are coming back out now, with someone strapped to the stretcher.

Not just someone. Ms. VanHill.

"Oh God," Casey gasps. He drops my hand and starts running toward the ambulance, but the EMTs block his way.

"She's my friend," Casey tells them. "Can I come in the ambulance with her?"

"Sorry," says an EMT not much older than Casey and me. "Only family is allowed in the vehicle. But you can meet her there if you want, and . . ."

The ambulance roars to life and the guy gets into the back with Ms. VanHill and closes the doors behind him.

Casey stands there looking lost as they drive away.

I have to help him. I have to snap out of this and make sure he's okay. And make sure Ms. VanHill's okay. This time I slip my hand into his. "Where's the hospital?"

"What?"

"I said where's the hospital?" I repeat. "Do we need bikes or can we walk there?"

For a second he doesn't answer. Then he says in a quiet voice, "We can walk. Let's go."

We hold hands till we reach what looks like a relatively small apartment complex. There's a sign hanging outside that says *Mackinac Island Medical Center*.

"*This* is the hospital?" I ask.

"Closest thing we have," Casey says.

He pushes the door open so we can both pass through. A sharp antiseptic smell hits my nostrils the second we walk inside the medical center. Something about it makes me freeze. Something about it triggers a memory for me . . . something I'd forgotten all about till now.

Sitting in a waiting room on my dad's lap. Moving her tubes and curling up in a hospital bed next to my mom. Rubbing my dad's hair to comfort him as he doubled over, sobbing.

Not understanding why he was so upset that Mom had fallen asleep.

Suddenly I can't breathe. Air won't come in. I can't push it out. I try over and over again but nothing comes.

I hear Casey ask about Ms. VanHill and the nurse say something in reply. All I can do is hope that if I stay very still I might be able to keep myself from exploding.

I don't want to leave Casey alone to deal with this and I don't want to walk away from Ms. VanHill, but I need to get out of here. Now.

Without saying a single word to Casey, I do it. I run out of the medical center. Down the hill. Gasping for breath, I put my hands on my knees and try to steady myself. Breathe in. Breathe out. I can do this. I just need to keep breathing.

As soon as my breath steadies, my feet take me into town and back out of it again. Past the hotel. I don't know where I'm going or why, but I have to keep moving. Only when I'm well past the hotel do I focus in on my surroundings . . . do I realize that I'm still on the man-icured hotel grounds. But there's no one else in sight, which feels . . . weird. Lonely.

Then I look up and I see it.

Built half into the side of the hill, with its glassy walls and ceiling jutting out into the lawn, is a greenhouse.

Not just any greenhouse, though. It's the one on the back side of the chest. I've only seen it before in mosaic form, but I know it's the same place.

Once again, I can't breathe. Something about this place feels almost sacred. It's a place my mother knew and probably loved. She made art of it and put her prized possessions inside it.

Now it's sitting there. Right in front of me.

I start walking again. The glass door is unlocked, so I head inside and look around.

There's a tree of some kind at the far end of the greenhouse grow-ing out of the ground rather than from a pot. Wooden shelves line the walls, each filled with dead plants and flowers. In the middle of the greenhouse is a lime tree that's laden with ripening fruit. The pot it's in has been painted with a scene of the lake on it.

I know I shouldn't, but I pick one of the limes and use my fingernails to carefully peel it. The smell of citrus hits my nostrils, making me sneeze. I sit on the floor and take a tiny bite of the fruit. It's tart and sweet and doesn't taste like the limes I've had before.

As I move to sit in a more comfortable position, my bare ankle scrapes against something. Looking down, I notice for the first time that the floor is a mosaic. Tiles broken into odd pieces (one of which scratched my ankle) and grouted together in a paisley pattern.

It's beautiful.

I run my fingers over the shards of tile and wonder if somehow Mom made this mosaic as well as the ones on her chest. I like to think that she did—that I'm sitting in a place that she loved, on a piece of artwork that she created with her own hands.

My phone dings once, twice. By the third ding, worry claws at me. I look down to see who's texting. Casey. Of course.

Guilt rushes through me. I can't believe I ran out of the medical center before I even got to find out how Ms. VanHill is. I can't believe I'm sitting in this, of all places.

"Everything is going to be okay," I tell myself. "Ms. VanHill will be. I will be. Everything will be okay."

If I say it often enough, I might actually start to believe it.

CHAPTER 35

Emma (Then)
Nine Months Later . . .

D o you think if we start making horrible faces they'll stop taking pictures with us in them?" Linda asks under her breath, her lips barely moving. "Or better yet, that they'll *publish* the pictures with us in them anyway?"

"No and no," I whisper back. "There's no escaping now."

Sadly, this is the honest truth of the matter. We're trapped until Mr. Desmond finishes his speech and the press finishes asking questions. It takes more effort than I like to think about not to fidget. Or shift my weight from leg to leg constantly. Or bolt. I hate the cameras—the flashes of the still photography, the blinking red lights on TV cameras that serve as reminders that we're being recorded. I'm constantly worrying that my dress is hiked up or that my bra strap is showing, even when I'm not at an official event. For what must be the hundredth time today, I reach up to smooth my hair but then stop myself when I remember that even this will be caught on camera.

It's awful. I don't like feeling this way—as if I'm being watched. I wish I could run away and just be at the beach. Or pretty much anywhere other than this makeshift stage facing down the press.

So I do what my mom told me to do when I'm feeling like this in public. I stand up straighter and take deep breaths in and out. Not so deep that you'd notice them, of course. Just enough to center myself. I try to picture the lake, the sunlight glinting off the water, the smells of sunscreen and pine needles and fresh water wafting over the sunbaked sand—the rippling of the lake water against the shore and then the chill of the water on my toes as I step into it on a hot day.

Ryan slips his hand into mine and squeezes it. I look up at him to find him smiling gently and nodding ever so slightly toward his dad. It's clear why. Not only have I stopped paying any attention to his dad's speech, but I've probably let my eyes, as well as my attention, drift away. Lost in Emma Land. That's what JR always used to call it.

JR. As I've done so many times these past few months, I push his name, his face, from my mind. Force myself not to think about how he's doing. *What* he's doing. Terry lost his job here as a result of the fire—something that's never sat well with me. So I don't even have his dad to ask about him.

NO. I shake my head. He doesn't deserve my thoughts—all the times I tried to write him. To visit him. But couldn't.

No, Emma. You're the most important person in the world to you. JR's words shake their way into my brain. All I can see in my mind is his face as he admitted what he did.

I try so hard not to think about him, but he always seems to sneak in. The only thing I can do is keep busy—helping with the campaign or at the hotel, doing whatever I can to stay occupied.

Ryan squeezes my hand again, but this time it startles me.

Oh God. Was it obvious I wasn't paying attention? Dad's going to be furious with me if the cameras pick up on that.

I immediately look in Mr. Desmond's direction and try to focus back in on his speech. But I've heard all of this before, too.

"What this country needs is a return to the values it was built on," he says. "The values of hard work. Of pulling yourself up by your bootstraps. Of grit and determination."

Next, he'll talk about lowering taxes to give business owners room to grow their companies and create jobs. It's all so predictable. Rehearsed. Meaningless. My eyes move away from him again, but the sea of reporters standing before us doesn't help me feel any better.

Stand up straight and take deep breaths. This can't last much longer, and then we'll be free.

By the time it's finally over, the urge to bolt is too powerful to ignore. The question remains, though: Where to bolt off to? Press surrounds the hotel. The horse-drawn carriages had carried in television satellite equipment from the ferry, and reporters and their technical people had set them up on the lawn so that the local networks could carry Mr. Desmond live. Even apart from the satellite dishes, there are cameras everywhere.

Summer used to feel magical. These days before the tourists arrived bustled with activity and anticipation. Even the air smelled of excitement. It was exhilarating—what I wanted to capture last summer one final time before I had to think about colleges and SATs and the future.

Instead it all shattered into pieces at my feet.

And this summer . . . tourist season doesn't even kick in until next weekend, but the island already teems with too many people, too many cell phones, too many ways to trip up while someone else is watching. My little corner of the universe has gotten eaten up by the outside world and I don't like it. I don't like it one bit.

Linda tugs me off the podium and I tug Ryan along with us. One furtive glance shows me that my parents are talking to the local reporter covering the Desmond campaign from the *Island Crier*. The coast is clear. We push our way through the throngs of reporters and people who came to hear their dad talk, finally breaking free of the crowd. But even that doesn't give me any real relief. As we pass the picnic tables where someone else now gives my arts and crafts classes, a twinge of longing pulls me up short. My steps slow so I can take a closer look. See the paint stains on the edges of the wood and on the benches. The purple patch on the grass where one of the kids must have dropped a tub of paint.

I loved those classes. I loved the kids and the things they created. Now someone else is teaching them, helping them, while I sit inside taking a tedious economics class Dad signed me up for or stuffing envelopes for a campaign I don't even care about.

My head turns so I can keep looking at the picnic tables till we've entered the stand of trees that separates the press area from the rest of the hotel. We move down the hill, through the playground, onto the beach. For nine long months, I've avoided this place as much as possible. Even now, the ghost of that night—of JR's lips on mine and my fingers tangled in his hair. His breath on my skin. It forces its way into my brain. Makes my chest throb.

I glance at Linda, at Ryan. Linda doesn't know—would never guess the truth. But Ryan knows what happened that night. Is he thinking about it right now, too? Is it dragging him down like a weight? Or is it just me? I can't believe it could just be me. I can't be here with them. It's too hard. I feel as if I'm letting them down with every thought I have when I'm here. Which means I have to keep them—to keep me—moving.

"What do you think, Emma?"

My head jerks up. "What?"

Ryan tilts his head to one side and sighs. "See, she says she loves me, but she doesn't listen to anything I say."

I have to physically shake myself out of my own head so I can answer him. "I always listen to you!" Deep breath in. Deep breath out. Have to act normal. "I hang on your every word."

Linda bursts out laughing. "If that were true, you'd know what he said," she points out. "Also, I probably wouldn't like you as much."

Ryan's smile fades into something disappointed. Something hurt.

"Just tell me what you said." I lay a hand on his arm and squeeze him gently. "And I'll tell you what I think."

"I asked if anyone wants to go into town and grab some lunch," he says sheepishly. "Press conferences make me hungry."

I twist my face into a smile. "I'd love to walk into town," I tell him. "It's the one thing my life is truly lacking right now." My attempt at keeping my voice casual doesn't quite succeed, but he doesn't seem to notice.

Or maybe he does. His eyebrows knit in dismay. "Do you ever take me seriously?"

"All the time," I reply. When my eyes meet his, though, I still see a hint of worry there. Why do I keep hurting him? Why can't I just be what he needs me to be? The person who's always there for him. Who wouldn't even dream of thinking about another guy when he's around.

I want to be that person so badly.

"I always take you seriously," I assure him. "I don't know what I'd do without you."

The worry—the knitted eyebrows—melt away immediately, replaced by his most dazzling smile. "Emma, I . . ."

"Nope," Linda interrupts. "This day has sucked enough without the two of you doing this while I'm here. This is a romance-free zone."

"Since when?" demands Ryan.

"Since right now," she tells him. "I've just declared it. New legislation. If Dad can play at being senator, I can play at making rules, too."

"He's . . . he's not playing at being senator." Ryan's voice is low. His shoulders deflate. "Why do you always say stuff like that?"

My eyes stray to Linda, but she just shrugs.

"He doesn't care about my life and my goals," she says. "Why should I care about his?"

"But you know how important this is to him!" Ryan argues. "He needs us to be more involved! I go to events with him, but you . . . you barely even show up anymore."

Linda's eyes bore into Ryan for a second. If she ever glared at me the way she is at him right now, I think I'd want the ground to swallow me up whole.

"What's up with you lately?" she demands of her brother. "Why are you always following Dad around like his little puppy all the time?"

Ryan's face turns a painful shade of red. "Dad does everything for us," he tells her. Then his voice drops to almost a whisper. "We owe it to him to help."

"He doesn't even pay attention to you anymore," Linda tells him. "Or Mom for that matter. Have you had a single conversation with him today?"

When Ryan doesn't say anything, Linda keeps going.

"You haven't," she says. "Because he was on the phone all morning talking about some stupid nondisclosure agreement and then he had a press conference." She pauses and breathes in deep. "You don't *owe* him anything."

Ryan's arms lay limp at his sides. "I do, though."

I sigh. They've had this same conversation so many times over the last few months. Linda puts her dad down, Ryan jumps in to defend him. It's a routine I can't handle right now, especially when the question of what I owe my own parents hovers over me all the time. How much of my life I have to give over to be what they need me to be.

"So . . . lunch?" I ask. "You two ready to go?"

Linda takes a deep breath and turns my way. "I could eat," she replies. "I'd rather have ice cream, but lunch works, too."

Mission accomplished. We're getting out of this place. Out of this conversation. Ryan holds his hand out to me with a strained smile, as if he hasn't put the argument with Linda quite behind him yet. But then he pulls me closer to him and kisses the top of my hand.

"Anything for you," he tells me.

"Ugh," groans Linda. "I thought this was a romance-free zone?"

He kisses my hand one last time. His eyes are full of love for me. As if none of the stuff with his dad or with Linda bothers him in the least. And nothing about this place brings back hurtful memories for him. My stomach lurches. Lunch might not be such a great idea after all.

As we walk down the path into town, I turn to look at the place where I broke Ryan's trust in me—where I broke JR's trust, too. When I turn back again, I find Ryan looking at me, a question in his eyes. He knows. He knows what I'm thinking and who I'm thinking about. I keep hurting him over and over again.

I don't want to hurt him anymore.

So I smile. I give him the brightest smile I can muster.

And it works. The smile that spreads across his face doesn't quite sparkle, but it's close enough. Ryan wraps his arm around me. I close my eyes and focus in on how good it feels to be close to him. I wrap my arm around his waist and sink into the warmth, the comfort of him.

When we finally get to Main Street, I have two things on my mind: a BLT and some fudge. Well, I have more than that on my mind, but that's what I'm focusing on right now.

"Emma!"

The sound of my name startles me. I turn around, trying to figure out who called me only to find Mathilde from the art gallery waving from across the street. Every time I think I've finally come to a kind of peace inside myself, something jars me out of it. Because I know what Mathilde wants. And I can't give it to her.

"Emma, I've been wanting to talk to you!" she calls.

Ryan and Linda and I come to a stop and wait for Mathilde to dodge a carriage and cross over to us. "I'm so glad I bumped into you!" she says. "Did you get the flier I mailed you?"

"I did," I tell her. "Thanks for letting me know about the exhibition."

"Let you know?" she says. "I want you to be one of the featured artists. Your work last summer was stunning." She smiles at me. "And if they happened to sell faster than anything else in the show, who am I to complain about it?"

I try to smile back. To force the corners of my mouth to lift. But my stomach ties itself into what feels like a giant knot. "I'd love to submit something," I tell her. "I just need to see what I have that could work. Maybe put a couple of new pieces together."

Mathilde squeezes my shoulder. "That's exactly what I wanted to hear!" she says. "Three to five pieces, like I said in my note."

With a nod, I say, "Got it. I'll see what I can do."

One more squeeze of the shoulder and Mathilde's gone. My palm slips against Ryan's, damp with sweat, but it's over. The whole conversation is over.

"You okay?" Ryan asks. "'Cause you look a little . . . not okay right now."

I square my shoulders. Take a deep breath. Mom's advice comes in handy in so many ways it's scary. "I'm fine," I lie. "Just thinking about the art show."

Linda squints her eyes at me. "You look like you could use some fudge."

My head falls back onto my shoulders as a weary laugh comes from somewhere deep in my gut. "I always need fudge."

She brushes a bug off her black pantsuit. "Some ice cream wouldn't hurt either," she says. "I think I need to eat my feelings after that press conference."

Linda slips her arm through mine and Ryan does the same on the other side of me. I pull them both closer to me, grateful that they're always trying to look out for me. But no amount of fudge or ice cream is going to help. Eating my feelings won't even begin to cut it.

CHAPTER 36

Emma (Then)

There is one thing I can do, though. I sit at my desk in the morning and lay out my best ink pens. A medium-weight tip seems good for a drawing of . . . who knows what. At least it's a good place to start. I put the nib of the pen onto the paper but nothing happens. But it's all okay. It's like writer's block but with art. Sometimes creativity doesn't just flow through you like some magical power. If I'm going to get out of this . . . rut . . . I'm going to have to *make* myself create.

A notepad sits at the edge of my desk by the phone. I've used these pads as blank canvases so many times, especially when I was little and the creativity did just flow from me. The paper's not that thick, but it's fine in a pinch. The raised embossing of *Palais du Lac Hotel* is stamped in black at the top of the page. The font is strong, but not too strong. Old-fashioned, but not *too* old-fashioned. Dad hired people to choose it for him.

I look at this font—this notepad—like it's going to turn into my muse or something.

Laying the notepad down, I pick up my pen again and put it to my real art paper. Rough rectangular outline. Barest hint of pages and the cardboard it's glued to. Then the lettering. Bolder lines, curving serifs. The *u* comes out wonky and the *H* is uneven. It's not even remotely anything Mathilde could use in her art show but at least it's a start.

I look down at what I drew and feel as if there's an opportunity here. To fill the blank page of the notepad I drew with . . . something. I close my eyes, willing myself to keep drawing, but the brief bout of inspiration feels as if it's already slipped through my grasp. I lay my head on my desk and try to push what's sitting in the drawer just underneath me out of my mind. It's been three months, four days, and twelve hours since I last made anything real. That whole time, not a painting, not a drawing, not a sculpture, not even the roughest of sketches. It's the longest I've ever gone without making anything. There's a restlessness in me that I can't quite figure out. It's hard to sit down and *do* anything that's real.

A knock sounds at our front door. No one's here but me so I have to force myself up. Force myself to make small talk and make excuses for my parents not being here.

I open the door to find Linda standing there, hair wet and smelling like chlorine. She still has her swim bag with her, so she must have come straight from practice.

"Hey," I say, holding out my hand to her. "I'm so glad it's you and not anyone else."

"Me too," she says as she takes it and pulls me into the living room. "What've you been doing?"

"Trying to draw."

"Trying?"

I shake my head. "Nothing's really . . . coming."

Linda throws herself down on the sofa and tosses the leftover fudge from last night onto the coffee table. "I brought early lunch."

"Sounds good to me." I sit next to her and break off a piece. It melts on my tongue, the sweetness slowly seeping into my taste buds and permeating my whole mouth. "This ish sho good," I mumble with my mouth full of fudge.

She leans into me, laying her head on the back of the sofa. "Look at me," Linda says. "Always knowing exactly what you need when you need it."

"You joke, but I really did need to see you."

She watches me as I break off another piece of fudge. "You okay?"

I start to shrug but then stop myself. This isn't something I ever did before but in the last few months I've started. I hate when I do it—I hate myself for picking up his mannerisms after everything that happened. After he'd gone. I don't want to think about him anymore.

"Emma?" Linda says. "*Are* you okay? Because you don't seem like you are."

Time to shake this off. The last thing I could ever tell Linda is that I'm thinking about JR. She would never want to talk about him after everything that happened. "I'm fine," I reassure her. "Just not feeling creative right now, I guess."

She chews on some fudge as she mulls that over. "So what's the deal?"

"I don't know," I admit. "It just feels like everything's changing, or about to change, and I'm not sure how I feel about any of it."

She puts her feet up on the coffee table. My mom would kill her if she was here to see this, which makes me smile for some reason.

"I get what you mean," Linda says. "The fact that you guys are going off to college in the fall and I'll be stuck here is . . ." She rubs both her eyes. "It's not good."

I turn to look at her. "But you like your job, right?" I ask. "And you had a date last night with ice cream shop girl, didn't you?"

"Yeah, yeah," Linda replies. "Lots of good things are happening. I'm really lucky to have this internship and Mae is . . . she's so cute. And funny." Linda pauses for a second. "Plus, she always smells like ice cream, which falls firmly in the *pro* column for me."

I laugh. "I can't believe *smells like ice cream* is one of the things you like about Mae."

"*Smells like dessert* is the number one thing I look for in a romance," Linda informs. "Isn't that how everyone chooses who to date?"

"Absolutely," I laugh. "Top criteria always."

She looks out the window for a second. "My mom wheedled me into doing a fundraiser later this afternoon," she tells me. "She got all misty-eyed when I said yes, like I'd just made all her dreams come true."

"Maybe you did?"

A weak laugh escapes from her. "I guess it's nice that one of my parents cares what I do."

Leaning my head on her shoulder, I wrap my pinkie around hers. It's time. I know it is. Time to come clean about the two acceptance letters lying in my desk drawer. One from University of Michigan, one from the School of the Art Institute of Chicago. A few weeks ago I accepted both. I know you're not supposed to do that, and I know it's wrong. But I just couldn't let go of the only dream for the future I've ever had. I couldn't. So I used some of the money my gran left me to put a deposit down for Chicago. My parents did the same for Michigan.

I haven't told anyone—not even Ryan or Linda—what I've done. The loneliness of that gnaws at me sometimes. A lot of things do these days. The repairs that insurance didn't quite cover. The loans my parents took out. The fact that I'm enrolled in two different schools for two different majors in the fall. Linda stuck doing events she hates doing. Ryan falling into line for his dad day after day. How angry my parents will be—how disappointed Ryan will be—when they find out what I've done.

I look at Linda again as she leans back into the sofa with her eyes closed. She takes a deep breath and lets it out in a loud *whoosh*. There's been so much on her mind lately. So many things expected or dismissed by her dad. And if I tell her—if I do come clean—I'll just add to that. How can I ask her not to tell Ryan? How can I drive another wedge between them?

The answer is that I can't.

"When's your fundraiser?" I ask.

Linda sighs. "Four o'clock. It's supposed to be happy hour. My dad's sense of irony knows no bounds."

Turning, I find her with a frown on her face. Neither of us is doing so well right now. "Want to run into town and grab some lunch?" I suggest. "Then we could spend some time together before you have to go make your mom happy?"

She takes one deep breath, then another. "Yeah, that would be good, actually." Her eyes meet mine. "You don't mind that I still smell like the pool, right?"

This makes me laugh despite myself. "If I minded that, we would never have become friends in the first place," I tell her. "You smell like chlorine for most of the school year."

With a shrug, Linda says, "Love me, love my chemical smell."

I just nudge her. "Drop your bag upstairs. I'll meet you outside in ten minutes. Okay?"

"Okay." She's up and out of the room faster than I could ever manage even without having been swimming laps all morning.

My fist wraps around the fudge wrapper. I crinkle it up in my hand and dump it in the wastebasket. Like a zombie, I walk to my room and open my desk drawer. There, my two letters of acceptance sit as they have for weeks. The drawer slides closed as I stare at the blank page still sitting on my desk. It's so frustrating to look at . . . nothing. Pen in hand, I scribble on the page within the page just to have *something* there. I put my pens away and pack everything back onto the shelves I got them from. Lunch. Lunch will be good. Being in town will be distracting.

Gone out for lunch, I write on a note for Mom. Instead of taking the stairs and running the risk of bumping into my parents, I head to the elevator. The hum of the motor is somehow comforting. When I was little I was mesmerized by this elevator, with all its shiny wood and brass-framed mirrors. I'd beg my mom to take me up and down, over and over again. Now, I hardly step foot in it.

As soon as I get to the lobby, I sneak out the side door and down the stairs of the verandah. I don't know why I'm being so stealthy. All they'd need to do is see the note I left for them to know where I'm going—yet I still don't want them to stop me from going.

They stop me from doing so many things I want to do.

Footsteps sound behind me but when I turn around I find Ryan instead of Linda. The second our eyes meet, his whole face breaks out into a smile, warming something inside me.

"Hey!" I call out. "Where are you off to?"

"Lunch with you and Linda!" he says. "She wouldn't invite me so I invited myself."

I look at him for a second. "And . . . she didn't mind that you invited yourself?"

"Oh no, she did!" he replies in a cheerful voice. "But I couldn't resist seeing you before I get swallowed up by campaign stuff later." He grins from ear to ear as he wraps his arm around me. "And aren't you glad I'm here?"

I lean into him. "I am, actually."

"Because you love me so much?" he asks as if he's a little boy seeking assurance. I don't mind giving it to him. I never mind. I'm the one who put this doubt in his mind in the first place.

"So much."

Ryan leans in and kisses me. It's just a soft brush of his lips at first. Then he deepens the kiss. His breath warms my cheeks. His hands feel like heaven in my hair.

"I love you so much, too," he whispers in my ear. His lips, his teeth, pull at my earlobe, making me shiver. "You know what I'm looking forward to?"

"What?" I gasp.

"September," he says. "College. When we'll be together with no parents, no curfews, no rules. I'll be able to wake up next to you every day and no one will care."

"Except maybe my roommate," I try to joke.

But he's not joking at all. "She won't mind," Ryan counters. "I'll be so fun and chill that she'll want me to be around all the time." His lips graze at the sensitive spot just under my earlobe. "Besides, we'll have my room, too. Between the two rooms, we'll figure it out."

I smile and nod, letting myself kiss him again rather than answer. I guess it's naive but I genuinely hadn't thought about what going to school together would mean for us in terms of that part of our relationship. He's already planning nightly sleepovers. And it's not that I don't want that, too, it's just that . . . well, there's something I still haven't told him.

"What would happen if we ended up going to different schools?" I ask. "Would you want to stay with me long distance?"

"Are you kidding me?" he says, his voice dripping with disbelief. "Of course I would. I want to be with you any way I can. Always."

"Okaaay." My voice sounds low and questioning. "Always is a long time, you know."

"I do know," he almost whispers. Ryan cups my cheek with his big, warm hand. "I said always and I meant it. Plus, we're not going to different schools, so it doesn't make any difference."

I need to tell him. Now. Right this second. But doubt creeps in again. Does he really need to know I haven't let go of Chicago yet? It's not as if my parents will let me go there anyway. It's a fairy tale—one that I can't help but cling to because I don't want to go to University of Michigan and I don't want to major in business. I don't want any of it.

"It's annoying that you're actually coming with us." Linda's voice cuts through the fog of my thoughts. Ryan and I break apart instantly. "It was supposed to be just me and Emma."

Ryan tenses up beside me. "But you don't mind because I'm an awesome brother, right?"

I lay my hand on him, trying to get him to stop talking. Ryan's eyes shift from Linda to me and back to his sister, eyebrows furrowed. "Wait, are you really mad that I'm coming?" he asks. "'Cause I can stay home if you really want me to."

With a dramatic roll of her eyes, Linda says, "No, you can come. You just have to promise not to piss me off while we're eating."

He crosses his hand over his chest. "You can count on me, little sis!"

Linda grabs my arm and starts walking. "You're already annoying me," she tells him. "That was strike one."

We walk in silence for a while. Me because I'm not sure what to say. Ryan because I think he's too afraid Linda will actually make him go home. And Linda . . . I glance sideways at her. "What's up?"

She shakes her head. "I still can't believe I let myself get talked into this fundraiser," she tells me. "Mom is a persuasive demon."

"She's so happy you're coming," Ryan assures her. "Dad is, too. You know he wants you to come to more events. Especially as the campaign heats up this summer and fall."

She turns and gives him a withering glare. "I don't really care," she admits. "Besides, what're you going to do when you start college? You'll be busy with classes and ROTC, won't you?"

"Yeah, but . . ."

A tense silence falls between them. I hate it when they fight. I always feel as if I'm being torn in two—expected to take Ryan's side or Linda's when it's a complete no-win situation.

"I'm just trying to do the right thing," he says. His voice is quiet, defeated in some strange way. "I want Dad to be proud of me."

This breaks my heart just a little, but Linda groans.

"Your constant need for affirmation is getting exhausting," Linda tells him. "You didn't used to be this way. You used to just be convinced you were awesome without constantly needing someone to pump up your ego."

His eyes drop down to the ground. "A lot has changed." He looks embarrassed—ashamed that he needs us to tell him that we love him, that he's important to us—and I don't want that for him.

"You've got me to affirm you," I reassure him. "I'll tell you how wonderful you are whenever you need me to."

A giant, irrepressible smile spreads across his face. "You really are the best, Emma."

"So are you." I smile back at him.

Linda groans again.

I take a deep breath and let it sweep back out of me. It's almost a relief to get into town, but then it's . . . not.

Everywhere I look, there are reporters or film crews. I know they'll all be gone again soon, but right now they're like swarming bees. By the ferry dock, a crew has just finished setting up a satellite dish that must've arrived too late for the press conference. A woman in a business jacket, blouse, and jeans tests her mic as she gets ready to go on air.

Early tourists—probably just arrived on the ferry—line up at shops to buy fudge and souvenirs even before they properly see the island. It's as if they're not even going to bother to get to know the place. They'll simply hit this one area and then go home to tell everyone about the carriages and how quaint everything is. The outside world is pressing its face against that glass of the windows here, fogging up the panes in ways that leave smudges in their aftermath.

Part of me has always longed for this. To meet new people and to see what the world off-island is like. Part of me, though, wants to cling to this little island for the few months I have left before I head off to college. Last summer ended in the worst possible way. I need this one to make up for that. As I watch the reporter straighten her jacket and put on a phony smile before she begins speaking to the camera in front of her, I know that some of the magic I longed for has already disappeared.

I close my eyes for a second, letting Ryan's strong hand pull me along the street. It's only when I open them again that everything falls apart in earnest.

So I slip away from his grasp and watch it all topple.

The dock for the fishing and tourist boats looks exactly the same as it always does—bustling with people working on their boats or bringing in their catches. An older man mends a fishing net. A woman hauls crates of freshwater salmon off her boat. The ferry pulls away from its pier, making its way back to the mainland. Everyone goes about their business as if nothing has changed.

Except that with something as simple as opening my eyes again, everything has.

I want to avert my eyes—to look away and pretend that what I'm seeing isn't real—but I can't. My own morbid curiosity forces me to keep watching.

He's not supposed to be here. Not yet anyway. He had two more months. And even then, I never really expected him to come back.

But there he is. Sweat-soaked T-shirt plastered to his back, scraping mussels off the bottom of a wildlife tour boat.

JR.

My hands ball up into fists. My fingernails dig into the soft skin of my palms. This is fine. Everything is going to be fine.

One glance at Ryan and Linda as they walk ahead of me makes it clear they haven't seen him yet. I just have to maneuver them away from the docks, and everything will be okay.

But why is he *here*? Why this island of all places? How could he come back? Doesn't he know how much damage he's done? Doesn't he know how much he hurt me?

Or does he just not care? I can't take my eyes off him, even though I know I should. There's a defiant look in his eyes, as if he's challenging the world—everything around him—for no reason. But I can read his face better than anyone else can. I can see what lurks just under the defiance. A lost little boy, trying to put on a brave face.

I will him to look up. To see me. I need him to know that I'm lost, too. That he made me feel this way.

Too many memories of him—of us—swirl through my head. His hands under my knees, around my back, lifting me onto him. His hand running over the back of my neck. His lips, his breath on my skin. His scowl as he heaped insults, accusations at me.

Heat surges through my chest and up my neck. I feel feverish. Not myself. I won't let him do this to me. I won't let him turn me into knots like this. Not now. Not ever again.

I run to catch up with Linda and Ryan, watching them to see if they'd noticed him. But they're still happily bickering. Which means Linda hasn't seen JR since before the fire. Before she ended up in the emergency room. Ryan hasn't seen him since that night on the beach when he saw us. . . .

My eyes dart around frantically, looking for something to distract them. Up the nearest side street, slightly uphill from where we stand, is the library. "I . . . I think I want to go to the library before we grab something to eat," I stammer out. "Would that be okay with you guys?"

Linda shoots me a strange look. "You want to get a book *before* we eat?" she asks. "Wouldn't it make more sense to go afterward?"

She has a good point but it doesn't matter. I'm going to the library and I'm taking them with me. Then I'll say I'm tired . . . that I need to head back to the hotel. Maybe even that we should just get sandwiches there so we can have a picnic on the lawn.

"I'd rather go right now if you don't mind," I reply, trying to keep my voice steady.

"Why? Do you need an art book so you can find new stuff to make?" Ryan asks.

Linda rolls her eyes at him. "She doesn't use instruction books," she reminds him. "How long have you been together and you still don't know that?"

"Hey!" he says. "Emma never talks about art with me. Do you, Emma?"

"Not really," I admit. As if that matters right now. As if it matters at all.

I glance sideways at him as we walk, but he's gone back to bickering with Linda and we need to get out of here. So I take them both by the arm and drag them in the direction of the library. If there's one thing I know I have to do, it's to get them out of here. I need to put a little distance between us and him. Between him and me.

CHAPTER 37

Lexi (Now)

I f there's one thing I know I have to do it's visit Ms. VanHill at the medical center. It doesn't matter whether I want to be there or whether it brings back painful memories my brain had pushed into the dark recesses of my head. Ms. VanHill is my friend. I have to get over myself and visit.

So I put Mom's chest in a bag just in case it might distract her, and then start walking.

The minute I walk through the medical center's doors the antiseptic smell hits my nostrils again and I stop breathing. The bare white walls feel so barren. So . . . clinical. Like this isn't a place to make people better at all, but just one to process them. A factory with doctors and nurses. I freeze for a second, clutching my bag to my chest.

I know I'm not being reasonable. Everyone here works every day to make people better. Broken bones and heart attacks. Routine check-ups and surgeries. This is a place that helps people.

Forcing myself to breathe, I take in the antiseptic smell again. It's just cleaning fluid. Like Windex or Mr. Clean. It's just to keep the place germ-free and clean.

It's not where Mom died.

I take one step, then another. The nurse at the front desk smiles at me. "Can I help you?"

One nod. One deep breath. I can do this. "Can you . . . can you let me know what room Clara VanHill is in?"

Then I hear it: Ms. VanHill's voice from down the hall.

"All this fuss over a wrist. You'd think I'd lost half my blood in that fall."

The nurse at the desk sighs.

"I bet I can find her myself," I tell her.

She smiles again. "I bet you can," she replies. "But just in case, she's in room 204."

I nod and follow the sound of Ms. VanHill's voice.

She's lying in a hospital bed, a huge bouquet of flowers by her side. She looks smaller, older in her blue robe and hospital gown. Like she's somehow shrunk since she got here.

But apparently nothing about her personality has shrunk.

"It's in a cast," she tells the doctor. "I don't know why you have to keep me here."

As I step farther into the room a young doctor starts patiently explaining that Ms. VanHill got bruised up in the fall. "And at your age, we want to take every possible precaution."

"At my age!" Ms. VanHill scoffs. "Lexi," she says as she spots me in the doorway. "Will you tell this woman that age is just a number and that I'm—"

But the doctor jumps in before I can respond. "I understand age is just a number," she explains. "But your number happens to be quite high. So we're going to keep you overnight for observation, just as a precaution."

The doctor gives me a tense smile as she leaves. "Enjoy your visit," she says. It doesn't sound like she thinks that's possible, though.

I grin at Ms. VanHill. "You should be nice to her. She's the one taking care of you."

Ms. VanHill sniffs, jutting out her chin. "She wouldn't be if I could go back to the hotel where I belong," Ms. VanHill tells me. "It is only a broken wrist."

My eyes shift down to the bright white cast on her left wrist. "What happened?"

"I fell" is all she says. "I put out my hand to break my fall. Wrist broken. Story concluded."

Ms. VanHill's stories never conclude that quickly. Something's up. "How did you fall?"

She sniffs at me again, as if I've greatly offended her. "The curtains in my sitting room were all akimbo," she tells me. "So I got on a chair to straighten them out."

This shocks me more than it probably should.

"You . . . *what?*"

She waves a dismissive hand at me. "Oh, don't make me repeat myself," she says. "And now that you're here, can you call for some tea and cake?"

"Um, no, I can't," I tell her. "The medical center doesn't do afternoon tea. But I'll bring you some from the hotel later today if you'd like."

This offer earns me a smile. "That would be lovely. I'd appreciate that greatly."

She gestures to the chair by her bedside and as I sit down, she holds her good hand out to me. I slip my hand into hers and give it a gentle squeeze.

"Now let's change the subject, shall we?" she says. "Casey said something about your mother's family but I can't remember what. I'm old now. My memory isn't what it used to be."

I grin at her. "I thought age was just a number?"

"Hmph." She waves the hand with the cast on it. "That's only when the doctor is here. I know how old I am."

Just as I open my mouth to tell her about my mother, Ms. VanHill opens hers as well.

"1924," she says. "That's when I was born. A war had ended, a depression was looming, and along came me."

I look at her for a long moment, trying to picture the time—the place, even. "The island must have been different when you were little."

"Not to speak of," she replies. "This place has always been stuck in a time warp." Ms. VanHill closes her eyes. "Attitudes have changed. People have more progressive ideas now. But this island . . . nothing ever really changes."

I mull that over for a second. For Mom, a lot seemed to have changed. She grew up here, she loved it. But she still left . . . and never came back again.

"Remind me of your mother's name again?" Ms. VanHill asks.

We're back on my mom again. I'll have to ask her about the island in the nineteen twenties and thirties later.

"Emma," I tell her.

"That's right," she says, nodding. "Emma Roth."

"Actually, that's part of what I found out," I say. "Her maiden name wasn't Roth. It was Wolfe."

Ms. VanHill sits more upright in her hospital bed. "Wolfe?" she asks. "As in the hotel Wolfes?"

With one deep breath, I admit to what I'm only just starting to believe myself. "It seems that way, yes."

She blinks at me. "Your mother was Richard and Jessica Wolfe's daughter?"

My mind searches for the right answer here. Jackson said that my grandmother's name was Jessica, didn't he?

"I think so." Then I look at her, trying to figure out what she's thinking. "Do you remember her now?"

It takes Ms. VanHill a long time to answer. "I remember Richard and Jessica," she says. "Very stuck in their own world. Very convinced the whole island revolved around their hotel." A shrewd glance accompanies this. "You don't mind my insulting your grandparents, do you?"

"I didn't know them," I remind her. "Insult away."

This makes Ms. VanHill laugh. "You're a spitfire, Lexi," she tells me. "And mind you, that's a compliment."

My cheeks burn. No one has ever called me a spitfire before. I kind of like it? "Um . . . thanks."

When she falls silent again, I wonder if she'll resurface somewhere else in time with different people in her memories.

"I didn't actually know them well," Ms. VanHill continues. "They were much younger than me. Ran with a different crowd." She sighs. "Your mother . . . I remember that they had a little girl, but . . ." Her face screws up like she's struggling to remember.

"It's okay, Ms. VanHill," I rush to assure her. "You weren't even living here then."

"No, that's true," she says in a distant voice. "I was already well into my career at that point, far, far away from here."

"Probably well into your first run of *Mame*."

Her hand slackens in mine. I'm about to get up to let her rest when she says, "Lexi, do you sing?"

The question makes me blink in surprise. "I mean, in the shower," I admit. "But that's about it."

"Ever been in a play at school or anything of that nature?" she persists.

This, unfortunately, hits a nerve with me and I'm not sure what to say in response at first. "No, nothing like that."

"But you know so much about my career," Ms. VanHill says. "So much about Broadway."

"I love musicals," I tell her. "I love the idea of breaking into song in the middle of a dramatic scene or singing to the person you love."

"But you don't do that yourself?"

"Um . . . it would be a little awkward if I just busted out in song in the middle of the school day," I reply.

She snorts out a laugh. "That depends greatly on where you go to school," she says. "But that's what the theatre is for. To give you a space to do things you wouldn't do in normal life."

Once again, it takes me a moment to respond. Because it's not like

I don't want to be in the school plays and to step outside of regular life. Doing so would, however, require something of me that I'm not prepared to do.

"Auditions terrify me," I say in a quiet voice.

"Anything worth doing in life will terrify you at some point," she counters. "That's how you know what you're striving for is worth attaining."

This trip falls into that category, I realize. Lying to Dad and Abby, sneaking around and coming here all by myself—it all terrified me. Now that I'm here, though, I'm making friends and finding out more about my mom and doing things for myself.

"Tell me your mother's last name again?" Ms. VanHill says.

"Wolfe. Emma Wolfe," I say. "Richard and Jessica Wolfe's daughter."

"Hm," she hums. "Where on earth did you get the other last name, then?"

"Roth?" I supply.

"Yes, that's the one," she says.

"I thought it was her name before she married my dad," I tell her. "I mean, I know it was."

Ms. VanHill nods. "The man in the picture," she says. "He must be the first husband."

Somehow I wish that were true. It would be less complicated if she'd married Ryan Desmond first. Mom and JR . . . it just doesn't make sense.

"I found out JR's real name," I tell her.

Ms. VanHill watches me with a squinting keenness in her eyes. "And?"

"His name was Jason Roth."

For a long second or two, Ms. VanHill looks out the window. Her eyes, her face, don't betray anything about what she's thinking. Then she gives me another piercing look. "So your mother was married to her friend JR before she met your father," she surmises. "That's one mystery solved anyway. Where's your phone? Have you looked the man up yet? What have you found?"

I sigh. "There are tons of Jason Roths. I have no idea which one is him."

"Hm . . . it must have ended badly or you'd have known she'd been married before," she tells me. "Almost no one knew about Fran and me or that I lost her the way I did. It happens."

I squeeze her hand. I wish I could turn back the years and find some way to let the two of them be together, but as Ms. VanHill said herself, that ship sailed long ago.

My thoughts stray back to Mom. To the fact that she married JR before she married Dad. But something's not adding up. I have no idea how that even would've worked. Mom and Dad had me when they were really young. They didn't even get married until a year after I was born.

A thought shoots into my brain. The worst one I've ever had. One that can't possibly be true.

I tear open the chest and start taking bits and pieces out. Her notepads and drawings, the fabric and unsent postcards.

Finally I find something I haven't looked at before. At least not carefully.

"What do you have there?" Ms. VanHill asks.

"It's another note she wrote," I tell her.

On one side is what appears to be her younger writing.

YOU ARE THE WORST.

You gotta stop complimenting me like this.

I can't. I'm really smart, so I know the worst person when I see him.

Emma.

JR.

I think you're the worst too.

On the other side of the paper, Mom's writing looks older.

I need to stop spending time with him. Now.

Why can't I stop spending time with him?

I put down the paper, not sure what to even say. Nothing makes sense anymore. JR caused the fire, but she was still friends with him? Or did she write this before the fire? Why can't any of the puzzle pieces fit together the right way?

Glancing up at Ms. VanHill to see what she thinks, I realize that she's gazing at me with intense sympathy in her eyes.

"If she married the arsonist," she asks, "then what happened to the boy in the picture?"

"Ryan," I almost whisper. I take out the picture of the two of them at the hundredth anniversary party. They lean into each other like they were drawn together like magnets. His hand lies so low on her backside. They were clearly dating, or else he wouldn't have his hand in that exact spot, not without her pushing him away. At least I hope she'd have pushed him away. From what I know now about Mom, it seems like she would have.

So she must have wanted him to touch her.

I rummage through the stuff in the chest until I find a picture Mom drew of Ryan, bypassing an old datebook. This time he's playing the guitar and looking up at—I guess my mom? Looking at her as if he'd like to have his way with her. Like, right at that moment. I've heard the expression "bedroom eyes" before, but never actually seen it in action.

Mom drew Ryan Desmond with bedroom eyes. He wanted her. Did she want him, too?

Every time one piece of the puzzle fits into place, another hole in the picture opens up again. And I'm starting to be scared of what I'll find when all the pieces finally end up in the right positions and the full picture emerges.

CHAPTER 38

Emma (Then)

The library. I just need to get to the library. I pull at Ryan and Linda again to get them to move faster toward the white-columned building. Only when we're inside with the door closed behind us do I let myself relax my guard even a little bit.

"Hey there!" says Caleb, the new librarian. He smiles. Linda blushes.

"Hi, Caleb," she says. "Um . . . nice day, isn't it?"

"It is, actually," he tells her. "I got some new books in. Go look in new releases and see if there's anything that catches your eye."

"Sounds good," Linda says. "And if I have any questions I'll definitely come find you."

"Great!" Caleb returns to checking books back into the computer system. I grab Linda and physically lead her to the new releases.

"What're you doing?" Linda hisses at me.

"Keeping you from throwing yourself at Caleb," I whisper.

"But he looks like Tobey Maguire in *Spider-Man*," she sighs. "All he needs is a Spidey suit and—"

"He's at least ten years older than you," I remind her. "Plus, aren't you dating Mae?"

"One date," Linda tells me. "We went on one date. That means all bets are still off."

"Let's look for some books," I tell her. "There really are lots of new ones."

"I'm going to look around, too," Ryan says before he wanders away. Very rarely does he take anything out to read—he just likes to see what's here.

Linda's interest in the new releases wanes, too, and she takes off looking for books about investment banking so she can contribute more at the company she's interning for. Left to myself, I pick up a new release at random and try to focus on the handwritten description that Caleb taped below it. Ryan and Linda didn't see JR. This really is going to be fine.

All I have to do is get a hold of myself. Just because JR's back on island does *not* mean I will let him throw me off this way. We can exist in the same place and still have nothing to do with each other. We already do exist on entirely different planes.

Apparently, that's what JR thought all along, anyway.

Another surge of heat courses through me.

Read. I need to read. I pick up the nearest book on the new release shelf. A biography of Shakespeare. It's probably interesting but it's not going to do it for me right now. Then I see a white cover with brightly colored shapes on it. Everyone always says you shouldn't judge a book by its cover, but I'm going to do just that.

I sit down at the nearest table and open up the book. I need to focus and block him out of my mind.

That's when I hear Caleb talking again.

"I'm so glad you could come today!" His voice rings with excitement. "It just arrived late yesterday. I stayed up all night reading it. What a fascinating case! And the whole appeals process was so unfair."

"I figured I'd stop in on my lunch break to pick it up," says a quiet voice I know all too well. "Thanks for getting the book for me."

Caleb says something else but my mind isn't working well enough for me to process what it is. He's here. We're in the same room. JR might be across the library but he's still sharing the same space, the same air, with me. I need to sit on the floor or duck behind a bookshelf or do *something* so that he doesn't see me. I won't let him see me. I won't look at him.

I don't even want to.

And yet I can't not look.

I turn to find JR standing at the front desk politely listening to Caleb's musings over whatever book it is that he requested. I freeze, gripping the book in my hand so tightly that the binding of it makes a crackling noise. Carefully—with painstaking care, in fact—I put it down on the table. Why bother pretending I'm reading anyway? All I can see is him. All of him. And how much he's changed.

JR's sweat-drenched shirt clings to his shoulders, his chest. He's filled out since I last saw him. He's not any taller, but his shoulders are bigger—more defined. His eyes are focused, serious, as he talks to Caleb. The dark mop of hair has been replaced with a close-cropped cut. The crease that used to come and go between his eyebrows looks as if he'd worried it into permanent existence over the months he was in juvenile detention. He holds himself differently. Straighter. More upright. He looks older. He looks . . . good.

God, why am I staring at him like this? Why am I even *thinking* any of this? He could've destroyed my home. Something must be wrong with me. That's got to be it. I am sick in some deep-rooted way that I need to figure out so I can get out from under it. Because right now it feels like a weight—an enormous, heavy burden that I'll never be able to carry with me.

But something must be wrong with him, too. *Why* is he here? What does he think he's doing anyway? What game is he playing? He talks to Caleb so calmly—as if he's never done anything wrong or he actually belongs here now. Back in this *bubble*. That's what he said after all. Just a land of make-believe that he had no place in. Yet here he is in it. Again.

So, yes, there's definitely something wrong with him, too.

Anger so strong that it makes my hands shake takes hold of me. I wish he was anywhere but here. Anywhere but this library. This island. This state.

JR looks up. He sees me. And I . . . I still can't tear my eyes away from him.

The serious expression that had been on his face morphs into a gentler expression. His chin relaxes. His eyes soften for a second. Then the crease between them deepens even more. There's something in his eyes right now—something so raw and vulnerable and full of pain that it makes my hands shake. I don't want him to look like that. I don't want him to feel like that. I want to hate him so much that it makes my eyes sting. But I don't. He once told me that he could never hate me and now . . . now I can't do it either.

God, I'm such a mess.

Someone touches my arm, breaking this spell JR has put me under. "Did you find anything?" Ryan asks. "It's so stuffy in here."

The tiny trace of vulnerability on JR's face disappears. His jaw tenses. Eyes harden as his mouth straightens itself into a grim line. And that's all it takes for my own anger to burn inside me again, too. What does *he* have to be angry about? That he did something terrible and got punished for it? That he single-handedly destroyed our friendship? My face is on fire. A bead of sweat runs down my cheek.

"Hey, are you okay?" Ryan asks.

"I'm fine. I'm always fine, aren't I?"

I try to angle myself so that Ryan has to look away from the front desk and JR. I have to protect Ryan from seeing him. I have to not hurt him again.

He sits down across from me, his back to JR. "You sure you're okay?"

"Yes, of course," I lie. "You're right. It is stuffy in here. I might go find the water fountain and . . ."

When I look up again, JR is gone.

Gone, but not for good. He's just gone back to his job at the docks.

He's staying on this island somewhere. We'll see him again—it's only a matter of time.

I stand up and hold out my hand to Ryan. "Let's go home," I tell him. "I think I'd rather get sandwiches in the café and eat on the lawn if that's okay with you."

"As long as sandwiches are involved, I'm all good!" he says. I look up at him. The smile in his eyes. The way he holds my hand in his. Gentle, as if I'm something precious to him. And I know I am. I know he's not pretending anything or hiding what he feels. There's no mystery, no anger when I'm with him.

I pull him into a hug, suddenly desperate to feel close to him.

"What's this for?" he says in a soft voice.

"For being you."

He holds me even tighter. *This.* This is what's true. What I need.

"Let's get Linda," I say.

But Linda's already standing by the door as if she's waiting for us. I take her by the hand and then grab Ryan's as well, tugging them outside. Not even pausing to say goodbye to Caleb or to see if JR is still in sight, I pull them down through the tourists on Main Street, up the hill, through the gates of the hotel. Only when I'm safely inside them do I feel as if I can breathe again.

"Lunch in the café?" I say again.

Linda stares at me with a pinched look on her face.

"What's wrong?" I ask.

She shakes her head. "I guess that wasn't what I was expecting you to say."

When I don't reply in any way, she stares at me again. "I think I'm just going to head upstairs. Shower up before the fundraiser."

"Are you sure?" I ask her. "Can I at least get you a sandwich and bring it up to you?"

She screws her mouth down into a frown. "I'm guessing you'll be fine without me." She looks me in the eyes. "You and Ryan probably have stuff you need to talk about."

Before I can ask what she means, Linda walks away from us at a fast clip.

I watch until she's out of sight before closing my eyes to blot out the world for moment. Ryan puts his hands on my shoulders—he gently presses his lips to my forehead, the tenderest of touches. I force my eyes to open again, to look at him. The worry that I see there almost breaks me. He knows something's wrong. And I can't even tell him what. I can't tell anyone. I don't deserve his worry and care. I proved that to myself in the library just now, and I'm proving it right now as JR still seeps into my thoughts.

I hold on to him as if I'm drowning and only he can keep me afloat. Maybe it's even true. "I love you so much," I whisper into his chest.

Ryan exhales a trembling breath. "I love you, too."

He smiles at me as I pull away from him.

"Do you mind if I skip out on lunch, too?" I ask. "I've got a little bit of a headache. I might just grab something upstairs and lie down for a while."

With one last kiss on my forehead, he says, "I'll see you tomorrow?"

I try to smile at him but can't quite get my mouth to move the way it's supposed to. "Tomorrow, yes," I manage to get out. Then I walk toward the hotel. With any luck my parents won't be around. With any luck I can just get to my room, close the door behind me, and finally have a second to *think*—to try to wrap my head around . . . all of this. The elevator beckons to me again, this time out of sheer exhaustion. My feet—my whole body—drag.

The relief of being home—in my room with the door closed—is almost too palpable. I've never wanted to shut the world out more than I do now. I lie on my bed and try to let myself rest.

I know with every atom in my body that JR cannot be part of my life anymore. Not after what he did. Not after all the things he said to me after the fire. I don't even want to think about him right now but I can't help it. The look in his eyes when he saw me. The memory of his lips on mine. All the times we fought and had fun together as kids. It all jumbles up in my mind, making my head ache. I close my eyes and breathe in deep.

I keep reminding myself over and over again that JR doesn't matter anymore. He's made sure that there can be no other way.

CHAPTER 39

Emma (Then)

I am having a difficult time convincing myself that JR doesn't matter. At breakfast with Mom and Dad, at the endless lunch welcoming new full-time residents of the hotel. At my desk afterward doing homework for the econ class. No matter what they make me do, my mind wanders back to him.

A restless, anxious tension knots around my insides like a snake coiling up tight before it strikes at its prey. It's just that there's no prey around and the only thing I'm eating away at is myself. I think—I think hard about how to make this feeling go away.

The only thing I can think of is to go find JR and make him listen to *me* this time. He had some hard *truths* to tell me last time we talked. Now I have some for him.

As soon as I finish my homework, I walk toward town and the docks. It's chillier than I thought it would be. The wind whips through my dress. I hold my arms around myself to keep from shivering as I walk.

The sky is a dull, eerie gray. So is the lake in the distance. The only difference between them is the ripples washing over the water. Later on—after I find him—I'm going to capture those gray-blues and the stormy light of this afternoon on paper. I'm determined to. A pale lavender pencil for some undertones to bring out the depth of the gray.

I picture it in my head. See the piece I'll make, when this is over.

Just as I'm about to turn into town, my eyes meet Ryan's. He gives me a quiet smile, its normal wattage dimmed. "I've been looking for you."

"I've been all over the place today," I tell him. I mean it, too—mentally and physically, I haven't been in one place all day long.

He falls into step with me. "Did you get some rest yesterday? Are you feeling better?"

It's a good question. I know he's only asking out of concern. I still can't answer truthfully.

"I'm fine."

A short pause follows, punctuated only by the cries of the seabirds.

"The thing is, you don't seem fine," he replies. "And we're a team, right? How are we going to last for the long run if we can't talk about how we're feeling?"

Something about the idea of us lasting for the long run bristles within me. And it has nothing to do with Ryan or our relationship. It's me. Or rather, it's my parents and their growing demands. The nagging feeling that underlying their support for our relationship, my parents are glad Ryan and I are together because it's useful to them. My poor, battered stomach churns again. I need to start doing yoga or meditation before I give myself an ulcer.

"Emma?"

I shrug and shake my head.

"I don't know what that means," Ryan says. "I don't know why you're shaking your head."

"Neither do I."

He angles himself toward me and brushes his lips against mine. It feels like possibly the worst-timed kiss in my entire life, and that's saying something given the events of last summer.

"I'm starting to worry about you. You haven't been yourself the last day or two." He lifts my chin so we're eye to eye. "And I'm leaving for a couple of days, so I . . . I just . . ."

That shocks me into speaking. "Leaving? Where are you going?"

"My dad wants me to go to Lansing with him," Ryan replies. "For a campaign rally and a dinner with his top donors there. He needs me to step up more."

Somehow the idea of him being so far away—especially with everything going on right now—is more than I can handle. "Can't you get out of it?" I plead. "I need you, too."

Ryan wraps his arm around me. "I know," he says. "And I'm sorry I have to go. But Dad's right. I need to step up."

I turn to look at him, my heart in my stomach. "Couldn't you step up next week? Or in a few days?"

He looks away. "Dad . . . he's so stressed out about the next few months. He needs me right now and I . . . I can't turn my back on him."

I search his face, wondering what's making him so dedicated to his parents lately. Linda keeps saying it's his need for affirmation, but it feels as if it's moved beyond that. "Ryan, what's going on with you?" I demand. "Just this once, why can't you say no?" Tears fill my eyes. I blink them back. After I talk to JR, I'll need Ryan at my side to help put the pieces of me back together.

"My dad . . . both my parents . . . they've done a lot for me this past year," he stammers. "They've made things possible for me that wouldn't have been without them so I . . . I want to be there when they need me."

That doesn't make any sense to me at all. What on earth have his parents done to make him roll over and do their bidding like this? He got fine grades senior year. He probably would have gotten into University of Michigan without them donating money to the school. And I know they're paying for him to go to there, but my parents are too, and . . . and I'm letting them fill up my days with the things they want me to do and the people they want me to meet.

I'm doing the exact same thing he is.

I'm not teaching my art classes this summer. Can't find anything inside me to create art anymore. The gallery exhibition will come and go and I won't have a single piece in it. And I'm just letting it happen.

My eyes stray out over the hints of lake and the clouds between the buildings. I was going to draw that—to put it all on paper and break through this . . . block . . . I've been having.

"Ryan, we have to stop living the lives our parents want for us and do what *we* need to do," I tell him. "Both of us. We need to break free from their . . . their expectations for us."

He gives me a sad smile. "I don't want to disappoint them."

"I don't either," I reply. "But I also don't want to live someone else's idea of what my life should be."

He kisses me again, the touch of his lips achingly soft. "I have to go. We're taking off soon. But I'll be back in a couple of days," he says. "Then we'll keep talking, okay?"

I sigh and turn away. "Okay."

With one last kiss, he starts walking back to the hotel. He seems . . . different . . . lately. Or maybe even not that lately? I can't quite put my finger on why he's different. His dad needs him, he goes. His parents want him to major in business and join ROTC, he agrees. He's so willing to let them carve out his whole life for him. He hasn't even broken out his guitar for months. I'd give anything to have him play again. I miss hearing him sing.

As I look up at the sky, a gnawing emptiness grows inside me. Everything's moving and changing so quickly that it makes me want to run away—to escape all of this and start over somewhere new. I want to travel and experience new places and people who I don't have all this . . . baggage . . . with. I want to make art again—to go to school in Chicago in the fall to follow my own path and make my own mistakes.

I turn away from the water to see the turrets of the hotel looming over the treetops. I love this place. It'll always be home to me. But other places can be home, too.

My stomach churns so much I think I'm going to throw up. I need to talk to someone who'll understand, but I'm not sure who that is anymore.

Then I realize that there's one thing I can do right at this very moment. One that will take at least one weight off me so that I can focus on more important stuff. I turn toward town again. My eyes scan the docks when I get there. The tourist boats and the little sailboats for rent. The workers and sailors coming and going. Even in this chilly, dank weather, there's still a constant bustle. What there isn't is any trace of JR.

I stand there for five minutes. Ten. Twenty. But there's still no sign of him. Maybe he's on break. Or has the day off. Or is working somewhere out of sight today. There are any number of reasons for him not to be here.

Even though I desperately need him to be here.

More and more minutes pass. Tourists talk and laugh and act like everything's perfect. One of them walks right into me, nearly knocking me off my feet. He doesn't even stop to say he's sorry.

I close my eyes for a second, willing JR to appear so I can yell. *Scream.* Tell him everything that's been pent up inside me all these months. When I open them, I see him at last.

He's coming out of one of the fishing sheds, talking to a coworker as they walk toward one of the boats. As desperate as I was to talk to him just a few minutes ago, now my feet feel glued to the sidewalk. And it's fine. As long as he doesn't see me, it's fine. As long as the ache that's building up inside me stays inside me where it belongs, everything will be okay.

He looks up. He sees me.

JR stops walking—stops talking—so abruptly that it's as if his feet are glued down, too. He's close enough that I can see his Adam's apple bob when he swallows. His breath mists in the chilly air. The same breath that once brushed against my cheek, my ear. The color drains from his face. Mine burns up with a feverish heat.

Neither of us moves or looks away. I'm not even sure I could.

I have no idea how long we stand there staring at each other before I finally start walking toward him. His shoulders tense up. A muscle in his jaw pulses. This is it. We are going to talk whether he likes it or not. And he doesn't look as if he likes the idea at all.

I'm ten feet away when his coworker taps JR on the shoulder. JR winces in surprise.

"You coming with me or what?" the woman asks. "Mussels don't scrape themselves off boats."

He nods at her. Without a word, without even another glance, he turns and walks away.

If anyone had told me when I left the hotel that I could feel *worse* than I did in that moment, I wouldn't have believed them. Now, though . . .

I have to keep walking. It doesn't make any difference where as long I get away from JR. Turning up a side street, I head to the nature trails. Choose the nearest wooded path and light onto it.

The leaves burst from their buds in that intense yellow-green that only happens this time of year, and I run my fingers over them absently as I go, wishing I could stop to paint them. To capture that color and keep it with me always.

As with many of the other things I wish for, though, I can't do it.

Without thinking, without even paying attention to where I'm going, I end up at Viola's bench. But the fact that Linda doesn't know JR is back weighs on me. I'm lying to her by omission every time I talk to her.

I have to keep moving.

A small path leads uphill. It's nice to get farther and farther away from the familiar. The trail forks and I have to look at the placard to decide which to take. They're both equally shady and flanked by evergreens, but the one to the right loops back into the town. The one to the left doesn't. Not yet anyway.

I veer left, following the blue blazes on the rocks and trees. At the end of this trail is the fort. I haven't been there since the eighth grade when we went on the last of three different field trips there. It grew tedious back then, always going on the same field trip. Now the fort feels as if it's the exact place I need to be. Somewhere I can be completely anonymous.

It's free to get in, which means I can just walk through the gates and explore. The buildings are a mix of faded wood and whitewashed brick from the early eighteen hundreds. A group of historical reenactors cleans their faux muskets. A small cluster of eager tourists crowds around a ranger.

Bypassing them all, I head up to the ramparts. From here you can see almost all of the island. The sun breaks through the clouds, illuminating the lake in the distance and the stark white of the buildings below me. Once again, I wish I had my watercolors, then I remember that even if I did, it would be no use. The urge to kick something is so strong I have to climb back downstairs and leave the fort so as not to do physical damage to a historic building.

With the tour moving toward me, I have to wade through them to get to the exit and out of the fort. Then I walk. I take a different path that leads me farther into the state forest and the dense old pine woods. The needles smell like heaven and my legs have that good kind of ache when you've used your muscles for the first time in a long time.

And I feel better—better than I have for at least a few days. There's a longer loop that passes by a small pond so I turn onto that. Frogs croak out for mates, birds sing. The whole forest feels as if it's just waking up after a long winter and I . . . I feel as if there may still be a way to deal with my life.

As I turn back toward town, the sun's lower in the sky. It must be close to dinnertime. My parents are going to wonder where I've been. The knot forms again in my stomach at the very idea that they need to know where I am every minute of the day. They weren't like this when I was thirteen. Now that I'm eighteen, they're tightening their grip.

The path lets me out right in front of the library. A slant of sunlight warms my face. It feels so good that I close my eyes, soaking it in for a moment.

"Jesus, are you following me?"

I turn to find JR standing a few feet away from me.

JR glances around to make sure no one else is here, then grabs me by the arm and pulls me behind the library. I try to yank my arm away but he holds me fast. As soon as we get back there, he lets go.

"What're you doing here?" he spits out. "What do you want from me?"

This is it. The moment when I finally get to talk to JR and tell him what I'm feeling. How angry I am at him. How I wish he'd go away and don't want him to leave at the same time. How completely and utterly confused I am.

I open my mouth to say all of this but what comes out is "I . . . I don't know."

He turns as if he's going to walk away from me, then stops again. "Emma, we can't do this. We have to just . . . just leave each other be."

As if I don't already know that. As if I wasn't infinitely better off before he came back. It's not my fault we've been thrown together again, it's his. *He's* the one who's here when he shouldn't be and . . .

All my anger comes rushing back. It starts in my chest and spreads outward to fill up my whole torso and even my limbs. My fingers tingle with it, as if one more step in the wrong direction will make lightning burst from them.

"So that's it?" I blurt out. "You're just going to yell at me and then walk away again?"

He stops once more. Balls up his hands. "That's not what I'm doing," he says through gritted teeth.

"Then what are you doing, JR?" I demand. "Because it's starting to feel like this is your whole *routine* now. Tell me what to do or . . . or how to think and then take off."

His head falls down onto his chest. "Yeah, that's me," he says, the sarcasm dripping from his voice. "Always leaving you all by your lonesome."

I huff out one breath. Another. I can't let him get under my skin this way.

"When did you get back, JR?"

A pause—a long one follows. He still won't turn around and face me.

"A week ago."

That stings even though I know it shouldn't. "I guess it never occurred to you to let me know you were here."

"No. It didn't."

Those words hang between us, a kind of tether that holds us together and pulls us apart at the same time. Because I can't let this go. I can't let him treat me this way.

"And now you think you can waltz back onto the island and . . . and . . ." My words falter. "You think this is all okay?"

JR pivots to face me, his cheeks stained red. "You really think that I'm okay with this?" he spits out. "You think I'm okay at all? Because I'm not. I'm really not."

I throw my head back in shock. "*You're* not okay? Are you kidding me?"

He squeezes his eyes shut and tips his head to the side as if he's trying to hide in the lengths of his hair. But the long hair's gone. JR seems to realize that at the same moment I do, and pushes his hand over his forehead.

"Emma, what do you want from me?" he asks again, his voice low. Defeated.

There's no backing away from this. I don't even want to.

"I . . . I want to know what happened, JR," I say. My voice sounds less steady than I'd like it to. "The real answer, I mean."

His arms rise up in frustration. "You think I didn't tell you the real answer?" he booms. "I don't know why I even bothered writing that stupid letter. I should've known it wouldn't make any difference."

I push my hand into my stomach trying to make the pain there go away—or least stop it from leaking into the rest of my body and destroying me from the inside out.

"Sure, you wrote me a letter," I snap at him. "Just like you've written to me all the other times you weren't here. I kept it in my mosaic chest so I could treasure it with your other correspondence."

He squeezes his eyes shut. "Oh my God." His voice is quieter but aching with exasperation. "If I'd known you'd dismiss every word I wrote I wouldn't've wasted the paper."

He turns to leave but this time I chase after him. This time I grab him. "No, you are *not* leaving yet. Not till we talk."

JR faces me again, his arms crossed over his chest "Then let's talk," he says. "I wrote you a letter, you ignored it. Now you're acting all innocent like you deserve an explanation that I already gave you. Is that what you want to hear?"

"*What* are you talking about?" I nearly scream.

The anger drains from his face, making him look younger—more like his old self—for a second.

"Did you really not . . . ?" he says, his voice practically a whisper. He looks at me again with an almost frantic expression in his eyes. "I wrote to you. I wanted you . . . I needed you to know that I . . ." He runs his hand over his eyes. He doesn't say another word.

Whatever storm had been brewing between us starts to dissipate. As if the dust settled in the middle of where we stand and everything is clear in a way it wasn't before.

"I didn't get any letter," I tell him. "If you sent me something I never got it." My voice is quiet, the fight has gone out of me.

"Okay," he says.

"Okay."

We stand there, only a couple of feet separating us, not moving, or speaking or . . . or doing anything but stare at each other. Our eyes lock and neither of us looks away.

"I wrote to you, too," I tell him. "So many times I did."

The crease between his eyebrows deepens. I want to reach out and smooth it away, the way I did so long ago. My fingers itch with it. But I can't. I know I can't.

"I didn't get your letters either," he says.

Shaking my head, I force myself to keep going. "I didn't mail them. I tried . . . over and over again I tried . . . but . . ." I fist my hands in the material of my dress to steady myself. "But I could never find the right things to say to you so I . . . I put it all away in the chest and . . . I should have just sent one of them. All of them."

His eyes are on fire now. Not in an angry way anymore, in a . . . I don't even know what way. I'm not sure I want to know.

"I wish you had," he says in a voice so soft I want to reach out and touch it. "I wish you'd gotten mine."

Silence falls between us. My heart's pounding so hard in my chest—rushing through my ears—that it's almost miraculous he can't hear it. All the pain, all the *everything* remains inside me. It won't leak out unless I let it. And I won't. I won't let it leak out.

We stand there, facing each other, neither of us sure what to do. At least I'm not.

"I'm sorry," he says at last.

I feel as if I'm back in the forest again gazing down two different paths that go in two different directions. I can walk away—not accept his apology or say another word to him. Loop back to life as I've known it over the past year. Or I can stay here and talk to him.

It's not even a choice, really.

"I'm sorry I yelled at you," he continues. "Just now and . . . and before, too." His hand rubs at the back of his neck a little too hard for it to be comfortable. "I'm sorry I said all those things to you, I . . . I was in shock that night I think and . . ." He sighs. "Not that it excuses anything. I know it doesn't."

He runs his hand over his eyes again. He really does look so much older than he did before. It's as if the juvenile detention center stole years of his life. The very thought makes me want to hold him close until something . . . somehow . . . is given back to him even though I know there's no way to ever do that. Whatever he went through, it's part of him now. Nothing can change that.

"I . . . I'm sorry, too," I stammer out. "I'm sorry I hurt you, and . . ."

Pain flashes in his eyes for a second before it evaporates, leaving him looking tired. Worn down.

"Can I ask you something?" he says.

I screw up my mouth, mulling this over. "Maybe?"

The question in my voice makes the edges of his mouth twitch. "You're unbelievable," he whispers. "You're so . . ."

"Just ask your question, JR."

A grim line forms across his mouth. "You and Ryan . . . you're still together, right?"

The hair on the back of my neck stands on end. I can't believe we're on this again. "JR, I don't . . . I can't talk to you about this, okay?"

He nods. "No . . . I know . . . I . . ." His eyes drop to the ground. "It just . . . it seemed at the library like you still are."

I take a deep breath, trying to find the strength to just say the simple truth. *Yes, we're still together.* But even the thought of saying those words to him makes my stomach tie itself up into an even tighter knot.

"Sorry," he almost whispers. "I didn't mean to . . . sorry."

"No, I . . ." Another breath. This is fine. I'm fine. "I am. I mean, we are. Still together."

For a long few seconds, JR doesn't move a single muscle. "And you're . . . you're happy?"

I know what the answer to this question is. So why is it so hard to get out one single word?

"Yes."

He leans his arm on a nearby pine tree, as if he needs help keeping himself upright. His forehead presses against the bark. He closes his eyes.

"JR, I . . ."

But he puts his hand out to stop me. "No . . . that's . . . ," he says. "I want you to be happy, Emma. I . . ." Our eyes meet again. All the fire, all the anger and annoyance and every other thing JR's eyes have contained since we first started talking have been replaced with an aching desolation. "I always want you to be happy."

There's an edge to his voice that eats at me. As if something got lodged inside my chest and is trying to claw itself out.

"I want you to be happy, too." My voice sounds so quiet—so small—that it seems almost impossible that he heard me. But he stiffens. He stands up straight again and faces me. There's a flinty resoluteness in his eyes.

JR steps farther away from me. "I've got to get home," he says. "My dad'll be waiting for me. But I . . . I'll see you around, okay?"

"I'll see you around," I echo.

He backs away another few feet before he finally turns and strides toward the front of the library. Back out of my life again. And I'm left standing here alone, picking up the pieces of my heart after he's shattered it once again.

CHAPTER 40

Emma (Then)

My walk back to the hotel is one of the hardest I've ever taken. I try to find the fierce fire I had earlier today. To not sympathize with him so much. For more than ten years, I've played at the playground, hidden in the greenhouse, told him what I thought and felt. Even when he was annoying me—being so sarcastic that I wanted to scream—I didn't really hold anything back. And in a weird way, we looked out for each other. We were always together when he was here. It's not easy to break practically a lifetime's worth of caring about him. I'm not sure I even want to.

The walls of the hotel feel as if they're closing around me when I get back there. Everything is too bright, too decorated. The voices of visitors echo too loudly in the lobby as if they're shouting at me. Even the smells from the bakery aren't comforting right now.

I need to get to my room so desperately it almost hurts. Mom's in the living room and greets me as I come in but I just ignore her. When I reach my room at last, I collapse onto my bed. I'm spending too much time on this bed during the daytime, which probably would worry me if I had anything left to worry with.

A knock sounds at my door. Mom walks in without me telling her she can.

"Are you feeling okay?"

"I'm fine," I lie.

She sits on the side of my bed. "You don't seem fine," she tells me. "I'm getting a little worried about you."

Echoes of my conversation with Ryan bounce around my head. He was worried, too. Just not enough to stay here with me when I asked him to.

"You don't have to worry," I reply. "I really am fine."

Mom brushes my hair off my face. "Can I tell you something that will cheer you up?"

Nothing's really going to do that, though I can't say that out loud. "What is it?"

"I had lunch with Eliza Desmond today," she informs me. "She dropped some pretty heavy hints that Ryan's planning to propose to you before you both head off to school this fall."

I sit bolt upright in my bed. "What?"

"I said—"

"No, I heard you," I say, cutting her off. "It just doesn't make any sense."

"What doesn't?" she asks.

She looks as genuinely confused as I feel at this moment. I can't believe she's confused by this. That I have to explain something so obvious to her.

"We haven't even started college let alone finished it yet," I explain. "I'm only eighteen. I'm too young to get engaged."

"It is quite young," Mom agrees. "But when you've found the right person, things like that don't really matter." A quiet smile spreads across her face. "Besides, lots of people meet their future partners in high school and get married young."

My head spins. I hear her words. I get what they mean. But I can't process that my mom is having this conversation with me. That she'd want me to get engaged before I'm even twenty. I have to explain this to her so that she understands.

"But I don't want to be one of them," I finally manage to get out. "I don't want to make decisions that will affect the rest of my life before I've had a chance to live any of it."

Mom folds her hands neatly over her lap. Her eyes drift toward the window. I sit next to her. Watching. Waiting for her to show any signs that she agrees with me.

"I understand," she says. The words come out slowly. Carefully. "I really do. But life isn't perfect, is it? Sometimes what we ideally want and what we get don't match up. We just do the best we can with what we have." She gives me a grim smile. "Life isn't always a fairy tale."

"Of course it isn't!" I'm trying so hard to tamp down my frustration—not to lose it with her right now. "I never said I wanted my life to be a fairy tale. All I want is . . ."

But what can I say here? What will make her really understand? My head throbs from all the hard conversations I've had today—from the sheer emotional energy I've had to use up over and over again. My fingers press into my temples. I can do this. If I could talk to JR, I can talk to Mom.

"All I want is to have a chance to live my own life for a while," I tell her. "Before everything gets so . . . settled."

Mom touches my cheek. "The Desmonds are dragging their feet about putting more money into the hotel," she says. "Dad doesn't like to talk about it, but we need that money. Badly. The damage caused by the fire . . . you know the insurance didn't cover all of it. And just to stay on top of the daily upkeep of the hotel . . . it's a lot." She pauses. Looks me in the eyes. "It's more than we have."

My head aches. The sick, heavy feeling returns in my stomach. I can taste bile as it rises to my throat. "That doesn't have anything to do with me and Ryan."

She raises one eyebrow. "Doesn't it?" she says. "You're a smart girl, Emma. I think you understand me."

The problem is, I do understand her perfectly. Not only are they telling me where to go to college and what to major in—now they're telling me who to marry and when. "Mom, I—"

"When I was your age, I dreamed of becoming a musician," she interrupts. "I was a violinist. A good one."

"I know, Mom," I reply. "I've heard the story."

She shakes her head. "No, you haven't heard the whole story. You have no idea why I made the decisions that I made." Her voice quivers slightly. She won't look at me.

"So tell me."

Mom pushes her shoulders back as if she's steeling herself to go into battle. "I was allowed to take lessons as a girl because my parents thought it was a harmless hobby for a girl of my . . . position . . . to have. But I loved it, Emma. I loved it so much." This time her voice doesn't just quiver, it snaps.

"I practiced all the time," she pushes on. "I kept changing to different instructors who could teach me more. It was my passion. I was . . . there haven't been many things I've loved that way in my life."

Tears form in my eyes. I've never seen Mom this emotional before. Even when Gran died she kept a stiff upper lip. She helped me grieve, but I never saw her grieving herself. This though—this is killing her to talk about.

"So why did you give it up?" I ask.

She laughs but there's no mirth in it. "I started auditioning right after college," she says. "So many auditions, Emma. Everything from the Detroit Symphony Orchestra to tiny chamber groups." She squeezes her hands in her lap so tightly it must hurt. "I didn't get any of them. I'd spent my whole life preparing for something that . . . that was never going to happen. I needed to get out of Gran's house. I needed to find a different path."

A horrifying realization hits me. One that has me backing away from her. "Dad?"

The grim smile returns again. "Dad had a successful family business, one I could throw myself into," she tells me. "He hadn't been subtle about his interest in me, and I liked him. So I had my parents invite him to things to bring the two of us together." Mom looks as if she's about to do battle instead of describe how she and Dad got together. "He asked me to marry him so quickly. It was . . . it was like being caught up in a whirlwind. Everyone thought it was so romantic that we got engaged so soon after we started dating."

I don't want to hear any more. I need to get out of this room—this *place*—before she says anything else. Mom grabs my hand. Grasps it hard in hers.

"I thought the violin would be my life, Emma," she continues. "But dreams like that . . . they're not sustainable."

The pain. The ache. In her voice. In my temples. My stomach. It gets so bad that I can't bear it anymore. "So what? You just gave up? You gave up your whole life because of a few failed auditions?"

"I did what I needed to do," she states. "You're so creative, Emma, and I know you want to pursue that. But you have to see that it's not realistic."

I tear up again. "I haven't even tried yet," I plead. "Why would you want me to give up before I even try?"

Mom squeezes my hand again, but gently this time. "Your dad and I have built a good life together. Plus, I've got you. It was the best decision I've ever made."

She wipes the tears that stream down my face. "I love you so much, Emma," she tells me. "And I know Ryan does, too. You're going to be happy together. And art will always be there for you as a hobby after college. After you get married."

And there it is. The permanence of that statement jars me out of my tears. Because she's not talking about *if* Ryan and I get married. She's talking about when. Everything's already decided in her mind. My future, tied up with a neat little bow to serve their purposes. I think about the acceptance letters in my drawer, about how much I want to go to Chicago and . . .

"You should think about what kind of ring you'd like," she says, breaking through my thoughts. "I'm sure Ryan will get you something lovely." Mom gets up and kisses the top of my head. "He's such a wonderful young man. You two are such a wonderful couple."

Mom gets up. She leaves my room—closes the door behind her with a soft *click*.

All this time I thought they'd listen. Not at first, maybe. In the end. I'd wear them down, make them see what I really need and that they'd want me to be happy and to live my own life. In a warped way, they probably think this is going to make me happy. I love Ryan, they want me to get engaged to him. Now.

I didn't even have a chance to tell my mother what I'm thinking or what I want. She told *me*. In her mind, probably in my dad's, too, it's all a done deal.

For a while it feels as if the walls are closing in on me, that I'll get crushed between the plaster under the pink-and-yellow wallpaper I chose when I was ten. It might even be better if it happened. Then I wouldn't have to face my parents again.

I close my eyes—block out the whole world for a second—though it doesn't help. Nothing will at this point. Spreading my arms out to the edges of my bed, I hold on tight. All I can do is lie here until the light changes outside. Until my parents' voices carry through the wall at the end of the workday—until I can figure out how to move forward.

CHAPTER 41

Lexi (Now)

Ryan Desmond, I type into Google. There are lots of them. One man comes up over and over again, but he doesn't look anything like the guy in the pictures. Some are too old, some too young. But their ages don't matter because I know what this Ryan Desmond looks like. And these guys aren't him.

I Google *Jason Roth* again, just to remind myself what a dead end it is. Scroll through endless pictures and news articles. Obituaries and LinkedIn profiles. Nothing that makes sense for the Jason Roth I'm looking for. Picking up the phone, I ask to speak with Jackson, but my call goes straight to his voicemail. His out-of-office message from last week is still on there, recommending that I talk to the assistant general manager about any pressing questions.

I leave him a message. My pressing questions will have to wait, I guess.

For a few minutes, I just sit on my hotel bed and stare out the window. Casey's working. Ms. VanHill's still in the medical center raising hell. Dad and Abby are hundreds of miles away. Chloe is even farther. I pick up my phone, but there are no new texts. Part of me needs Chloe so badly that I start typing.

Feeling so lost with all this right now, I send to Chloe. I watch my phone. I wait. But nothing happens. No phone calls or texts. Looking at the time, it's not all that surprising. She's at work, probably too busy to check her phone.

Or maybe she put it on mute so I wouldn't keep interrupting her during the day?

I close my phone and toss it across the bed. Then I pick it back up again.

Ahoy, matey. Soon we'll be searching for treasure! I pad in the message and hit send to Abby's number. Then I look down at what I sent with a blank stare. **That was for Connor. Obviously.**

Right away the three dots start bouncing. **I figured! He can't wait till you get back! We're all looking forward to having you home again!** Abby writes back with about fifteen heart emojis.

It's impossible not to smile at her text, but then when I open up Dad's, it's impossible not to be struck by the difference in them. Never once does he say he's looking forward to me coming home or he misses me. It's all questions about colleges and asking how the car's holding up. Reminders to text him once a day so he doesn't think something's happened to me.

I close my eyes and picture the look in his eyes when I asked about Mom right before I left. The pain in them. He's still hurting over losing Mom. I am, too. A desperate, aching part of me wishes we could share that together. I have so many questions, and he has the answers to them, but he's locked it all up so tight that there's no way I'll ever be able to get in.

Which leaves me here. In a hotel room far from home. Alone.

One last time, I thumb through his messages. Then I send him off one. **Consider this your daily reminder that I'm a.) alive; and b.) being responsible and letting you know that I am.**

Off the text goes.

I wait. And wait. And wait. He doesn't text back.

I guess at least that means he hasn't found out where I am yet?

My foot jitters on the end of the bed. I start humming "Oklahoma" under my breath, like somehow Rodgers and Hammerstein will solve all my problems. Or any of them.

Then I get up. I need to walk or run or to do *something* other than just sit here feeling sorry for myself. So I fill up my water bottle and wrap up the muffin I stole from breakfast this morning. Just as I'm about to leave, my eyes catch on Mom's mosaic box and hold there. I walk over, open the top of it, and dive inside. Under the drawing of Ryan Desmond giving Mom *the look* are three or four hotel notepads filled with writing. I grab those, too, and put them in my backpack as gently as I can. Then I leave.

The lake is beautiful at this time of day, with the late afternoon sun slanting over it. It's also crowded. Like really crowded. Families swim around in the water. Little kids dig in the sand. All kinds of grown-ups lie in lounge chairs soaking up the summer sun. There's a jarring combination of yelling and splashing and running . . . of the smell of sunscreen and pine trees and water.

I know Mom loved the lake and canoeing with her friends. I want to feel her presence here. But mostly I feel overwhelmed.

Time to keep walking. Without thinking, I walk into the trees and follow a path that seems to be heading back into town. One look at the map and I can see exactly what lies before me. Shops and restaurants. The town green. The ferry dock. But beyond all that, there are hiking paths marked. I stop and look at that for a second. Never once in my entire life have I been hiking. I don't think the idea of hiking ever even occurred to Dad or Abby.

So I guess I'm going hiking.

I open up my phone and look for a more detailed map of the trails here as I'd rather not get lost as I wander into the woods. Okay, and now I have the song "Into in the Woods" in my head like I'm Sondheim's Little Red Riding Hood and somewhere out there lurks a wolf. I shake my head as I think about Mom and JR pretending to be wolves together again. I wish any of this made sense.

But it doesn't, so I try to get my bearings on the map and start

walking, humming the song under my breath. I pass a couple of inter-
secting paths, but the one I'm on loops around eventually, so I stay on it.

Just as my mind wanders back to Mom . . . to whether or not she
ever walked down this path or even if she liked the woods at all . . . I
see a rustic bench just off the path. Only when I get closer do I realize I don't have to wonder if Mom had ever been here. She drew this
place, though I didn't pay any real attention to it before. This exact
bench, with the name "Viola Benson" inscribed on a plaque. Except in
Mom's sketch, a blond girl was lying on the bench as if she'd just collapsed from the weight of the world pressing on her. Was it Linda from
her stories? Or someone else I haven't found yet in the mosaic box?

I run my fingers over the caption.

TO THE MEMORY OF VIOLA BENSON WHO LOVED THESE WOODS SO MUCH SHE WANTED TO SPEND ETERNITY IN THEM. MAY HER FIERCE SPIRIT WALK AMONG THE TREES IN DEATH AS IT DID IN LIFE.

For a few seconds all I can do is stare at it. Like the hotel . . . like
the ferry pier and the town itself . . . this is somewhere I *know* she's
been. I sit down and close my eyes for a second or two. Birds chirp
overhead. The wind rustles through the trees. The air smells damp
and piney. Clean. Mom probably sat here and listened to these same
sounds. Smelled these same smells.

Tears well up in my eyes. Maybe she loved these woods like Viola
Benson did. Maybe she came here a lot. All the time, even. *Maybe.*
Maybe. Maybe.

All I still have are maybes. And questions. Some I'm not even sure
I want the answers to anymore. I feel like every time I try to give my
mind a break . . . to rest a little . . . the same thought shoots though
my head. She got married to JR. And dated Ryan.

I unzip my backpack and take out the notepads I stowed in there before I left the hotel. This seems like as good a place to read them as any. Probably a better place than anywhere else.

The first one has a tiny picture of the greenhouse on top, sketched in pencil. Underneath it lies what looks like a whole story that she wrote out.

All I asked was, "Want to go exploring?"

The usual snark and arguments followed. JR didn't want to wander around in the heat. There's no place to explore anyway. On. And on. And on. He was on a tear. But he also came with me. (I love it when he gives in.) He even had a place to explore in mind, even though he didn't see fit to tell me that till we got there.

When I asked where he was going, all he said was, "Exploring."

Because he's JR, he wouldn't say anything else. Not a single word. Even when I asked him. A lot.

I turned the page. The writing is clearly from when she was younger. Back before the fire and things got weird between them.

We walked for so long it got hot. And sticky. And buggy. Then I saw it. A greenhouse built into the hillside as if it were half cave, half human building. Some of the glass is broken and the roof tiles are all cracked. It felt as if no one had been there for years till we showed up.

"You knew it was here," I whispered.

JR didn't respond, so I took that as a yes.

Then I made a squealing sound that made him wince. But I didn't mind him being dramatic and negative for once. Not with this place to explore.

"I can't wait to go inside!"

I started to take off again, but he grabbed my arm. "You can't go in there. There's probably broken glass everywhere."

If there's one thing that drives me up the wall, it's when he tries to tell me what to do. Which he knows. And does anyway.

"I have shoes on," I told him. "I'll be fine. Plus, I really want to see what's inside."

He tipped his head down so he could hide in his hair again. God, I wish he'd get a haircut so he wouldn't be able to do that anymore.

"And you really like getting your way." JR tells me this all the time.

And he's not wrong.

"Don't be boring, JR," I told him. "We came to explore, so let's explore!"

I didn't bother waiting for him to say anything rude to me. I just went and opened the door. The whole place was full of smells. Good ones—green, wet things growing, and flowers in full bloom. Well, and there was also kind of a gross smell of rot and mold.

JR sneezed. Three times. Violently.

I hadn't even realized that he'd followed me in till he sneezed.

"Bless you," I whispered.

But I didn't turn around to look at him. There was too much to see in the greenhouse. A Juneberry tree growing up out of the tiles on the floor. A huge geranium that's burst through the little pot it had been placed in. Grass and daisies. Wildflowers everywhere.

And so, so much green.

"JR, you found the Secret Garden," I told him.

I looked over to the corner of the greenhouse and saw a lime tree. An actual lime tree with tiny limes hanging off it. "Want to eat one?" I asked him.

His whole face screwed up like he tasted something bad. "Yeah, sure," he said. "Worst that'll happen is we poison ourselves on lead paint that's seeped into it. No big deal."

When I accused him of being a giant glass-half-empty person, he had the nerve to disagree. Sometimes he really does just argue because he likes to argue.

So I ignored him and picked one of the limes. When I gave him half, JR looked at it suspiciously. "Count of three?"

"One, two, three."

It tasted stronger than the limes at the hotel. Extra lime—y. I'm going to go back tomorrow and eat more. I'm going to make him come with me whether he wants to or not. I really do love making him do stuff.

I flip through the pages and read it all again. They drove each other batty, but they also seemed to do a lot of stuff together. And knew each other for a long time. I tuck the notepad into my bag and look at the other two to see if there might be more clues. More anything, really.

On the next one, her writing looks older. Messier. There're no drawings or painting this time. There's nothing at all but a single page of her words.

Talked to Jackson. He kept saying over and over that if I don't tell people how I'm feeling and what's going on with me they'll never actually know. No matter what else I told him—and I told him a lot—he kept coming back to this. But no one is ever going to understand this. And when I think about Ryan, I just . . . I don't even know what to think, actually. I love him so much. I always will. But I know he won't understand. He has no reason to. Talking it out is never going to change that.

I drop the notepad on my lap. She loved Ryan. She did something to upset him. I wish I still had the postcard so much, my stomach hurts. Because it has to be him. She wrote to Ryan but never mailed it. So does that mean they broke up? Or were they still together after she wrote it and there was no point in mailing it because everything was already okay between them?

The last notepad has two or three pages of her writing so I pore over them.

Tomorrow. I leave this place tomorrow. I'm sad about it but

also . . . not. I've been reading all about Chicago. All about school and the neighborhood and the art scene there. It still seems unreal that it's happening. That I made it happen. But tomorrow I'm getting on the ferry. Jackson rented a car to drive me there.

I've never been to Chicago. I've never been anywhere. The more I think about it, the more that knot coils up in my stomach again. I'm going to live somewhere I've only read about. Seen pictures of. In a tiny room with a complete stranger of a roommate. That seems like a bad idea. At least right now it does.

But I made my decision. Now I have to live with it. And I think . . . I hope . . . it'll be good. Fingers crossed anyway.

I keep looking at pictures of the lake there and the pretty art deco buildings. At pictures of the art in the museum—at all the pieces I've read about and seen only in books. It'll all be waiting there for me. That's exciting. Logically, I know that.

But I still feel so alone right now.

Jackson took her to school, just like he said he did. He dropped Mom off there by herself. No Ryan. No JR. No mention of her friend Linda. So how did she go from being Emma Wolfe alone in Chicago to being Emma Roth? What changed?

That question . . . the one I can't quite get out of my head . . . keeps coming up again and again. When she was dating Ryan. When she married JR. When they got divorced.

And how Dad fits into all of it.

CHAPTER 42

Emma (Then)

My economics class starts at three o'clock in my old high school. Dad's reminded me maybe a dozen times that I should be there early to make a good impression. So I've tried to do what he wants me to do. To be on time and do my homework. To let go of the art classes at the hotel and make the best of this.

I even tried to keep an open mind. Maybe I'd like taking business and econ courses. Maybe I'd find something in myself I hadn't known about before. But what I've found is that economics is so tedious that it's slowly eroding me from the inside out. That I'm letting my art and everything I love about it just . . . slip away because that's what they want. And I love them both so much I don't ever want to let them down.

But as I stand outside the building and look up at the window where I'm supposed to discuss microeconomics with the other twelve or so students signed up for the class—I just can't do it. Instead I wait for Linda to come out before I head in to make my good impression. I haven't seen her in a few days anyway.

When I finally spot her walking out with a group of other girls, a small pang hits me in the gut. I know I shouldn't be jealous of her swim team—that her teammates in no way threaten our friendship. But being on the outside looking in—literally right now as I stand outside the high school—it's hard not to feel that she's going to move on without me once I go to college. I even want her to. Even though I don't.

It takes a few seconds for her to see me, but as soon as she does, she says something to her teammates and then heads my way as they walk toward the pool.

"You going to your class right now?" she asks.

I nod. "Are you going to the pool?"

"Yeah. To swim off some steam."

"Is everything okay?" I ask. "What are you trying swim off?"

Linda bunches up her fists in her shorts and looks off in the distance. "Nothing worth talking about," she says at last. Then she turns back and looks me in the eyes. "What about you? Anything new happening?"

There's something in her voice—something in the way she asked the question and looks at me that makes my cheeks burn. For the first time, I wonder if she saw JR in the library or somewhere else. If she knows already and is waiting for me to bring it up.

She crosses her arms over her chest as she waits for me to say something—anything—in response to her question. Part of me even wants to come clean and let her know that he's back and we've talked. How everything is so weird and confusing and . . . not good. But all that would do is hurt her. JR caused the fire that made her get rushed to the hospital. And yes, she was fine. But that doesn't take away from the fact that it happened.

"So, I'm guessing since you haven't answered me, it means nothing's new." Linda's voice is flat. Emotionless.

"Just class," I tell her. "And Ryan being away."

We stand there and stare at each other for a long second or two.

"Yeah, okay," she says, her eyes straying to where her teammates just disappeared on their way to practice. "Well . . . I've got to go. See you back at the hotel?"

"Yes. Yes, of course," I reply. "Maybe . . . maybe we could have breakfast together tomorrow or something?"

Linda shakes her head. "Early debate practice," she says. "I'm having breakfast here."

"Oh."

Something feels as if it's broken between us but I don't know what. My mind strays back to the questions about JR—about whether or not she's seen him—but I can't bring myself to ask her. To tell her.

I am a coward.

"I've really gotta go," she tells me. "But we'll catch up tomorrow night, okay?"

"Okay."

As I watch her leave, the pang hits like a blow to my chest. For the longest time, I just stand there with my backpack over my shoulder. Kids pour out of the doors, their numbers trickling down to a tiny stream of stragglers. In the distance, teachers ride off on their bikes or walk home to wherever they live. The whole school starts to fall silent.

One of my econ classmates calls my name. "Are you coming in?"

"In a minute," I call to her. But I know even then that I'm not going in that building today. That there's no way I can sit through this class feeling the way I do right now. My parents won't expect me home till after five. Dinner won't be till six thirty. I have plenty of time to do . . . I don't even know what.

What I do know is that the decision I'm about to make is the wrong one. A bad one, even. I turn around and walk away from the school anyway. This should bother me. A normal person would feel bad about this. I just keep walking. Skirt through the edges of town, head up past the library. Out into the woods.

There's a certain freedom to being alone with the trees and the fresh air. I find myself coming to the woods more and more often, maybe because the beach doesn't hold the same comfort it used to. It can't.

By the time I get to Viola, the air is already cooling off. For a split second, I feel it in my bones that Linda will be lying down on the bench there, relaxing and waiting for me. I'm so convinced of it that it comes almost as a shock when she's not there.

A strong wind blows around my hair, my ankles, tossing my dress around my shins in a swirl. I push the hair back out of my eyes and sit down. Plopping my backpack on the bench, I lie on my side and lay my head down on it. I close my eyes and just breathe for a while. Maybe this is what I need. Linda might not be here right now. Viola might never be again. But this place—it's still one that means so much to me.

I'll just rest for a little while. It'll all be okay.

When I wake up, the change in the light through the trees around me disorients me for a second. Then I remember how I got here and why.

I also realize it's already 5:05. Class is out. I need to head home.

The woods are nearly silent as I walk back toward the library. The road into town is as well. Only when I hit Main Street do the tourists and the noise hit me like a brick wall. I stand at the corner for a second or two, trying to gather up the strength to launch myself into it again. But what other choice is there? I have to get home and this is the way there.

As I walk past the dock, my steps slow just a little bit. My eyes scan the area looking for him but he's probably already done with work for the day. Just as I pick up my pace again, though, there he is. Sitting bolt upright on a park bench in the tiny area of grass just to the side of the dock, his backpack by his side. His eyes roam around as if he's looking for someone. Probably his dad or someone from work. Some new person he's friends with now that I'm not a part of his life anymore.

My jealousy pulls me up short. What is *wrong* with me today? First I got all edgy because of Linda's teammates, now over JR. I'm not even friends with JR anymore. Not really. I just need to keep walking and pretend I never saw him there.

As I get closer, though, I can't help myself. Each tiny piece of him comes into focus for me, bit by bit. The eager look in his eyes. The late-day sun warming his short brown hair. The T-shirt that's not anywhere near as baggy as it used to be. The holes in his jeans that leave little blocks of his knees exposed.

When I look up again, our eyes meet. JR watches me for a second before he gets to his feet, shouldering his backpack as he does. He starts to move my way. I stop and wait for him.

"What're you doing here?" I ask him.

He shrugs. "I work here."

I look down at my hands. "No, I mean, what are you doing here right now? Aren't you done for the day?"

The crease between his eyebrows deepens. "I've been waiting for someone."

The words make me wince a little, even though it was exactly what I expected him to say.

"Well . . . I guess I won't keep you then," I say. "Have a good night."

As I move away from him, JR calls, "Wait, Emma . . ."

I turn to look at him. To see what he wants. But all he does is stare at me with that deep crease between his eyebrows. God, why does he have to look like this? So worried. So . . . sad.

"Um . . . the thing is . . . ," he stammers out. He tilts his head as if he's still hoping for the long hair he cut off to fall over his eyes and hide him. "The thing is, I was actually waiting for you," he blurts out. "Or . . . I guess . . . hoping I'd see you?"

When I don't respond, JR keeps talking. "I mean, if that's okay? I . . . I don't even know, Emma. I just wanted to see you."

Our eyes meet for just a split second before I glance over at all the people moving around us. Past us.

JR watches me the whole time. "Is there somewhere else we could go to talk?"

I nod but I can't think of anywhere to go. He nods, too, just before he starts walking. Only when he turns back with a question in his eyes do my feet start to unglue themselves.

Neither of us says a word. We just keep moving.

It feels as if I've been in motion all day long and never getting anywhere.

The old observation tower looms in the distance—a relic of the days before tourists could take biplane tours to see the island from above. It's three stories tall, all wood and steel connectors, with an observation station up top.

Glancing at JR sideways, I catch him just looking away. A tiny flush of . . . something . . . hits me. We shouldn't be spending time together, let alone by ourselves in a deserted area. I shouldn't trust this situation—trust *him*.

Yet when we reach the stairs to the tower, I lead the way up.

The wood creaks with every step I take as if the tower itself is protesting that I shouldn't go up there. At the first landing, I stop for a second and squeeze my eyes shut. The creaking behind me stops, too. JR stands there, waiting for me to be ready. For me to lead the way again.

Without turning to look at him, I open my eyes and keep climbing. By the time we get to the top, my calves burn and my face is flushed. I walk to the edge of the tower. The view of the island, the lake, is beautiful. I can see both the Grand Hotel and the Palais du Lac—my home—in the distance.

JR stands next to me but not close enough for there to be any danger of us touching.

"This is pretty," he says. "You should come back and paint it sometime."

My shoulders stiffen as I shake my head.

He turns to look at me. "No?" he asks. "You don't like good light and beautiful scenery anymore?"

"No, I just . . ." I shake my head again. "I just haven't been doing a lot of painting lately. It's been . . . I just can't anymore."

Not a word comes out of JR in response. I wrack my brain to find something else to talk about.

"Um . . . how are the Earthsea books?" I ask, a little desperately.

He squints at me in the bright light. "I finished them all before . . ." His voice trails off. His fingers play at the edges of his T-shirt. "I haven't been reading much fantasy anyway."

I look over at him in surprise. "Really?"

A shrug meets my question. He doesn't say a word.

My mind strays to Linda. To Ryan. To my parents. To all the people who'd be hurt and upset if they ever found out where I am right now.

"JR, why are we here?" I ask at last.

For a long time, a silence falls between us.

"Maybe we shouldn't be," he says in a low voice.

His words hit me hard. Cold. Right in the chest. For a second, it's hard to breathe.

"Okay, then," I say. "Good to know. I . . . I'll see you around, I guess."

The moment I turn to leave, he touches my arm again but I shake him off. JR pulls his hand away. Takes a step backward.

"Sorry, I . . ." He starts the sentence but he never finishes it.

I step back toward him, making his eyes blow wide open. I don't even care.

"Why were you waiting for me?" I demand. "Why did you want to go somewhere to talk if you weren't actually going to talk?"

He runs his hand over his eyes. "I . . . I just wanted to see you."

I spread my arms wide. "Well, here I am! I'm right here. I'm not even sure why anymore."

A cold wind whips around us, tangling my hair around my face and making me shiver. Goose bumps break out over my arms. I hold them around my abdomen to try to keep warm.

Even though I can hear him rummaging through his backpack, I keep my eyes out over the lake. It's time to make a decision. Stay and try to talk or leave and not turn back.

Something soft and warm slips over my shoulders. JR moves away from me just as I raise my arms to see what it is. A gray sweatshirt—his gray sweatshirt—lies over my shoulders. I run my fingers over the soft material. Pull it closer to me to shield myself from the wind.

Finally I look up at him. "Thanks."

He nods. Then he smiles. JR actually smiles. There's none of the bright sparkle of Ryan's, but something about it makes me swallow hard. Maybe it's because I haven't seen him smile for so long. Maybe that's why my eyes fill with tears.

"So . . . ," he says. "Um . . . how're things going with you?"

A tiny, wet laugh bursts from me. "Way to break the tension, JR."

"I'm a master conversationalist," he replies. "You should know that by now."

"Yes," I agree. "You've been talking my ears off for years now."

When he doesn't respond, I glance over at him. "JR, why did you come back here?"

He looks away—out into the distance. "My mom wouldn't let me come home," he tells me. "Said she already lived with a criminal once and wasn't looking to do it again."

This time it's me who can't find anything to say. I watch him for a long minute, wishing I knew what he was thinking. But his face doesn't give anything away.

The wind picks up again so I pull the sweatshirt tight around me. The material smells like him—like the lake and sweat and pine needles. I breathe in again and close my eyes. I remember this scent up close. His arms around me. His hands on me as we kissed. My eyes open wide. I glance over at him. Find him watching me. It's time to really talk. That's why we came here.

"What was in your letter, JR?" I ask. "The one you wrote to me when you were away?"

A long silence follows my question. A tourist boat cuts through the water in the distance. A cloud obscures the sun. JR doesn't say a word.

"You wanted to come here to talk," I remind him. "And this is what I want to talk about."

He nods, then shakes his head as if he can't decide if he's agreeing or saying no. "It doesn't matter anymore."

"Maybe to you it doesn't," I tell him. "But it matters to me." My voice dies down to almost a whisper. "It matters a lot to me."

He does that tip of the head again, as if he could still hide in his hair and avoid me. But I'm standing right here so there's nowhere for him to go.

"I don't want to talk about this, Emma," he says in a low voice. "I can't talk about this."

"But you could write about it?" My voice comes out harsh. Cold.

He rubs his mouth, the back of his neck. "Look, you're happy, aren't you?" he says. "Your life is . . . it's good, right?" Without waiting for me to answer, he keeps going. "And I served my time," he continues. "So can we just . . . just let the past be in the past?"

Everything about him is shrunken right now. Small. His shoulders, his eyes. It's as if he's disappearing—collapsing into himself—before my eyes.

And yet I can only answer that question one way.

"No. We can't."

He nods again. "Okay," he says. "I understand." But he doesn't say anything else. We're at an impasse. We might always be at an impasse.

"I . . . I should go," I sputter out. I look down at my watch. I was supposed to be home from my class over an hour ago. "Oh God, I should really go."

"Okay."

At first I'm not sure if he's going to follow me or stay up here, but then I hear the steps creak behind me as he comes down with me. It's strange—this sensation of *knowing* he's nearby and feeling that he's there, even if I can't see him.

I really need to get home.

At the bottom of the tower I hand him back his sweatshirt. In an instant, the cold hits me again, giving me goose bumps again.

"Keep it for now," he says, handing it back to me. "You're still all shivery."

Do I really want to have even this small piece of him? It takes me a while to reach out and take it from him once more.

"Thanks."

Our eyes meet. He nods and I do, too.

Then I turn and walk away.

As soon as I turn onto the hotel grounds—as soon as I know for sure that he's not looking—I slip my arms through the sleeves of the sweatshirt and let its warmth envelop me. The comfort of it doesn't last long.

"Where have you been?" my dad demands. "I've been worried sick about you."

I slip the sweatshirt from my shoulders and hold it in a ball, hoping he won't notice it. "Dad, I'm only an hour late," I remind him. "It's not a big deal."

"An hour, huh?" he says. "Because you were so diligently working away in your class before that?"

This stops me cold. I should have known this was coming and prepared myself for it, but I hadn't thought about it at all.

"Your teacher called after class to tell you what the assignment is for next time," he goes on. "I was confused at first. Why would she need to call when she just saw you? Then I put two and two together."

Even as Dad paces the room ranting about how irresponsible I am, I still find it possible to let other things occupy my mind. If I'm being completely honest with myself, to let JR occupy it. As I walked home, I found I had more and more questions. Like what are we doing spending time together? How could this possibly be a good thing? And what would Ryan think if he knew? My parents?

"Are you even listening to me?" Dad shouts.

I nearly jump out of my skin. "Sorry," I say. "And sorry I worried you." But part of me wonders what I should be sorry for. Do they need to keep tabs on everything I do? I didn't even want to take this class. He signed me up for it, then told me it was already paid for without consulting me. Without giving a thought to the fact that it would mean giving up my art classes. Or maybe he had thought that part through.

He stops pacing for a second to stare me down. He doesn't look angry anymore so much as frustrated. "I *was* worried," he tells me in a softer voice. "So was Mom. We had no idea where you were. . . ."

I walk over to him. Tell him what he wants to hear. "I really am sorry. I just couldn't sit in that stuffy classroom today. I should've let you know I wasn't going to class."

I don't tell him that I needed to escape. That I couldn't handle the weight of his expectations on me. He wants everything in my life to be exactly the way he orders it for me. Everything perfectly in its place, with me perfectly falling in line.

Dad nods as he puts his hand on my shoulder. "Yes, you should have." His heavy sigh isn't so forgiving. "Dare I ask where you've been all this time?"

I squeeze the sweatshirt up into an even tighter ball. His eyebrow lifts as if he can tell that I'm carefully thinking over my answer. Or more importantly, careful of who not to mention in my answer. "I needed some air," I say. "So I went for a walk and then went up the old observation tower for a while."

Dad stares at me, baffled, with his blue-gray eyes that can be so intense that they force you to stumble backward. But this time my feet stay glued to the floor. I wonder if he can tell I'm lying, or at least telling only part of the truth. But when has my dad ever really paid attention to what's in my mind? In my heart?

"Fine." He rubs his hand over the stubble on his chin. "Just don't skip class again, do you hear me? I paid good money for it. And you have to start preparing for the future."

I could remind him that I don't want the future he's carving out for me. That I don't want to stay or run the hotel and marry who they choose at the time of their choosing. But he already knows I don't want any of that. He just doesn't care. Neither of them does.

Dad looks at his watch. "I have to go. Town meeting tonight." He grabs his suit jacket and leaves.

Because of course he can do whatever he wants to when he wants to. I collapse onto the couch. My head hurts from all of this, but there's nothing I can do to make myself feel better.

CHAPTER 43

Emma (Then)

My parents are both up and out early this morning, so I have the place to myself for a little while. I grab my sketchbook and a tin of pencils and set up on the living room floor to brainstorm ideas for the gallery show. Three to five pieces might not be possible at this point, but at least I could manage one or two—just enough to prove to myself that I can still do this.

As soon as I open up my pencils, there's a knock at the door. I close my eyes and sigh. Does someone always have to be knocking at the door, needing something from me, telling me what to do?

The knock sounds again, louder this time. I sigh and drag myself off the floor.

"Just a second," I call. Then I open the door.

On the other side of it stands Ryan, hand raised as if he was just about to knock a third time. His hand lowers and slides behind my back. It skirts my backside, down my thigh. "Mmm . . . ," he breathes into my ear. "Just who I was looking for."

"Ryan, what are you doing?"

"I'm showing you how happy I am to see you after two whole days apart," he tells me. "Is that so wrong?"

"No, of course not, but . . ." I look around the hallway to see if anyone's seen us. "Could you maybe do it somewhere a little more private?"

"If you want me to," he says.

As soon we get the door closed behind us, I take a good look at him. He's wearing a suit, which means he must have just gotten home.

His blond hair is styled so that it sweeps over to one side, giving him a dramatic, rakish look despite the fact that Ryan might actually be the least dramatic, rakish person in the entire world. And he seems . . . handsy. He's already reaching for me again, pulling me toward him.

"How was your trip?" I ask him. "I thought you weren't going to be home till later today?"

He smiles at me. "Our breakfast this morning had to be postponed," he says. "And my trip was really good. Kind of amazing, actually. Dad introduced me to tons of state reps and senators. Even to the governor."

Despite how emotionally weary I feel, I force myself to smile back—to be as happy as I would be on any other day. "I'm really glad you had fun. It wasn't the same without you here."

Ryan appears to almost melt when I say this. I like him this way—I miss him this way. It's been so long that I've almost forgotten what a sky-high enthusiastic Ryan looks like.

"It wasn't the same without you in Lansing either," he tells me. "I missed you so much." He lifts my chin so he can kiss me. "God, I missed that, too. Come to the beach with me so we can make out all day."

Something in my stomach falters. Drops. He's been thinking about me. Wanting to be back home with me. And the whole time he's been gone I've been fighting with my mom about whether or not I want to marry him. Or arguing with my dad. Or with JR.

Whatever Ryan sees in my face, it provokes a puzzled look from him.

"I wasn't joking," he says. "All I want is to get you somewhere our parents aren't and to kiss you till I have to stop to breathe." He pauses as if in deep consideration. "Or to maybe eat, 'cause, you know, I do like my food."

"Yes, I do know," I say absently.

The grin that spreads across his face is so hard to resist. I can feel my chest, my stomach loosening up. Crackling open for him again.

"So the beach, then?" I say.

I wouldn't have thought it possible, but his eyes brighten even more. He starts looking around the living room. "Do you have a blanket we can bring?" he asks. "I don't want to have to make out standing up all day."

"Ryan!" I say. He never talks like this. I don't know what's gotten into him.

Just this one word from me stops him in his tracks. "What? Do you not want to make out with me?" he asks. There's a hurt expression in his eyes that I put there. When he finds out that I've seen JR, it'll only be worse. I don't want to hurt him. I don't ever want to hurt him.

"No, that's not what I meant at all," I reassure him. "You're just usually not so . . . so . . ."

"Dying to be close to you?" he asks. "I hate to break it to you, Emma, but I always am."

With that, all of my remaining resistance falls away. Why not try to relax and not worry so much all the time about my parents and the future and JR? Why not let him sweep me off my feet and tell me how much he loves me? Everything feels so hard so much of the time that I crave this kind of easy.

"Then . . . let's go, I guess?" I say. "But you have to stop saying *make out* because you're starting to make it weird."

Ryan crosses his hand over his heart. "As you wish, Buttercup," he says solemnly.

I do a double take. "Excuse me?"

"You really need to see *Princess Bride*," he tells me. "I can't spend the rest of my life with someone who doesn't know *Princess Bride*."

The comment throws me off. "The rest of your life?" I repeat. My mother's words echo in my mind: *Ryan's planning to propose to you before you both head off to school this fall.* That can't happen right now. I won't let it. "That seems like a steep period of time to plan for when we only just graduated from high school," I say, trying to laugh it off.

All he does is kiss me again. "When you know, you know, right?" he says. "And I *know*. We're going to get married and have kids. We're going to stand for something."

Alarm bells go off in my head. "Ryan, you sound like your dad."

Instead of disagreeing, Ryan nods. He actually nods. "We got to spend so much time together the last couple of days," he tells me. "More than we ever do. And we talked the whole time." He caresses my cheek. "About you and me. About the future."

Ryan's face flushes with an excitement that I can't even begin to share. "I'm going to go into politics like Dad, but even before that . . ."

"Ryan," I interrupt. "I'm glad you're figuring things out for yourself. But we can't decide on a future together until we both know what we want, right?" He's diving headlong into territory I don't want to travel. Not yet anyway. I have to stop this while I can. I have to get some space.

"But I . . . I finally know what I'm going to do," he assures me. "I'm going to take over the business someday. Then I'm going to run for office just like Dad. But first I'm going to—"

I tug at his arm to get him to stop talking. "Ryan," I say. "Ryan, that's wonderful. I'm happy that you've figured all this out, but . . . but what about my plans? Where do I fit into this?"

My questions—my doubts—don't dampen his enthusiasm at all. "Dad and I talked about that, too," he tells me. "You could help design all my campaign stuff when the time comes." He sweeps his hand across the room as if he's taking in the whole horizon. "We'll be one of those power couples, except we'll be totally in love with each other."

The walls feel as if they're closing around me again. Holding me back. Holding me in place.

"No. No, you're not hearing what I'm saying, Ryan," I tell him.

"I still don't fit into that. I don't want to design campaign logos. I don't want to be in the public eye. Not even a little bit."

The smile fades from his face. "Then what do you want?"

That's a harder question to answer. Ryan's happiness brimmed over just a few minutes ago and now it's . . . diminished. I diminished it. I want so much for him to be happy but I want to be happy, too. I have to be able to tell him what I need or none of this will work at all.

"I want to go to college," I say. "But for art, not for business. And then . . . then I want to travel all over the world and see the places I've only ever read about."

Relief is written all over his face. "We can do all that!" he says. "We can take trips all over the place before we have kids if that's what you want."

Before we get married. Before we have kids. And he runs for office. And my whole life gets planned out in a completely different way—but still not a way I want. "Ryan, I . . . I can't talk about this right now," I protest. "It's too much to think about. I'm not *ready* to think about it."

Those normally smiling blue eyes watch me with a question in them, as if he's trying to figure me out but is coming up short. "But I need to talk to you about this," he says. "Today."

There's something in the tone of his voice that makes me look up at him, suddenly worried. "Is something wrong?"

He comes to stand in front of me but he doesn't reach for me the way he was just a few minutes ago. "No . . . no. Nothing's wrong," he tells me. "It's just that . . . before all that other stuff happens, there's something I have to do first."

My heart drops into my stomach. I force myself to breathe—to get control of myself and be ready for whatever he says next. For if he's really going to propose.

Ryan gives me a sad smile. It's not the face of someone who's about to drop down on one knee. "I know we're supposed to start school together in the fall," he says instead. "I know it's what we've been planning all along, but . . . but I'm going to enlist instead."

"What?" My head tries to wrap itself around what he's just said. To understand and process the words. I blink again and again, trying to make sense of this.

"I said I'm going to enlist instead." His voice is steady. Calm. It makes me anxious that he's so calm about this.

I place both hands on his chest to steady myself. Maybe even to steady him.

"But you're already going to do ROTC!" I slide my hands up to his face and pull him down to me. "You're going to be in the service anyway! Why rush into it?"

Ryan shifts his head so he can kiss the palm of my right hand. "Dad never joined up," he explains. "And we talked it over. A lot, actually. We think it would help his campaign if I do it now rather than later."

My eyes widen in shock. This can't be happening.

"You're going to enlist . . . t-to help his campaign?" I stammer out. "Ryan, listen to what you're saying. It doesn't make any sense!"

The sad smile on his face nearly breaks my heart. "I'm trying to do the right thing, Emma," he explains. "Not just for him, for the whole country. Dad . . . he'll be a good senator. I think he could really help people. And I'll be helping, too, just in a different way."

A small part of me freezes in fear. This is what happens when we live our lives according to what other people want. What placing family duty over everything else looks like. His college, his freedom . . . possibly even his life—Ryan's sacrificing all of that. For a senate campaign.

"Ryan, don't do this," I plead. "No campaign is worth risking your life over."

He smiles again. "It's all been decided," he tells me. "I . . . I owe it to him. He's done everything for me. Everything." His hands slip up over mine. "Dad's going to get my entrance expedited so I can leave sooner rather than later. It's what I was going to do anyway, just a few years earlier." His lips press against my forehead. "I need you to understand, Emma. I . . . I need to know you'll be waiting for me when I come home." His voice is low. Desperate.

Tears stream down my face. "Don't do this, Ryan," I say again. "Please don't do this."

"I have to," he says. "It's only for a couple of years. I'll be back before you know it."

It's not true. We both know it's not. He'll be gone a whole tour of duty, maybe more. He's lying to me or deluding himself or . . . something. But I know that sometimes you lie to the people you love to make them worry less. To keep their lives from being harder. I do it all the time, after all. Now he is, too.

One look at him and I know I'm going to let him.

"I need you to understand, Emma," he pleads. "To wait for me. Then we'll do all the things we talked about. Get married and . . . and travel all over." He takes both my hands in his. "Whatever you want. Can . . . can you do that? Please say you'll do that, Emma."

"I understand," I tell him. "And I . . . I'll be waiting for you when you come home."

Relief floods his face. His lips brush against mine over and over again. His hands run up and down my arms. "It's all going to be good, Emma," he breathes into my ear. "Once I do this . . . once I serve and then come home . . . we'll have such a good life together. I promise we will."

I nod. Lean into him. Let his strong arms wrap around me and hold me close. He'll go away for a few years and I'll go about my life. We'll write and call, talk as much as we can. All this time I've been worrying that if I ended up going to school in Chicago, I'd be letting him down. Now it's him who's walking away from it.

But it's going to be good. Ryan said so. He promised.

I really wish I could believe him.

The whirlwind surrounding me reaches a kind of gale force. At some point it has to stop. I'm more and more worried about what that point will end up being.

CHAPTER 44

Emma (Then)

The lights in the ballroom shimmer and sparkle in the soft light. It's the same scene in the same room at the same time of year that it always happens. There's never any reason to have this particular dance. It's not opening night of the season, or midsummer—it's barely summer at all—yet this dance persists.

Never once has it been as painful to face it as it is right now.

For most of the afternoon, I hid in my room pretending to be asleep even when my mom knocked on my door to check on me. I don't have the energy anymore to fight with her and Dad. They've worn me out with their demands that I do something I'd probably do anyway if they'd only give me the space to make the decision for myself. And there's no way I can talk to them right now about Ryan enlisting. My eyes droop. I can barely stay awake and on my feet.

Only when I spot Linda entering the ballroom do I perk up at all. Then I see who she's with and my eyes aren't drooping at all anymore. Because holding hands with her is a petite girl with short purple hair and a long magenta dress. Her dark skin glows in the chandelier light as she looks up at Linda. Mae. Linda brought Mae.

I run across the dance floor, dodging waltzers as I go, until I reach them.

"Hey!" I say. "I'm so glad you're here."

"Um . . . thanks?" Linda says.

Her voice has an edge that I try to ignore.

"No, not you," I tell her with a forced smile. "Well, I mean, of course you. But I really meant Mae."

Linda's not-girlfriend grins at me. There's nothing at all forced about it. "I'm glad I'm here, too," Mae replies. She nudges Linda. "This one kept saying she'd be busy tonight and that there'd be a dance, but I didn't think she'd ever get around to asking me to come with her."

"But I did, right?" Linda says. Her whole face softens when she looks at Mae. Even her jaw looks looser than it was before. "And believe me, if I didn't hate these things so much I would've asked you much sooner. I just didn't want to subject you to it."

Mae's eyes wander around the ballroom for a second before settling back on Linda. "Yeah, I can see why you hate this," she replies. "Too much pretty music and delicious-looking food. It must be agony for you."

Linda's eyes follow the same path that Mae's did but with considerably less enthusiasm. "It's a sacrifice I have to make," Linda concedes. "But for you, I'll do it."

Their eyes meet. Linda's eyes, her mouth—every part of her seems to melt into a smile. And . . . this . . . this is wonderful. They are wonderful.

"So . . . have you had any of the delicious-looking food yet?" I ask. "Because it is actually pretty good."

"I heard dessert's the best part," Mae says. "And any dessert that's not ice cream sounds like heaven to me."

"French pastries?" I tell her. "Or maybe chocolate-dipped strawberries or tiny tiramisus?"

"Mmmm . . . ," Mae groans at the very thought of them. "I want everything. Let's eat all the things!"

Linda smiles at her for a second. Then her eyes flicker to me as if she just remembered I'm still here and it fades. I take a step back from her.

"Um . . . you two should go eat dessert till you're stuffed full," I say.

Mae's whole face lights up. "God, I love it here," she sighs. "I *really* love it here!"

Linda looks over at me again. "See you around?"

Then they're gone. Just as I think I'm going to get out of here, Ryan steps into the ballroom with his parents. His dark blue suit that perfectly fits around his shoulders and waist, the golden glow of his hair in the ballroom's light—he really is beautiful.

I watch him stand by his dad's side, shaking hands with strangers and accepting their congratulations as Mr. Desmond shares the big news with everyone. He doesn't even see me. He doesn't even look.

It suddenly feels too hot in here. Sweat seeps through the armpits of my dress. My breath comes in shallower and shallower bursts. For a second, I think Ryan's going to come find me at last. He's walking in my direction, a smile on his face. But his dad moves forward to grab him by the arm. He leads Ryan away to meet someone else in the crowd.

Ryan turns back to me and mouths *Sorry*. He still goes with his dad. A lump forms in my throat. I have to force myself to breathe.

I spot my mom standing near the orchestra, as always, watching them play. The whole scene has a new poignance to it now. I'd feel sorry for her if I could feel anything right now except for a roiling stomach. So I wait till I can breathe normally again, and then walk over to her, resolute about what I need to do.

"Mom, I'm getting overheated," I tell her. "I'm going to head outside for a little while to cool off."

A look of concern passes over her face. "You do look flushed," she says. "Are you sure you're feeling all right?"

I once again force a smile. I've been doing this a lot lately.

"I'm fine," I reply. "I just need some air. I'll come back in after I cool down."

She starts to say something else but I can't stick around to hear it. I'm getting out of here now, before anyone does anything to stop me.

The cool air on the verandah feels beautiful—almost miraculous— after the sweat I worked up inside. It doesn't take long, though, for the relief of it to wear off and for my sweat to evaporate leaving me shivering in the cold night. I've got to keep moving or this is going to become a problem very quickly. The lights of town glow above the trees and I follow as if I'm a moth and can't resist their call. Actual moths—early ones—dive-bomb the lamplights that line the hotel's front drive as I pass by them. Then the buildings of Main Street lie before me like perfect pastel shells washed up on the beach that I could pick up and put in my pocket if only I had the strength to lift them. I stop and admire the view for a minute.

Then I press on.

Though I know JR won't be there I walk to the docks anyway. Or maybe because I know he won't be there I go?

Despite the late hour, the place buzzes with people working to prep their fishing boats to go out on the lake at dawn. A whole world I've never seen before unfolds in front of my eyes. I don't know any of these people, though JR probably does at this point. The thought makes jealousy surge through me again that they might get to have new, uncomplicated relationships with him when I can't.

We left things so . . . unsettled when we talked in the observation tower. He wouldn't talk about the fire. I can't force him to. His sweatshirt still lies on my closet floor, balled up in a heap. Otherwise, it's almost like the conversation yesterday afternoon never happened. Almost. I press my hand to my stomach to stop the churning that's started up again.

A flag catches my eyes. Flying over one of the dilapidated houseboats is a flag with an arch curving over the top of it covered with elaborate symbols. I can't read the writing, but I know what it says, nonetheless. It's from *The Lord of the Rings*. The Doors of Durin. *Speak friend and enter.*

I walk toward the houseboat, quickening my pace with each step I take. It has to be them. Who else would put an Elvish saying on their houseboat? Without letting myself stop to talk myself out if it, I trip up to the door and knock on it.

When it opens, JR stands there in the darkness. For a second the crease between his eyes furrows so deep that it's worrisome. For a second I think he's going to close the door on me and leave me alone out here.

"What're you doing here?" he says in an undertone. "How did you even find me?"

I shake my head. "The flag. I saw the flag."

He glances around the dock, then pulls me inside the boat. I don't wait for him to ask me to sit—I just collapse onto a lumpy couch.

JR watches me for a second, concern in his eyes. "What's wrong? Are you okay?"

"I feel sick." Just saying it makes me feel a tiny bit better. As if admitting there's something wrong might have taken a little of the weight off me.

JR's on the couch next to me in an instant. "Why're you wandering around by yourself if you're sick?" His voice is low, urgent. "Do you need to go to the medical center?"

My head shakes back and forth again. "No, I always feel this way now," I explain. "My stomach . . . it hasn't been good for a while. And I got all sweaty and couldn't breathe and . . ."

He moves closer to me. Looks me over before meeting my eyes again. "Were you having a panic attack?"

This startles me out of the need to vomit words at him for a second. "What? No," I say. "I don't have panic attacks."

He gets up and grabs a small bottle of water—the kind little kids put in their lunchboxes—from the galley kitchen at the end of the room. "Drink this," he tells me. "Slowly."

I gulp it down too quickly and cough some back up again.

"Good to know you're still so good at listening to other people," he sighs. "Some things never change, I guess."

"What's that supposed to mean?" I choke out.

"It means," he says, "that you used to talk at me till I did whatever you wanted me to do all the time when we were kids."

I sniff indignantly. "Well, I'm not like that anymore," I inform him. If I was, we'd be talking for real. About what matters. Instead, we're back to arguing again.

The whole thing just makes me tired.

He shoots me a questioning look. "Then what are you like?" he asks. "It's been a while. Enlighten me."

I can't tell if he's serious or if he's mocking me. "If you're going to be a jerk, I'm going to leave."

"Emma," he says, his voice dead serious. "You shouldn't be here anyway."

The words sting. His whole demeanor stings. "You want me to leave?"

JR leans his head back on the sofa. "That's not what I said."

"It's what you implied, though." The hurt lingers in my voice as much as I try to push it away. JR must hear it, too.

"What's going on?" he says in a gentler voice. "Something must've happened for you to show up here like this."

I shake my head. "I don't know," I say. But in reality, I do know. All I have to do is tell him. "Have you ever felt as if everyone wants something from you that you're never going to be able to give them?"

"Story of my life," JR replies.

He's being sarcastic and I really need him not to be sarcastic right now. "No, but really?"

"Really?" he repeats. "I'm more in the wanting things I can't have camp."

"That's just as bad," I say softly.

"It is what it is."

There's something in his voice that makes me look over at him, worried.

"Are *you* okay?" I ask.

He swallows down a breath. "Do you really want to know?"

"How can you even say that?" I question. "I'm here, aren't I? I didn't ask you because I didn't want to know."

He sighs again. "Then no, I'm not okay. I haven't been okay for a long time. Is that what you want to hear?"

"I want to hear the truth," I reply. "And if you *ever* tell me again that I don't really want to hear the truth, I . . . I'm going to . . . to . . ."

"You're going to stammer me to death?" he offers.

I push him, hard.

He pushes me back much more gently. I go to get him again, but he grabs both of my hands and holds them fast. "No more shoving, okay?"

"Okay."

We sit in silence for what feels like a long time. He doesn't let go of me.

His hands are warm and rough. JR rubs his thumb over the delicate skin of my palm. Something like a cross between a laugh and a sob comes out of my throat. I've got to get out of here before it turns into just sobbing.

"I should go," I say.

"Yeah, probably."

He still doesn't let go of my hands.

"My parents will wonder where I am."

"My dad will be home soon."

"So."

"So."

Silence falls again. Our silences used to be comfortable because we didn't need to talk every second of the day when we were together. Nothing about this is comfortable.

"I should go," I say again. This time he lets my hands loose. They feel cold without him holding them anymore.

He gets up and I do, too. As I start to walk to the door he says, "Emma?"

I turn back again.

"Would you . . . I mean . . . instead of hoping we bump into each other or . . . or finding each other by accident, maybe we could . . ." His voice trails off.

I don't respond—I don't move a single muscle. I need him to be the one who says it—I need him to want to see me, too. He won't even talk to me about anything real and I still need him. Our friendship. Or at least whatever remains of it.

"Maybe we could meet for lunch or something?" he finally gets out. "Maybe even tomorrow?"

And there it is. It feels almost as if I've exhaled for the first time in months.

"Tomorrow would be good."

JR nods. "Um . . . I take my break at twelve thirty. Meet me behind the library?"

"I'll bring lunch."

"No. Just come," he tells me. "I'll take care of it."

"Okay."

We stand there just staring at each other for a moment or two.

"Want me to walk you back?"

My jaw drops for a second. "What? No, of course not," I say. "Wouldn't you get in trouble if anyone saw you at the hotel?"

And there it is again, hanging between us. No matter what we do or how much we want to see each other, the night of the fire looms in the background.

The damage he did to the hotel. To me.

JR knows it, too. I can see it in the slouch of his shoulders right now, in the downward turn of his eyes as he watches me leave.

But instead of saying anything—instead of just telling me what he's thinking—he holds the door open for me. I pass through it and out into the night again. I don't look back, I don't stop once until I get through the gates of the hotel again and back up to the verandah. The music wafts out to greet me. Lights and laughter slant through the open ballroom doors. Inside my real life waits for me. I should be in there. Getting to know Linda's girlfriend. Standing by Ryan's side as he explains his decision to join the military to people. Being who my parents want me to be.

I kind of wish I didn't have to face it.

CHAPTER 45

Lexi (Now)

S o, to recap," Chloe says. "Your mom was getting it on with a
rich, gorgeous guy, but also with the criminal who caused the
fire?"

"Yes," I say. "No, I mean . . . it's complicated."

God, this all makes me so tired.

"Yeah, I can tell," Chloe laughs into my ear. I love her so much, but
her laughing about this is not helping.

On top of that, I'm in the business center of the hotel right now
since cell coverage is spotty everywhere else. The only other person
here is a woman about Dad's age who's giving me death looks because
I'm interrupting her work with my soap opera life.

I guess she can deal, though, can't she? All she has to do is work
right now. I'm dealing with an emotional three-ring circus.

"I think she was with both of them at different times, but . . ." I
don't even how to talk about this. Like, if I say it out loud, it might
make the whole situation worse.

"But what, Lex?" Chloe says. "I'm on my lunch break. You've got
to get to the point."

I take a deep breath. "So, you know how we thought my mom's
maiden name was Roth?"

There's a pause on the other line. "Yessss," Chloe says, her voice
dubious about where this is going. I feel her pain.

"So, that wasn't her last name," I tell her. "It was Wolfe. Emma Wolfe."

Chloe huffs out a surprised breath. "Then where'd you get the
Roth from?"

I squeeze my eyes shut. I can do this. I can tell her. After all, I already basically told Ms. VanHill. And this is Chloe. She'll understand no matter what. "That was JR's last name. Jason Roth. They . . ." My voice gives out. "They may have been married before my mom and dad got married."

There. It's out there. She knows now. She can help me deal with all of this.

Instead she lets out a low whistle. "I can't believe that the woman who married *Matthew* of all people had this dramatic love life before she met him," she says. "Your mom must have gotten tired of all the excitement and wanted someone stable."

For a second I just close my eyes. I have no idea how to respond to that or whether or not I should be defending Dad. I could fall asleep right here. Just curl up in a ball and drift away for a little while. The lady in here probably wouldn't even mind, if it meant that I'd stop talking.

"Now that I think about it, *both* our moms married him," Chloe goes on. "And I mean, you know I love Matthew. But he's not exactly a sparkling personality."

Okay, now I definitely have to defend him. "Stop insulting Dad."

But it's like she didn't even hear me.

"Oh my God!" she almost yells in my ear. "He must be really good in bed. That's probably it, right?"

I sigh. The carpet doesn't even look dirty. I bet Jackson makes sure it's cleaned all the time. I really could just lie down and pretend none of this happened.

"Lex?" Chloe shouts. "You still with me?"

"I'm still with you," I sigh again. "Just . . . can we please not talk about my dad's sex life?"

Chloe barks out a laugh. "I mean, it's my mom's, too," she reminds me. "You think I want to ponder the intricacies of how Connor came to be?"

"Chloe!"

I collapse onto the nearest desk chair. "Chloe, this isn't helping. I just . . . really need you to help me."

She doesn't say anything for a second or two. Then she clears her throat. "Okay, then let's be serious here," she tells me. "Your mom may, in fact, have married this guy. But it was probably a stupid teen romance where they think they'll last forever even though everyone else knows they'll break up in a hot minute."

I let the thought that Chloe chose her college only because her girlfriend wanted to go there slide away rather than comment on it. Besides, they seem happy. Mom and JR seemed . . . problematic. At best.

But maybe Chloe's right. Maybe they were only married for a month or two. Just two ridiculous kids not old enough to make any real decisions about their life, then moving on. Even if Jackson didn't know they'd gotten married before they left for college, maybe they did it in secret and then broke it off afterward.

Honestly, I feel like anything's possible at this point.

"The important thing here is not to panic because your mom was a romantic drama queen, right?" Chloe says. "Everyone makes bad dating decisions in high school." She pauses. "Well, everyone but you because you don't make *any* dating decisions."

"Okaaayyy, well, I'm going to go now," I tell her. She laughs, but I mean it.

A text dings in my phone. Casey. **Ms. VH is back. Bringing tea up. You coming?**

"I'll stop being obnoxious," Chloe promises.

"No, actually I do have to go," I say. "Casey just texted and we're going to go visit . . ."

She's laughing in my ear again, even though this really isn't funny.

"Okay, maybe you are going to make some bad relationship decisions after all," she says.

"Goodbye, Chloe."

"Goodbye, Lex," she replies. "I'll text you later about your date with Casey."

Her laughter is the last thing I hear before I hang up. Next time she calls maybe I'll just let it go to voicemail.

Be right there, I text back to Casey. Then I try to get myself centered again.

Stop to catch my breath. Try not to let Chloe get to me. Or to think about Casey like that. Or to panic about Mom.

Then I take off to the Lake Suite at a run. Only when I get to the third floor of Ms. VanHill's wing do I realize I should have brought Mom's mosaic chest. So I go back to get it and then much more slowly make my way to her suite.

A visiting nurse is just leaving as I walk in. She smiles at me wearily as she goes.

"Are you going to have help now?" I ask Ms. VanHill.

"Pssht." She waves her hand dismissively. "My godson insisted that she come today, but it's all nonsense. I keep telling all of you, it's just a broken wrist. Nothing like the time a whole unit of stage lighting fell on me." She actually smiles at the memory. "Now *that* was an injury."

I look at her for a second, stunned. "You mean they fell from overhead?" I ask. "And landed on you?"

She gives me a dramatic eye roll. "You young people all think every bump and bruise is a shocking setback," she replies. "I'll have you know I was back in costume and onstage three days after that happened."

Okay, now I'm just confused. "Oh . . . so you didn't really get hurt?"

"No, I fractured my tibia in three places," she serenely informs me. "They only kept me in the hospital for one day after the surgery, though, and you couldn't see the cast under my costume. I saw no reason to sit out show after show under the circumstances."

I open my mouth to tell her that was a bad decision. A risky one.

That she could have hurt herself further. That she *definitely* should not be operating under this mindset at her age.

But she chuckles under her breath, interrupting my thoughts. "To be perfectly honest with you, it was much harder trying to have sex with that cast on than it was acting in it."

Just as my jaw drops to the floor, a knock sounds at the door. I go to answer it, glad to have something to do other than respond to that last one.

"You look so shocked," Ms. VanHill says to my back. "But a woman has needs. Even one with a broken tibia."

"I don't doubt it," I reply, holding the door for Casey.

"What don't you doubt?" he asks.

"That she's a woman of steel," I tell him, skipping over Ms. VanHill's declarations about her sex life. Why is everyone talking about sex today?

Of course, then Casey smiles at me, and my cheeks feel hot again. I try to force Ms. VanHill's *a woman has needs* comments out of my head. I am partially successful.

"Well, even women of steel need lemon cake sometimes," he tells me. Thankfully, he doesn't have ESP, or he would not be answering so lightly right now.

"Even though we young people think every bump and bruise is a shocking setback," I add.

Ms. VanHill rolls her eyes at me again. "Pour some tea and keep your sarcasm to yourself, young lady."

I do as I'm told and we all help ourselves to cake.

"What have you discovered since I've been under lock and key at that godforsaken medical center?" Ms. VanHill asks. "Are you going to read to me from your mother's things today?"

Suddenly I feel shy about this. I brought the chest, assuming they'd want to hear more—that they're as interested as I am. But can anyone be as interested as I am? What if I'm just pestering them with the constant stories about my mother?

"Only if you want to hear more," I tell her. "I completely understand if you don't, because, I mean, I . . . you know . . ."

"Use your words, Lexi," Ms. VanHill says.

"I don't want you both to feel like you have to keep doing this with me," I blurt out.

Ms. VanHill and Casey exchange a glance.

"I'll leave you to reassure her, Casey," Ms. VanHill says. "I'm too old to be coddling youngsters."

Casey grins at her and then clasps his hands together as if he's praying. "Please read us more, Lexi," he pleads. "You can't leave us hanging like this!"

"Hmf," Ms. VanHill grunts. "It's not how I would have phrased it, but I suppose it does the trick."

I look from her to Casey and back again. "So . . . it's okay to keep talking about her?"

Ms. VanHill holds up her good hand. "I'm not even going to dignify that with an answer."

"So why don't you fill us in?" Casey adds.

I bring Casey up-to-date as I open the chest and sift through what we've already looked at together. Under the picture of Ryan Desmond is an ad cut out from a newspaper for an art show at a local gallery. Mom is one of five local artists listed in the show. Honestly, I knew she was a good artist but I hadn't realized that she ever got to put-stuff-in-a-gallery good.

Next in the box is an old datebook, so I flip through the pages.

"There's not much in here," I tell them. "One page has a dentist appointment penciled in, but then there's nothing for what looks like months."

"So not the most fascinating item in the chest," Ms. VanHill asserts. "What's after that?"

Just as I'm about to put the datebook aside, something slides from out of the last page of it. For a second I can't answer her. I mean, I should have seen it coming, right? Condoms. A boy with bedroom eyes. More than one relationship swirling around. It was all there if I'd bothered to read between the lines.

It's just that it hadn't ever occurred to me to read this *much* between the lines.

Gingerly I pick up the flimsy printout that's been lying inside the datebook for who knows how many years and touch my mother's name in the corner of it.

Emma Wolfe

6 week ultrasound

The picture in the center shows a tiny blob that's still too small to look like anything yet. It's circled in red with *baby!* labeled as if the doctor knew she'd never be able to decipher it on her own.

"Lexi, are you okay?" Casey's voice sounds as if he's at the other end of a long tunnel, reaching me only as a distant echo.

When I don't answer, he touches my arm. "Lexi?"

I glance up at him, only to find him leaning over me, his eyes filled with worry.

"What is it?" he asks.

Rather than having to answer, I hand it over to him and watch as his eyebrows knit together. He in turn hands it to Ms. VanHill but his eyes never leave mine.

"Is this you?" Ms. VanHill asks.

I shrug. "I have no idea."

"There's no date on it," she says. "Just the weeks she's pregnant."

"Which means it's probably you," Casey adds with a smile.

But according to Jackson, when Mom left for college she wasn't pregnant. It didn't sound like she was even dating Ryan or JR at the time. And Mom definitely didn't even know Dad when she lived here.

The only way it makes sense is . . .

Oh God.

I swallow down a painful gulp of air before I can speak again. "I don't think it's me."

Silence falls in Ms. VanHill's sitting room. "Do you have an older sibling?" she asks.

I just shake my head.

"Well, then perhaps she miscarried," Ms. VanHill suggests in a soft voice. "She wouldn't be the first woman who had. Or the last. People don't talk about it much, but that doesn't mean it doesn't happen all the time."

I nod my head a little too hard. "Yes," I breathe. "That's probably it. She got pregnant and lost the baby."

"Or ended the pregnancy," Ms. VanHill adds with a flourish of her hand. "That's also more common than you'd think. Why, on the stage actresses have to make hard decisions all the time, especially when . . ."

Casey actually elbows Ms. VanHill. She shoots him an outraged look, but doesn't say anything else.

"Maybe," I say. "It must have been one or the other, right?"

"Right," Casey reassures me.

Ms. VanHill takes the ultrasound from me. Examines it closely. "Or she gave the child up for adoption and you have an older sibling out there somewhere."

"Ms. VanHill!" Casey says.

She sniffs, offended. "I'm just trying to help."

I take the ultrasound picture back and look at it long and hard. Maybe it's me, maybe it's not. Maybe she lost the baby, maybe she didn't. Anything could be possible since I have no real way of finding out the truth. It's not like the medical center is just going to hand over someone's medical records. I'm not the police or anything. All I have is this chest.

"I've got to go," I tell the two of them. "I'll catch up with you later."

They both call out. Try to get me to stay. But I can't. I need some time to think and I need to do that alone.

. . .

By the time I reach my room, sweat runs from my hair and down my back and I'm out of breath. Casey's already texted twice, but I don't respond. This is one part of the mystery that I have to solve by myself.

I dump the rest of the contents of the chest out onto my hotel bed. There are more drawings of Ryan Desmond, a news article about the gallery show I found the ad for before, even an envelope full of pressed wildflowers.

There are no other ultrasound pictures anywhere in the chest, no other trace of anything having to do with a pregnancy.

Does that mean Ms. VanHill might be right and Mom lost her first baby? How could I possibly find that out?

I fall backward onto the pillows and knock the envelope with the pressed flowers in it to the floor. Absently I lean over the bed and pick it up.

On the flip side of it are words Mom wrote in all capital letters.

WHY DO YOU HAVE TO BE THIS WAY?
WHY DOES EVERYTHING HAVE TO BE SO HARD?

Was she talking about Ryan Desmond? JR? Or was it her parents? I'll never know, and the never knowing is beginning to tear a rift inside me that I don't know how to stop anymore.

I have no idea what to think or what to do.

There's a single bar on my phone and I press Chloe's number, hoping against hope that the call will go through and she'll pick up.

The call goes to voicemail.

The same happens when I call Jackson again.

I sit on the floor, at a complete loss.

CHAPTER 46

Emma (Then)

For once in my life—maybe even literally the first time—I don't want to be late. JR only has an hour for lunch after all and I don't want him to waste it. At noon I leave my room with a library book to use as an excuse in case anyone asks where I'm going. Now all I have to do is get past my parents.

"Where are you off to?" Mom asks.

"I'm heading to the library to return a book," I tell my mom.

She barely looks up from the spreadsheet she's got open on the computer. "It's almost lunchtime. Why don't you eat something first?"

I can do this. It's barely even lying. All I need to do is get the words out. "I might just grab lunch in town and read whatever book I get next."

This time she looks up. "Really?" she says. "I know Ryan's been busy, but you could still have lunch here."

I shrug. "It's nice to do something different sometimes," I reply. "And I like having time to myself."

Mom knows this is true so she just nods at me. "Okay, have fun with your quiet time."

"Thanks, Mom." I walk at what I hope is a normal pace toward the door and then run down the stairs.

It takes me all of ten minutes to get to the library.

"Back already?" Caleb asks. "That might be a new record!"

"I need something different," I tell him. "Something that won't stress me out."

He tents his hands under his chin for a second before smiling at me. "Have you read any Jane Austen?"

"None," I admit.

"The public education system has gone to the dogs," he sighs. "But today, it's going to work in your favor. Come with me."

Caleb leads me to the fiction section and pulls *Pride and Prejudice* from the shelves.

"You really think I'm going to like this?" I ask.

"There are times in life when you discover a small, perfect thing," Caleb replies. "It doesn't happen often, but when it does you have to savor it. This book is a small, perfect thing."

"Okay, I'll read it."

Caleb nearly jumps in excitement. "Excellent! You won't regret it, I promise."

As he checks the book out for me I glance at the clock on the wall. 12:25. I walk out of the building and head straight back to wait for JR. I don't have to wait long. The humming hits me first. I have no idea what song it is, but I know it's his voice even at a hum. I turn in the direction it's coming from.

"You're late," I tell him.

JR's eyes widen in surprise. Then a low laugh escapes from him. I haven't heard him laugh in a long, long time.

"You were dying to do that, weren't you?" he says.

"You have no idea."

He shakes his head at me. "Let's go eat lunch."

It feels like the old us for a second—like the way we used to be before. I want that feeling to last, but after we walk into the woods behind the library to a little clearing between the trees, JR opens his backpack and spreads out a blanket. We're apparently not going to sit in the grass or the pine needles like we used to when we ate outside. We're having a real picnic.

"You . . . um . . . really came prepared." The surprise in my voice makes him look over at me.

"You have no idea." There's a tiny, sly smile on his face. I can tell he's pleased with himself.

When he goes back into the backpack, though, I see why he said I have no idea. He takes out two freshly wrapped sandwiches and napkins. Underneath those are two bottles of iced tea and a tiny box of fudge. All semblance of what we used to be like has blown away on the late May wind. This isn't just coming prepared. This is . . . like a special occasion.

My first date with Ryan flits through my mind. The backpack of stuff. The food he brought. The blanket. I glance back over what JR's spreading out under the trees and shiver, just a little. He probably spent a couple of hours of his pay on all of this and he shouldn't have. He just shouldn't have.

"I feel bad that you did all this," I say. "I could have brought some stuff too and . . ."

"Emma?"

"Yes?"

"Just . . . come sit, okay?" JR pats the space next to him on the blanket. "Everything's all set. All you have to do is eat."

There's something almost funny about the fact he thinks I can actually eat when I had to sneak out to meet him. When I'm with him at all. On this blanket. In the middle of the woods. When he did all of *this* for me.

Screwing open the cap of my iced tea, I gulp down a swig of it. I look around at the trees and play with the hem of my dress.

"What's your book?" he asks at last, breaking the silence.

He smiles when I hold it up. "I read it last winter. It's hilarious."

I squint at him. "Are you being sarcastic again?"

"No, it's really funny," he insists. "Wait till you read it. You'll see."

I think about everything he just said and realize I skipped over a detail. "You read Jane Austen when you were in the detention center?"

A shrug is his only response. He hands me a sandwich. He arranges his iced tea so that it won't topple over on the uneven ground. What he doesn't do is answer my question.

At least not at first.

"I read a lot of stuff while I was there," he says. "Whatever I could get my hands on. *Emma*'s pretty good, too. I didn't love *Mansfield Park*."

"They had that many Jane Austen books there?"

"They had that one." He points to my book. "The librarian there requested more for me. He seemed pretty excited that I wanted to read them."

It's such a tiny window into his life over the last nine months, but even this breaks my heart a little. I don't want to hear any more, yet part of me knows that I have to. I want to at least try to understand what he went through.

"Were the other kids there okay?" I venture.

He opens up his iced tea. "I mostly kept to myself. Kept my nose down and my eyes focused on the possibility of getting out early for good behavior."

"And you did?" I say, despite already knowing the answer to the question. He's here two months earlier than he should have been, after all.

"I did. I'm known for my good behavior, you know. That's why I was there in the first place." His voice drips with a sarcasm edging on bitterness.

"JR," I say, "are we *ever* going to talk about—"

"Aren't you going to eat?" he cuts me off.

My shoulders droop. "Yes . . . yes, of course." I unwrap my sandwich—a BLT on rye—and take a huge bite. "It's really good."

The faintest of smiles teases at his lips. "It's not like I don't know what you like."

I watch him for a few seconds, but he's not eating at all. He's just fiddling with the blanket and looking down at his crossed knees.

"We don't have to talk about the detention center," I say. "I'm not trying to push you to talk about something painful."

JR swirls his iced tea around in its bottle. "It's okay," he tells me. "It might actually be . . . good . . . I mean healthy. I probably should talk about it sometimes." His foot nudges mine. "Thanks for checking, though."

Belatedly I realize this really wasn't a great way to ask about the fire. It seems like I just let him off the hook, but I can't. I take a deep breath.

"But I do want to talk about why you ended up there," I blurt out.

His eyes rise up to meet mine abruptly. "I told you I—"

"You don't want to talk about that either," I finish for him. "I know. But maybe you have to. Maybe *we* have to if we're going to . . ." My voice trails off.

But JR nods. "I get it," he says. "I know you want answers. I would too if I was you. It's just that . . ."

Those words hang in the air. He never finishes the sentence.

Time to keep pushing. It's exhausting to always be pushing for something and never get it. JR's answers about that night. Being able to create art. Being able to carve out my own life.

"I read the police report, JR," I begin. "I know it was an accident, but . . ." I take a deep breath. "But what were you even doing there? Why . . . why did you walk away when you could see that the curtains were . . . ?"

JR squeezes his eyes shut. "Can we just leave it at me being angry that night?"

"No, JR."

When he opens his eyes and looks at me, I shrink away. There's a look of pain there. Of defeat. I haven't seen him look like this since that night. Since he admitted what he'd done and we'd . . .

"I'm trying to do the right thing here, Emma," he says in a soft voice.

"For who?" I ask. "Who are you trying to do right by? It can't be me because I want to talk about this." I rub my hand over my eyes. "JR, I *need* to talk about this."

But he looks away from me. Again.

"I . . . I'm sorry," he almost whispers. "I'm so, so sorry." He shakes his head. "But you . . . you have to know I'd never intentionally hurt you, right?" JR leans toward me on the blanket. "I need you to know that."

Part of me does know that, I guess. No matter how much we used to tease each other or get under each other's skins, I never doubted his friendship. But what does that matter? What do intentions matter if bad things happen anyway? Hurtful ones?

I pick up my sandwich but have lost my appetite. He doesn't seem to be eating his, either. This hasn't been much of a lunch.

We sit in silence for a few minutes—on the same blanket, a chasm between us. I never once take my eyes off him. He doesn't even look like the same person anymore. The rigid shoulders. The short, neat hair. The constant worry in his eyes. It's as if I'm sitting here with someone else. Someone who won't talk to me about the one thing that matters.

JR doesn't notice me staring at him at first. When he does he gets immediately defensive.

"What?"

"I don't know," I reply. "You look . . . different now."

His eyes roam over me and he shakes his head. "Not you. You look exactly the same."

A twinge of sadness snags in my chest. He's completely different; I'm the same. "I don't know if that's a good thing or a bad thing."

JR gazes at me long enough that I have to look away.

"It's a good thing." My eyes meet his for a brief moment. "It's definitely a good thing."

It's what I wanted to him to say. Now that he's said the words, though, I have no idea what to say in response. Or at all. He thinks looking like me is a good thing. My mind wanders to the night when everything fell apart, the one he won't discuss anymore. I think about the way he kissed me. He didn't kiss me back out of surprise or to be polite after I kissed him first. He wanted to as much as I did. He wanted me as much as I wanted him.

What is wrong with me that *this* is what I'm thinking about right now?

My cheeks blaze into what I'm guessing is a horrible blush.

"Have some fudge, Emma," he says, completely changing the subject.

Maybe it's for the best. My mind's not where it should be. There's enough to deal with in the present without trying to relive what happened in the past. Maybe that's why he won't talk about it.

I break the little slab of fudge into two pieces and give him one. He nibbles at his, one tiny bite at a time, his eyes on the sky.

"You know what I missed the most?" he says. I wait for him to answer his own question. "Being outside. I missed being able to just walk outside whenever I wanted to and looking at the stars or the clouds."

"I can only imagine," I reply. "I bet you missed a lot of things."

JR takes a swig of his iced tea. "I missed my dad." He looks back up at the sky again. "I missed you."

My whole world narrows for a moment to the blanket we're sitting on and JR next to me.

"I missed you, too," I admit. "Even when I was furious at you, I did."

He glances down at his watch. "I've gotta go," he says. "But this has been . . . good. It's nice to do something normal like have lunch with you."

All I do is nod as he starts packing up the blanket and our stuff from lunch. He's so meticulous about all of it—bottles in his backpack, trash left out for him to throw away. Even the way he folds the blanket has a strange precision about it.

When he's done—when he's back on his feet again with his backpack on his shoulders—our eyes meet again. I don't know what to do right now. How to leave off with him.

"I'll see you around?" is what comes out of my mouth.

He inhales sharply. "Okay."

I squeeze my eyes shut as he begins to walk away. It's clear what I need to do—I need to let him leave and to limit our time together. All it does is frustrate me and make my life harder. I'm just torturing myself and probably him, too, but . . .

"JR!"

He looks at me, a deep crease between his eyebrows.

"When?" I ask. "When will I see you?"

For a long second or two he doesn't say anything. Eyes on the ground, shoulders stiff, my question seems to have thrown him.

"I have Memorial Day off," he says. "Want to do something then?"

"Yes."

He bites at his lower lip. "Okay. Meet you here on Monday. Same time."

Then he's gone.

I lean against the back of the library clutching my book to my chest. The wind whispers through the trees, the faintest of breezes. I lift my face toward it, needing to cool my cheeks. What I *should* do and what I'm *actually* doing are so far apart at this point that it's as if I'm having an out-of-body experience. I have to go home now and pretend nothing happened. To come up with an excuse to get away on Monday, during one of the biggest weekends of the year at the hotel. I have to lie again.

A tiny voice in my head questions—over and over again—why I'm doing this. But as often as I try to come up with excuses for myself, or to explain it all away with more complex reasoning, it always comes back to the same thing. Because I want to.

Pushing myself off the library wall, I head toward home. All I need to do is avoid everyone when I get there so I don't have to lie. The book slips farther down in my arms and I press it into my stomach in a vain attempt to hold myself together.

My parents, Ryan, Linda—I know I'm letting them all down by continuing to see him.

I still don't want to stop.

My feet take me home on autopilot. I don't remember long stretches of my walk at all, while others come back vividly—the manure I almost stepped in, the smell of the lilacs.

I shut myself in my room and open the book Caleb recommended. Not focusing on my own life and all of the swirling mess it entails might not be such a bad thing.

CHAPTER 47

Emma (Then)

am losing touch with reality. Or maybe it's that I don't want to deal with reality anymore because it's too complicated. It's easier to run away and hide, which is what I keep doing. I am a coward, a terrible human being, to avoid my parents, Linda, even Ryan, the way I have been. But when I'm with them it feels as if I'm lying to them simply by not telling them that I've seen JR again. Not only that I've seen him, that I've sought him out. An accidental meeting is one thing. Actively making plans to see him over and over again—that's on me.

As I sit in the dining room this morning with my parents, I come up with a radical plan to keep me busy and out of their way.

"Is there anything I can do to help with the Memorial Day preparations?"

Dad's hand stills as he lifts his coffee cup to his mouth. "Are you serious?"

The fact that my own father is shocked that I'd willingly help out around the hotel probably doesn't say anything good about me as a person. Add to that the tiny detail that I'm only offering for selfish reasons makes me hate myself a little. But there's no turning back now.

"Yes, I'm serious," I reply. "I know there's a lot to do, right?"

"Right." Dad puts his coffee cup back on the table. "Did you have something specific in mind?"

"Honestly? Not really," I admit. It feels good not to lie about something anyway. "Whatever needs doing the most, I guess."

My parents exchange a glance. When a slow smile spreads across Mom's face, the knot in my stomach starts to twist again.

"That would be wonderful, Emma!" she says. "I'm so happy you're taking an interest in the hotel."

I have to physically stop myself from wincing at her words. "So . . . what can I do?"

"Go talk to Clarice when you're done with breakfast," Dad tells me. "I know her team has a lot to set up for this weekend's activities and you've worked with her before. She'll know how best to use your skills." He reaches across the table and takes my hand. "This means a lot to me, Emma. We could really use your help."

The knot rises up, catching my lungs, my heart. My ribs ache. It's hard to breathe. Dark spots form in front of my eyes as less and less oxygen comes in.

"I've got to use the bathroom," I tell them, stumbling to my feet.

I run, as fast as I can, to the family bathroom down the hall where no one will see me or find me. Sliding down the wall, I gasp for breath. I close my eyes to make the dark spots go away. Put my head between my knees to keep myself from passing out. *I'm* fine. Everything is.

Except everything isn't.

I force myself to take one deep, tremulous breath after another into my lungs. To focus only on breathing for now. And it works—it gets easier to breathe again. The shaking subsides a little and my eyes don't feel as wonky.

JR's words echo in my mind. *Were you having a panic attack?*

No. That can't be what this is. I splash some water on my face and press a damp paper towel against the back of my neck. As I prop myself up on the sink my eyes stray to my reflection in the mirror. My hair's a mess. Dark circles hang under my eyes.

We have to just . . . just leave each other be, JR said.

Maybe he's right. This is making me physically ill, which means I can't see him again. If I stay away from him I won't have to lie to anyone, I won't have to feel this way. All I'll have to deal with is my parents and the hotel and college and Ryan and the future. My hands start shaking again. It's as if I'm watching my own life spiral out of control with no way to stop it.

Breakfast. I have to return to breakfast. I splash more water on my face, then pat it dry.

I walk back out into the wide hallway in a daze and rejoin my parents at their table.

"You were gone a long time," Mom remarks.

"I started talking to someone in the ladies' room," I lie. "You know how it is."

She laughs just a tiny bit. "I do, actually."

They talk. We eat. As soon I can reasonably be excused, I head to the second floor to Clarice's office. She'll give me something to do—something to get my mind off everything else.

By the end of the day, I'm covered in wood stain with achy arms. It's the best I've felt in weeks. Maybe even longer than that. All day long, I chatted with the activities staff as we worked and not once did I ever have to say anything about myself. Add to that the satisfaction of actually painting something again, even if it's just the play structure, and it hasn't been a bad day. I look up at the hotel, its pale blue turrets and lacy white woodwork gleaming in the late afternoon sun, appearing every inch the palace it describes itself to be. My heart swells just looking at it. Yet I know I can't go home yet—back to lying and avoidance and my life.

So I walk.

It shouldn't surprise me at all that I end up at JR's houseboat, but somehow it still does. I'm just like the moths in the lamplight at night after all. I'm always getting drawn back in, even when I know I shouldn't.

I knock on the door but Terry, not JR, answers.

"Terry!" I wrap my arms around him. "I'm so happy to see you!"

He gives me a one-handed pat on my back. When he pulls away, he doesn't return the compliment. Instead he shakes his head and walks away from me into the houseboat. Each footstep is halting. Uneven.

Before I can ask if he's okay, he says, "You two. I don't know what to do with you two."

I follow him inside. "What do you mean?" I ask even though I'm not sure I want to hear the answer.

Terry doesn't seem to care. He settles onto the sofa and glares at me. "What do you want from him, Emma?"

The question startles me. "I don't know what you're talking about," I tell him. "I don't want anything from him."

Another shake of Terry's head greets this statement. "I think you do know what I'm talking about," he says. "And I think you need to figure this out."

"Terry, I—"

But he cuts me off again. "You need to think about what you want your life to be and what kind of people you want in it," he spouts at me. "The kind who'd sacrifice himself for someone he loves." His dark eyes bore into me. "Or the kind who'd force him to take the fall for something he didn't do."

His words hang between us. Every muscle in my body freezes. I couldn't move right now even if I wanted to. I can barely breathe. His words. I heard his words but . . .

"Terry," I almost whisper. "What . . . what do you mean?"

An exasperated huff of breath spills out of him. "You want to know what I mean?" he demands. "Then maybe you should start asking someone other than my son what really happened that night."

"Dad!"

I turn so quickly that my head spins a little. "JR."

But he doesn't so much as look in my direction.

"Dad, I told you to mind your own business," he says. "That doesn't mean the minute I leave you're allowed to butt in again."

Terry gets up, his ascent slow and painful. "I hope you two know what you're doing," he tells us. "Because it doesn't seem like you do."

JR and I both reply at the same time.

"I know exactly what I'm doing," he says.

"I have no idea what I'm doing," I say.

I stare at JR. Watch him go and get two little bottles of water.

"Since when do you have no idea what you're doing?" he asks me.

"Since . . . a long time, I think." The knot in my chest is almost unbearable. I don't want to let it spread this time. But Terry's words keep spinning around in my brain. *The kind who'd sacrifice himself for someone he loves. Or the kind who'd force him to take the fall for something he didn't do.*

"JR?"

He looks up at me, the deepest crease between his eyebrows. "Let's go for a walk," he says. "You look like you could use a walk."

"Good Lord!" Terry mutters. "Well . . . have a good walk, I guess."

"Dad!" JR sputters again.

Terry waves his hand dismissively at JR as he walks through one of the two doors of the room that serves as their kitchen and living room. JR watches him, a pained expression in his eyes.

"JR, what was he talking about?" I ask. "What did he mean about taking the fall?"

He shakes his head. "This isn't a conversation I want to have right now."

"Then when do you want to have it?" I demand. "Because it doesn't seem like any time is a good time for you."

Instead of answering, JR hands me one of the water bottles. "I really need to get out of here," he tells me. "I can't . . ." His eyes meet mine, a look of desperation in them. "Please can we not do this right this second?"

I reach out and take the bottle from him, not sure what else to do.

"You ready?" His voice is low, unsteady.

"Yes."

Paranoia takes over the minute we leave the houseboat together, though. Someone might see us together. Someone might tell my parents or . . .

I feel JR's eyes on me as we walk. "Want to get out of town?"

I follow him over the dock. Through an alley between two shops. Out onto the town green. From there, we walk onto a dirt road to a trail that leads deeper into the woods. It's much cooler here. There's been so little rain that dust rises up between us as we walk. JR sneezes. We just keep walking.

"Where are we going?" I finally ask.

He takes a deep breath. "Somewhere we can talk."

We walk onward in silence.

Soon. Soon we'll reach some kind of destination and we'll talk about this. About the fire and about everything that happened after it. *Maybe you should start asking someone other than my son what really happened that night.* I have no idea who to ask other than JR. What I even should be asking.

Now that this is really going to happen, a strange unease settles in my stomach. Each step I take seems to be moving me further and further away from home and everything it entails. Something is so wrong here that I can't begin to wrap my mind around it.

Maybe I don't want to talk about it after all. I'm afraid if I do, everything inside me will finally burst. It'll corrode everything around me and I'll have ruined all the people and things I care about. Maybe even myself.

"Want to go to Mirror Rock?" JR asks.

"Okay."

We come out of the tree line for about half a mile. Just as I start to build up a sweat, we're back under the trees again.

"JR, are we really going to talk about this, or . . . ?"

The crease between his eyes deepens again. "Can we talk about something else?" he says. "Just for now, I mean?"

I wrack my brain trying to think of something else we could possibly talk about. All I come up with is "Um . . . how are you doing?"

His face turns red as if I've asked a difficult question. "Fine, I guess," he says. "Trying to figure out how to pay for college."

I let that sink in for a second. "You're done with high school?"

"What do you think I did while I was locked up?" His voice has an edge to it, as if he's holding back as much as I am right now. Then he lets out a deep breath. "There aren't a lot of options in juvie, Emma. You can be bored. You can get into trouble. Or you can study."

Our hands brush together. He blinks back his surprise.

"So you studied?"

With a nod, he goes on. "I finished school. Took a few classes through Michigan State," he says. "They gave me some money to go there this fall. Just not enough."

"So what're you going to do?"

He shrugs. "I'm going to keep working. I'm going to figure it out."

We move into a thick wooded area.

"I saw the flier for the local artist exhibit," he says. "Wondered what you were submitting this time."

All I can do is shake my head.

He glances at me sideways. "Does that mean you're not submitting anything?"

"It . . . it means I haven't painted for a while. Or even drawn anything."

That sits in the air between us. "Like a creative block or something?"

"Like that, yes."

I can still feel his eyes on me but won't look his way. There are things he doesn't want to talk about? Well, there are things I don't either. At least not right now.

The trees open up again as the tall, slim Mirror Rock towers over the scene before us. It's so beautiful here—so pure in its beauty—that it's almost a respite from what's hanging over us right now. With my eyes closed, I spread my arms out to capture the wind.

"Sometimes I wish I was a bird and could soar out over the lake on the wind," I whisper.

"I know." JR's closer to me than I'd realized.

When I turn to look at him, I find him staring out over the lake. The wind rifles through his short hair. It blows his loose-fitting T-shirt up around him, exposing a sliver of his abdomen.

"JR?"

He nods at me. "Let's talk."

Neither of us says anything. I wonder what he's thinking. Where he's going to start in this swirling mass of questions. I guess there's only one way to find out.

"What did your dad mean, JR?"

His eyes remain firmly on the lake. He won't even glance my way.

"I wrote to you," he says at last. "I . . . I tried to explain but then . . ."

"I didn't get the letter," I finish for him. "I know."

When he doesn't say anything else, I put my hand on his shoulder. "Tell me, JR," I whisper. "Tell me what you wrote."

"I . . ." He swallows hard. "I would never have done anything, *ever*, that would've put you in danger," he says. "Or that would've hurt Linda or the hotel . . . or . . ."

I wait for him to keep talking but he doesn't. "Then why did you tell the police you did?"

His eyes close. "They accused my dad of setting the fire," he says. "He already had a record. He was an easy target."

Something about this doesn't make sense. "Who would seriously believe your dad would do something like that? He's so—"

"They were going to arrest him," he cuts me off. "And he was already sick, Emma. He'd had a stroke just before last season started."

"I didn't know," I say softly. "I had no idea he . . ." But it all makes sense now. The limp. How much he labored to do what used to be easy for him in the garden. It's all starting to make horrible sense.

"He wasn't in any kind of place where he could go back to prison,"

JR says, so quiet that I barely hear him above the wind in the trees.

All of the air rushes out of my lungs. Pieces of this puzzle begin to fall into place in a way they never had before. It's an even uglier puzzle than I'd thought it was.

"So you said you did it?"

"I did what I had to do." His voice, the resolute way he's standing, tell me more. The pain he went through. The sacrifice he made. The months he wasted for something he didn't do. It's all there. Just waiting for me to understand.

It took me too long to understand. Now I do. At least partly I do.

"If you didn't cause the fire then who did?"

JR shakes his head. "That's not a question I can answer."

"Because you don't know?" I ask. "Or because—"

"I had to sign paperwork, okay?" he blurts out. "They made me promise I wouldn't say anything to anyone about it or . . ." JR squeezes his eyes shut as if that will somehow make something different. Better. "Don't ask me to talk about this, Emma. Because I can't, okay? I just can't."

He walks away from me. Leans against Mirror Rock with his head in his hand.

JR didn't cause the fire. Whatever he signed, whatever else he can't tell me, he didn't do anything wrong. He protected his dad. He sacrificed himself. And someone forced him to do it. More than one someone. *They*, he said. My eyes take in every move—every tiny shift—he makes as he stands there.

I want to go to him. Comfort him. But how do you comfort someone who lost so much? How do you even attempt to give some of what he lost back?

The answer—sadly—is you can't. I can't. All I can do is try to be his friend.

So I walk over to him. I slip my hand into his. Without looking up, he moves so that our fingers intertwine. Our palms press together.

"I'm so sorry, JR."

He squeezes my hand. "There's nothing for you to be sorry about," he says. "You're not the one who . . ."

"I'm still sorry."

He looks over at me at last. We see each other. We both know now. I reach up with my free hand and pull him close to me. Wrap my arms around him.

Something like a sob escapes from him. "I wanted to tell you," he says into my neck. "I wanted you to know." He holds on to me. Tight. "I wouldn't have ever done anything to hurt you. Not if there was anything I could do to help it."

"I know," I whisper. "I know, JR."

He sniffs loudly. Pulls away from me to wipe at his eyes. I'm out of his arms. Out of his reach now, even. And I don't know what to say or how to say it. Neither of us does. We just stand there and watch each other as the sun dips lower in the sky.

I look down at my watch. It's dinnertime. I'm late. Again.

"I need to go," I tell him. "My parents . . . they'll be worried if they don't know where I am."

He looks at me expectantly, but I don't say another word. My problems with my parents are nothing. Nothing at all compared to what he's gone through over the last year.

"Let's hit the road then," he says.

I glance down the path that will bring me home again. I can't believe that so much could have changed in the time since we got off that path. But it has. Everything has.

We start the walk back into town. He doesn't say a word. Neither do I. We retrace our steps back to the dirt road, then step aside to let two bikers pass by.

One of the bikes stops short just a few feet away from us. The rider gets off and lets it fall to the ground as the other rider glides to a stop in the distance. I look up to find Linda staring at me.

"I knew it," she says. She walks right up to me. "I kept trying to get you to talk to me. To tell me that you'd seen him. But you know what, Emma? You just kept lying about it. Right to my face."

I cower back from her. From her anger and the hurt in her eyes and how right she is.

"I . . . I didn't realize you'd . . ."

"Didn't realize I knew?" she supplies for me. "Didn't think you'd get caught?"

Something's building up inside, about to explode. I hold my stomach to keep it all inside but it's not working anymore.

"Linda, I . . ."

"No," she spits out. "You know what? Don't say a word. There's nothing you could say at this point that would make this better."

Mae comes up behind Linda and puts her hand on her shoulder.

Linda glares at me—a look that I never, ever thought she'd direct at me. That I'd make her direct it at me.

"You know what he did to me, right?" she says. "You know I ended up in the emergency room. Or did you conveniently forget that part when you decided to spend time with him again?"

Her anger—her accusations—linger in the air. I want to tell her the truth. That it wasn't him. That someone else hurt her, not JR. But I can't. She probably wouldn't believe me anyway.

"Ryan was looking for you earlier," she tells me. "Bet he has no idea where you've actually been. That you're with *him*." She throws her hand out, gesturing wildly at JR as he stands behind me.

The knot's so tight I can barely breathe anymore. "You won't tell him, will you?" I plead. "You won't tell my parents?"

Linda lets out an angry laugh. "You're unbelievable, Emma," she tells me. "You sneak around behind my brother's back. You *lie* to him. And then you want me to cover your ass?"

"No, that's *not* what I meant!" I protest. "I'll tell him myself, I just . . ."

I have no idea how to finish that thought. What would possibly make any of this better.

"You know what he did to me," she says again. "But you're hanging out with him anyway."

Mae starts to pull Linda away from me, but she turns back again. "You better tell Ryan soon," she says. "Tonight. Because if not, I will. And believe me, I won't gloss over anything when I do."

Another tug, then another—Mae finally gets Linda to move. They walk back to their bikes. In one second . . . two . . . they climb on them. They ride away. Neither of them looks back.

"Guess you should get home before anyone else sees us together," he says. I turn to face him again but he won't meet my eyes. "Or your boyfriend gets the wrong idea."

The edge in his voice makes me shudder. "JR, I . . ."

"Emma, don't," he says. "Please don't."

I want to explain to him—I *need* to explain to him—that it's not because I'm ashamed to be seen with him or have anything to hide. It's just that they don't know. So they don't understand.

"Will . . . will I still see you on Monday?" I ask.

He finally looks over at me; the sadness in his eyes almost overwhelms me.

"We shouldn't," he says.

"But we will?" The hope in my voice is almost as bad as the despair in his.

JR sighs. "But we will."

CHAPTER 48

Emma (Then)

My hands shake so much that my fork clinks against my plate when I try to spear a piece of broccoli. The noise echoes in my ears. No one else looks over.

Carefully—aware of every move I make—I put the fork down. I hide my hands under the table. Squeeze them into fists to stop the trembling. My eyes dart around the table. My parents, Mrs. Desmond. Linda. None of them know. They still think JR is someone who caused destruction and hurt. But now I know. And there's no possible way to turn back from that.

"Aren't you hungry, love?" Mom's voice startles me. When I look up at her, there's worry in her eyes.

"I . . . I had a late snack," I lie.

That's all I seem to do these days. Lie after lie after lie. The only way I can tell them the truth is to break JR's trust and make him break whatever agreement he signed. I have no idea what would happen if he broke the agreement. What whoever made him sign it would do to him.

A shudder overtakes me. I squeeze my hands harder into fists. There has to be a way to make this better without getting JR in trouble. I just have no idea what that way is.

Linda sits directly across from me tonight. She doesn't speak to me, she doesn't even look my way. It's as if I don't even exist anymore. I sit here and watch her, willing her to look up at me. She never does. Instead she pushes her food around her plate. She stares at the wall.

After dinner. I'll talk to her after dinner and then everything will be okay again. I'll make her understand even if I can't tell her about JR. Explain as much as I can and then . . .

Then it still might not be enough.

The distance between us only deepens when Ryan and his dad arrive late.

He plunks down in the chair next to me, draping his arm around me. "Did you miss me?"

Finally—*finally*—Linda looks up at me. The resentment in her eyes makes me shudder again. So I turn to Ryan instead. I tell the truth for once. "Of course I missed you."

"Oh my *God*." Linda pushes her plate again with a clank of silverware. "Can I be excused?"

Mrs. Desmond blinks at Linda for a second as if she's confused by the question. Then she says, "If you need to be."

"I do," Linda tells her. "I need to get out of here."

Without waiting for her mother to respond, Linda slams back her chair and peels out of the dining room. Silence falls at our table.

Ryan freezes with his menu half open. Watches her go. "Is Linda okay?"

Everybody at the table just goes on eating. It's as if he never said a word.

"Well, Ryan and I had a productive afternoon," Mr. Desmond says to no one in particular. "You're going to be so proud of him, Emma. He's going to change the world."

I have to squeeze my thighs to keep myself from screaming at the man who'd bully his son into a career he doesn't want. Who'd convinced him to join the military just to save his own face.

"I'm already proud of him," I manage to get out. "He doesn't have to do anything other than be himself for that."

Mr. Desmond raises his eyebrows at me, but his wife misses the tension altogether and smiles at my mom. "They're so sweet together," she says. "It's so nice they found each other so young, isn't it?"

Mom rushes to agree. "They're adorable," she says. She keeps this conversation going, distracting Mrs. Desmond.

Ryan puts his hand over mine under the table. "What would I ever do without you?" he whispers.

I try—I try so hard—to smile at him. But I can tell from the look on his face that I'm failing. And how could I not? I know what I need to do after dinner. What I need to tell him. And that no matter what I say or how I say it, it's going to hurt him.

"You know what the situation is, Jack." My dad's voice cuts through my thoughts. Through Mom and Mrs. Desmond's conversation. "You know it's not going to be enough."

Mr. Desmond in no way rises to my dad's state of agitation. "We all do the best we can, Richard," he replies. "And that's what I'm doing. I have a campaign to think about. November is just a few short months away. I have to invest in the future of our state."

Silence falls around the table. Mom takes a long drink of water. Mrs. Desmond awkwardly smiles at everyone.

Finally Ryan turns to me. "Dad and I were dropping in at diners and talking to people," he says. "Best part of the campaign."

"You do love to talk," his mother says faintly. "Even as a little boy you did."

Mom jumps on the opening. "Emma was like that, too," she tells Mrs. Desmond. "Always so chatty and full of imagination."

Mrs. Desmond's smile settles into something more sincere. "I guess that's why you became an artist," she says to me, digging in as deep as she can to make this dinner even worse.

"I guess so," I agree. Time to change the subject before she gets on a tear about my art. Turning to Ryan, I say, "How many places did you go today?"

He's only too happy to tell me about it. The moms chat on. The dads eat silently—one glowering, the other with his best campaign smile on his face. I watch Ryan as he tells me about how great his dad was. His eyes are bright. His hands move without any trace of shaking. He seems comfortable. At ease right now.

As soon as dinner ends, I am going to shatter that ease. Me. The person he doesn't know what he'd do without. My hands dig into my thighs so hard they're probably going to bruise. This dinner is never going to end.

When it's finally done, Ryan pries my hands from my legs and pulls me aside. "Want to go for a walk?" he asks. "Maybe somewhere private?" He steps in closer to me. Whispers in my ear. "I've been thinking about you all day long." He runs his fingers down the back of my neck, leaving goose bumps in their wake.

"Yes, let's go."

Time to finally tell the truth. Or at least part of the truth. The part that's mine to tell and won't mess up JR's life any more than it already has. I look up at Ryan as we walk. He's humming under his breath. Stepping out of the dining room, I take a deep breath. I can do this. If I don't tell him, Linda will. A physical pain shoots through my side at the thought of how angry she is with me. I have no idea how to make that better, but I will. After I talk to Ryan, I will. My hand presses into my side to hold the pain in.

"I'm going to hit the ladies' room," I tell him, and pull away from him before he can answer.

The ladies' room bustles with women and girls of all ages. Putting on makeup. Changing diapers. Laughing as they splash water at each other at one of the sinks. I slip into a stall and just sit on the seat for a minute or two to gather myself. I have to do this. I *want* to do it. No part of me wants to lie to Ryan. The only way forward is to tell him the truth.

I get up and wash my hands. Ryan's waiting for me in the hall with such a tender smile on his face that I nearly have to turn around and go back into the bathroom again. He's going to be so hurt. He's not going to understand. And there's no way I can explain to him in a way that'll make sense. I'm stuck between a rock and a hard place as they slowly flatten me into a tighter and tighter spot.

I hold out my hand to him. Ryan takes it, raises it to his lips for a whisper-soft kiss before slipping his hand into mine. I'm not going to cry. I'm *not*.

We head out through the verandah, over the lawn. The *Welcome to the Palais du Lac Hotel* banner waves above the gate, ready for tomorrow and the onslaught of guests. The chairs are set up by the pool. Croquet wickets stick up out of the grass. The whole hotel waits—poised and ready—for Memorial Day weekend to begin.

"Want to grab some ice cream?" Ryan asks.

I pull him to an abrupt stop. "Can we not go into town tonight?"

"As you wish," he says. "Where to?"

The question pulls me up short. We can't go anywhere we might see JR. That much I know. But there are more places I *don't* want to go than places I do. "Not the beach or . . . or town," I tell him. "Maybe we could just walk around the grounds for a while?"

He smiles at me. "If that's what you want," he says. "We can find a quiet spot even in this old fortress if we try hard enough." Ryan's eyes brighten. "Actually, there's an old abandoned greenhouse right at the edge of the grounds. We can go there." He moves in closer. Whispers in my ear. "I can't wait to be alone with you. I'm leaving so soon . . . I want to spend every minute with you I can."

And that's it. That's all I can take. We can't go to the greenhouse. The very idea of him having been there before makes me feel sick again. The knot tugs—*yanks*—at my insides. So much that I almost double over.

"Ryan," I gasp.

Only now does Ryan seem to realize that I'm not okay. "Come on," he says. "Let's find somewhere to sit." With one arm around me, he lifts me up. Supports me.

I don't deserve this boy. I probably never will.

"Right here," he tells me. "This bench has your name written all over it." He eases me down on a weathered marble bench and sits next to me. As the sun sets, he watches me with worried eyes. "Do you need something to drink? Or something else? Tylenol?"

I shake my head. "No . . . no, I'm fine," I tell him. "I just need to sit for a minute."

"Okay, but if you change your mind, I'll . . ."

"*Ryan.*"

His eyebrows knit together in surprise. "Yeah?"

This is it. Time to do the right thing. For both of us. "There's something I need to talk to you about," I begin. "Something kind of important, actually."

With a quick nod, he says, "Okay."

He has no idea what's coming. How could he know or even suspect that I've been hanging out with the person I cheated on him with? The one person he might actually hate in this world?

Press my stomach. Breathe. I can do this.

"So, I know you've been busy," I say, but then I stop myself. "No, that makes it sound like what I'm going to say has anything to do with your schedule and it doesn't."

He touches my cheek. "Then what is it?" he asks. "You can tell me anything, Emma. You know that, right?"

"I do know," I agree. "And I am going to tell you, I just . . . I just need a second, okay?"

A reassuring hand on my knee. A tender smile. God, why can't he be horrible or scolding or do *something* to make this easier? Why does he have to be so . . . *Ryan* right now?

"So . . . the thing is," I begin again. "The thing is, JR is back."

Ryan's whole face falls. "Oh."

"And I went to go find him," I continue.

"Oh." He moves just far enough away that his hand slips off my knee.

"At first I just . . . I had to talk to him and . . . maybe even to yell at him. I don't know, I . . ." My voice falters for a second. "I just needed to see him."

"At first?" Ryan's voice is small. Barely above a whisper.

"I . . . I've seen him a few times."

He looks down at his hands and inhales deeply. For a second, he holds his breath. Then it comes out in a whoosh. "Has anything . . . happened?" he asks. "Between you guys, I mean."

"No! Of course not!" I reassure him. "Nothing. We just talked, Ryan."

His eyes bore into mine as he tries to read whether or not I'm telling him the truth. It makes me sad he has to do that, but I know why he does. Because even now, I'm not telling him the whole truth. I'm protecting JR and keeping his secret.

Ryan shakes his head. "I just . . . you guys . . . ," he trails off. "You guys . . . before I mean, I . . . I saw you with my own eyes and you were . . ."

That halting sentence never gets finished, but I can read between the lines. We were kissing. We were wrapped up in each other as if nothing else existed in the entire world. I remember. God, I remember all of it.

"Ryan, I . . . I promise you all we've done is talk." This much, at least, I can do. "I promise nothing else has happened."

His eyes close and he shakes his head. "You guys were such good friends," he says at last. "It makes sense that you miss him. That you'd want to see him. But Emma . . ."

"I know," I tell him. "I know everything you could possibly say about it, and I understand if you're angry with me. But I need you to know that . . ."

His hand slips over mine. "Emma?" he asks. "Did it . . . did seeing him give you any closure?"

"Not really."

Another nod. A grim smile. "Maybe closure is a lot to ask for after everything that's happened."

I press my eyes shut, wishing all this pain would go away.

"I'm sorry," I tell him. "I'm . . . I'm so, so sorry, Ryan. And I know on top of . . . everything else . . . he was your friend, too, and I . . ."

But he shakes his head. Vehemently. "I'm glad you told me," he says. "I'm glad we can talk, even about hard stuff."

I watch him in the gathering dark, wondering what he's thinking. If he could really be this forgiving.

"My mom . . . she told me once after she and Dad had a big fight that relationships aren't always easy," he adds. "That they take work and you have to always keep communicating." He smiles at me. None of his usual joy is in it. "So that's what we have to keep doing, right? Just talking stuff out and . . . doing the work. Right, Emma?"

Doing the work. I've read this about relationships in books and in magazines—that relationships are hard work. But I wonder if that has to be true. If it isn't possible to find someone who things are easy with. Ryan probably wishes he'd found that with me. He's leaving so soon and all I keep doing is making things hard.

As I sit here in silence, Ryan watches me. Eyebrows bunched over the bridge of his nose. Eyelids drooping with sadness. "Right, Emma?"

And I'm weak and I'm a coward and I'm a million other things. All I know is that I can't hurt him again. I love him too much.

"Right, Ryan."

A sigh of relief rushes out of him. "Good. That's . . . that's really good," he says. "We'll figure this out as we go."

In an instant, he's got his arms around me. I clutch at him as if I never want to let him go. I probably never will. We'll figure it out as we go. For now, though, I'll let him hold me and I'll protect him from my own corrosion and rot. I . . . I'll let JR know that I can't see him on Monday. Or ever again. That it's too hard to keep his secret from the people I love and we have to stop spending time together. And I'll make this right with Ryan.

It's the least I can do for him. The very, very least.

CHAPTER 49

Lexi (Now)

A loud ring goes off in my room, scaring the crap out of me. It takes me a few seconds to realize that it's the hotel phone. The one plugged into the wall like it's 1980 or something. Then I realize it's still ringing.

"Hello?"

"Ms. Carter?" A man's voice comes through the receiver.

"Yeah, that's me."

"This is Max from the front desk," he says. "You have a guest down here to see you."

For a second I think he must have the wrong room. "A guest?" I ask. "But no one even knows I'm here."

A long pause follows that statement. I shouldn't have told him that. I can't *believe* I just said that out loud. To someone who works here.

"Nevertheless, you have a visitor," he pushes on, as if I hadn't just admitted I'm a minor hiding out at a pricey hotel.

I stand by my hotel bed with the phone still in my hand, not knowing what to do or say. It's Dad. It's got to be. Who else would have figured out where I am and what I'm doing? The credit card company must have tipped him off. And now I'm probably not going to be allowed out of the house again for the rest of my life.

"Okay," I say at last. "Tell him I'll be right down."

Max starts to say something else, but I hang up before I hear what it is. If I don't head down to the lobby right now, there's a chance I'll make a run for it. I'm not even kidding.

Grabbing my hotel key, I lock up my room and walk down the hall.

My stomach clenches more and more with every step I take toward the lobby. This is the stupidest thing I've ever done. It'll be the most trouble I'll ever be in. He's probably standing in the lobby right now, trying not to scream at everyone around him as he waits for me.

Not that he ever really yells. He just gets that stone-cold look on his face when I've done something wrong. Just the thought of it makes me feel sick. This is why I never break the rules. I should've just stuck with that approach. Everything would've been okay if I'd just stuck to the rules.

As I head down the grand central staircase of the hotel, I try to come up with a plan. I'll just come clean and tell him the truth. That I came here to find out more about Mom. That it's been the single most confusing thing I've ever done in my whole life and then . . . then I'll show him Mom's mosaic box and everything inside and pray he doesn't flip out.

As I enter the lobby, I need to take a few deep breaths. Sunlight streams through the windows. Someone's playing the piano off in the distance. The soft tones of it just reach my ear. Hotel guests are coming and going. Talking and laughing.

And I'm going to have to face Dad.

Finally I look around to find him. Every corner, every sofa and chair . . . I can't find him anywhere. I take out my phone to text him and then I see her.

A woman about Dad's age stares at me from across the lobby. She's about as white as a person could get. Pale blond hair with skin almost the same color. Tall, slender. She's wearing a business suit and has a fancy bag slung over her shoulder.

I recognize her . . . I've seen her face before. Wracking my brain, it finally comes to me. The girl lying on the bench in Mom's sketch. I blink my eyes a few times to make sure that what I'm seeing is real. But when I look back at her again, she's still there clear as day. And she's still staring at me with furrowed eyebrows.

She starts walking toward me. I should head over to meet her or at least start moving in her direction. Instead I stand here watching her get closer and closer. Something about the way she's looking at me makes my palms sweat. She doesn't look happy to see me or anything even though she clearly knows exactly who I am. It's more like a determination in her eyes. Like she's steeling herself to talk to me.

Maybe I should do the same. I wipe my palms on my shorts and straighten out my shoulders as she stops in front of me.

"Lexi," she says. "I thought it might be hard to find you but"—she takes a deep breath—"but you look . . . just like Emma."

"I know."

The woman nods. Stares at me like she's studying every inch of my face, which is . . . weird.

Then she reaches out to hand me something. When I look down, I see Mom's postcard. The one she never mailed. But I did.

This woman has the postcard.

I try to wrap my brain around this. The woman in the sketch. She has the postcard I mailed out. But . . . but . . .

"Who *are* you?"

She grimaces. "I guess I should've led with that." Then she holds her right hand out to me. "I'm Linda Desmond."

Linda Desmond. The Linda in Mom's stories. In the picture. The one who gave her the bracelet.

The one she wrote the postcard to.

"I . . . you weren't who I was expecting," I manage to get out.

A single eyebrow goes up. "You thought it would be my brother?"

"Maybe." I'm not sure who I thought it would be. Or why I'm so shocked it's her.

"Why don't we go for a walk, Lexi," she says. "And we can talk about where you got this postcard."

Linda leads the way out onto the verandah but stops at the railing and looks out over the lawn toward the lake. "It hasn't changed at all," she murmurs. "Nothing has changed."

It's hard to tell if she means that as a good thing or a bad thing. The expression on Linda's face has barely altered since I first saw her . . . shock mingled with sadness. It doesn't change now.

She shakes her head and turns back to me. "Let's take that walk."

So we walk. She clearly wants to go to the lake so I follow her there like a puppy. But even when we get there, she doesn't say a word. The silence is starting to eat at me.

"Linda, I . . ."

"You want to know who I am," she supplies for me. "And what I'm doing here."

"Pretty much."

There's another pause, long enough that I start to think she's not ever, in fact, going to tell me anything.

Then she sighs. "I was . . . well, *surprised* seems like too tame a word for it," she begins. "I was stunned when this postcard arrived in the mail."

For the first time it occurs to me what a rash thing it was to send it. I never once thought about how it would feel for whoever got it to suddenly find a postcard from my mom in their mailbox. To get a postcard from a ghost.

"Just Emma's writing . . . ," Linda goes on. "Just seeing it again." She glances over at me. "And then your note at the bottom. It was . . . well, it wasn't what I'd been expecting."

Guilt begins to eat at me. "I'm so sorry," I tell her. "I . . . I didn't mean to do anything to upset you and—"

"No, it's good that you sent it," she interrupts. "Hard. But good." Linda attempts to smile at me. She doesn't quite stick the landing. "I had no idea she'd tried to write to me. That . . ." Her voice cuts out and we stand together looking out at the lake in a tense silence.

I ache to talk to her. To find out more. But she doesn't seem like she really wants to talk.

"Where did you get the postcard?" she asks in a quiet voice.

"Um . . . my grandmother died a couple of weeks ago," I tell her. "The nursing home she'd been living in sent me a chest with mosaics all over it filled with Mom's stuff."

Her eyes flash to mine. "You have it?" she demands. "It's . . . it's still around?"

"Still around."

"And the mosaics?"

I narrow my eyes, trying desperately to figure Linda out. "The mosaics are all still there."

First a nod, then a shake of the head greets my words.

"Emma was so talented," Linda says at last. "I've never known anyone as talented."

I glance at Linda. "Can I ask you something?"

"Go ahead." She sighs again, like she knows what's coming.

"What happened between you and Mom?" I ask. "What happened with Ryan?"

Linda winces slightly. One side of her mouth turns downward. "Life happened," she said. "My father happened." She looks at me again. "I guess your father happened, too."

My eyes widen in confusion, but she just keeps going. "Ryan died," she says in a pained voice. "He was killed when an IED exploded in Iraq. Did you know that or . . . ?"

Ryan Desmond. The boy with the bedroom eyes. The one who sang to her, sat under the stars with her. The boy who might have been the father of the baby she lost or gave away. He's gone.

"I didn't know that." My voice sounds small. Hopeless.

She gives me a curt nod. "I can't imagine Emma told you about him before she died," she tells me. "You were so young, and he . . . he was already gone. He wouldn't have mattered to her at that point anyway."

Her words have an edge . . . a bitterness that throws me off. There's something here that I'm not quite understanding.

"Linda, what happened?" I ask again. "Why did Mom write this postcard to you? What happened with Ryan?"

That one-sided frown is back again. "You know they were together, right?"

I nod. "Mom wrote about him. About all of you," I tell her. "There are stories and drawings in the chest. I . . . I recognized you from there."

Her hand passes over her eyes. "They were together," she says again. "For a long time, actually. I thought they'd get married. We all did."

This is . . . it's a whole new layer to a story that was never quite complete. It's . . . more than I ever knew before. And I need to know more.

"Was she in love with him?"

Linda's jaw tightens. "That's not an easy question to answer," she says. "I think she was. Probably only Emma could have answered that question for certain." She looks out at the lake again. "I know that he loved her."

Suddenly my hackles rise up like I'm a cat being threatened. I don't like what she's implying about Mom. "They must have been really young when they got together," I tell her. "That's probably why it didn't last."

Linda turns to face me for the first time since we got to the lake. "Maybe," she says. "But Emma had . . . other things . . . in her life. She was never committed to him the way he was to her."

There's an accusation in her words and in her tone. But I have one of my own.

"And he got her pregnant," I spit out. "So I guess they both had their issues."

She flinches at my words. "Who told you that?" she demands. "Who told you that lie?"

I take a step back. Away from her. Fist my hands up so tight my nails dig into my hand. "No one told me," I admit. "I found the ultrasound."

"And you actually think it was Ryan?" A bitter laugh escapes from her. "If it had been, he would've stepped up. He would've made sure he was part of . . . of everything. Even after they'd broken up. He loved her so much, Lexi. He would've done anything for her."

The air rushes out of my lungs. It's hard to push any back in. Over and over again I try until I have to hit my chest to make something happen.

Linda sighs again. "I didn't mean to raise my voice," she tells me. "I thought this was all . . . all ancient history. That I could come here and see you and put the past to rest."

One breath. Two. In and out. Again and again. I slowly get my breathing back under something that resembles control.

"Is that why you stopped being friends with my mom?" I ask in a small voice. "Because she left Ryan?"

Linda shakes her head. "I would've been sad that they broke up," she says. "Disappointed we wouldn't be sisters. But Emma was my best friend. She . . . she was luminous. Like something out of a fairy tale, spinning everything she found into gold." She closes her eyes for a second. "She helped me see the world as . . . as lighter than I'd thought it could be. She made our move here bearable. More than bearable."

She swipes at her eyes, turns away from me again. "I didn't think anything would ever change that."

"Then what happened?" I need to know the answer. To understand this piece of Mom's life.

Linda's eyes look up at the sky. "JR happened. She chose him. Over all of us." Even after all these years, the hurt lingers in her voice. "She left with him and never came back."

Everything is swirling around, like I'm dizzy in the worst possible way. I knew JR happened. I knew they ended up getting married, at least for a little while. But I also know part of this story isn't true. Part that she might need to know.

"I talked to Jackson Murray." Linda's eyes sear into me. I keep going anyway. "He said that Mom went to Chicago and JR went to school in Michigan. He drove her there himself." I take a deep breath. "Whatever else happened, she did *not* leave here with him."

Linda shakes her head again. "I have something you should read."

She reaches into her bag and hands me a crumpled old envelope. "Emma sent this to Ryan," she continues. "Years ago. Before you were born. Maybe it'll help you understand."

As carefully as I can, I take the letter from her. It's made out to Ryan Desmond with lots of letters and numbers under his name.

"He was in basic training," she tells me. "She sent it to him a few weeks after he left."

For a second, she doesn't say anything else. Then she clears her throat. "He must've taken it with him to Iraq because it was in his things when he . . ."

I look down at the letter in my hands. I can't open it. I don't want to know what happened anymore. I want to keep Mom in mind just as she is now. To preserve what little I have of her and not look any deeper.

"Just read it," she tells me. "Maybe it'll help. Maybe it won't. I don't even know anymore."

So I do. I take the letter out. If I want to know Mom . . . really know her . . . I guess I need this part of the puzzle, too.

Dear Ryan,

I have no idea where to begin or what to say to you right now. All I know is that I wish you were here for so many reasons—one of which is that I could talk to you in person rather than having to send you this letter.

But no shooting star, no birthday candles can make that wish come true. So here we are.

When you left, there was still so much unresolved. So many questions we never answered because there was no time and because I think neither of us wanted to face them. Or find out the answers.

Things have changed since then, though. Things always do change. Sometimes for the better. Sometimes not.

This time the change is one I never saw coming. I thought you were the hero of my story. Of everyone's story. The kind of person who'd always try to do the right thing, even if it was hard. Even if it was terrible. But I was wrong.

It hurts me so much to write that. To even admit it, Ryan. But you're not the person I thought you were—the person I loved so much I'd have given up almost anything for him.

And I know I'm not blameless here. I know I hurt you and disappointed you. I love him, Ryan. I didn't mean for it to happen. I didn't even want it to. I didn't want to hurt you. Ever.

But it turns out you've hurt me, too.

Which means I can't be with you. Not anymore. I'm so sorry to tell you that through a letter and while you're training. There's no help for that, I guess, but I'll always regret that I couldn't tell you this in person.

Stay safe, Ryan. Take care of yourself, and please stay safe. Even after everything that's happened, I still worry about you—and will wish on every possible star that you come home safely.

Emma

For a minute I stand here, frozen. I read through the whole letter again, trying to figure out what all of this means.

"What did he do?" I ask Linda. "Why wasn't he the kind of person she thought he was?"

She stiffens. "I can't answer that," she says. "All I know is her part in all this. The reason she wasn't blameless."

"So that's all you acknowledge, too?" I push the letter back at her. Yes, Mom said she'd done something wrong. But so did Ryan. Why does Linda blame her but not him?

"Look, Lexi," she begins. But she stops herself and breathes in deep. "I don't want to argue with you. That's not why I came here."

My anger goes down as hers does. "Then why did you come?"

Linda shakes her head. "I have no idea," she admits. "I guess I . . . I thought this might let me lay the past to rest but . . ." She looks up at me. "But you look so much like her, and . . . and this is all a lot harder than I thought it would be."

She finally takes the letter back from me and then reaches into her bag and takes out the postcard again. "At least she tried to make things better," Linda says. "She tried to write, even if she didn't send it. That means something, right?"

Despite the fact that I was furious at her a minute or two ago, I find myself wanting to comfort her. "It means a lot."

Linda tries to give the postcard to me, but I push her hand back. "Keep it," I tell her. "It was supposed to be yours anyway."

Her eyes stray down to the words on the card. They move as she reads it over again, line by painstaking line.

"Thanks," she says. "I think I will."

Once again, she looks around the lake. Out at the people on paddleboats and canoes. "We were all happy," she almost whispers. "For a while, we were all so happy."

Shaking herself out of her own thoughts, she looks at me again. "You should talk to your dad about all of this," she tells me. "I'm sure he can fill in all the missing pieces for you."

That swirls around in my brain for a second. "How would my dad know any of this? He wasn't even here when it happened."

Linda's eyebrows gather like a storm on her forehead. "Of course he was here," she informs me. "He's what came between them. He was the whole problem."

I need to explain it to her. Everything will be okay if I just explain it to her.

"Linda, JR isn't my dad," I tell her. "My dad's name is Matthew Carter. *My* name is Lexi Carter."

The postcard crumples in her fist. "Then you?" She shakes her head like she's trying to clear it. "JR . . . Jason Roth . . . he's not your . . . ?"

I can barely move enough to shake my head. "No."

Her hand closes over her mouth. Rubs at it a little too hard. "Then it was all for nothing," she murmurs. "She didn't even want JR in the end. She didn't want any of us."

CHAPTER 50

Emma (Then)

Memorial Day weekend comes whether we're ready for it or not. Visitors swarm the hotel even though the lake's not warm enough to swim in yet. Even the heated pool isn't heated quite enough. No one cares. They're here for the carriage rides and the old-fashioned ambiance—for sweeping hotel vistas and gourmet food. No one cares about the weather or the temperature of the lake.

I wander through the guests, trying to make sense of my life. Ryan's leaving in less than two weeks. Linda won't talk to me. I still don't know who really caused the fire last summer. I walk backward for a second or two so I can look back at the hotel. It's unusual for mail to go missing. Neva, who runs the mail operation at the hotel, wouldn't stand for anything less. So maybe JR's letter got lost before it even got on island. Maybe it's still stuck at the bottom of some bin in a post office somewhere between here and Detroit. Or maybe not.

My feet come to an abrupt stop as I stare at this strange place I call home. The place my parents want me to dedicate my whole life to.

Most of the weekend has passed in a blur. Ryan's been busy with his dad. My parents have been busy with the onslaught of guests. I left Linda a note asking her to meet me at Viola's bench so we could talk. I sat in the woods for hours. Till it started to get dark and I got nervous about walking home through the woods by myself.

She never came.

More than once, I've tried to tell JR that we're off for today—that we need to be off altogether so I don't continue to hurt the people around me any more than I already have.

I never do it, though.

Instead I find myself leaving the hotel this afternoon as planned. There's a certain inevitability about it. As if I can't help myself. JR and I have always been friends. I can't walk away from him now.

Ryan's words echo in my brain. *Maybe closure is a lot to ask for after everything that's happened.* The pull of what we had then—what we have now—is too strong. I keep walking.

As I round the corner to the library, I see JR standing just off the road, looking out toward the water. In one hand he holds a tiny bouquet of wildflowers. They're for me. They must be. Why else would he have them? But then, why would he? He's never given me even a single dandelion before. We didn't have that kind of friendship. We don't now.

Even though I know I should say his name or get his attention, I stay stock still. He stands with his feet slightly apart, his free hand balled up in the pocket of his faded jeans. The flowers he grips too tightly in his other hand are starting to droop from the pressure of it. He seems tense. Rigid.

Then he turns around. He doesn't say hello. He doesn't say anything at all. We stay on opposite sides of the road, watching each other. There's a buzzing in my ears, as if my brain's sending me a warning signal. Walk away now. It's not too late to just walk away.

But I don't walk away. I don't even move a muscle. His eyes soften. He steps across the road, into the space I occupy.

"Emma."

"JR."

A smile—one that hints at some secret happiness—spreads across his face. For once, he doesn't fight it. He just lets himself be happy. The buzzing in my ears returns. But as I look over at him—at his smile right now—I know I'm not going to heed its warning.

"These are for you," he says, holding out the flowers to me.

"They . . . they're really pretty." And they are. Pinks and yellows and the palest of lavender colors, with greens of lots of different shapes and tones.

"I picked them on the way here," he admits. "There were so many colors and textures, I . . . I thought you might like them."

Colors. Textures. Who else in my life thinks about things like that? Only JR. I wish I could tell him how much it means to me—how much I appreciate that he did this—but I can't. Not right now anyway.

"I'm going to paint them when I get home," I tell him.

His smile deepens. "I . . . when I picked them, I mean . . . I hoped they might help you get out of the block you've been having."

I step toward him to take the flowers from his hand. The moment my fingers touch his, I stop breathing. Something about it is electric.

Just to have something to do, I bury my nose in the flowers, trying to let the scents carry my thoughts away from his touch.

JR shifts from one foot to the other in front of me. "Um . . . my boss said I could use one of the older sailboats today," he says. "We could go out on the lake as far as we feel like." His eyes drift to the ground. "If you want to, I mean."

I try to imagine what it would be like on the lake today. The chill of the wind blowing past us. The sun glinting off the water. JR by my side.

"Yes," I tell him. "Yes, I want to."

JR's face flushes red. Mine feels as if it's burst into flame. A storm swirls inside me. Churns up my stomach and twists my insides into the knot that never quite goes away anymore.

Nothing good can possibly come from getting on a boat with JR and heading out onto the lake by ourselves. Ryan will be hurt. Linda might never speak to me again if she ever finds out. And my parents . . . I don't even want to think about my parents. I know in a deep-rooted way that this is a terrible idea.

I go with him anyway.

• • •

We head to the dock in a silence I'm grateful for. A fear lingers in my mind that if I start talking I might say something that will burst the little bubble surrounding us. I glance over at him only to find him watching me with serious eyes. He knows. He understands.

One deep breath. Two. More. I try so hard to ground myself again that I might end up hyperventilating from it. Then I see it up ahead. The town's only ambulance. The last time I saw it was the night of the fire—the night Linda inhaled smoke and had to be taken in for observation. Something must be really wrong if the ambulance is here.

We push through the crowd without a word to see what's happened.

"I have a pulse," someone calls out in front of us. "Lifting on three!"

The crowd clears to let the EMTs through with a stretcher between them. I blink my eyes. It takes a second to process what I'm seeing.

The person on the stretcher is Terry. His eyes are closed. He looks sunken. Depleted.

I grasp JR's arm, but he's already moving toward the EMTs. "This is my dad," he tells them. "What happened?"

"Not sure yet," the closest EMT tells him as she keeps moving. "He wasn't breathing. No pulse. We stabilized him, though."

They push past JR and me, already loading Terry into the ambulance. Slipping an oxygen mask onto his face and hooking him up to monitors. The doors close. They drive away with Terry inside.

My heart pounds in my chest, but how I feel doesn't matter at all. I turn to JR. "He'll be okay," I tell him. "I'm sure he'll be okay."

But he shakes his head. "You don't know that." He sounds dull. Faded. As if some part of him left with Terry in the ambulance.

I take him by the hand and pull him away from the dock. JR lets me lead him up the hill to the medical center, his hand limp in mine.

"I'm sure everything will be okay," I tell him again.

He shakes his hand free. "We don't even know what happened," he says. "And I . . . he . . ." His voice cracks as he comes to a stop in front of the emergency room entrance.

For a split second I have no idea what to do or how to help him, so I do the only thing that comes to me. I hug him, tight. JR doesn't resist at all. His arms wrap around my shoulders, my lower back as he presses me even closer to him. I reach up and run my fingers through his hair. A choking sound comes from somewhere deep inside him.

I just keep holding him close. Willing him—willing Terry—to be okay.

"Thanks," he cries into my neck. "I don't know what I'd do without you."

My fingers run down the back of his neck. He shivers. I freeze. But I still don't let go of him. Instead I pull him even closer, holding on tight.

Someone clears their throat behind me. JR lifts his head, then lets go of me abruptly. When I turn to see why, I find Ryan standing there, his face sickly pale.

My stomach drops down into my feet.

"Emma, I . . . I had no idea you were . . ."

I close my eyes for a second, steeling myself for what's coming next. He thought after we talked that I wouldn't see JR again. That it was all over and that we were moving forward without JR coming between us anymore. I can almost *feel* his thoughts roiling through his mind as he looks at me.

"I . . . I was in town and I . . . I heard what happened," Ryan stammers out. For a few seconds, he doesn't say anything else. He just stares at me with stunned eyes. I wonder what he sees right now. If he can tell how sorry I am that I hurt him again. Or if he even cares at this point.

Part of me can't believe I'm standing here with both of them. My chest, my stomach tie up in a knot—tear themselves in two. I want to be there for JR. I want to reassure Ryan. I end up doing neither.

Ryan clears his throat again. "I . . . I didn't know you were here, Emma," he says. He looks at JR for the first time. What he sees seems to shock him. I try to look at JR with fresh eyes as Ryan is right now—the cropped hair, the set of his shoulders, the lock of his jaw. But I've already grown too used to the way he looks—the person he is now—to be shocked by it.

"So . . . um . . . I came to say," he sputters. Ryan looks straight at JR. "I mean . . . I have no idea what your insurance situation is but . . ."

JR stiffens next to me. "If you have something to say, just say it, Ryan. I don't have time for this right now."

My eyes widen in shock. "JR!"

Ryan holds out a hand to stop me. "No, it's okay," he says. "It's . . ." He takes a deep breath. "It's just that I've heard emergency room visits cost lots of money and I know that you might not . . . I mean after what happened last year . . ."

The money never even occurred to me. How could it have? There was no time to think or do anything else but get JR here.

For some reason JR's face has hardened into a hostile mask. A muscle on the side of his face pulses. Ryan doesn't seem to notice. He knocks his fists nervously against his thighs.

"And I can pay the hospital bills," Ryan finally manages to get out. "You don't have to worry about the money, JR, because I'll . . . I can take care of it."

If I was shocked before, now I'm staggered. Ryan comes here. He finds the two of us together. Then he does this. It would solve so many problems for JR—make his life so much easier.

"I don't want your money, Ryan." JR's voice rings out clear and cold. He looks from Ryan to me. Stares at me for several long seconds. Then he wipes his hand over his eyes. Without another word he turns and walks toward the emergency room. Away from us.

"Go home, Ryan," he calls behind him. "No one needs your charity here."

The door slams behind him. The noise makes my breath catch in my throat.

For a long moment or two I stand there with my eyes fixed on the door he walked through trying to figure out how to convince him that he should take Ryan's help.

Something touches my hand. I wince away in surprise.

Ryan stands there with his hand still outstretched to me, an ache behind his eyes.

"Sorry, I . . . I'm just . . ." But I have no idea what else to say to him.

"Emma, I . . . ," he begins. "When we talked the other day, it seemed like . . ." Ryan looks away from me. "I thought you just needed closure. That you . . . you wouldn't see him again."

The hurt in his voice leaves me numb. I put that hurt there. Again. I know he thought I wouldn't see JR again. I thought it, too. And I know what question is coming next even though it'll be nearly impossible to hear it. To answer it.

"What were you doing with him?" I expected to hear hurt in his voice again, but Ryan sounds upset. Angry. "Why were you with him like . . . like *that*?"

"Like what?" The sound of my own voice seems far away. As if I'm hearing it through the end of a long tunnel.

Ryan tosses both of his hands in the air in frustration. "Emma, you were . . . embracing him," he tells me. "Like, passionately." He looks away from me. "Like you were the last time."

This feels like an accusation. With a shake of my head, I try to set things right. "I was just hugging him, Ryan."

"I know what I saw."

And I know what I felt. I'm lying to him. I'm even trying to lie to myself. Why can't I just tell him the truth? Just for one minute stop panicking about my life. Is wanting to be friends with JR again really that horrible? Even if Ryan doesn't know JR's innocent, is it worth all this . . . this sneaking around? Making plans no one else knows about. Why is everything so hard?

Ryan rubs his eyes. "I guess at least you weren't kissing him this time."

The words—the steely anger in his voice—hit me like a slap. I stand there. Hands shaking. Knees trembling. Not sure how much longer I can stay upright on my feet.

Because he's right. I'm the one who messed up. Again and again and again.

"Emma, you have to stop seeing him," Ryan tells me. He blows out a stormy breath. "Hasn't he done enough damage already to make you see that?"

I shake my head. "I wish I could explain this to you." Even my voice sounds unsteady right now. "I wish there was a way to make you see that he . . . he . . ."

But there is no way. JR signed the paperwork. He promised to not tell anybody that it wasn't him who caused the fire. The fact that I'm so tempted to tell Ryan anyway doesn't say much about me as a friend. The fact that I was with JR again doesn't say much about me as a girlfriend.

And in the end, there's nothing I could say about JR or the fire or anything else that would make this better. So I go with the part of the truth I can tell without betraying JR's trust.

"I met him at the library," I begin. "I was on the dock when the EMTs were taking Terry away." I take a deep breath. "And I hugged him because . . . because his dad's pulse had stopped. And he's my friend, Ryan." Something inside me sinks into itself. As if I'm imploding before I collapse. "He's my friend. I couldn't just . . . just . . ."

I shake my head. At Ryan. At myself. "I'm sorry."

Ryan rubs the heels of his hands over his eyes. "All I wanted to do was help him," he tells me. "That was all. And then I get here and . . ."

"I know," I reply. "And I appreciate it. I appreciate that you're the kind of person who'd . . . who'd let the past be the past and still try to do the right thing."

This time it's Ryan shaking his head. "No. You're making me out to be a hero, Emma, and I'm not," he tells me. "Don't . . . don't put me on a pedestal for trying to do the right thing. If you could see inside me right now, you'd know that I'm no hero."

Neither of us says anything for what feels like a long time. There's not much left to say anyway. I'm all talked out. Depleted from having to admit things that hurt him. From having *done* things that hurt him. All that's left is this . . . this emptiness inside me.

"Emma?"

I look up, waiting to hear what he'll say. Knowing I probably deserve whatever it is.

"Emma, I'm leaving so soon," he says. "And I . . ."

"Ryan, it's still not too late to change your mind," I say in a pleading voice. "It's not too late to stay here."

"It is too late," he tells me. "And I don't want to back out. I want to do the right thing. Please don't ask me not to do the right thing, Emma."

My eyes stray to the door where JR went into the building. Ryan tried to do the right thing with him, too. To make this easier for JR so that he wouldn't have to worry as he sits in there all alone waiting to hear if his dad is okay. It's more than I'm doing right now. I'm the one who left him alone to deal with this.

"Emma, don't go in there," Ryan says. "Don't go to him." He steps away from me, leaving me a cold shell without him near me. But then he stops. He holds out his hand. "Come home with me," he says. "Come home and everything will be okay. We'll *make* it be okay."

I glance down at his hand for a second. His eyes plead with me. His hand trembles as he holds it outstretched. I've hurt him so much. Done so much damage.

I won't do it again.

"Yes," I say. "Yes, I'll come home with you."

CHAPTER 51

Emma (Then)

Ryan's going-away party is a less-than-celebratory occasion. It's just our two families in one of the smaller function rooms and even there we're still lost in the emptiness surrounding us.

"I'd like to propose a toast," Mr. Desmond says. "To Ryan, a true American hero!"

"To Ryan," we all parrot.

Everyone takes a drink except for Mrs. Desmond, who's clinging to Ryan's arm as if you'd have to pry her cold, dead hands from him. I guess not everyone in the Desmond family is happy he's leaving.

Not that it will make any difference. He's going whether we want him to or not.

Tom enters the room pushing a large cart of food in front of him. Even though the placement makes no sense at all in terms of distributing the food, he somehow lands right next to where Linda leans against the wall. I watch as he tries to engage her with no luck. Finally she snaps at him.

"Can't you see that now's not a good time?"

Clearly Mrs. Desmond isn't the only member of the family who's not happy about this. Tom moves away, so I take a chance. We have to move beyond this at some point. Maybe that point is now, while we're both finally in the same place at the same time. While we can help each other deal with the fact that Ryan's leaving. I take a few tentative steps in her direction. Linda rolls her eyes and looks away. She's not making it easy for me. But then why would she, given what she thinks she knows about the whole situation?

"Hi," I say as I stand against the wall next to her.

"Hey."

My mom's watching us with a strange look on her face. It occurs to me only then that she already knows something's wrong between Linda and me. She sees what's going on. It makes me wonder what else she sees without me telling her. I'll have to figure that out later. After I make this right with Linda.

"I . . . I haven't seen you in a while." I blink my eyes, trying to put together what to say next. "Did you get my notes?"

Linda shrugs. She watches her mom cling to Ryan on the other side of the room. One side of her mouth turns down.

"Are you okay?" I venture.

"Do you even care?"

The sharp tone of her voice takes me aback. "Of course I care. Do you really doubt that?"

She balls her hands in the pockets of her shorts. "I never used to," she says. "But things change."

"They don't change that much," I press on. "I don't change that much."

Her eyes roll. "Is that why you're still hanging out with your little friend?"

I touch her arm but she elbows me away. "Linda, please can we talk about this?" I plead. "Or are you just willing to write off our friendship?"

Everything shifts in an instant. Her posture—the set of her jaw. The fire in her eyes as she turns to me.

"*Me?*" She points at herself. "*I'm* the one writing off our friendship? It takes a special kind of delusion to think that, Emma."

Desperation begins to set in. I *need* her to understand—or barring that, at least to forgive me. I can't lose her. Not if there's anything at all I can do to fight for this friendship.

"Does Ryan even know you're spending time with him?" she spits out. "Or is that something you neglected to share with him the same way you didn't share it with me?"

My hand finds its way to my stomach, once again trying to hold in the pain that's growing inside me. "He knows," I say. "I told him."

"And?" she demands.

"And he understood," I tell her. "He wasn't happy but he understood."

She makes what sounds like a hiss. "Good thing he's such a saint, isn't it? Otherwise you'd be out of luck."

"Linda . . . I . . . I wish there was a way to explain it to you, I . . ."

Her eyes move over me, taking me in. "Are you still spending time with him?"

"No . . . ," I protest. Then I think about it. I haven't seen JR, but it's not because I don't want to. That I don't feel as if I've abandoned him when he needed me the most. But that's not what Linda wants to know—and I have to be honest with her. "I mean . . . yes, I saw him again . . . but I haven't seen him since his dad . . ."

"Then I guess there's no way to explain it to me." Linda pushes herself off the wall and walks over to where her mom and Ryan are sitting. My eyes meet my own mother's from across the room. She's seen all of it. I can tell just from the look in her eyes. For a second, I freeze, not sure what to do. I know I'm not going back to sit next to her right now, that's for certain. So I head to the bar and ask for a Coke with lime and I sip at it slowly, trying not to choke on it, as I wait for Tom to get the food on the table.

Ryan chose the meal for tonight, which means we're having a lop-sided, mismatched feast of fish tacos, French fries, and crème brûlée for dessert. Not a single person in this room won't have indigestion by the end of the night. Not a single person in this room cares. All that matters is that Ryan's happy.

He gets up to lead me back to the table. "Come sit with me," he says. "I need you here right now."

I don't even try to argue the point. He'll be off in the morning, spending one last night in their old home in Detroit—"I just want to see it again before I leave," he told me—and then he'll be gone. To basic training, to his regiment. Possibly to a war zone. I slide my hand into his and hold on tight. If I could physically hold him back, if I could keep him from leaving from sheer force of will, I'd put every ounce of my strength into doing it. I can't even look at Mr. Desmond tonight without wanting to wipe the smile off his face as violently as possible. No one should push their child to do something like this. No one.

Linda rolls her eyes again as I join her at the end of the table with Ryan, though she doesn't say another word to me. She doesn't even look my way. It's as if I don't exist anymore.

Mostly Mr. Desmond and Dad carry on the conversation, and even that's pretty stilted. I'm not sure Dad even likes the man anymore—he's just playing at being a good friend and a good host. But they make small talk, they include the rest of us in the conversation here and there so no one's left out. Dad's got to be a conversational genius to pull this off.

There's a polite veneer over the whole proceeding until Tom takes the dessert plates away. Until the party comes to an end.

"Mom, I'm gonna walk Emma home," Ryan says. "I'll be upstairs soon."

While his mother responds, I look to my own. "I'll see you upstairs in a little while, Emma."

"Yes," I agree.

My parents leave. Linda and Mrs. Desmond leave. Only his dad remains with Ryan and me.

"Well, I guess I'll let you two have a little time to yourselves since you clearly could use some," he prattles on. "But don't keep your mother waiting too, too long, Ryan."

Just the sound of his voice makes my teeth grind, but Ryan smiles at him.

"I won't, Dad. I promise."

Then, very suddenly, we're all alone.

Pushing a strand of hair behind my ear, he says, "Want to go get some air?"

"Yes, please."

We put our arms around each other and head outside. The night is cool and dry—perfect weather for this time of year—as we sit down on a settee on the verandah.

"The first time I ever saw you I was sitting right there." Ryan points to a spot near the French doors. "I'd come out here to get some air and calm down. I was so angry my parents made us move here in the middle of junior year." He smiles at the memory. "Then I saw you." He pulls me so close that it's hard to see anything but him anymore. "I thought you were the prettiest girl I'd ever seen, even before I met you." He smiles again. "It's funny how things work out, huh?"

"Ryan, you—"

"Then my mom introduced me to you," he presses on. "And there was something about you, Emma. You were light as air when we first met. You were . . ."

He kisses me, his lips soft. Achingly soft.

"I'm sorry I won't be with you in the fall," he tells me. "I'm sorry we won't be waking up next to each other every day and going to classes together. I'd thought . . . I had all these dreams about what college was going to be like for us." For the first time tonight, his voice falters. He swallows hard. "But we'll be together when I get back."

I can't take it anymore. I bury my face in his shoulder and hold on tight. "I just want you to be safe."

Rubbing the back of my head, he murmurs, "I know. I know. And I'll do my best to stay safe for you, I promise." He lifts my chin so our eyes meet again. "I really will be home on leave before you know it."

I want to believe this. To head to school at the end of the summer knowing in my heart that everything will be okay and he'll come back soon. The problem is, even if he does come home soon, he won't come back the same. He'll never be the same Ryan he is now. How could he be? They're going to train him to fight. To kill people. And the idea of Ryan Desmond knowingly, willingly hurting anyone is impossible for me to fathom.

"Listen, I have to head upstairs." His fingers run down my neck, over my shoulder. "My mom . . . she's not in a good place right now."

"I could tell."

He nods, his mouth a grim line. "So what I want to do right now is kiss you," he tells me. "Kiss you so it lasts me a few months and so you don't have to come to the ferry tomorrow."

My eyes widen in shock. "Ryan, I . . ."

"Emma, I don't want you to come to the ferry," he says in a low voice. "It'll be too hard to . . ." His lips press against my temple. "It'll be too hard to get on the boat if you're there."

Tears sting my eyes as I hold him closer. "Okay."

"It's going to be hard enough as it is." His voice trembles. His hands do, too.

So I kiss him. I hold on to him and breathe him in and kiss him over and over again until I'm lightheaded from it.

Ryan leans back against the wall, his eyes closed. "That's the kind of kiss I was talking about," he whispers. "The kind that lasts."

We get up. He makes good on his promise to walk me upstairs. Then he's gone. I stand in the hallway, unable to move.

Mom opens the door. Without a single word, she and Dad both are out in the hallway with their arms around me and I cry till I can barely stand up anymore. Till they lead me inside and Dad gets me a glass of water while Mom eases me into bed, holding me close.

As soon as she's gone, I get out of bed and sit on the little love seat by the window. The moon is full, bright tonight. I watch it move, ever so slowly, across the sky. I watch it set. Then the dawn as it peeks over the lake. I sit at my window keeping vigil till I know the ferry has come and gone, taking Ryan and the rest of his family away with it.

After—after he's gone—I lie down in bed again pulling the quilt up around me, terrified that he's never going to come back.

CHAPTER 52

Emma (Then)

Ryan called right before he left for basic training, but I haven't heard from him since then. I haven't heard from Linda at all, and I've left her messages. Lots of messages. The last time I called, Mrs. Desmond answered and told me in a fretful voice that Linda's been very busy.

So I do my homework. I go to class. Whatever needs doing at the hotel, I do it. Filling in at the canoe rental. Monitoring the playground. Helping organize food at a bonfire. I thought if I kept moving, kept doing something—*anything*—it wouldn't hurt as much.

It doesn't really work, though. I'm not really sure why I thought it would.

Because keeping the pain at bay during the day only means that I push it back into the nighttime. And nights have been long.

Every day I think about going to find JR. Every day I want to. But I keep stopping myself. I haven't seen him for this long. Maybe it's for the best. He's probably better off without me in his life. If I walk away now, there'll be nothing to regret later. He'll be fine. I will be, too. Eventually. Otherwise there'll always be this *thing* hanging between us—the night of the fire and the secret I have to keep about it. The parts of the story he'll never be able to tell me. *You shouldn't be here anyway.* That's what he said the first time I showed up at their new place. Maybe he was right.

At least I try so hard to convince myself he was.

I can't stop thinking about him. I want to know how he's doing. What he's doing. Where Terry is in his recuperation. About the medical center bills I'm sure are piling up. That will keep piling up if what I heard about Terry's leg breaking when he fell and the surgery he needed is true. And why he wouldn't let Ryan pay them.

As I sit on the beach, I look down the path to Main Street. I swore to myself that I wouldn't go knocking on JR's door again, but I'm not sure I can take this anymore. I get to my feet. I'm going to find him.

By the time I do, all my brashness and courage begin to slip away. It disappears altogether when the expression in his eyes hardens the moment he sees me.

"What're you doing here?" he asks as he clocks out for the night.

"I need to talk to you."

JR turns and gives me a searching look. "So you didn't want to talk me last week or the week before that, or . . ." He dips his head down. "Do you want me to go on, because a lot of time has passed, Emma."

The words sting. Mostly because they're true.

"I'm sorry," I say in a low voice. "I didn't mean to . . . I . . . I wanted to see you."

"Just not enough to actually do it."

When I don't say anything else, he lets out a sigh. "Come on," he beckons to me. "Let's talk."

I walk by his side till he unlocks the houseboat and lets us in.

"How's your dad doing?" I ask as he holds the door open for me.

"Better."

My eyes roam around their houseboat. "Is he home?"

"He's still in rehab after his surgery," JR says. "Something you'd know if you hadn't disappeared on me."

I press my hand to my heart. Try to curb the pain there.

JR looks at me for a second and his eyes soften. "He's still got a lot of physical therapy ahead of him and he's on all kinds of medication," he tells me. "But he's on the upswing."

"That's good. That's really good."

As he watches me, some of the fight seems to go out of him. "Where've you been?" His voice is small. Hurt.

I press my hand harder to my chest. "I've been trying to figure some stuff out."

JR squints his eyes at me for a second. Finally he shakes his head. Tosses his backpack into the corner of the room before pulling at the bottom of his T-shirt. "I need to change," he says. "I can't deal with *this* feeling so grubby."

"Oh . . . of course," I reply. A moment later, though, when he turns his back to me and peels off his shirt, I wonder if I really meant that.

I can't take my eyes off him. The muscles in his shoulders, his back, move and shift as he bends down to get a clean shirt from his duffel bag. I turn away, forcing myself to look out the window at the boat tied up next to Terry and JR's. A resolution forms in my brain to keep my eyes looking this way. To make sure I don't see him like this again.

But I don't. I just . . . don't.

My eyes wander back to him. Thankfully, he's got a shirt on again. This isn't why I came. I can't get distracted from the reason I came.

"I need to talk to you."

"So I've heard," he says as he sits on the other end of the sofa. "So why don't you get to the point, Emma."

Deep breaths. If I keep taking deep breaths I can get through this. I just need to figure out where to begin. "I . . . I've been thinking about you and your dad and the . . ."

JR gets up again. "I don't want to talk about this. There's nothing else I can tell you."

I walk over to him. "Why?" I persist. "Because you don't trust me?"

He lets out an exasperated sigh. "You know what? I shouldn't trust you," he tells me. "I shouldn't trust you at all," he says. "But it doesn't matter anyway. I signed an agreement, remember? I'm under legal obligation to shut the hell up."

I stare at him in confusion, not sure how we got back here again. To the fire. To whoever or whatever caused it.

"What are you talking about?" I ask. "I want to know why you wouldn't let Ryan pay Terry's medical bills, not about the fire."

A deflated "Oh" is the only answer I get from him.

I eye him warily. "Why did you think I was talking about the fire, JR?"

He walks to the tiny kitchen and gets a bottle of water, holding it out to me on offer. I shake my head, so he gulps it down himself.

"JR."

"Emma."

"Why wouldn't you let him help you?" I can't let this go. I need to know the answer.

"You don't get to show up after all this time and demand answers from me," he says. "That's not how it works, Emma. That's not how friends treat each other."

I wince at his words. Even at the word *friends*. A whole chasm of emotions opens up in my chest.

He walks over to the tiny porthole window in the kitchen area. "I don't know what you want me to say here. What you want from me."

"First, I want you to know that I'm sorry I disappeared." I take a deep breath. "Then I want you to tell me the truth."

"Fine," he says. "Apology accepted. Is that what you want?"

I get to my feet. Walk over to him. "It's . . . it's part of what I want. But not all of it."

"Yeah, well, life's hard, isn't it?" he snaps. "Sometimes we don't get the stuff we want."

"JR, I'll figure it out eventually," I say in a quiet voice. "So you might as well just tell me." My confidence wanes down to almost nothing again. "I promise I won't tell anyone."

He throws his hands up, frustrated. "Emma, my life's not some . . . some mystery . . . and you're not Nancy Drew."

Back and forth, he paces the living area of the houseboat. An idea forms in my brain that never occurred to me before—something so horrible I don't know how to ask about it. I don't even know if I want to. It would be better not to know the truth if there's any chance it could contain what I'm thinking right now. I'm going to leave it alone. I'm not going to ask.

Then I do it anyway. I ask the question that looms over this whole conservation because I need him to tell me it's not true—that I'm being paranoid and should take a deep breath and get a grip on reality again.

"Is it . . . is it because they're related?" I whisper.

The knot—the knot that keeps me up at night, that makes me sick all the time—twists in my chest. I sit down at the little kitchen table. The night of the fire, the night I'd been so confused and hurt and . . . and furious. It's all starting to make sense.

"Ryan caused the fire, didn't he?"

JR winces. It's all the confirmation I need.

"He caused the fire and they were going to blame your dad so Ryan wouldn't have to deal with the consequences." The words rush out of me now. "But then you confessed and took the blame instead."

After a long sigh, JR sits down across from me. "Maybe you are Nancy Drew after all."

The words fall like lead. Like they could crash through the table, the floor, and sink the boat underneath us. "So I'm right?" I choke out. "It was Ryan?"

He reaches over, taking both of my hands in his. "His dad made me sign paperwork . . . even my dad had to sign, and . . ."

He squeezes my hands. "They were threatening to have me arrested anyway and tried as an adult, Emma. You know what that would've meant?" His head presses against the cold Formica of the boat's wall. "It would've meant prison." JR lets out a bitter sound. "For God knows how long. But if I signed it . . . if I shut up and took the fall . . . I could go to juvie. Minimum sentence, no record afterward. My . . . my whole life wouldn't've been ruined and Dad would be safe and . . ."

"You were trapped," I supply for him. "You had no choice."

"I had no choice."

The words hang in the air between us.

"Ryan got drunk that night." The voice that comes out of me doesn't sound like my own anymore. There's a cold, dead feeling in my stomach. "He got in a fight with his dad. He . . . he saw us on the beach."

JR tries to catch my eyes, but I can't look at him.

"Then what?" I murmur. "Fill in the blanks for me."

"I don't know exactly what happened, Emma," he tells me. "It sounded like he threw something and knocked over a candleholder. The curtains caught fire."

I listen to the words. I even know what they mean. But I can't . . .

The foundation that I thought was underneath me—solid and sturdy and unshakable—it turns out it was built on . . . on nothing. And I have to salvage some of it. Whatever of it I can.

"But he didn't remember doing it." It comes out as a statement even though it's not. I can no longer assert with any confidence that the person I've spent almost a year of my life with didn't do something so horrible. "He was really drunk and he didn't know what happened."

I wait for JR to agree with me—to put Ryan back in his proper place in my mind and let me at least have that. JR leans toward me. He squeezes my hands again. He doesn't say a word.

"JR, tell me that he didn't know," I plead. My breath trembles as I try to get it in and out of my lungs. "Tell me he wouldn't do something like that."

Lifting one of our clasped hands to my chin, he gently guides my face upward so we're eye to eye again. "He knew what he did." JR's voice is heavy with grief I can't even feel yet. "He sat across from me when I signed his dad's paperwork."

The finality of those words leaves me cold. Hollow. He knew. He *knew* he was destroying JR's whole life and he did it anyway. All this time I thought Ryan had offered to help JR because he was a good person when the reality was . . . it was . . .

Things start slotting into place that didn't before. Ryan saying he's no hero. Linda overhearing her dad talking about a nondisclosure agreement. The offer to cover Terry's medical bills.

"I wrote to you," JR says. "I told you everything then, but when I got back . . . you never got the letter and . . . and you said you were still with him. That you were happy and I . . ." He looks away. "I didn't want to take that away from you."

He didn't want to take that away from me—was willing to let Ryan go about his life and be happy if that would make me happy, too. Pain blooms throughout my body.

I struggle to keep breathing normally. To take in air and blow it out again. But I still have one last question that needs to be answered. "And . . . and my parents?"

JR's eyes are full of sadness. He slides his hands up my arms and doesn't let go. "Emma, I don't want to talk about this anymore."

"No. You have to," I cry. "I need to know. You . . . you can't leave me to wonder my whole life if they did or . . ." My voice trembles. Shatters. "I won't be able to think about anything else, JR. Not ever." What's left of my sanity, of my control over myself or anything, is slipping away. "God . . . *please* just tell me."

He closes his eyes. "They knew."

I choke on my own breath. A sound comes from somewhere deep inside me and I choke on that, too.

"I don't believe you. They wouldn't . . . they would never . . . my mom . . . she loves you and . . ."

JR kneels beside me and pulls me into his arms. "I'm sorry, Emma," he whispers. "I'm so, so sorry."

That's all it takes for the knot in my chest to tie itself so tightly that it finally . . . snaps. Everything I've tried so hard to hold back—to hold in—explodes into a million pieces. My eyes squeeze shut. I can't get air in my lungs anymore. I'm suffocating . . . dying . . . I . . . oh God . . .

"Emma, listen to me, okay?" JR's voice reaches me from across some strange void. I'm not in his arms anymore. I don't know why. "Just listen to the sound of my voice. I need you to stay with me. I need you to breathe."

I try to nod. Nothing happens. Nothing comes.

"Now take a breath when I do, okay?" He sounds calm. I don't know why he sounds calm. "Do you hear me, Emma?"

This time I nod.

"Now breathe in deep," he tells me, taking in a breath himself. "And let it out."

Together we exhale.

"Good. You're doing so good," he assures me. "Now let's do it again. Breathe in . . . and now out."

I follow his voice—his breaths—till I can do it on my own again. Even after I come back to myself, he's still breathing too heavily.

"I'm sorry," I mumble. "I didn't mean to . . ."

"It's okay, Emma." He holds me close to him. Rubs my back. "I'm right here."

So I let myself lean into him. Into the one person I can still believe in. He's being so nice . . . looking out for me even after I . . . even after everything.

I hold on to him even tighter.

"I'm so sorry," he says. "I didn't want to tell you but . . . but then you guessed. And I don't want to lie to you, Emma. Not now. Not ever." He eases my aching head onto his shoulder. "But I didn't want to hurt you."

I push him away and stagger to my feet. "I have to go home."

His eyes widen in horror. "Yeah, that's *not* a good idea right now," he tells me. "You're not in any shape to go back there."

"No, I'm going to."

"Emma, you just had a panic attack. You should stay till . . ." I press my hand to his cheek and he stops talking.

"I have to. I have to talk to them."

"Then I'm walking you home."

Something about the determination in his voice brings me up short. "You can't," I tell him. "They'll throw you out if they see you. They'll . . . they might try to hurt you again, JR . . . and I . . . I can't let that happen." A sob wells up from deep inside me. "I won't let them hurt you ever again."

JR closes his eyes. "Emma, I need you to stay here, just for a little while," he says again. "*Please*. I need to make sure you're okay."

The desperation in his voice finally shakes me back to reality. I won't worry him. I won't leave him. So I collapse onto the couch. Hold my head in my hands.

The couch shifts as JR sits down next to me. He keeps trying to comfort me but it should be the other way around. I should be the one taking care of him after everything that happened. Everything that my family did to him. That Ryan did.

"I'm so sorry," I whisper.

"I know."

He brushes my hair off my face. Holds his hand out to me. "Come here."

So I take it. And when he pulls me into his arms, I let him do that, too. I let the comfort—the aching warmth of being so close to him—wash over me. JR shudders as I wrap my arms around him. Little by little, he relaxes into me. Muscles unclenching. Heartbeat slowing.

Eventually I'll have to go home and deal with my life again. But right now, we're here together. I'll make sure he's okay and he'll do the same for me.

I close my eyes and ease into his shoulder.

The rest I can deal with later.

CHAPTER 53

Lexi (Now)

I stand here watching Linda Desmond grappling with her past like I'm not having my own crisis. Like she didn't just lob a horrible accusation at my mom. She doesn't seem to notice that, though. For a few minutes, she's lost in her own little world. And that's fine. It's better than fine. I don't want to talk to her.

Because whether she realizes it or not, things are not okay right now.

If Mom never came back here. If she went to college and dropped off the face of the earth, then one question keeps nagging at me. *Why?*

My phone rings in my pocket but I hit silence without even looking at it.

Linda glances back up at me and blinks like she still needs to clear her head. "I'm sorry, I . . . I guess I thought all this time that she was with JR and . . ." She stares across the lake. "But that wasn't even why . . ."

I turn to start to walk back to the hotel, but she calls out, "No, Lexi, wait."

Then she reaches into her bag again. "I should go. It's going to take a good four hours to get home and this was . . . harder than I'd thought it would be," she admits. "But this is my business card. If . . . if you ever want to talk more. About your mom or . . ."

She takes my hand and presses a card into it that says *Linda Desmond, CEO Desmond Automotive*. "Or about anything. You . . . You can call me, okay?"

"Okay," I agree, not sure if I really mean it.

With one last nod, she moves to leave but then holds back. Reaches out her hand to me. "It was really good meeting you, Lexi," she says. "Emma . . . I was devastated when I heard she'd died. Even after everything that happened, I still regret that I didn't get to see her one last time."

I take her hand and she gives me a quick squeeze. "Take care, okay?" she says. Then she's gone.

I watch until she disappears into the trees. That was much harder than I thought it was going to be, too. My phone rings again. Chloe. It's got to be Chloe.

But when I pick up, all I get is static on the other line. "Chloe?"

She doesn't reply. "Chloe, if you can hear me, I . . . I can't hear you," I stammer out. "I'll try to call you later because I . . . I really need to talk to you." My voice quivers at the end. I hang up before I start crying for real. I walk along the beach, right through the hotel's property. Right to the edge of town. A dock looms in front of me, smaller than the one I got off the ferry onto. There are fishing boats unloading their catches. A couple of houseboats are moored to it. People constantly on the move. Someone handles the mechanisms to offload the fish that was caught today. A woman yells at the crew of her boat about what slackers they are. A man mops the deck of his houseboat.

Everyone's going about their days as if nothing's wrong. They're all doing what they're supposed to be doing. They're in the place they belong.

Everyone but me.

I keep walking till the shore gets rockier and I have to scramble up to find a safer path. There's a fork in the walking path and I keep right so I can stay by the water. The trees start to fade away. Then they're gone altogether as the lake opens up in front of me. A tall, thin rock stands straight up at the water's edge. I read about it before I came here. Mirror Rock. It's called that because it looks like some giant hand placed a standing mirror in front of the lake so it could gaze at its own beauty.

I walk around the edge of it, then lean against the rock as I face the water. The sun is so high in the sky . . . so bright . . . that I have to close my eyes to block it out. I wish I could somehow stay still enough to seep into Mirror Rock and become part of it like people used to do in Greek myths. Rocks, trees, flowers . . . so many gods turning so many humans into inhuman things. I wonder if that happened if you'd still feel human thoughts and emotions or if they'd go away? I wish there was a way to find out so I wouldn't have to deal with the aching numbness inside me.

But myths aren't real and magic doesn't happen. People don't just become trees or stars, and I can't hide from my life forever.

That song from *A Chorus Line* comes back to me again. No matter what I do to try to feel nothing . . . no matter how many times I've tried over the years . . . I still feel too much.

At the moment, I feel so many things at once that it's hard to function.

Back in my room, I start to pack. There's no reason to stay here and waste more money. All I have to do is get my stuff together and go say goodbye to Ms. VanHill. Well, and probably Jackson, too.

Then there's Casey. I know he's working today but have no idea when he'll be able to take a break. And it's not like I can just waltz into the kitchen and demand to see him. He's got work to do. Money to make for school in the fall. He doesn't need me interrupting his day.

The thought of him, of Ms. VanHill, makes tears well up in my eyes. I only just met them and the thought of not seeing them again hurts something deep inside me.

None of this seems fair. But I guess life isn't fair.

If it was, Mom would still be alive. I'd never have come here by myself because she would've told me all about her life and the people in it. I'd know her through her actions and words. Through the way she loved me and Dad. Maybe I'd even have come here with her and have seen the island and her memories of it through her eyes.

Instead all I have is this chest. These few days on the island where she grew up.

In desperation, I sift through the things in the chest again. But of course there's nothing new. I rub at my rib cage like that will somehow erase the growing ache there.

I pick up the datebook again and flip through the pages, hoping that there's something in here I missed before. There's an entry in January for an orchestra concert. Another for a haircut on February twenty-eighth. March, April, May, June, July . . . there's nothing at all. Only when I get to August is there more. A doctor's appointment. Then another one the next week. A red star next to the day she was leaving for college.

The whole fall has almost nothing in it. She must have been in school then, with this datebook left far behind. I flip through to the end but only find a page with a full calendar for the next year printed on it. I'm about to flip the book closed when I see it.

The tiny square for May twenty-third circled in purple ink. Around it, in tiny, perfect letters, are the words *Alexandria's due date!!!*

I stare at it. Alexandria. Me. I was born six days after that. May twenty-ninth.

The baby in the ultrasound is me.

My hands shake as I put the book back in the chest. With each drawing, each notepad they shake even more. I ball them into fists but even that doesn't stop the tremors.

She got pregnant while she was still living here. Before she went to college and met Dad. They got married a year after I was born. The timing of it is . . . it's not right. Something's not right but I . . . I just . . .

My phone rings again but I don't make any move to pick it up.

There's nothing I could say to anyone right now. There's nothing to say, period.

When the phone starts ringing again, I finally look down to see who it is. Chloe, of course. I hit the green button on the phone. I instantly regret that I did.

"Where have you been?" she demands. "You leave me a weird message, then start crying when I finally get in touch with you. Then you ghost me." She lets out an annoyed huff of breath. "What the hell is going on?"

And that's it. That's all it takes for me to start crying again.

"Oh God, Lexi, talk to me," Chloe says in a softer voice. "I didn't mean to yell at you, I was just so worried and . . ."

"No, it's not you," I manage to choke out. "I just . . . I met someone. My mom's old friend Linda Desmond from the chest."

A hush falls on the other line. "Ryan's sister?"

"Yeah, her," I agree. "She came here when she got the postcard I mailed."

"Linda was your mom's ex?" Chloe asks. "Talk about a plot twist."

"No. *No,*" I tell her. "That's not it at all. Mom wrote to her because their friendship ended, not because they were dating."

"Oh." The disappointment in her voice is clear as day. It makes me want to hang up. To stop having this conversation or thinking about any of this.

"Lex, you still there?" she asks. "I'll stop obsessing over your mom's dating drama if you keep talking." A pause follows this. "Okay?"

I let out a low breath. "Okay."

Once we come to this deal, though, neither of us says anything for a while.

"Did you find anything else out?" Chloe ventures. "Because the postcard thing doesn't seem that dire."

I press at my heart, at the ache that won't go away there. I close my eyes to try to block it all out. Mom. My due date. Dad.

"She was pregnant while she still lived here," I almost whisper. "She . . ."

"But . . . but what does that mean?"

"It means she got pregnant before she even met Dad," I tell her. Then I face up to it . . . the thing that's destroying me from the inside out. "It means he's not my biological father."

My voice doesn't just crack this time. It breaks. It fractures in a way that feels like it'll never get better again. That I won't.

"Lexi." Chloe's voice is low. Serious. "You don't know that. You have to talk to Matthew. I'm sure he'll be able to explain everything."

I shake my head, the phone still pressed to my ear. "There's nothing left to explain. She was pregnant with me. Dad wasn't in the picture yet."

Silence falls on the other line.

"Even assuming that's true," Chloe begins. "I mean, who else would be your bio dad?"

I suck in a breath. Let it out slowly. It hurts to even breathe anymore. "JR. I think my birth dad was her friend JR."

Now that I've said the words . . . said them out loud . . . the reality of them weighs me down. My hands grip at the bed to keep me from falling through the wood under my feet. Crashing into the floor below us.

"Lexi?" Chloe says my name with such sadness. She knows. She already knows it's true. "Lexi, you need to talk to Matthew. You need to tell him what you found out."

"Maybe."

I lie down on the bed, letting gravity hold me in place. I hug the mosaic box to my stomach. "Mostly I need to leave here."

"And go home, right?" Chloe says. "To talk to Matthew."

My mind can't work well enough to have a plan, though. It's barely working at all. "I don't know."

A rustling noise hits my ears. Like Chloe's moving around or . . . or . . .

"Listen to me, Lexi," she says. "You cannot go anywhere right now. You can't drive. You can't go home. You can't go anywhere else, okay?"

"Chloe, I've got to get out of this place."

"No," she says. "What you've got to do is promise me that you won't go anywhere till at least tomorrow, okay?" She sighs into my ear. "I'm worried about you, Lex. I don't think you're in any shape for a road trip."

I hear her. I want to promise her whatever she wants. But I also can't stay here anymore.

"Lexi, are you listening to me?" she spits out. "I want a promise. A solemn vow that you're not going anywhere till tomorrow. Understood?"

The worry in her voice feels like a punch to my gut. She's my best friend and I'd . . . I'd never want her to be worried if I'm okay or not.

"I promise."

A long exhale comes through the receiver into my ear.

"Good," she says. "Now here's what I want you to do. Get something to eat. I don't care if you have to order room service and then work three jobs to pay for it. You need some food."

I shake my head again. "I have a muffin from breakfast."

"Nope. Real food," she insists. "Some water, too. Then . . . then go for a walk, okay?"

"Sure," I say absently.

There's another long pause.

"Lex, I love you so much," Chloe tells me. "I need you to be okay."

My eyes tear up again. "I love you, too."

Chloe tells me again to order food. To take care of myself. Then she's gone.

I sit on my bed staring at the quilt. A text buzzes in my phone. But when I see that it's Casey and not Chloe, I toss the phone aside.

Part of me wants to text him back. To run to Ms. VanHill's room and cry everything out in her arms. But I can't bring myself to move and I'm not sure I have any tears left to cry.

Instead I think about what Chloe wants me to do. Eat. Hydrate. Maybe take a walk.

It's not an escape from this . . . this mess my life has become, but it's something. And I need to do something.

CHAPTER 54

Emma (Then)

When I wake up it's dark outside, and my arms are still around JR. Little by little, I become aware of where I am. My body twists in a strange position. His shoulder presses into my left arm, which tingles on the brink of falling asleep. The muscles in my chest ache from holding them tense for too many days and weeks. There's a cramp in my side.

But that's not all I'm aware of. JR's hand on my knee as my legs curl up over his. My head tucked under his chin. The steady beat of his heart under my hand as it presses against his chest. Warmth radiates off him as if he's a bonfire on a cold night. It seeps into me.

Despite the pins and needles in my arm, the cramping—despite it all—part of me wants to stay exactly where I am and never move again. JR stirs beside me and I shift just enough to look up at him in the one dim light shining in the kitchen. Still fast asleep, his dark eyelashes brush against the tops of his cheeks. There's a tiny hint of a frown on his face. That deep crease between his eyebrows, as if he's still worrying, even as he sleeps. But there's a softness about JR at rest. The tinge of pink on his cheeks. The way the light plays across his face. The way he holds me.

As soon as his eyes open that hint of frown disappears, replaced by something gentler.

"You good?" I ask him.

"Are you?"

I shift, moving my left arm at last and leaning my head against the sofa. "I asked you first."

His eyes flutter around my face. "I'm good."

At some point we need to get up and give each other some space. At some point I need to go home.

Last night comes crashing over me again as I realize what going home will mean now. Facing my parents. Knowing what they did to JR—how much they hurt him. I press my eyes closed trying to block it all out for just a little while longer.

"Emma?"

When I don't open my eyes, he touches my cheek.

I force my eyes open. He's looking at me with such concern that it almost breaks me. If I stay much longer, it might.

"I should go home."

JR doesn't say a word. He just watches as I untangle myself from him. I smooth out my dress. Slip my flip-flops back on. Get my bag and look around the room.

"Are you sure you're okay?" he asks.

I have to think that over for a second. "Not really," I tell him. "But I still need go home."

"Can I walk you?" he says. "At least to the gate?"

My chest tightens. What if someone sees him? What if he gets in trouble again?

"Emma." JR's voice is soft. Low. "It's past three. You had a rough night. I'd feel a lot better if I could walk you to the gate."

So I nod and he does, too.

With one last deep breath, I walk to the door and hold it open for him.

Even at this hour, there are people working on the dock. JR says quiet hellos as we pass. None of them says a word about him walking me out of his houseboat at this hour but I can feel their eyes on us. The daughter from the hotel and the boy who caused the fire.

Relief floods through me as soon as we're on Main Street and solid land. It takes only a few minutes to reach the gate, where we both come to a stop. JR shifts his weight from one foot to the other and back again. I rub my hands, almost itchy to touch him again, on the sides of my dress. We fell asleep in each other's arms and that hangs between us now.

As does the knowledge of what the people in my life did to him.

"You should get some sleep," he tells me.

"You too."

"And I'll see you . . . soon?"

I think about that. When will I see him again? When is too soon or not soon enough? How will this work now that I know the truth? All of it.

"Tomorrow night?" I venture. "When you get off work?" My eyes drop to the ground. "I . . . I have some stuff I have to deal with at home before that."

Silence falls, making me look up at him again. "Emma, you . . . you won't tell them I broke the agreement, right?"

"I won't," I tell him. "I promise."

He nods one last time. "I'll see you tomorrow night."

JR doesn't move to hug me so I don't either. I just walk up the drive to the hotel. I'm sure my parents haven't gone to bed. Not with me out this late. Not when they have no idea where I've been. And that's fine. They can be as angry as they want.

I'm angry, too.

I turn one last time before the road bends up the hill to find JR still standing there. I give him a small wave. Then I walk around the bend.

The hotel looms ahead me, lit up like a lantern in the dark of the night. For a second, all I can do is stand here and stare.

Home.

It used to be a fortress to me—the one place where nothing bad could ever touch me because it was my place and because my parents were here looking out for me. Loving me. Tears well up in my eyes, but I quickly wipe them away.

I know they love me. Nothing about that has changed. Could ever change.

But everything else has.

The lobby is practically asleep at this hour, but Lianne at the front desk gives me a puzzled smile as I walk by. The grand staircase looms before me, all impeccably shined wood and spotless carpet. I grab the handrail and walk upstairs. Soon I'll be home.

As I fumble with the key at our door, it swings open. My dad stands there, his face livid.

Right behind him is Mom, her tired eyes creased with worry.

I push past both of them and head toward my room.

"Oh no you don't." Dad catches my arm and pulls me back. "You're not going anywhere till you tell us exactly where you've been tonight."

My eyes settle on him before shifting to my mom. "Sorry I made you worry."

Wrenching my arm free, I start walking to my room again.

"Emma!" Mom calls out. "We've been worried sick about you. We . . . we almost called the police and . . ."

When I turn to face the two of them, something Mom sees in me makes her wince.

"I *am* sorry that I worried you," I tell them. "That wasn't my intention at all. But I *am* going to bed. I *am* going to sleep for a while. And if you try to stop me, I can just find somewhere else to sleep."

A stunned silence falls in the living room. Mom grabs Dad's arm for support. A vein pulses in his temple. I look at the two of them— the two people I trusted most in the world. The ones I thought would always be there for me.

"Good night," I tell them.

Then I walk into my room and shut the door, locking it behind me. Now that I'm here, though, I have no idea what to do with myself. I stand in the middle of my room. Arms limp at my sides. At a loss.

They knew. They let him get locked up. I think of all the years I've been friends with JR, all the times Mom has made a point of calling him by his actual name to make him happy. The times she got us fudge or made us sandwiches when we were little. When my dad held JR up as the example of what it meant to be responsible. How good he's always been to Terry.

But they were clearly okay with letting Terry take the fall for Ryan. Then they were okay with forcing JR to.

I sit down on my bed. Kick off my flip-flops. For a long time I don't move at all. The sound of my parents' muffled voices carries through the closed door. Then even that noise stops. The silence in my room is almost suffocating.

I know I should get up. Change into pajamas. Wash my face and brush my teeth. I should do all the routine things I never give a second thought to on a normal night. I don't do any of them.

Pulling back my quilt, I crawl into my bed. Wrap my pillow around my head.

Rest. I just need some rest. Everything will be better, more bearable, in the morning.

Sunlight streams into my room, waking me up again. It feels so good to stretch out my achy muscles that it's all I can think about for a minute. Then it all rushes back. Last night. JR. My parents.

I lay my arm over my eyes to block out the sunlight and give myself a little time to think.

If last night was too quiet, today everything seems too alive. The creaking footsteps of the people upstairs from us. The sounds of kids yelling on the lawn through my open window. The brightness of the sun, even through my closed eyes. The rumbling of my stomach.

I glance at the clock. It's just before noon. I need to get up and shower. Eat. In the bathroom I turn up the shower to a high heat and finally peel off yesterday's clothes. The hot water runs down my skin, through my hair, washing away some of the tension clenched inside me. It clears my mind and helps me focus on what I need to do and how.

Teeth brushed. Hair combed. A new dress, a new day. I take my School of the Art Institute of Chicago acceptance letter out of my desk drawer and smooth it out on the desktop.

Then I shake my head at myself. I can't avoid this any longer.

When I finally emerge from my room, both of my parents are sitting in the living room. A plate of pastries lies on the coffee table and three cups of tea steam by their side.

"I heard the shower go on," Mom explains. "I thought you might want some breakfast."

"Thanks."

I sit down across from them on one of the plush chairs and take a sip of tea. Reaching for a croissant, I sink my teeth into the lush buttery layers of it. It feels good to eat.

My parents sit there watching. Waiting.

After a few bites of croissant, I put it down and brush my fingers off on my napkin.

"I guess you want to talk about last night," I begin.

"Yes," Dad agrees. "We absolutely do."

My eyes shift back and forth between them. Dad pulls at his tie as if it's too tight. Mom rubs her hands on the legs of her capri pants.

"Then let's talk," I say. "I fell asleep and I came home as soon as I woke up again and realized what time it was." I suck in a breath. "As I said before, I'm sorry I worried you."

"*Where* were you?" Dad persists. "You weren't just out in a lawn chair, because we looked."

"We looked everywhere, love," Mom adds in a quiet voice. "The beach, the pool house. All around the hotel."

It's funny to me that they still think I'm the one who's on the spot here. That I've done something wrong that needs to be accounted for. But I'm not going to explain myself to them anymore.

"I was out," I tell them again. "I was doing some thinking. About college. About the hotel." I press my hands into my knees to keep myself steady. "About the night of the fire."

Dad's eyes flint with irritation. "So you stayed out all night . . . thinking?"

"Yes."

The silence that falls after that single word is thick with tension.

"And you have nothing else you want to tell us?" Mom asks.

This is it. All I have to do is say the words I mulled over in the shower and then it will all be done.

As done as it can be.

"There is actually more," I reply. "I've been doing some research." I have to choose my words carefully so as not to give them any ammunition against JR. "About the night of the fire."

They share a look that has just a glimmer of concern in it. It makes me feel bold. I'm in control now—of my life, of my decisions. They can't do anything to stop me anymore. They've lost the right to.

"What about that night?" Mom asks in a measured voice.

"I've been looking into what happened and when and how," I explain. "Things I overheard and police and fire department stuff. None of it adds up."

Dad's face pales. "Adds up to what?"

"To who the police arrested for causing the fire."

Once the words are out of my mouth there's no taking them back. I think I've done enough to protect JR, but the knot ties up in my chest again. I might have gone too far—said too much.

Dad clears his throat. "I know it was hard for you to accept that your friend would—"

"Just stop, Dad. Stop before you say something you'll regret."

He sputters out, just as I asked him to, his hands digging into the sofa.

"Emma, love, you have to believe that the—"

"Mom, I'm not going to pretend that I don't see what's right in front of me anymore," I say. "I'd appreciate it if you both would do the same."

Dad's hands are so deep in the sofa cushion it might rip. Mom twists her wedding rings in circles. Neither of them says a word.

"So just this once can we . . ." My voice cracks. I close my eyes. Breathe. I have to get through this. There's no going back now. "Just this once can we be honest with each other?"

My dad stares at me like he's looking at a stranger. "I don't know what you want from us," he plainly states. "I don't know what you need."

Pressing my hand to my rib cage, I force myself to ignore the pain. "I need you to tell me the truth."

Something in my mom's eyes solidifies. Hardens. She takes a sip of tea. She clears her throat. "So you know."

"I know enough."

"Which means your friend broke his agreement," she continues.

The knot twists in my chest. I have to force myself not to react to it. Not to give them anything they can use against JR. I told him I wouldn't let them hurt him again and I meant it.

"I have no idea what you're talking about," I lie. "I did some research. I found things that didn't make any sense." One breath in. One breath out. "And then it did. Then I could see."

"And . . ." Dad's voice trips on the single word. "And what is it you think you see?"

Tears fill my eyes. "Not the people I thought you were," I choke out. "Not the people I . . . I always hoped I'd see you as."

Dad reaches out, but it's not to me. He takes Mom's hand. They share a glance. They may not have gotten married because they were madly in love with each other, but they're a united front, nonetheless.

I just never thought they'd unite against me.

"You . . . you have nothing to say to me?"

Mom looks at Dad again. "I don't know what there is to say," she tells me. "I'm not going to try to justify our actions to you. We . . ." Dad squeezes her hand when her voice falters.

"We're your parents, Emma," she goes on. "We have to protect you. To protect our family and . . . and our home." She reaches her free hand to me. "We did what we had to do."

The temptation to take it—to pretend this never happened and go back to the way things were before—is so strong it eats at my insides. I know deep down that part of me will never be the same again. I'll never regrow what's been devoured.

They watch me, waiting to see what I'll do. I look at her hand. I don't take it.

"We all have to do what we think is right," I tell them. "It's just that you knew it wasn't. You *had* to know it wasn't." I curl into myself to stop the pain in my chest, my stomach.

"I have to do what I think is right, too," I continue. "So I feel I should tell you that I'm not going to University of Michigan in September."

They both gasp. I keep going. "I'm enrolled in the School of the Art Institute of Chicago."

"Emma, that's not an option," Dad blurts out. "You have to be responsible here."

Anger flares up inside me, sparking a fire. "*You* are trying to talk to *me* about being responsible?" I spit out. "I don't think you have a leg to stand on, Dad."

I get up and walk toward the front door. "I'm going to use the money Gran left me and take out loans for the rest," I tell them. "But I *am* going to art school."

"Emma!" Mom calls. "We can pay for college. There's no reason for you to—"

"I don't want your money," I cut in. "I couldn't go to school knowing that you were paying for it on the back of . . . of . . ."

I can't bring myself to say JR's name in front of them. So I unlock the door and push it open. "Thanks for being honest with me. I guess."

"Emma, *please!*" Mom shouts. It kills me to hear her like this—not to respond or to take her outstretched hand. But it's not possible anymore. I know that, even if they don't yet. I walk through the door and close it behind me.

CHAPTER 55

Emma (Then)

I need to talk to Ryan. To ask him about that night and what happened and to at least give him a chance to hear me out. But I can't exactly call him up to chat while he's in basic training so I call his mother instead.

As the phone starts to ring, my stomach clenches up more and more. Linda might answer. Mr. Desmond might. No one might be home and I'll have to leave a voicemail that any one of them might hear. That Linda might.

I hold my breath, counting a second ring. A third. I'll just leave a message and . . .

"Hello?"

The sound of Mrs. Desmond's voice throws off my carefully planned words. I can't help but wonder if she knows, too. If everyone in their family does but Linda.

"Hello?" she says again.

I clear my throat. "Hi, Mrs. Desmond. It's Emma."

"Emma!" she exclaims. "I'm so happy to hear your voice. How are things on the island? How are your parents?"

There's no way to answer that truthfully so I don't even try. "Everything's fine," I tell her. "Um . . . have you heard from Ryan at all?"

"I did," she says, her voice softer now. "He called two nights ago."

My eyes widen in surprise. "He called?" I say. "So I can talk to him?"

"Emma, I wish you could," she tells me. "He only gets one five-minute call a week. We won't hear from him again for days."

Something deflates inside me. One call. Five minutes. There's no way he's going to call me instead of his mother. No way I'll be able to talk to him.

"Um . . . do you have an address for him yet?" I venture.

The sound of Mrs. Desmond riffling through paper is the only one on the line for a while. I drum my fingers on my desk, trying to be patient.

"Okay, here it is," she says at last. She reads me off a bunch of numbers, and even explains what needs to go on which line of the address.

I thank her quickly but then linger a moment or two, trying to figure out what to say next. "How is he?"

She lets out a sigh. "He says he's good," she replies. "But he sounded so tired." Another sigh. "Jack says this will be good for him, but . . . I don't know if he's cut out for the military, Emma."

The defeat in her voice makes my chest ache. "I worry about that, too."

That sits between us for a second. "He misses you," she tells me. "He said he already sent you a letter." A small laugh comes over the line. "And believe me, for my son to sit down and write a letter, he must miss you a lot."

I try to laugh along, but it comes out as more of a cough.

"Um . . . is Linda home?" I ask at last. "Can I talk to her?"

A longer pause than I expected follows. "Oh . . . well, she's been very busy, Emma," Mrs. Desmond tells me. "But . . . but I'll tell her you called again. I'm sure you'll hear from her soon."

I thank her. Say a polite goodbye before I hang up.

A deep despair settles in my stomach. If Linda won't talk to me now, she definitely won't when she finds out I've been spending time with JR again. I pillow my head on my arms on top of the desk. There has to be a way to make this all work. To make it better.

I just have no idea what that is.

But I need to do something productive—something to help me move forward. I fill out my roommate form for school. I calculate the loan interest to see how in debt I'm going to be at the end of four years.

The answer is a lot. Enough to make me wonder if this is a really good idea. I haven't even been able to make anything for a while. What if I get there and can't *do* anything? I might just sit in my classes and stare at blank canvases with no idea how to fill them.

I glance at the alarm clock by my bed. 4:17. Too early to meet JR, too late to do much of anything else. But with a restless energy building up inside me, I need to move now. So I grab my bag and slip on flip-flops. I have about forty minutes now before I meet JR and I know how I'm going to fill them.

By the time he gets off his shift at five, I'm waiting by the dock with a bag of sandwiches in one hand and a houseplant in the other. JR smiles the minute he sees me.

"New plant?" he asks. "You doing some redecorating?"

Confusion washes over me for a second. "Oh, no . . . it's not for me," I reply. "It's for your dad. When he gets out of the medical center, I mean. I thought . . . I know he liked being in the garden before so I thought he might like to have something green at home."

JR stares at me long enough for me to wonder if getting the plant was a good idea after all.

"That's . . . ," he begins. "He'll really like that."

My cheeks burn up as I hand it over to him. JR gazes down at it. "Thanks for doing this."

When he finally looks up, there's confusion in his eyes. "Mind if we head to my place first?"

I know why he wants to. My mind immediately goes to the last time he needed to change. The way I couldn't keep my eyes off him. "No . . . um . . . of course not."

He nods toward the houseboat and we walk over there together. This time I don't look around to check if anyone sees us together. I honestly don't care anymore if someone does.

"What's in the bag?"

"Oh . . . um . . . I got us BLTs," I stammer out. "And iced tea. I . . . I figured you'd be hungry after working all day."

Why am I acting like such an idiot? Tripping over my words. Blushing at the drop of a hat. He's got to have noticed. He must think I'm acting weird. I mean, I am acting weird. As he unlocks the door I wipe the sweat from one palm and then the other onto my sundress, switching the bag from hand to hand as I do.

"Dad's gonna love this," JR says as he puts the plant on the table. "You'll have to come over when he gets home so you're here when he sees it."

I'm not sure Terry would really want me here—not after our last conversation—but I don't say that to JR. I don't want to burst his bubble when he looks so pleased.

"Um . . . what do you want to do tonight?" I ask just to change the subject. I don't honestly care what we do but JR's cheeks flush red, so he must.

"Since we never got to take a sailboat out," he begins, "would you maybe want to tonight?"

A flood of emotions rushes over me. Pain. Embarrassment. A strange sense of . . . hope.

"Yes," I reply. "I really would."

He nods and puts the plant down on the table.

"Just let me change." He pauses as he gets to his duffel bag. "Then we can head out."

I nod—one, twice . . . twelve times? I brace myself for him taking off his shirt again, but when he grabs a new one, he glances back at me for a second before heading to the bathroom instead. A few minutes later, he comes back out with the clean shirt on, smelling like soap.

"You ready?"

Once again, I nod like a fool.

"Then let's go."

. . .

Out on the dock again, people call out his name. Greet him as we walk. He waves—tells them to have a good night. It once again hits me with a pang that there are whole swaths of his new life here that I'm not a part of. I'm not used to him having a life here that I'm not a part of.

"Sandy!" he calls out to an older woman. "I'm gonna take you up on the offer to use a sailboat."

She turns and looks first at me and then at him. "Got a hot date?"

My cheeks turn to fire, but he just smiles. "Yeah, with my best friend."

Sandy stares at me with one eyebrow raised but I can't really bring myself to care what she thinks. Because he just called me his best friend. Without a hint of sarcasm or irony. *His best friend.*

JR nudges me. "You coming or what?"

I shake myself to come back to reality. "Oh . . . yes, of course!"

He shoots me a confused look. "Were you in Emma Land again?"

"Something like that," I murmur.

Instead of teasing me, JR just nods toward the other end of the dock, where a fleet of tiny sailboats lie. He gets one ready to take out—notches up a mast and gets the sails up.

The boat rocks as I step on. I nearly lose my footing, but JR reaches out and steadies me.

"You good?"

"I'm good."

After he stows our dinner in a tiny compartment, he works with fast hands to secure a bunch of different ropes while I sit here doing not much of anything.

"How did you learn how to do this?" I ask.

"Sandy makes us learn how to work everything," he says, never looking up from the knot he's tying. "Have to be able to deal with an emergency. To help out."

That makes perfect sense. Yet it's still jarring to see him so expertly working these ropes—doing something I had no idea he could do. I keep discovering these new pieces of him. We were apart for less than a year but so much of him has changed. So much of me has not.

"Come here for a second," he says to me. Then he lights into an explanation of how we're going to have to move from side to side depending on where we need the wind in the sail.

"I thought this was supposed to be relaxing?" I say absently.

"I'll do all the work," he tells me. "You just have to get up off your butt now and then."

I nod. "Sounds fair."

A nudge is the only response I get, but I don't really mind. I don't mind having to move back and forth either. The last time we were supposed to do this a kind of dread laid under the anticipation—a knowledge that every single thing I was doing was wrong. Now, I know the truth. Now I'm his best friend. There's nothing to worry about anymore, I guess.

Then I look over at him. The sun shines in his dark hair making it come alive with colors you can't normally see—copper and tiny glints of silver. His cheeks are pink from the sun. He practically glows. I have to close my eyes for a few seconds to block out the sight of him, trying not to think about what it feels like to run my fingers through his hair. To touch him.

My pulse races through my veins. It pounds in my ears.

My best friend. That's what he called me and I . . . I'm happy that I can be that for him. I'm grateful he thinks of me this way after everything that's happened. But it also means this pull toward him—the one I can't quite shake—it's all on me.

"Emma?"

I nearly jump out of my skin.

"You gotta stay with me so you know when to move, okay?" The words could be stern. Commanding. But his voice is soft. His eyes are, too, as he smiles at me.

He spent almost a whole year in a detention center for something he didn't do. His mom won't let him come home and his dad's sick. They're in debt. He doesn't have any idea how he'll pay for college in the fall. So many things have gone wrong in his life but he smiles at me as if nothing in the world has ever gone awry. In a way he never would have before.

"I'll stay with you."

For a second, the crease between his eyebrows deepens but then he looks at the water and pushes off. Away from the dock and his coworkers, my parents and the hotel. Slowly—very slowly—we move away from every part of our daily lives. The farther we go, the more it feels as if a weight is lifting off me.

JR tells me once, twice, to switch sides. Our knees touch. Our hands do too. The boat feels tiny now that we're out on the lake. There's no way to hide from him or even from myself. Heat blooms around my neck, up my cheeks. My earlobes itch.

I close my eyes and try to focus on the wind as it whips my hair back and the brightness of the sun under my eyelids. JR hums under his breath— tells me to switch sides again. He steers us at an angle to the wind.

"Are we going somewhere?" I call to him.

His eyes crinkle up. "Wait and see."

The island blurs as we sail past it. The water's beautiful—the teal and green and gray depths of it. I want to paint this—the colors of the water right at this very moment. I want to so badly it hurts.

After about an hour, we leave the island behind as he steers us into open lake.

A growing swirl of anticipation—of nerves and something like elation—flares up in me. We are so alone right now. More than we've ever been before. Even in the greenhouse, Terry always knew we were there even if no one else did. If he needed to find us, he always could. But now . . . now it's just us. My stomach rumbles but I'm not sure I could eat a bite of my sandwich.

The water changes color underneath us, the gray depths receding till it's just the warm teal of the sunlight over some shallower water. Rocks peek out of the lake not far away. One glance at JR and I know we're at our destination.

"How did you know this was here?" I ask.

"One of the boat captains calls it the nature cruise gate to hell," he replies. "Get caught out here and you're stuck with complaining tourists till someone can tug you out again."

I smile at that. "But we won't get stuck, right?"

"Not in this thing."

He works to tie down the sail, then drops a tiny anchor, tethering us here.

"Dinner?" he says.

I grab the bag and we each take an iced tea and a sandwich. JR and I sit on opposite sides of the boat and eat in silence, surrounded by blue—the undulating pale tones of the late afternoon sky, the changeable blue-green of the water. It's as if we're in a dome of color that goes on forever. I gulp down some iced tea and lean my head back to soak it all in for a minute before I have to ruin the peace we sit in.

"I talked to my parents," I say at last.

He stiffens, hands gripping the boat. "And?"

"I told them I did some research and figured out it wasn't you," I continue. "When the agreement came up, I said I didn't know what they were talking about."

JR lets out a long breath. "Thank you."

I just nod. I can feel his eyes on me but I can't look up.

"How'd it go?"

"Not well."

He waits as if he thinks I'm going to say more. "You okay?"

Another nod. "Are you?"

For a long second or two JR gazes out over the water. "Sometimes." He turns back to face me again. "Right now I am."

Something under my ribs . . . shifts. Like two plates under the earth letting hot magma seep out between them. "Right now I am, too."

Another long silence hangs between us.

JR finishes his dinner and puts his trash back in the bag. The boat bobs up and down gently on the lake. Tiny fish swim around us. There's no way I'm going to be able to eat any more without throwing up so I carefully rewrap it and slip that in the bag, too.

Leaning over the boat, I run my fingers through the water. It's cold, but not so cold it's uncomfortable at this time of year. And in this shallow spot, the sun's warmed it up a little.

"I haven't been in the lake for almost a whole year," I say under my breath.

"Me neither," JR says. "I used to close my eyes and think about what it looked like. Pretend I was neck deep in the water." He twists his body so he can get a better view of the expanse behind him. "Think about canoeing at night under the stars."

Part of me wants to apologize again and again, but I don't think he wants to hear it. Not from me, anyway. Not now. So I think about what he might actually want. What might help him.

"We could go swimming right now."

He lets out a sad laugh. "We could," he says. "If we'd worn bathing suits."

I shrug as if I'm so nonchalant about this, even though no part of me is. "Can't we just jump in with our clothes on?"

JR turns back to face me. Slowly. Deliberately. "Are you serious?"

"I'm serious."

A frown arches downward on his mouth. He rubs the back of his neck. "How's that gonna work with that long dress?"

I glance down at the thin cotton sundress I have on. Something quivers in my chest, but I ignore it. "It'll be fine," I tell him. "Just a little . . . clingy . . . when I get out. I'll put on one of the sweatshirts."

As soon as I say it, though, I wonder if it will be fine. If we should go swimming. Over and over again the image of him changing shirts burns into my brain. I shouldn't feel this *want* for him. This isn't how a best friend acts—itching with the need to touch him.

He squints his eyes at me as if I'm a puzzle he's trying to figure out. "Are you sure? 'Cause you don't seem sure." His eyes stray out over the water again. "We could just sail around more."

I take a deep breath. Maybe it's not a good idea, but . . . "No, let's do it."

Now that I've said the words out loud, the quivering turns to racing. My heart races.

When he doesn't say anything, my nose wrinkles in disgust with myself. He knows it's not a good idea. I know it, too.

"Okay, let's do it."

JR takes off his T-shirt. Less than two feet separate us. The pounding in my chest grows so strong that it makes my ears buzz. I shake my head at myself. In two steps, I dive off the side of the boat.

Cold water envelopes me. Shocks my body back to its senses. I dunk under, letting it close over my head for a second. I swim underneath the surface for a few strokes to get some space between me and JR. When I come back up, he's already in the water.

"It's freezing!" he yells. "How did I let you talk me into this?"

I pull back my arm and slosh water at him. JR dunks under to avoid my attack. He laughs as he cuts back through the lake's surface again, splashing at me as he does.

As I leap away, laughter pours from me. It seeps out of every crevice of my body. Maybe this is what happens when that pain in my chest cracks open—not seething magma, but *this*. I kick my legs to make a giant tidal wave hit him, but he grabs my ankles and pulls me under. Swims away fast to avoid my revenge.

"Why don't you come back here, JR?" I call to him. "Afraid of how I'll retaliate?"

He laughs again. "Um . . . yeah."

I shoot JR a grin. "You should be!" Then I launch myself at him, using both arms to surge water over him.

More laughter sputters out of him. I'm about to launch another water attack when he calls out, "Time out! Time out!"

I swim around him, circling. "Was that too much for you, JR?" I tease. "You couldn't handle the heat?"

He shakes his head at me, grinning from ear to ear. I like him like this. No sarcasm, no hiding when he's happy. As if he's shed some hard outer layer—even if just for this one moment—and JR shines through. He gazes up at the sky, a look of awe on his face.

"I really needed this," he says in a quiet voice.

"Me too."

He kicks his legs up and floats on his back, eyes still on the sky above him as if he's never seen anything so beautiful in his entire life. As he watches the sky, I watch him. The lazy kick of his legs through the water. The way his hands cup at it as if he could capture the lake in them. The curves of his shoulders. His chest.

A tiny smile spreads across his face. Just the barest upward turn of the corners of his mouth. The urge to kiss those upturned corners—to taste the lake water on his lips—hits me. Hard. Longing for him sparks inside me.

I shouldn't feel this way about him.

But I do. I really do.

God, I love him so much.

I choke in a breath. Cough on it.

I have to swim away from him—to put some space between us. Try to catch my breath.

Because I love him. It's not just the longing to touch him. That's there, too, vibrating just under my skin. But this goes beyond just wanting him. It's a bone-deep need to talk to him, laugh with him. To be close to him in every possible way.

How could I not have realized this before? Was it just lying there, dormant inside me, waiting for me to wake up? I have to sit with it for a while—live with the knowledge of it before I can even begin to cope with it.

So I let him peacefully float, blissfully unconscious of the storm surging inside me. I tread water and swim till my teeth chatter.

Till JR finally surfaces out of his own thoughts. "I'm freezing," he says. "Want to dry off?"

The only thing I can do is nod. I look over at the boat, unsure how we're actually going to get back on without capsizing it.

"I'll give you a leg up," he says as if he's reading my mind.

I nod again even though I'm not sure how that's going to work either. How he won't get a huge eyeful of my wet dress plastered to my body. As soon as we get to the boat though, JR interlocks his fingers to give me a leg up, then turns his head away from me and looks out over the water.

Holding his shoulder with one hand, I try to ignore how close he is—the fact that his bare skin lies just under my fingers. Even if his eyes aren't on me, he's still so near. It would be so easy to let my body slide against his. To wrap myself around him and lose myself in him.

A chill runs down my spine.

I push my foot off his fingers and launch myself onto the boat. JR swims away so I can squeeze the water out of my dress. He only comes back when I call him. When I hold out a hand to him, he takes it. The boat rocks dangerously as he climbs on board but doesn't tip.

Water drips from JR's shorts. He keeps his eyes carefully averted. Throws me a sweatshirt and puts his shirt back on.

"You ready to go?" he says.

When I turn back—when my eyes meet his again—heat spreads over my face. It curls down my neck and into my chest. I am on fire.

"I'm ready."

Untying the ropes, he gets the sail back where he wants it. The anchor's up at last and the wind catches in the sails. It cools down my cheeks. Whenever I can—whenever we're not on the move to keep the sail going—I close my eyes and just let the wind take hold of me.

JR never says a word.

When we finally reach the shore, the sun's starting to go down. "Thanks for the sail," I say. "And the swim. It was . . . I mean . . ." That's as far as I get.

"Thanks for the sandwiches," he adds. "And the plant. My dad really is gonna love it."

I force my face into a smile. He returns it, just barely.

"So . . . um . . . I was thinking. We haven't been to the greenhouse in a long time," he begins. My mind flashes to the last time we were there. To everything that happened that night. From the crease between his eyebrows, it looks as if he might be thinking the same thing.

"But I . . . I wondered if maybe tomorrow night after I have dinner with my dad," he continues. "Maybe we could meet there?"

When I don't answer, the crease deepens between his eyebrows. I want to massage it away so badly my fingers twitch.

"Yes," I say at last. "When can you be there?"

"Eight o'clock?"

"Okay."

We stand facing each other in silence. Seconds turn into minutes. We still don't move.

Then he wraps his arms around me. I cling to him so hard I might leave marks on his shoulders. With my eyes closed, I can just *feel* him.

I love him so much it's a miracle that it doesn't burst out of me, spilling all over everything around me, including him.

JR can tell something's changed. He pulls back and narrows his eyes as he studies me—tries to figure out what went wrong.

"So . . . I'll . . . um . . . see you tomorrow?" I say.

His lips form a grim line. "Are you sure you want to?"

"I'm really, really sure."

He takes another step backward, toward the houseboat. Away from me. "See you at eight."

Then he turns to go. I watch as he walks away, willing him to turn back. To kiss me till I can't breathe anymore and tell me he loves me, too. He doesn't turn. And it seems too far-fetched to believe that he could possibly love me after everything that's happened. I'm his best friend, after all—something I both long to be and long to throw back at him and demand more. But there's no *more* to demand. Even if there was, I would never ask it of him.

So I walk back home. I let myself into our place. Freeze as I walk into the living room and meet my mom's eyes. I try to ignore the pain I see in them. Try to ignore my own—the dull knife-edge of it—as I stand here, just staring at her. Long moments drag on. And on.

"Good night, Mom."

A deep breath rushes out of her. "Good night, Emma."

But even leaving the room doesn't make the pain go away. Closing my door and locking it behind me doesn't either.

Too many emotions are tearing my heart apart. It's as if my mind— my heart—decided to feel everything at once, just to see what would happen. How I'd cope with it.

I'm not coping well.

CHAPTER 56

Lexi (Now)

There's only so much walking I can do before my feet get tired. Only so much food and hydration I can worry down before my stomach churns.

I'm not doing a good job with the self-care Chloe told me I should tackle.

Back at the hotel, locked in my room, I feel as if I'm beginning to lose my mind. I should have just left after I talked to Chloe. The four walls of this tiny space feel like they're closing in around me. The bright yellow of the wallpaper throbs behind my eyes. All I want is to be home again, watching weird train shows with Connor. I want the comfort of my bedroom and the kitchen and the living room. I even miss the bathroom. The cracks in the tiles. The old medicine cabinet that falls off the wall if you shut the door too hard.

I had no idea that it was possible to miss a bathroom. It doesn't make any sense that I do. But I'd trade all the shine and new fixtures of the bathroom here for the one at home in a heartbeat.

If it weren't for Dad, I'd want to just get on whatever boat I could and drive through the night so I could sleep even for a little while in my own bed before I woke up to the sounds of my family getting ready for the day.

But home equals Dad and I can't face him right now.

I stare out the window of my room at the fire escapes and rooftops. There's nothing left for me here except this ugly view and more wasted money.

A knock sounds at the door. Someone in a hotel uniform stands on the other side holding an envelope. "A note for you," she tells me. "I was told it was urgent."

My eyes widen. Dad. It's got to be Dad. "Oh . . . okay . . . I . . ."

The woman smiles at me as she hands it to me. "I think it's only urgent in the mind of the sender if that helps."

I shake my head to clear it. "Um . . . thanks."

A second later she's gone, leaving me with a cream-colored envelope with my name in shaky writing on it.

Ripping it open, I find embossed initials on the top of the page.

CVH

Well, at least it's not Dad.

Dear Lexi,

The front desk is irritated with me for not simply calling you, but a note is so much more commanding than a phone call. It's much more difficult to say no when a request is made in writing.

I've already placed an order for tea, so I expect to see you soon. Bring your mother's things.

Yours,
Clara VanHill

A wet laugh comes from deep inside me. She thinks this is just a note, but I'm going to keep this forever. The time Clara VanHill wrote to me and demanded that I come see her.

I press the note to my chest. Maybe I should start a box to keep important memories in, too. Maybe when I get home. After I make a treasure chest with Connor. And in between working three jobs to pay my hotel bill.

This is not helping. I put my shoes back on and carry Mom's chest with me as I walk to Ms. VanHill's room.

She answers the door almost immediately with a smile on her face, but it fades when she takes a good look at me.

"What happened?" she asks as she leads me into the room. Ms. VanHill gestures at the sofa by the window and then sits next to me.

When I don't respond to her, she takes the story chest from my lap and gently lays it on the coffee table next to the tea tray. Her cast is already looking dingier, the white of the plaster fading as the days wear on.

"Lexi, tell me what's going on," she says. "You don't look as if you've come ready to enjoy your tea."

"No, I did. It's just that . . . that . . ."

She puts her good hand on my arm.

"Breathe," she tells me. "Have some tea. And you and I will talk."

I open my mouth to start talking again but she holds up one finger to stop me. "Tea first," she declares. Ms. VanHill sets out two dainty cups and begins to pour dark tea into both of them. "I had an old friend," she says. "Ginger. She was always in a dither about her dance partner." She sighs. "I can't even begin to tell you how many cups of tea I had to practically pour into her to get her to calmly talk the situation through."

A pause ensues as she's deep in thought. I guess I am, too. She can't mean Ginger Rogers, can she?

Ms. VanHill hands me a cup with milk and sugar in it. "To be fair to Ginger," she continues, "he could be a crotchety old walking stick. Though he was a lovely dancer."

For a minute or two, she seems lost in her own memories of times gone by and friends long gone. I take a sip of tea. The sweet warmth fills my mouth, my throat as I swallow. I close my eyes and take another sip and another.

"Now," Ms. VanHill says. "You look ready to talk at last."

I blink my eyes in surprise. She told that story just to get me to drink tea and get myself together?

"Like Ginger?"

She shrugs. Only Ms. VanHill can make a shrug seem dignified. "Sometimes we'd have something stronger than tea," she admits. "But since you're still in high school, we'll stick with tea." She pauses. "For now."

I choke on a sip of my tea, almost sputtering it out my nose.

She gives me a second to get myself back together. "What happened, Lexi?"

I take a deep breath. Then I let the floodgates open, describing my meeting with Linda Desmond and the evidence I found in the datebook that the baby in the ultrasound is me.

That JR, and not my dad, is my biological father.

Ms. VanHill sighs. "It would sound like the plot of a melodrama if it weren't your real life."

"I don't know what to do," I admit to her. "I don't know how to tell my dad."

Ms. VanHill puts her tea down on the table with an elegance I don't have now, and definitely won't have when I'm in my nineties.

"Come here, Lexi," she says. She opens her arms. I lean into them willingly.

"Everything will be just fine in the end," she says in a soothing voice. "Your father will understand." She runs her hands down my hair over and over again. "None of this is your fault, Lexi. He won't love you any less because you don't have half his genes."

The very thought of how he's going to react, though, leaves me struggling to stay calm again. Sucking in deep breaths and letting them out again. That's the best I can do right now. Because Dad's not exactly effusive on a good day and he does think I'm his biological daughter. With this . . . I shudder.

"Lexi," Ms. VanHill says again. "I know what it's like to despair. I know what it feels like when you think you've lost everything. But you have not lost everything. I promise you that."

I start to shake my head, but she holds me even closer, as she starts humming under her breath. The tune sounds familiar to me. I can't quite place it, though, until she sings some of the words.

I've only ever heard Ms. VanHill sing in recordings up till now. Her voice, when she was much younger, sounded like nothing I'd ever heard before. Now, worn with age, she sounds beautiful in a completely different way. It rasps a little, trills notes it probably wouldn't have before. It gives me chills.

I let her voice seep into me and fill up the gaps that have broken inside, even as the words she's singing tear me apart.

"Sometimes people leave you, halfway through the wood."

She keeps singing, about mothers who aren't around anymore and parents making mistakes. I know the song. "No One Is Alone." It's sung after every possible disaster has struck in the play by the people who are left trying to pick up the pieces of their lives.

"I didn't know you'd been in *Into the Woods*," I say in a choked voice.

"Hmf . . . well, I wasn't," Ms. VanHill sniffs. "But just because Steve Sondheim didn't have the good sense to cast me in it doesn't mean he didn't write some lovely music."

I snort out a tiny laugh. "I bet you would have been a better witch than even Bernadette Peters."

This time Ms. VanHill laughs as well. "Well, I can't disagree with you," she replies. "But don't ever tell her that."

I finally sit up so I can look at Ms. VanHill. "Next time I see her, I'll keep my mouth shut."

She touches my cheek. "You're going to be just fine, Lexi," she says. "I know you are. And you really aren't alone, do you understand? I'm here for you. Casey is, too. Your family."

I manage to get out a quiet "Thank you."

We drink tea. I nibble on a slice of lemon cake. We talk about Casey and the hotel and she tells me more outrageous stories about her career.

Finally she raises her chin at the mosaic chest. "Aren't you going to read me anything today?"

The emptiness returns, worse than it was before because for a few minutes she'd distracted me and let me think about something else.

"There's nothing left to read," I tell her. "I've reached the end of her stories."

"No," Ms. VanHill says. "There are always more stories. Always, Lexi."

After another hug, I grab the chest again and say a quick thank-you. I'll come back when I'm all packed up to say goodbye. I'll have one last cup of tea with her before I leave.

I start walking back to my room, but the idea of sitting with all the yellow and blue makes my eyes ache, so I stop. My feet take me down the stairs and out onto the verandah. I clutch Mom's chest closer to me, even as I wish I could toss it into the lake that's lazily rippling in the slowly setting sun. I wander toward the water but when I get there, I can't sit still. There's a restlessness under my skin . . . something itching at me that I can't scratch away.

I know where I need to go.

Turning back toward the hotel, I walk right past it and over a small grassy hill till I finally reach my destination.

The greenhouse sits tucked into the far hill, light reflecting off every pane of glass, making it glow. It calls me, this place. Draws me in like a magnet. Mom loved it here. I just know she did. And I need to be here one more time before this whole trip turns from a lovely horse carriage back into a pumpkin again.

Once I'm inside, though, I have no idea what to do. The mosaic on the floor has to be my mother's doing. It's not the work of a run-of-the-mill tile layer but something deeply intricate. A piece of art made from broken shards and remade into something new and beautiful.

I wonder for the first time if that's what happened in Mom's life, too. She got broken by Ryan and JR but then she put the pieces back together with Dad and made something new with him. It's hard to imagine Dad being the kind of person you make something beautiful with, but what do I know? I've never had any relationship, let alone a broken one.

Easing myself onto the mosaic floor, I lay the chest down next to me and start to go through the contents of it all over again hoping that I missed some clue—some detail—that would prove me wrong, but I empty it out in frustration.

Only when there's nothing left in the chest do I notice something I never had before.

There's a slit in the silky material that covers the inside of it, right in front. I've never opened the chest from this angle, so I never spotted it before. It doesn't look like a rip or a tear, but rather as if someone took a sharp knife across the material.

I kneel beside the chest and run my fingers over the slit. There's something bumpy inside the material, so I slip my finger in to see what it is.

After a few tries, I worry out a letter addressed to Mom.

It's still sealed up, like no one ever opened it. The typed return address is from a juvenile detention center in Detroit. My heart pounds in my chest as I turn it over in my hands. JR. A letter from JR. Even after reading all the stuff in the chest, opening something she never read herself feels strange.

I turn the letter over again and again in my hands. Remind myself that I've been following all these tiny breadcrumbs since I got here and maybe this will fill in some important blank that's still gaping in front of me.

There's only one way to find out. I slide my finger under the seal and break the envelope open. The paper inside is thin and yellowed with age, but still perfectly intact. My hands shake as I unfold the letter. It's completely typewritten. Even JR's signature is. Single-spaced in small type as if he tried to cram as much as he could onto this one page.

Emma,

There are so many things I want to say to you. I should have said them to you in the greenhouse that night. I should have told you the truth. But I was too angry at the time to realize it. I had a whole year in this place staring me down and I took it out on you.

I'm really sorry I took it out on you.

Yeah, you shouldn't have kissed me and I was mad at you. But you're not the one who put me here. You didn't deserve what I said to you.

I've spent so many hours trying to figure out what to write and how to make you understand. I guess in the end, it comes down to this. I didn't cause that fire. I wouldn't have done anything like that. Ever. But especially not with you inside the hotel.

I'd never want to hurt you. I'd do anything for you.

I worked on the floor of the greenhouse for weeks thinking I'd surprise you with it and finally tell you how I feel about you. But there was Ryan and he made you happy. So I kept my mouth shut.

I tried to stay out of the way because I could tell you liked him even before you got together. I didn't want to be sulking around the edges of your happiness, so I tried to give you some space. But you wouldn't let me. The whole situation was impossible because I didn't really want to stay away from you. It physically hurt to.

So when you kissed me I let myself hope for a second that you felt the same way, even though I knew it wasn't true. I was a mess afterward. I was hurt and angry. But I would never, ever have been a big enough mess that I would've put you in danger.

But it didn't matter in the end. Your precious boyfriend screwed up, and everyone closed in around him to make sure he wouldn't have to deal with the fallout.

Mr. Desmond had already told the police he'd seen my dad lurking around inside the hotel and they were only too happy to believe him. Why would they doubt a future senator's word over an ex-con's? My dad was sick, Emma. He was struggling just to get his work done and he was going to end up in jail again because Ryan screwed up.

But if I said I did it and signed Mr. Desmond's paperwork, they'd leave him alone. I'd get a minimum sentence and no record. All it would take was a few months of my life for my dad to be okay. If I kept my mouth shut about what happened and followed the terms of the agreement, everything would be fine.

Except here I am. Breaking the agreement. Telling you the truth and hoping it won't get me more time here. Or worse.

And while I'm here, Ryan's probably still pretending like nothing happened and comforting you about how terrible it is that your old friend caused the fire.

But you have to know it wasn't me. That I love you and wouldn't have done anything to hurt you. You know that, right?

Although, I guess everything I'm writing here is going to hurt you. I just hope it helps you see who Ryan really is. Because he doesn't deserve you, Emma.

I'm running out of paper, so I've got to go. If you want to write back, my address is on the envelope. I really hope you write back. I miss you so much.

Love,
JR

I let the letter fall into my lap. He didn't cause the fire. He could have stayed in jail for telling Mom the truth. He told her anyway.

My heart aches for JR and for my mom. Something's cracking inside me. Breaking into pieces. I rub my hand over my heart trying to make it stop, but it doesn't work. Nothing will work.

Because Mom and JR are gone. But Dad's not. And I'm going to have to tell him all of this. Just like JR had to tell Mom what would hurt her, I have to tell Dad. I close my eyes and start to hum . . . to lull this ache in my heart. What comes out is "No One Is Alone," the same song Ms. VanHill just sang to me. The words run through my head, giving me something else to focus on, to distract me, until I start singing them out loud, too.

Just softly. Just for me.

"Lexi?"

I have to shake my head to clear it, because when I open my eyes, I can't possibly be seeing what I'm seeing. But there he is, standing in the doorway of the greenhouse.

"Dad."

CHAPTER 57

Emma (Then)

Ryan's address sits on my desk waiting for me to use it. I take out a pen and some paper. I sit down at my desk—but don't know what to write.

There are two things I'm sure of, though. That Ryan sat by and let JR get locked up rather than taking responsibility for the fire. And that even if JR doesn't feel the same way, I'm still in love with him. I can't be with Ryan—even if he hadn't done what he did—with that hanging over us.

It's not right for me to be in love with someone else.

It's not right that he lied to me all this time. That he hurt JR the way he did.

Two sides of the same coin. No matter how I flip it, the outcome doesn't change. Me writing to Ryan. Telling him that we're through.

My fingers tremble as I wrap them around the pen. I have to do this.

Dear Ryan,

I stare at those two words on the page. Will them to multiply and arrange themselves into exactly what I need to say. But nothing else comes. My hand stalls. My fingers tremble again. It would be so much easier if he was still here. If we could sit down and talk until there was nothing left to say. But he's at basic training and I'm here. He'll use his five minutes every week to talk to his mom, and I'll know deep down that it's what he should be doing. Five minutes wouldn't be enough time anyway.

Focus. I just need to focus. Tell him the two reasons why we can't be together anymore.

Dear Ryan,

I know you sent me a letter, but it hasn't gotten here yet. I got your address from your mother instead. So this definitely isn't any kind of reply to what you wrote. Not at all, actually.

Looking down at what I just wrote, I know it's not what I really want to say or how I want to say it. I crumple the paper up in my hand and push it to the side of my desk.

Another sheet of paper, another start.

Breathe in. Breathe out. I have to let him know how I feel.

Dear Ryan,

I never thought you'd be the kind of person who'd hurt someone else. Who'd willingly—knowingly—harm anyone. I can't believe I let you lie to me all this time while I stood by like a fool while you deceived me.

I throw down the pen. Hold my head in my hands. *Why* can't I do this? I get up. Pace the room. Once. Twice. Over and over again. Frustration—anger—crackles inside me. At Ryan. At myself. At my parents. At a world that let something like this happen. The boy who has powerful parents walked away from a crime. The boy who doesn't paid for it.

The smooth pane of my window cools my forehead as I press against it. The only way this is going to get done is if I stay calm.

It's so hard to stay calm.

I head to the bathroom and tie my hair back in a ponytail. I splash some cold water on my heated face and look at myself in the mirror. Examine my face—the sharp angles, the dark eyes, the tired smudges underneath them. It's the face of someone who's made a mess of her life and needs to fix it.

I have to do this, I tell myself.

After drying my face and hands, I head back to my desk.

Dear Ryan, I write. But this time I keep going.

I have no idea where to begin or what to say to you right now.

All I know is that I wish you were here for so many reasons—one of which is that I could talk to you in person rather than having to send you this letter.

But no shooting star, no birthday candles can make that wish come true. So here we are.

I reread the words. I study every one of them to see if they all make sense.

Then I keep writing. Making it clear I can't stay with him. Being vague about JR and how I could possibly know Ryan's role in all of this. Telling him I love JR.

I can't even bring myself to reread it. The letter's finished. I'm going to send it. My hands shake again as I stuff the letter in an envelope. The bitter taste of the glue lingers on my tongue as I seal it shut—write his name, his address at the base. All I have to do is mail it.

I take the letter to Ryan, grab the roommate paperwork for the Art Institute, shoving them both into my bag. Just as I'm about to leave, a twinge of doubt creeps into my chest. If I mail these two envelopes everything in my life is going to change. Irrevocably. I don't even know if I can make art anymore, let alone go to school for it. How can I make decisions this big? How can I *know* I'm making the right ones?

Walking back to my desk, I take my little watercolor set out and grab some paper. I fill a bottle of water. It's the only way to be sure. At least the only way I can think of. Everything in my bag, I finally leave.

I walk out into the warm air but I'm not really sure where to go anymore. I never thought my life would fall apart this way—that I'd be left to pick up the pieces of it all by myself. But here I am, shards of what I thought I knew about my world and nearly everyone in it lying at my feet.

So I walk. Let my feet move beneath me down to the lake, along the shore. I skirt around town, looking out over the Tolkien flag that flies from JR's houseboat for a second before I head toward the dirt road behind Main Street and onto the path. By the time I get to Viola's bench, sweat streams down my back. As much as I need to sit, for a while all I can do is stare at the bench. The inscription. Her friends must have been grieving terribly as they scattered her ashes and put this here to honor her.

Now I've come to mourn the loss of another fierce spirit. As soon as I mail the letter in my bag—as soon as Ryan gets it—any chance of having Linda back in my life will shatter into a million pieces. And I'm not sure how to deal with the reality of that.

I lie back on the bench and clutch the wood. Linda will never come here with me again. Never share dessert or snark about her day to me. She doesn't want me in her life anymore. Breaking up with Ryan is only going to seal what was already a done deal.

Tears well up in my eyes, but I wipe them away. She'd be furious if she could see me right now. Tell me I'm being ridiculous. That this is what comes of being an arty, overly sensitive person in flitty dresses. But I can't help myself. I thought we'd always be friends. I want her back in my life so much it hurts. I swallow down a sob, holding my stomach to try to keep myself from falling apart. I had to lose Ryan. Linda, though . . .

Things could have been different. If Ryan had never thrown anything and knocked over those candles. If they hadn't lit the curtains on fire and Linda hadn't ended up in the hospital. If he'd taken responsibility and JR had never been locked away. If I'd known—seen—been stronger, maybe this all would be different.

I slip the two friendship bracelets off my wrist and lay them on the bench. But as I start to walk away, I run back and grab them. Shove them into my bag. I may have to let her go, but I can't let this tiny piece of her slip out of my hands.

After tucking them safely in my bag, I look around me at the woods that Viola and Linda and I all loved so much. I let my fingers run across the inscription on the bench.

"Take care, Viola," I whisper. "I'll miss you, too."

• • •

Another place, another path calls to me. So I walk. And walk. The heat of midday chafes between my thighs.

I've walked this path before lots of times but never like this. Never alone.

I feel so, so alone.

Only when I get to Mirror Rock do I sit. Only then do I let myself mourn for my parents, for Ryan, for Linda—for all the things I've lost, and all the things I'll still lose as the days and months stretch out in front of me. Things I'll never get back again. I lean against this giant slab of stone and watch the sun dapple on the lake.

With painstaking care, I lay out my paints and brushes. I set the bottle of water on a level piece of rock and smooth out the thick, textured paper I brought. Now all I have to do is paint.

I stare down at the page.

Never in my entire life has so much depended on one little painting. But if I can't do this, I can't do Chicago. I can't make that part of my life happen. The knot forms in my chest again, slowly twisting till it feels as if it's cutting into me from the inside out.

I close my eyes and just breathe. Air comes in and pushes itself back out again. The waves lap, over and over again, against the rocks below. Gulls call as they fly out over the lake. Everything moves, changes. This is no different. Brushes of color where there was nothing before. Something new. Something simple. Just forms, colors—*anything* at all at this point.

When I open my eyes again, I let them settle on the horizon where the water meets the sky and the different blues meld into one big swath of color. My mind wanders to yesterday. To sailing and swimming and the colors of the sky and the water. Teal and gray. Ice blue and cerulean. Silver.

I open my water bottle and dip my brush into it. Swirl some on my little palette. Then I add cyan and cadmium. Viridian and steely gray.

I layer it on, color by color—tease the colors of the lake and the sky out of these tiny cakes of pigment. I make art again.

With each stroke of the brush, something releases inside me. The knot begins to uncoil. My organs ease into something more like normal. I put my brush down so that I can stretch out my hand, then I brush more color onto the page. The wind picks up the bottom of my dress, making it dance around the edge of my watercolor paper. I close my eyes. Let it wash over me. For a second I wish I could spread my wings and fly away. Then I look back at what I'm creating and know I don't want to be anywhere but here.

By the time I put my paintbrush down, relief so deep it makes me dizzy brightens the corners of my mind. I can do this. I can move forward and carve out a life for myself.

Leaning back on Mirror Rock, I close my eyes and wait for the paint to dry on the paper.

Then I pack everything up—I stow the painting carefully in the bag—and I move on.

Main Street hits my senses a little too vibrantly. There are too many colors and sounds. Smells so potent I can taste them. I don't want to be here right now, but I have one last thing to do before I can fall back into quiet again.

Standing in front of the post office, I lay my hand over the place in my bag where the two envelopes lie. Two tiny slips of paper that will change so much of my life. I take one step forward. Then another. Hear my voice ask for two stamps. Hand over my money to pay for them.

Two stamps, two letters. One mail slot.

Ryan's letter slips so easily from my fingers through it, ending one of the most important relationships of my life. I have to keep reminding myself that it's not just an ending.

All the pieces of my life will get rearranged into something new like the tiles in a mosaic. I never thought that from those pieces I might be able to choose something different. Something that's mine. But I can—I will. There's just one more person I have to talk to and then everything can start over again. A new beginning.

CHAPTER 58

Emma (Then)

The door to the greenhouse is open when I get here so I quietly step inside. JR slumps against the far wall. His eyes are closed, his shoulders droop forward as if it's too hard to hold himself up anymore. A slight frown turns the corners of his mouth downward.

"Sorry I'm late."

He looks up, startled. Checks the time. "Only five minutes. I'll let it slide this time."

The words themselves sound like they're supposed to be a joke but there's a weariness in his voice—his eyes.

"Is your dad okay?"

"He's fine, but . . ."

I sit down next to him on the floor, waiting for him to finish. Worry creeps into my mind. Maybe Terry's not okay after all. Maybe something else happened—some new health issue they didn't even know about before. The worry begins to edge into panic.

JR gulps down a breath and starts again. "Um . . . there's something I need to tell you," he says. "And I don't know how you're going to feel about it." His hand passes over his mouth. "I don't know how I feel about it, to be honest."

The coil of panic snakes around my chest, making it hard to breathe. I won't let the knot come back. I won't. No matter what he's going to say, it'll be okay. I'll *make* it be okay.

"Your mom came to see my dad today."

My whole body flinches as if I've been punched. *"What?"*

"Dad said she was there for a while," he goes on. "They . . . um . . . had a long talk."

I watch him, muscles tense, waiting for the next bomb he's going to drop.

"What did she do?" I ask. "You have to tell me what she did so I . . . I can . . ."

"Emma." JR lays his hand on top of mine. "Emma, it's okay. She didn't do anything you have to fix, all right?"

The hand he's not holding shakes in the folds of my dress. "Then why was she there?"

"She offered to pay Dad's medical bills," he tells me. Just as I'm about to bark out a protest, JR keeps talking. "He said yes."

The greenhouse—the trees and the flowers and the windows— they start to spin around me. Slowly at first. Then faster. I'm going to throw up.

"Emma?" JR squeezes my hand. "I know you're shocked. I was, too. But it's all done. She brought a check with her." His head falls back against the glass with a thud. It startles me. Brings me back to myself.

"But . . . but why?"

He sighs. "She told Dad it was her fault he had no insurance any- more," he says. "That she wanted to try to make things right."

Anger—hot and electric—courses through me. "Is she also going to give you back all the months you were locked up?" I say. "Or take away the fact that she tried to ruin your life?"

He turns to face me on the floor. "I said the same thing, Emma," he tells me. "I was . . . angry . . . when I found out."

JR shakes his head over and over again. "Dad said he wasn't going to let my stupid pride or his get in the way of me going to school this fall so . . ." His eyes close. "So it's all done now."

I think about my mom—about what she and Dad did to JR. About how defiant they both were when I confronted them about it. My head hurts.

"Um . . ." He tilts his head in that way he used to when his hair was longer. "Um . . . your mom told my dad that you're going to art school in Chicago." JR's eyes meet mine. "Is that true? Are you really going to . . . ?"

"I mailed my roommate form today," I tell him. "I'm really going to."

He stares at me for a second. "I'm so happy for you, Emma. I can't believe they're letting you go."

It hits me all at once how much he still doesn't know about what I've been doing and what it all means. I have to tell him. Now.

"They didn't really have any say in it. I . . ." My voice falters. I have to swallow down the lump in my throat. "I didn't ask permission. I told them that I'm going."

JR's eyes widen so much it looks painful. "You did?"

"I did."

He leans back against the wall of the greenhouse again. Nods in approval. "You were always good at talking at people till they did what you wanted them to."

"You would know."

When he doesn't reply—when silence falls between us—I run my fingers over the floor, skimming my hand over the mosaic I laid out and he grouted. I let this one part of the hotel that still feels as if it's *mine* remind me why I'm here. What I still need to do.

"I was actually going to tell you tonight," I say. "And give you this."

As carefully as I can, I pull the watercolor out of my bag.

JR takes it from me, his eyes roaming over the painting. "You did it," he says in a hushed voice. "You worked through the block."

"It was the colors of the sky and the lake yesterday," I tell him. "I wanted to paint them." I bite the inside of my mouth for a second. "I want you to have it."

For a long time he just stares at it. "You sure you don't want to keep it?"

I take a second or two to think that over, but in the end, I know what the answer is. "No, you keep it," I tell him. "To remember the day with."

He winces slightly for some reason but murmurs a quiet "Thanks."

"Um . . . and there's other stuff I need to tell you, too."

His eyes close. The warm lines that had just been on his face—the almost contentment I'd seen there—slip away. "Why don't you tell me, then?"

I glance around the greenhouse, our clubhouse for so many years. The one place that was always *ours*. "I wrote to Ryan."

JR's shoulders stiffen. "And?"

"I broke up with him."

My eyes drift shut so I can't see his reaction to this. And I know that's cowardly. I know I should face this head-on, but right at this moment, I can't. I just can't.

"Are you okay?" The worry in his voice makes me open my eyes again.

"I think so," I tell him. "Yes."

When he leans in closer to me, I wonder if he's going to hug me. Maybe even kiss me. Instead he says in a pained voice, "Is it because of me? Because of what he did to me?"

Pressing my hand into the tiles again, I force myself to keep talking. "Partially," I admit. "I . . . I can't be with someone who'd do something like that. Who'd treat anyone that way, let alone you."

He bends down and tries to catch my eyes but I won't look up. I have to just say what I need to say and let him react however he does and then move on. The fact that I don't know how this will end makes my dinner churn in my stomach.

"What's the other part of the reason?" he asks. "You said 'partially.'"

Tears brim in my eyes. Run down my face.

"Emma?" he says. "Whatever it is, you can tell me." He sucks in a breath. "Whatever it is it'll be okay."

I wipe the tears off my face. "I told him that I love you."

My eyelids squeeze shut again, pushing out more tears. It takes so much effort not to cry that I feel overheated—feverish—from it. Only when he doesn't respond does a trembling take hold of my chest. It was a risk. I knew it was. I knew he might not still care about me like that.

But I hoped so much that he would.

"You . . . you told him that you love me." JR says the words carefully, enunciating each one as if I might misunderstand him otherwise.

I just nod.

"And you wrote that because . . . you do?" he goes on. "You do love me?" Opening my eyes again, I look directly into his, trying to be brave. Trying to tell him the truth, no matter what.

"I do love you."

JR's shoulders start to shake. He covers his eyes with his hand. Leans back again to let the wall support him.

"JR, I'm sorry if you . . . ," I start, swallowing down all the panic welling up inside me as I try to keep talking. "If I put you on the spot. But . . . but I need you to just rip off the bandage if you don't feel the same way. I . . . I really need you to tell me."

Never in my entire life have I felt so sick. I can't possibly come out of this okay.

"Emma?"

He reaches over. Lifts my chin so we're eye to eye. "You can't really think I don't love you, right?"

The words wash over me but there's too much *can't* and *don't* for me to be able to make sense of them. "I thought it was obvious. Like . . . painfully obvious," he tells me. "My dad figured it out ages ago. I'm pretty sure your parents and Linda did, too. Even the people at work know. So I . . . I thought you must, too, but . . ."

He smiles at me. That beautiful little smile that just barely tips up the corners of his lips. "I love you so much," he breathes. "For so long and . . ."

I reach up to touch his cheek. He presses his hand over mine.

"All I've ever wanted is to be with you."

And that's all it takes. A laugh bursts out of me. A sob. Tears fill his eyes, too.

When I finally pull him into my arms, his tears spill out onto my shoulder. Seep into the strap of my dress. I run my fingers through his hair and let my other hand roam down his back. He shivers at my touch. Slides his fingers down the bare skin of my arm.

Our eyes meet. JR's eyelashes are still wet from his tears. There's a hint of doubt lingering in his eyes—doubt that I want to erase so that he never needs to feel it again.

So I kiss him. Just a gentle brush of my lips against his. Then another, till his lips are soft. Open. He sighs into my mouth, breaking something inside me. My resolve maybe. Any desire to fight this anymore. I deepen our kiss.

When he pulls away from me to catch his breath he smiles so widely—so unabashedly and un-JR-like—that it makes me laugh. Then JR starts, too. We double over, toppling into each other, laughing just for the sheer joy of it.

I slide both of us down onto the floor so we can lie next to each other. So I can wrap my leg around him, feel him pressed against me. Kiss him again and again till I'm dizzy from it.

We are an explosion. We're fireworks.

We're the Fourth of July.

I can't get close enough to him—can't stop touching him. I slip my hand under his shirt and scrape my fingers down the smooth skin of his back, gasping at how good it feels to finally be able to touch him.

A new beginning. A new chapter. One we'll start together.

There's nothing in this whole world I want more.

CHAPTER 59

Lexi (Now)

D ad stands in the doorway looking like he sees a ghost. His face has gone pale. His eyebrows bunch up over his nose. I wait for the explosion to happen, bracing myself against the glass wall. Then I realize it's not me he's looking at. His eyes roam around the greenhouse taking in every detail, snagging here and there on something . . . the lime tree . . . the broken pot of the geraniums. He takes a huge breath. Then he finally steps inside.

When he looks over at me my stomach drops.

For a long few seconds, he doesn't say anything at all.

"Chloe called," he says at last. "She was worried about you."

I can't believe she'd do this to me . . . get me in trouble like this. I look away, waiting for what comes next. How angry he is. The lies I told. The money I wasted. The trouble I'm in.

Instead he comes and sits down next to me. He doesn't say a word. I can't believe he came all this way and won't talk to me even to tell me how mad he is. Tears sting my eyes. I have to press my palms into the tiles on the floor to keep myself from crying.

"I looked for you all over the hotel," he said. He clasps his hands over his knees. "I was worried about you, too."

Gulping down the lump in my voice, I say, "Sorry."

Dad nods. "Me too."

But I have no idea what he's sorry for and he doesn't seem to want to tell me, so it's like we're standing on the opposite sides of a long hall, neither of us taking a single step forward to meet each other.

"Chloe said you have your mom's mosaic chest," he says at last.

His voice is low. Too calm. But I know what's coming.

"It's mine now, Dad," I say. "You can't take it away from me, I . . ." I have to blink the tears away so I can keep going. "I need to have something that was hers. I *need* to."

When my voice cracks, he turns his head to look at me. "I know, Lexi," he says. "I wouldn't . . . I never wanted to . . ."

He blows out a breath.

"Can we back up a little?" he asks. "Maybe start this conversation over again."

I shrug, not sure what else to do.

"I'm going to take that as a yes," Dad says. He tips his head to the right and closes his eyes. "I'm not much good at this." Another pause. "But I guess you already know that."

My pulse races as I wait for him to keep going . . . hope that he will. That he'll talk and talk so that I don't have to start talking myself.

"I . . . I never meant to keep her from you," he tells me. "I never meant to cut you off from her. It's just that . . ."

When Dad swipes at his cheeks, I finally look over at him. Tears run down his face. He brushes them away again. It hurts to see him this upset. To know that I made him this upset, and keep pushing him to talk about Mom when he clearly doesn't want to.

I reach out a hand to him. For a second, it seems like he's not going to take it. That even this tiny attempt to bridge the gap between us will be rejected. Then he wipes his hand on his pants and holds on tight.

"When she . . ." He gulps down a breath, like he can't bring himself to say the word *died*. "When we lost her. I was . . . not good. I wasn't in a good place for a long time."

"I know but, Dad . . ."

He nods. "It's no excuse," he says. "I know that, Lexi. I really do."

Dad squeezes my hand. "I'm just trying to explain," he tells me. "Not to make excuses."

I watch him in the afternoon light of the greenhouse. The sun illuminates his face. The crease between his eyebrows and the tense set of his mouth.

Explanations, not excuses.

"Then tell me, Dad."

He nods again. "My dad died," he says. "He'd been living with us. His health wasn't great." He closes his eyes. "I was devastated when he died. Emma was, too." Dad glances at me. "Do you remember him at all?"

I shake my head. "Not really."

"He adored you," he tells me. "I wish he'd lived long enough for you to remember him."

Dad's hand trembles in mine.

"Me too."

His eyes squeeze shut like he has to block everything out so he can keep going.

"Your mom's heart gave out six months later."

That hangs, heavy, in the air between us. Because I do remember this. The ambulance. The hospital bed. Mom falling asleep and never waking up. Dad's sobs echoing in the room.

My shoulders shake. I don't know how much longer I can keep myself from falling apart.

"Six months, Lexi," he says. "That's all it took to lose them both." He shrugs. Wipes more tears from his face. "She was so young. We thought we had our whole lives to spend together, but . . ."

I want to be able to say something . . . do something . . . to make him feel better but my mind blanks. I have no idea what would comfort him. Neither of us knows how to help each other.

Dad turns again and gives me a grim smile. "And I had to take care of you," he pushes on. "I had to fight to keep you, even. And it . . . just making sure you had what you needed and the bills were paid and the house stayed even reasonably clean, I . . . I wasn't in a good place."

The knowledge that he did all this—that he fought to keep me—eats away at my insides. My stomach collapses into my spine. I have to tell him. I have to, but I have no idea how to do that and not make it destroy him.

"So I tried to just . . . soldier on, you know?" he says. "I didn't have time to grieve or to deal with Emma being gone, I just . . ." He shakes his head. "I did what I had to do to stay sane."

I swallow down the tears and try to steel myself . . . just enough so I can tell him. So that everything's finally out in the open.

"Dad," I say. "Dad, there's something I need to tell you."

He nods. "I know. We'll figure it out when the credit card bill comes in."

God, he's not making this easy.

"No, that's . . . ," I begin. "I mean, I know I have to pay you back. And I . . . I really am sorry I worried you, but . . ."

Silence falls in the greenhouse. This time he's waiting for me to talk. Giving me the space I gave him before.

"I've been going through Mom's stuff," I get out. "And talking to people here." I bang my head back on the glass wall. "God, I don't even know how to say this to you, but . . . but I don't think you're my biological father."

I turn away from him so I won't have to see how he's taking this or what he looks like right now.

"Lexi." His voice is calm. Even. Like he's not upset at all. "That's not true."

Shaking my head, I keep going. "No, I think it is. I . . . I found some stuff, and . . . and she was with someone else and he . . ." Breathe in. Breathe out. I can do this. "I think that's when Mom got pregnant."

Dad squeezes my hand. "I promise you she wasn't cheating on me."

Pulling away from him, I almost yell, "Dad, it was before Mom met you! Her friend JR . . . when she still lived here . . ."

He unfolds his knees. Turns on the mosaic floor to face me. "Lexi, look at me."

When I shake my head, he says, "Open your eyes. Please."

My eyes flutter open to find him . . . smiling? Just a tiny hint of a smile. A sad one, but still. Why can't he take me seriously and just for once hear me out? Why does everything with him have to be so hard?

"Lexi, I'm JR."

I shake my head at him again. "No. That's not possible," I tell him. "He used to be here during the summers and they were friends before she met you."

"I know," he assures me. "My dad worked here. I used to come for holidays and for the summer. Emma and I . . . we used to raise hell sometimes when we were kids."

Something's not making sense. I hear him talking. I even know what he's saying . . . the words are all computing. But it can't be true. I think of the kids who howled at the moon. Who burned Mom's itchy dress on a Viking funeral pyre. The rift that came between them. The fact that she married him before she met Dad.

"His name was Jason Roth, Dad. And yours . . . isn't," I reply. I'm trying to reason with him . . . to explain why he has this wrong, but he's got this ridiculous calm look in his eyes. He's clearly in denial.

"My name was Jason Matthew Roth," he tells me. "JR for short." A tiny secret smile passes over his face. "I hated it when she first started calling me that. But then . . . then I didn't anymore. I loved that she had this special name for me."

It feels like my whole body might melt into the tiles and seep into the grout. This can't be true. "Dad, I don't understand."

Any hint of a smile fades from his face. "I know and I . . . I'm so sorry you were worried," he sighs. "I'm sorry I've been so bad at . . . at everything, I guess."

He reaches out his hand to me this time. I don't hesitate to take it. He sighs again. Squeezes my hand.

"Let me try to explain," he says. "Jason Matthew Roth and Emma

Alexandria Wolfe . . . we fell in love," he tells me. "Things . . . they weren't good here. With her family, I mean. So we left and never came back."

"No," I say again. "Jackson told me Mom and JR didn't leave together. That he drove her to Chicago and JR went to school in Michigan."

The crease between his eyes deepens. "Jackson?" he exclaims. "You talked to Jackson Murray? But . . . but how?"

"He owns the hotel now," I explain. "And he told me that—"

"It's true," Dad cuts me off. "We found out she was pregnant but I had to spend at least a semester at Michigan State before I could transfer to be closer to her. But then I did. We . . . we got a tiny apartment together. My dad, he moved in with us, and . . . and then we had you."

Something about these words . . . the way they fit in with what Jackson said . . . with what I already found. It sinks into me, deep. Dad was JR. He's my biological father. And they . . . he . . .

"Dad, you went to jail for no reason!"

His head jerks back like someone slapped him. "How do you know that?"

Instead of answering, I pull the mosaic chest onto my lap. I hand him his own letter.

"Lexi, where did you get this?" he whispers. "Emma, she . . . she never read it. It never got to her."

With one hand he holds on to the letter. The other clutches at his stomach. "I can't . . ." But he shakes his head instead of going on.

"It was hidden in a slit in the inside of the chest," I tell him. "It wasn't with her other stuff."

A hard look passes over his face. "Of course they hid it from her," he says to himself. "Of course they were too afraid I'd . . ."

After a few deep breaths he seems to get back in control of himself again. "God, I can't believe I'm really here," he murmurs. "I never thought I'd ever . . ."

"The greenhouse is in a lot of her stories," I tell him. "In the chest, I mean."

He nods. "It was our clubhouse." His voice is soft but there's pain still hidden behind it. Now I finally know why. "We were always in here." He raises his shoulders in a slight shrug. "You were conceived in here."

My breath. My shoulders. My eyes . . . everything seems to blow backward.

"Too much information, clearly," he continues. Then his mouth drops into a frown again. "I haven't talked about Emma enough," he says. "I haven't talked about her at all with you, and I . . . I guess I'm rusty on what to say anymore."

Now that I've recovered from the bomb he just dropped, I feel like I can supply ideas about what he can say. "Why don't you start with why you have a different name now?"

He gives himself a little shake, then nods again. "I had it legally changed," he says. "I wanted a fresh start when I went to school, so I told everyone to call me Matthew. Then later, when Emma and I both changed our last name to Carter, to my dad's name, I dropped the Jason, too."

Dad raises his free hand to rub his eyes. He's too pale right now. The crease that's always between his eyes is almost painful to look at.

"I'm sorry I dragged you back here," I tell him. "I . . . I just wanted to know more about her. And then her mother's nursing home sent me the mosaic box when she died and . . ."

A startled noise escapes from him. "Jessica's dead?" he whispers. "I didn't know that."

It's hard to tell if he's sad or just surprised. I'm not sure I want to know. She and my grandfather did try to take me away from him. *I had to fight to keep you,* he said.

We sit in silence for a while, probably because neither of us knows what to say.

"What were you singing when I first came in here?" he says, breaking the quiet.

"Oh . . . it's from *Into the Woods*," I tell him.

One look at his face and I can tell he has no idea what I'm talking about. "It's a musical, Dad," I explain. "Ms. VanHill had just sung it to me and I . . ."

Then I remember that Dad has no idea who Ms. VanHill is either.

"You sounded beautiful," he says, glossing over her name. "You should think about joining chorus this year. Or maybe trying out for a play."

And be in a musical. Where people burst into song and dance in the middle of conversations. "I think I'm going to, Dad."

He nods. "Are you also going to tell me who Ms. VanHill is?"

So I do. I tell him about her and about Casey. About bumping into Jackson. Dad's eyes narrow when I tell him Linda Desmond came, but he doesn't say a word. All the while, he runs his fingers over the tiles on the floor.

"Dad, did Mom make this mosaic?" I venture.

"This one, the ones on the box," he says, his voice far away. "The painting over the mantel at home. The little sculpture in the backyard. This." He takes a tiny basket made of woven pine needles out of his pocket. "She . . . she could make something out of nothing."

Tears fill my eyes again. I can't believe he's finally talking about her. A tiny sliver of hope spreads through my chest. Maybe things will be better now. Not that he'll suddenly talk about her all the time, but maybe he'll at least answer my questions.

"Lexi, I'm sorry you had to come all this way just to . . ." His voice cracks again. "I'm sorry I didn't share more of her with you. And I . . . I'll try to do better, okay?"

The tears overflow . . . stream down my face. "Okay."

"And you need to promise not to run off like this again," he continues. "It's not okay that you lied to Abby and me."

"I know. And I'm sorry."

Dad pulls himself to his feet and holds his hand out again to help me up.

As I walk through the door, though, he turns back. His eyes roam all around the greenhouse one more time, taking in every last detail again like he's trying to memorize something he already knows so well.

Then he turns back to me. "Let's get going."

CHAPTER 60

Lexi (Now)

As we walk across the lawn my name rings through the air. I turn to see who's calling me. When I see that it's Casey, something loosens inside my chest. He runs over, still in his hotel uniform.

Then he throws his arms around me. For a second, I stand there shocked. Limp. Then I hug him back. Lean into him and lay my head on his shoulder and just sink into this moment. Into him.

"I was so worried about you," he says in a quiet voice. "I saw you leave and you looked so upset, but my manager wouldn't let me take a break and I . . ."

Someone clears his throat behind us. Dad.

"Are you going to introduce me to your friend?"

As I pull away from Casey, his eyes fill with confusion. Then we both turn to face Dad. He's got his hands crossed over his chest, his eyebrows knit together.

"This is my friend Casey," I tell him. "Casey, this is my dad."

If it was possible for someone's jaw to actually drop, Casey's has.

"Oh . . . um . . . I didn't know you were coming?" he says to Dad before looking back at me. "Did you know he was coming?" he says in almost a whisper.

"Nope. It was a total surprise."

Casey turns to Dad again. "Um . . . It's nice to meet you, Mr. Carter?" His eyes dart between us as Dad shakes his hand. I wish there was a way to explain to him everything that's happened right now, but I can't. Not with Dad here.

"Same," Dad says, still eyeing Casey with furrowed eyebrows.

"So . . . um . . . want to head inside?" I say at last. "Maybe go see Ms. VanHill?"

Finally Dad's arms drop to his sides again. "Yes, I'd like to meet her," he says. "And to see Jackson. Though I'm not sure he'd want to see me."

Jackson's office is so quiet when we get there that I'm afraid he's off in a meeting or done working for the day. Then I see him sitting on the sofa under the windows with his arms around Caleb the librarian.

Caleb's hot husband. The girl at the library said he was leaving early to see his hot husband. I just had no idea it was Jackson.

"Hey!" Caleb says when he sees me. "Did you find what you were looking for at the library?"

"Oh, I . . ."

Then he sees Dad standing behind me. For a second, his nose . . . his eyes crinkle up like he's confused about something.

"Caleb," Dad says. "I'm sure you don't remember me. It's been a . . . long time. But you were always really kind about ordering in books for me."

Caleb smiles. "You . . . I do remember you," he says. "I remember your voice." His eyes stray from me to Dad, confusion in them again.

"You need new glasses," Jackson tells him. "Or you would have recognized Lexi right away."

Caleb's cheeks pinken up as he turns to smile at Jackson. "Maybe you're right."

The room falls quiet for a few seconds before Dad's voice cuts through it.

"Jackson."

Jackson approaches from behind Caleb, an unreadable expression on his face.

"JR."

Casey lets out a startled *"What?"*

Both Dad and Jackson turn to look at him at the same time. Casey's hand rushes to cover his mouth, like that will make his outburst disappear. I really need to explain all of this to him.

Dad shakes his head before looking at Jackson again. "I didn't know if you'd remember me."

"You'd be difficult to forget" is Jackson's response. Then he straightens his tie and sighs. "My condolences about Emma. I know how much she meant to you."

I watch Dad, not sure how he'll respond to this and if he'll shrink back up, away from talking about her again.

"Thank you." His voice is low, barely controlled. But it's progress. God, I really hope it's progress.

Casey edges closer to me. "What is going on here?" he whispers.

"I'll tell you everything later," I promise. "When we can be alone."

When his eyes widen at what I've said, I clear my throat. In a much louder voice, I say, "Why don't we all go up to see Ms. VanHill? I want to introduce her to Dad."

Jackson holds up one finger before walking over to his phone. "Yes, I'd like to have tea and cake sent up to the Lake Suite," he says into the phone. "Lemon cake and some vanilla, too. Enough for . . ." Jackson looks around the room at all of us. "Six people," he says. "And if there are any of Mischka's truffles left, add those as well."

After saying a quick thank-you, he turns back to us. "Shall we?"

The elevator is crowded with all of us on it together, but at least Dad and Jackson seem to be thawing out with each other, as one describes his latest updates to the hotel and the other talks about his work as a public defender.

Casey still seems confused, but that's not terribly surprising under the circumstances.

Ms. VanHill, on the other hand, doesn't look at all perplexed when she sees the group of us standing outside her door.

She reaches out to take my hand as she throws a deadly glare at Jackson. "How kind of you to stop by," she says to him in an icy voice. If she ever talked to me like that I think I'd roll over and drop dead where I stood. "It's not as if we live in the same hotel or anything, or that you have miles to travel in order to visit an old woman."

Instead of being offended by this, Jackson grins at her. "Sorry I haven't been up in a while." He leans in to kiss her on the cheek. "I had a business trip, as you know. Then a million things were waiting for me when I got back."

Ms. VanHill waves a dismissive hand at him. "Yes, yes, I heard all about it," she replies. "Your *husband* still comes to see me even if *you* don't have the time to anymore."

My head once again feels like it's spinning.

She gestures to indicate that we should all sit down. "Have you met Lexi?" she says to Jackson and Caleb. "Lexi, this is Caleb and his husband."

"Or as I prefer to think of myself, your godson," Jackson adds.

The spinning abruptly stops. Jackson. Her godson. The one who promised to write to Frances Marley.

The glare she gives him could probably kill someone much larger than me. Much larger than Jackson, even. He remains unmoved.

"I've already ordered tea and dessert for all of us," Jackson tells her.

This time, she sniffs in approval. "Well, at least you're good for something."

Ms. VanHill slips her arms through mine and Casey's and leads us to the nearest sofa. "Is anyone going to introduce the man you dragged in here, or shall I do the honors myself?"

"Ms. VanHill, this is my dad, Matthew Carter," I tell her. I take a deep breath, knowing how much this is going to shock her. "Or as my mom used to call him, JR."

Her eyes narrow at him for a split second, but being Ms. VanHill, she doesn't miss a beat. Instead, she raises her chin majestically.

"JR," she intones. "The former arsonist."

Jackson coughs into his sleeve, but Dad steps forward with a grim line across his mouth.

"The accused arsonist," he tells her. "Who was innocent of the charges."

She instantly looks to me for confirmation, and I force myself to smile at her. "It's true," I tell her. "He might look like a criminal, but he didn't actually do anything wrong."

This time Dad coughs awkwardly. Ms. VanHill completely ignores him.

"I assume this means you've resolved the issues surrounding your paternity?" she asks me.

"I have."

A sudden burst of relief rushes over me. Because I *have*. All the worry . . . all the panic even . . . about what I found and how to tell him. It's gone now. I'm going to keep Mom's stuff. We're going to try to start a new chapter. He's going to try to do better.

Another cough from Dad startles me out of my own head. "Anyway . . . ," he says. "I've heard a lot about you, Ms. VanHill."

She looks him up and down. "Not as much as I've heard about you."

Dad looks at her, puzzled, for a second before shaking his head. "No wonder Lexi likes you so much."

"Well, I am a legend after all," Ms. VanHill informs him. "Everybody likes me. Except the foolish ones who don't."

The two of them strike up a conversation while Jackson and Caleb talk to Casey about when he starts school. A knock sounds at the door, and Caleb gets up to help with the tray of treats being delivered. As we sit at the tea table, I look around at them all. It's a group I never would have imagined mingling with each other, a mix of people who knew and loved Mom and people who know and love me. Somehow I think she would have been happy to see us all here together.

We talk and eat and drink tea. We all look at the things in Mom's mosaic chest. Dad cries twice as he sifts through the treasures in there, but he still forces himself to do it. He forces himself to remember.

He's going to try to do better, after all.

Abby and Connor call Dad. It's so good to hear their voices again.

"Are we still going to build a treasure chest?" Connor asks me.

"Argh, matey. Of course we are," I reply. "We'll start the minute I get home."

"*After* she finds another job to help pay for this little trip of hers," Dad adds, making me groan.

But Jackson loudly clears his throat. "Actually, Lexi is about to inherit a stake in the hotel," he informs Dad. "So all room charges will be cleared, under the circumstances."

Dad gives him a blank stare for a second like the words aren't processing. "You . . . you're going to own part of . . . of this?" he asks me.

"It seems that way."

A long enough pause follows this that something twists in the pit of my stomach.

But Abby asks him to take her off speaker and he walks into the corner, talking some, but mostly listening. Nodding.

After Dad hangs up the call and comes back to the table he seems calmer. Less like he's in shock. He goes back to talking to Ms. VanHill again, while Jackson and Caleb talk about how our call kept breaking up and the right level of Wi-Fi in the hotel.

Casey moves his chair closer to mine so that our legs touch under the tea table. He doesn't move away. Neither do I. When he leans in even closer, my cheeks burn. "I'm glad you found what you were looking for."

I think about that for a second. I came here to find out more about Mom. To be where she'd been and to feel closer to her. Despite everything—despite all of the drama and hurt and confusion—I do feel closer to her.

"Me too," I say to Casey. "Me too."

ACKNOWLEDGMENTS

Two timelines, two narrators, and a mystery to put on the page—this story has been a journey and I have so many people to thank. First and foremost, I want to thank my brilliant (and very kind) editor, Nicole Ellul, and the whole team at Simon & Schuster, including Dawn Cooper and Laura Eckes for the gorgeous cover. Jim McCarthy, thank you for making this opportunity happen and for your support through the whole process.

In terms of critique partners, I couldn't be luckier. Pat Bridgeman, Chris Brodien-Jones, Pat Lowery Collins, Laurie Jacobs, Nancy Kelley, Laurence King, Valerie McCaffrey, and Linda Teitel heaped on so much support, advice, and feedback as I was writing this story, working too much, and running on adrenaline for far too many months. And then there's Mary Lee Donovan and Jamie Michalak—amazing editors and writers, as well as dear friends.

Speaking of dear friends, I'd be remiss without sending hugs to Courtney O'Connor, Belinda Thresher, Megan O'Connell, and Sabrina Fedel. A special shout-out is necessary for two colleges at which I teach—the whole crew at Lesley University's MFA in Creative Writing program as well as the community at Montserrat College of Art.

Stephanie and Jill, my best friends of more than thirty years, consistently make me laugh more than anyone else, and were always available to shoot a few arrows (okay, a *lot* of arrows) while I was in the midst of complicated revisions.

I'm also blessed to be part of a group of family without whom I'd be lost, including my wonderful parents, Beatrice and John Platt; Barbara, Mike J., Caroline, John, and my uncle Anthony; and, of course, Barbara, Doc, Dan, and the entire O'Brien-Miller-Rowell crew.

I want to send all the love in the world to my daughter, Char, who is always my biggest and best cheerleader—and who's also a pro at reminding me to take occasional deep breaths and breaks. And last but by no means least, my husband, Mike, read every single draft of this story, kept me sane throughout it all, and never ceases to amaze me with his patience and seemingly bottomless supply of love.